DEEP TIME

DEEP TIME

A Novel

Susan Sizer Bogue

SHE WRITES PRESS

Published 2025
Printed in the United States of America
Print ISBN: 978-1-64742-916-4
E-ISBN: 978-1-64742-917-1
Library of Congress Control Number: 2025900939

For information, address:
She Writes Press
1569 Solano Ave #546
Berkeley, CA 94707

Interior Design by Kiran Spees

She Writes Press is a division of SparkPoint Studio, LLC.

To THB, an extraordinary friend

Chapter 1

Grand Canyon

Lauren, 1972

Never or always. Fact or fiction. Animate or inanimate. A list of contrasts was the only way Lauren Brown could make sense of the magnitude of the divide she felt between her prior life and her life to come when she first experienced the West. Instead of preparing for the Graduate Record Exam, she had studied Grand Canyon river rafting brochures and created an elaborate comparison chart of smooth-water versus white-water trips, oars versus motors, number of days, and embarkation points. The trip would be the start of the adventurous life she and her husband, Kenny, planned to live after college.

They'd finished final exams, skipped graduation ceremonies, and flown to Denver, where they'd borrowed Kenny's brother's 1963 Volkswagen Beetle to make the fourteen-hour drive to Page, Arizona.

Going west from Denver on Interstate 70, they watched the landscape transform from grassy knolls to forested hills and from rocky outcrops to high mountains. When they drove under an overpass, its massive pillars framed a postcard view of snow-capped peaks in the distance.

"Wow! I wonder if those are fourteeners," Lauren said, thumbing through the guidebook she was reading.

"What the heck are fourteeners?" Kenny asked, glancing at her.

"Mountains higher than fourteen thousand feet. Colorado has fifty-four."

"Wait. Wasn't Blue Knob only three thousand feet?"

"Yep."

"That mountain beat us up pretty bad. A fourteener would've killed us."

They looked at each other and laughed. Kenny's sense of humor was one of the things Lauren loved best about him. Last Christmas, with no instruction except the ski rental guy's pigeon-toed demonstration of the snowplow technique for stopping, they had tried to teach themselves to ski at Blue Knob, Pennsylvania's highest skiable mountain. Early snowplow attempts on actual snow had ended in crossed skis, followed by falls and struggles to get up.

By early afternoon, Lauren had fallen once getting off a lift and once getting on. Kenny had crashed into a tree at low speed to avoid running into a child. On their last run, they had collided with each other, ending in a heap. One of Lauren's skis had headed downhill by itself. They had laughed until they were almost too weak to right themselves. Limping down the bunny hill looking for the missing ski, they had watched four-year-old children glide past them.

Lauren had added "first time skiing" to all the other "firsts" she and Kenny had experienced together. "Firsts" were hilarious, humiliating, romantic, exciting, or maybe all of them combined.

"Damn, this is embarrassing," Kenny said, downshifting.

Their little yellow VW fell back with tractor-trailers and Winnebago campers in the right-hand lane as they drove up Vail pass. On the uphill climb, he hunched forward and gripped the steering wheel as though moving his weight forward would speed the engine.

"Yeah, we're not making very good time," Lauren said, watching the speedometer drop to thirty miles per hour. "But look at the incredible mountains."

Kenny exhaled and relaxed his shoulders as they reached the summit and headed downhill at a faster speed.

She looked over at him with his shaggy, end-of-finals hair and unshaven stubble and marveled at how handsome he was. But for the gearshift and the gap between their seats, she would have scooted over to be closer to him. As it was, she reached across and massaged his neck.

"That feels good," he said, giving her a quick smile.

She couldn't imagine anything better than sitting side-by-side with her husband on a trip to somewhere they'd never been, to try something they'd never tried, and with college behind them.

As tired as they were, they both seemed energized.

On the other side of the Continental Divide, a sign on a bridge identified the Colorado River, whose grandest work was their destination. It meandered beside them for a time before roaring through the fortress-like, pinkish-tan rock walls of Glenwood Canyon in Western Colorado. They caught glimpses of river rafters below them.

"Look how much fun they're having," Lauren said, leaning toward the driver's side to better see down the canyon.

"Hey, they're paddling their own rafts. How come we're going in a motorboat?" Kenny asked, looking at her.

"We're not going in a motorboat!" she said, laughing. "It's a rubber raft with a small motor at the back to steer it." After a dramatic pause, she continued, "Some of the rapids in the Grand Canyon were named for people who died there. We'll be glad we're in a big raft."

>>

When they crossed from Colorado into Utah, Lauren felt a spaciousness of sky and land she had never experienced. Even though she and Kenny had been married since Thanksgiving, this trip was the actual start of the life they would create together. It seemed fitting to travel through the otherworldly landscape of Utah.

"I feel like we're on a different planet," she said.

"Yeah. A very strange one."

"All this empty land makes me wonder why people live crowded together in cities."

"Jobs, of course."

Lauren's lighthearted mood faded.

She remembered what her adviser had described as the "exquisite agony" college seniors suffered deciding what to do with their lives. Lauren had never experienced it. The "exquisite" was considering all the wonderful possibilities after college. The "agony" was actually making a decision to get a job or go to graduate school. *Am I doomed because I missed both phases?* she wondered.

"With finals and planning for the trip, I repressed thoughts of jobs and the real world."

"Hey, we've got till the end of the summer before we have to worry about permanent jobs," Kenny said.

"I know. But let's face it, I have no idea what I want to do. I'm interested in everything a little bit but nothing for very long. I need to find something that keeps my interest."

"You grew up with wealthy grandparents. You think the way you make money should be your passion. When you're raised in a family like mine where there's never enough money, your goal is to get a good-paying job. Period. My passion isn't business, but it'll give us a good life."

Dear, practical Kenny, Lauren thought. *He's not suffering any agony.*

"You're right, of course, but I loved all my art and philosophy classes. I'm not sorry I took them. I'm just sorry waiting tables is the only thing I'm qualified for."

>>

After arriving late, the next morning they drove to the Page Airport, where a pilot would fly them to their embarkation point of Lee's Ferry. A battered, single-engine Cessna 172 Skyhawk sat on the runway.

"That plane looks like it came through World War II!" Lauren said, taking hold of Kenny's arm.

"I don't think the Skyhawk was manufactured till the nineteen-fifties, but I hope to God its engine is better maintained than its exterior!"

When they met their pilot, he looked even worse than his airplane. Chuck was at least sixty years old, with a potbelly and a florid face that hinted at years of boozing. Lauren felt her throat grow dry and her knees weak. Kenny gave her a meaningful look that she interpreted as, *We're going to trust our lives to this man?* When they bent down to pick up their backpacks, they stayed low for an extra few seconds to confer about how to meet their rafting party without meeting their Maker.

"This guy looks like he starts drinking in the morning," Lauren said in a low voice.

"But I didn't smell any alcohol on him. He seems alert."

"Geez, I don't think I can do this."

"What's the alternative?" Kenny asked.

"Flying is the only way to get to Lee's Ferry."

"Then we have no choice."

They climbed aboard.

>>

The airplane barreled down the runway and lifted off amid much shuddering of the frame and whining of the engine. Kenny sat up front with the pilot, and Lauren rode behind him next to their backpacks and sleeping bags. In shouted conversation above the engine noise, they learned they were all from Pennsylvania. Chuck had moved from Harrisburg to Arizona because of his wife's asthma.

"The missus feels a heck of a lot better in this dry climate," he told them, turning his head around, owl-like, to include Lauren in the conversation.

Lauren gripped the seat and nodded mutely. She wished he'd watch where he was flying. She saw they were following the Colorado River as it cut deeper into the canyon.

"Below us is Lee's Ferry, but we're going to make an extra little loop. I can't let you see the Grand Canyon from the river without first seeing it from the air."

Before Lauren could object, the plane swooped, tipped a wing, accelerated, and climbed higher. The shortness of the flight was what had convinced her to get on the plane. Now they were being hijacked by the pilot. She groaned under the roar of the engine.

When she looked out the window, her fears receded. Below lay mesas painted in ribbons of glorious colors. Light tan rock ran along the top; then layers of pink, coral, terra cotta, and a broad swath of maroon descended in order. The same color scheme echoed across the canyon.

Could the mesas be cut from one massive plateau? Lauren wondered.

To the north a rock wall glowed incandescent in the morning sun. Gold, copper, and russet bands melded in the sun's fire. As an art major, Lauren had studied the world's greatest masterpieces. Even these dimmed in comparison to Earth's artistry.

"This is incredible!" she said in a voice loud enough for Kenny and Chuck to hear.

"I thought you might like the view," Chuck said, turning his head and grinning.

"Do they find dinosaur bones here?" she asked.

"You'd think so because the rock's ancient—so ancient it's before the dinosaurs. Down at the bottom it's over a billion years old. Geologists do find marine fossils in the top layer of Kaibab limestone."

Lauren couldn't fathom what a billion years meant. Her idea of ancient was when dinosaurs had roamed the earth. The Grand Canyon was older than dinosaurs! Her heart beat fast. The beautiful layers of rock in the canyons below represented mysterious eras of the past. Why hadn't she studied geology for her college science credits? It hadn't seemed relevant to life on the East Coast. Now it seemed essential to understanding the West.

She and Kenny learned Chuck was a member of the Raggedy-Ass Miners Club for geologists and rockhounds. He spent weekends prospecting for gemstones. That Chuck's rosiness might originate from the desert sun and the red rocks he hiked among, rather than from whiskey, relieved his passengers' anxiety. His enthusiasm for Arizona geology soon infected Lauren and Kenny, who were mesmerized by the grandeur of the canyon walls.

"You two should make a side trip to Sunset Crater Volcano near Flagstaff. You'd see lava flows like they just happened, even though the last eruption was almost nine hundred years ago."

A volcano in Arizona! Why had she thought all volcanoes existed on islands in the Pacific? She wondered if any of the mountains they'd seen in Colorado were volcanoes.

Chuck circled the plane in a leisurely U-turn. Lauren and Kenny relaxed as he chatted about his recent adventures prospecting for turquoise. Near-disasters while rock climbing were his favorite stories, and he laughed louder at his escapades than his audience. Below was a geography lesson in buttes, spires, towers, and castle rocks. The greenish Colorado River wound through the land.

"What's that straight line down there?" Kenny asked Chuck.

"Dang! That's our airport. Almost flew right past."

He shoved the control stick forward and the plane made a sharp dive. Kenny and Lauren braced themselves. In a few seconds the plane leveled out and lined up with the badly rutted runway.

The moment their wheels touched down they knew something was wrong. The end of the tarmac was coming too quickly.

Chuck jerked the stick back and gave the plane full power. The plane stuttered and struggled to get airborne. Lauren grabbed the back of Chuck's seat, closed her eyes, and waited for the worst. When she opened them, the plane was slowly gaining altitude.

She let out her breath. *That was almost a disaster.* She reached over and touched Kenny's shoulder. He turned and gave her a raised eyebrow look. Soon they were circling the airport and making their final approach. This time they landed near the start of the runway and bumped to a stop at its end.

"That was more exciting than I planned," Chuck said, by way of apology, as he exited the plane.

Holy shit! That was scary. Landing was always the worst part of any flight. But two landings! Lauren sat immobilized for a minute or two. Gradually, her fear gave way to relief they were safe. She hefted backpacks and sleeping bags to Kenny before climbing down from the plane.

They stared with disbelief at Marble Canyon Airport. There were no runway lights, buildings, or control tower. Two-foot-high brush marked the edges of the narrow tarmac. A hump in its middle kept one end of the runway out of sight of the other end. A faded-orange windsock dangled from a pole. Cliffs to the west, northwest, northeast, and east of the airport contributed to beautiful scenery but added nothing to clearance or survivability odds for airplanes. Solid ground felt wonderful under their shaky legs.

When they said goodbye to Chuck, Lauren gave him an extra twenty-five dollars for the air tour of the Grand Canyon.

"I can't believe you gave him more money than he asked for—after that landing!"

"Oh, but he's such a nice man. And thanks to him, I now have a career plan."

"You're going to be a pilot?" Kenny asked, his eyes round and incredulous.

Lauren laughed. "God, no! I may never fly again. No, I want to be a geologist."

>>

Years ago a ferry service had operated at Lee's Ferry, but now it was the staging area for Colorado River trips. Piles of life vests, backpacks, coolers, and waterproof containers lay on the ground. Lauren recognized the name of an outfitter whose brochure she had studied. Georgie's River Rats, two of whom wore matching gold T-shirts, were gathered near their raft. Lauren had wanted to go with this company since it was run by a woman, but, at seven to ten days, all of Georgie's trips were too long.

After inquiries, they located their guides, Ben and Zack, who were loading groceries and gas cans onto a large gray rubber raft. Kenny held up two six-packs of Budweiser he hoped to bring aboard. Ben gave him two thumbs up and showed him where they tied on food and drink to keep cool in the river. Lauren and Kenny stored their backpacks and sleeping bags in army green rubber sacks they were given. Over the next hour the rest of their rafting party arrived: three middle-aged men from Wisconsin and a young medical doctor and his girlfriend from Atlanta.

The scenery from river level was awe-inspiring even before the raft trip began. Lauren had to stop herself from using too much film on the Vermilion Cliffs, which she identified from a guidebook. She wouldn't have known the word vermilion except in last semester's Italian Renaissance Art class, her professor had noted that Titian had used vermilion, a flaming red, to paint the robes of the main figures in *Assumption of the Virgin* so viewers' eyes would be drawn to the drama in the painting. The Vermilion Cliffs were similarly compelling with their intensely red layers interspersed with purples, pinks, and tans. At the bottom of the cliffs were rows of red rock whose texture could only be described as ruffled. In the painting, Mary was carried to Heaven on a pink cloud borne by cherubs. Linking Titian's glorious vision of Heaven with this phenomenal landscape did not seem strange.

She put down her camera when Zack started his talk. He demonstrated the proper way to wear their life jackets and warned that survivability time in forty-six-degree water was only a matter of minutes.

"If you're thrown from the raft, try to position yourself on your back with your feet down river. Wait to be picked up. Any questions?"

"But you just said we would die in the cold water," one of the men from Wisconsin said. "Shouldn't we at least try to swim to shore?"

"If you're thrown from the raft, it means we're in rough water. Swimming is futile. Your life jacket is designed to keep your head above water. Don't panic and we'll be back to you within a minute or two."

"Where's the snow?" Kenny asked, gesturing at the surrounding desert.

Lauren gave him a puzzled look. The guys from Wisconsin chuckled.

"What are you talking about?" Zack asked, cocking his head.

"Snow melt must be the reason the water is so cold. Where does it come from?"

"Oh, good question. The water is so cold because it's released from the bottom of Glen Canyon dam—almost five hundred feet deep. No desert sun shines down there." He pointed toward the raft. "We can finish orientation while we're cruising this stretch of quiet water. Let's launch."

>>

Under a hot noonday sun, the group waded into shallow water and climbed into the raft. The river was cold and smooth. Zack used an oar to guide the raft into deeper water as Ben manned the motor. Lauren and Kenny found places along one side of the raft. They grinned at each other as they got underway. Their love of outdoor adventure was a strong bond between them. When they first met, Kenny was the one who had nudged Lauren out of her protected life as an only child. Now she initiated adventures as often as he did.

"Colorado River rapids are rated on a scale of difficulty from one to ten, with eleven being unnavigable," Zack said, continuing his briefing. "Today we'll experience three or four pretty good ones in the four-to-six range. They'll get your attention."

It wasn't long before they splashed and bounced over the choppy water of the Paria Riffle, where the river was shallower and rocks were barely submerged. Canyon walls rose on both sides of the river, creating deep shade. Lauren stored her camera in its black waterproof container. They floated under the five-hundred-foot-high steel arch of Navajo Bridge, the last place cars could cross the Colorado River for hundreds of miles. The bridge spanned the opening of Marble Gorge—the beginning of the Grand Canyon. It felt momentous.

A low thrumming sound was the first hint they were approaching Badger Creek, a major rapid. To better balance the raft Zack asked Kenny to move to the front while he positioned himself at the back with Ben. The sound grew to a roar. Lauren felt her heart beating fast. Ahead the river seemed to disappear over a ledge. They approached the drop-off slowly.

"Hang on. We're going over!" Ben shouted.

Everyone hunkered down except Zack, who half stood to assess the best passage. The raft plunged ten or twenty feet into roiling water, and a big wave threw it sideways. Ben skirted some boulders by gunning the motor. The raft bucked and veered but soon rode the rapids in the right direction. When they made a slight turn, a wave washed over the front of the raft and doused Kenny. His loud laugh could be heard above the tumult.

Lauren chuckled and shook her head. Kenny's raucous laugh was irresistible.

>>

By the end of the day, they had covered twenty miles and survived four major rapids. Repeatedly splashed and soaked by the river, Kenny had dried in the burning sun, but still looked like a drowned man revived. The front of the raft, people realized, was a sacrificial position.

"Don't worry, everyone will take a turn," Zack said to Kenny at the end of the afternoon.

"I didn't mind. Going over the falls first was a blast."

Ben skidded the raft onto the beach above the mouth of North Canyon, their designated campsite for the night. After helping unload supplies, Lauren and Kenny rolled out their sleeping bags on a level site away from the main camp area. Zack set up the portable toilet while Ben gathered driftwood to fuel the camp stove.

With the fire blazing, the guides prepared dinner like people unused to cooking. Nevertheless, slightly sandy steaks, fried potatoes on the far side of crispy, and deli salads tasted fabulous to the famished rafters. After dinner everyone sat around the fire drinking and talking until late. The Wisconsin men—Woody, The Hawk, and Nelly— passed around a bottle of Jack Daniels. Dr. Mike and his girlfriend, Collette, split a bottle of wine, while Lauren and Kenny shared their cold, forty-six-degree Budweisers with Ben and Zack.

Ben was a senior at Arizona State University, and Zack, a grad student at Northern Arizona University in Flagstaff. They ran river trips all summer.

Lauren was curious whether Zack knew about the volcano since he went to school in Flagstaff.

"Our pilot mentioned Sunset Crater Volcano near Flagstaff. Is it worth seeing?"

"Absolutely. My freshman geology class took field trips there. If I hadn't majored in archaeology, I might have considered geology."

"I wonder what you can do with a degree in geology."

"I don't know, but I bet you could work for a mining or oil and gas company. Maybe government. The guy who taught us geology did fieldwork every summer. It sounded pretty cool."

Teaching sounded exciting. Summers she could spend outdoors doing geology fieldwork. She couldn't believe she was considering going back to college when she'd just gotten out.

After a pause, Zack continued, "Of course, there aren't many places like the Grand Canyon, where millions of years of Earth's history is exposed. Archaeologists work in the time scale of humans, but geologists work in deep time."

So many times! Lauren thought. *Ancient time, dinosaur time, and now human time and deep time. Maybe ancient time and deep time meant the same thing?* She let conversations swirl around her while possibilities for the future competed with each other in her mind. She leaned against Kenny for warmth as the evening grew cool.

By the time they crawled into their sleeping bags around midnight, the night had turned cold. They were too tired to zip their sleeping bags together, and both fell asleep immediately, despite the lumpy ground on which they lay.

>>

By day four, Lauren and Kenny were seasoned river rats, their new straw hats severely misshapen. Both had taken extra turns being deluged up front when no one else volunteered. Around lunchtime, their raft pulled ashore where the Little Colorado River flowed into the Big Colorado.

"While Zack and I organize lunch, the rest of you might want to swim. The temperature will surprise you. We'll probably hang out here until three or four this afternoon," Ben said.

Not only was the water in the Little Colorado clearer and bluer than that of the Big Colorado, it was as warm as a swimming pool in late June. After bathing in paralyzingly cold water the past few days, the rafters immersed themselves in the luxuries of temperate water and unhurried time. Their final night's campsite above Unkar Rapid was only a few miles downriver, so they lingered until the sun dropped out of sight. Reluctantly, they climbed back into the raft for a short run to camp.

After dinner that night, Lauren slept fitfully, the roar of Unkar Rapid intruding in her dreams. Around midnight a full moon rose above the canyon wall. It was as though someone had shined a floodlight into a dark room. Everyone jolted awake. Laughter and exclamations emanated from sleeping bag outposts around camp. Lauren propped herself on one elbow and surveyed the newly visible night. The river shone silver and gave off sparks where submerged rocks created ripples. Their rubber raft lay like a beached sea creature on the far side of the campsite. Across the way, layers of sedimentary rock, whose subtle color changes were visible by day, now were delineated by varying textures under the light of the moon. *This night is irreplaceable*, Lauren realized. She lay down beside Kenny, who had drifted back to sleep, and put her arm across his warm chest. The swim in the Little Colorado, the beauty of a full moon rising, and her husband's presence made her want to savor the happiness she felt. Nevertheless, she soon fell asleep to the sound of the bellowing giant downstream.

At breakfast Zack prepared the group for what the morning held.

Lauren shifted her weight from one foot to the other while she listened to him. It was hard to stand still when she was consumed by nervous excitement, as though she were at the starting gate of a race. With her heart pumping and adrenaline flowing, she wished they would hurry and launch.

"So even though you're leaving the trip halfway through the Canyon," Zack concluded, "you'll experience Hance, the most exciting rapid on the river. And don't worry, we haven't lost anyone yet."

Once underway, they navigated Unkar and Neville without a

problem. As they approached Hance, Zack moved to the front near Kenny. Lauren and The Hawk were on the left side and the other two Wisconsin men, on the right. Dr. Mike and Collette occupied their usual places at the back near Ben.

Lauren could see rough water ahead. Her stomach did a little flip. Ben swung the raft to the right to avoid a big pile of boulders in the middle of the river. The raft then skirted the right side of a vortex called "the hole." Lauren caught a glimpse of an inverted tornado. A whiplash of energy propelled them into chaos. The raft wallowed out of control over waves. When they plunged into the trough of a giant wave, the raft swung around sideways.

"Hey!" Dr. Mike yelled.

Lauren turned to see what he was yelling about and caught sight of Collette in the water just as a big wave washed over her. *Oh, God, she's going to drown*, Lauren thought.

A few seconds later Collette surfaced, flailing her arms. Ben turned the raft and gunned the motor to get to her, but it was powerless against the waves. Zack stumbled to the middle of the raft to grab the paddle, almost going over the side himself. Lauren and the others clung to the rope around the perimeter to avoid getting thrown overboard.

"What the fuck!" Dr. Mike yelled at Ben. "She's going under!"

A wave threw the raft sideways. Ben maneuvered to the left side of the river where there was less turbulence and inched upstream to within a few feet of where Collette had resurfaced. Zack reached her with his paddle, and she grabbed hold. He pulled her into the raft just as it bucked and swung in another direction. Lauren realized she had been holding her breath and exhaled with relief.

By happenstance, the raft avoided another big vortex. When they finally reached quieter water, Ben cut the motor. Everyone cheered Collette, who looked bedraggled and continued to shiver despite being wrapped in numerous towels.

>>

In late morning, the group disembarked at Phantom Ranch. Lauren and Kenny tied their sleeping bags onto their backpacks and followed the path that led to the South Rim trail.

Shortly, The Hawk overtook them, calling, "See you at the top."

"Wow! He's amazingly fit for somebody who must be in his late thirties," Kenny said after he had gone by.

"No kidding. Hey, I think I figured out how he got his nickname," Lauren said in a conspiratorial tone.

"Because he's got a hawk nose?"

"Yeah, that, but did you notice at night when we were all sitting around the fire, he kind of perched rather than sat? And just now he didn't walk around us, but swooped?"

Kenny laughed. "Well, he is The Hawk."

Lauren and Kenny picked up their pace. The trail consisted of gentle switchbacks for the first couple of hours, but the direction was relentlessly upward. They refilled their canteens at Indian Garden and would have rested, but they had hopes of catching The Hawk, so they didn't linger. When they reached the steep part of the trail, Jacob's Ladder, the sun emerged from the clouds. Their T-shirts were soaked with sweat under their backpacks, and with the rising heat, sweat dripped from their faces. They were hungry and exhausted. On a narrow part of the trail they stepped aside for a mule train carrying people down the canyon. Lauren was happy to rest, even for a few moments.

Kenny said, "Now that would be embarrassing. I'm glad you didn't book us on mules."

By the time they reached the South Rim, they were ravenous. It had taken them five and a half hours. Lauren regretted not waiting for the sandwiches Ben and Zack had offered to make. Instead, she and Kenny had survived on a bag of raisins.

"Hiking twelve miles with five thousand feet of altitude gain requires more than a few raisins," Lauren said.

They headed straight for the bar at the lodge without a backward glance at the Grand Canyon, one of the most beautiful places on Earth.

>>

After the shuttle returned them to their car in Page, Lauren and Kenny had made a side trip to Sunset Crater Volcano near Flagstaff. The two hours spent at the volcano had been tantalizing hours for Lauren. Unlike the Grand Canyon, which flaunted its eras in colorful layers of rock, the volcano hid its mysteries deep within the earth. The geology of both places fascinated her more than she ever remembered being intrigued by classes in art and philosophy.

She felt strangely whole and happy as they drove across Arizona via US 40 on the long trip back to Denver to return Kenny's brother's car before flying home. Maybe the beauty of the Grand Canyon had permeated her soul. Worries and insecurities fell away. Painful thoughts of never having known her father and having been raised by a crazy mother and a domineering grandmother often intruded in her life; now that narrative seemed to belong to someone else. The high sky of the West did something to a person.

While Kenny drove, Lauren studied a map of Arizona and noticed they would pass a few miles north of Petrified Forest National Park before crossing into New Mexico. She was intrigued. *What mysterious processes turned a tree into stone?* She had to know. But she couldn't ask Kenny to make another stop. He had been a good sport about changing their route to see the volcano. Instead, she added Petrified Forest to her ever-expanding mental list of places to explore.

"I feel like I belong in the West," Lauren said after a long, companionable silence as they drove toward Albuquerque. "Look at the blue sky and fluffy white clouds that stay on the horizon, as though they know their place."

"It's not Philly, that's for sure."

"Exactly. The clouds at home are heavy and gray. They block the sun half the time. It's depressing."

She turned to face Kenny and said with excitement, "Let's move to Arizona so I can get a degree in geology!"

"Working construction isn't my life's goal. But I can make more money—at least this summer—than I could at a financial planning job," he said, keeping his eyes on the road. "It's too soon to think about moving. I want to explore jobs posted at the business college."

Lauren slumped a little in her seat. Sometimes she wished Kenny would show enthusiasm for her ideas—even if they were impractical. It was fun to talk about possibilities and imagine them into the future. She frowned. "Of course, but I don't want to be stuck waiting tables forever."

"We need time to figure things out."

After a long pause, Lauren said, "Science has always fascinated me. I think I will like being a geologist."

"What does a geologist even do?" Kenny shrugged.

"I know it would be interesting. Learning how the earth works." She smiled when she thought back to their side trip to Flagstaff that morning. "Wasn't the volcano incredible?"

>>

That night she lay awake pondering their trip. The West was not a Hollywood set. It was real. Its magnificence lived up to her memories of the mountains and canyons in Roy Rogers movies she had watched as a child. Earth's beauty had always moved her. She loved the lush green lawns, shady trees, and flowering shrubs surrounding her childhood home in Philadelphia. Now she understood the difference between the East and the West. Dirt. Pennsylvania had a lot of it. Arizona and Utah had less.

Exposed rock was ripe for study. It was exciting to think of the antiquity of the earth and its millions of years of history waiting for geologists to explore. Kings, queens, conquerors, and cruelty dominated much of the record of civilization she had studied in college. Nature's greater forces weren't always benign, of course, but they weren't rooted in evil or greed as were human events. She was inclined to side with nature.

Chapter 2

East Texas

Chris, 1976

Chris Connor was running late the day Lauren Brown was scheduled to make a presentation in Geo Chronology class on the formation of the Himalayas and the disappearance of the Tethys Sea. As he took a seat, he could sense tension in the air. Seven or eight male students from oil-producing countries in the Middle East had positioned themselves in front-row desks.

He turned to his friend Bryan and whispered, "Hey, what's going on here? Why are all those guys in the first row?"

"No clue."

Chris didn't know their status in class, but it was rare for more than one or two of them to attend class on any given day. It seemed they were auditing rather than enrolled in the course.

Bryan whispered, "It's weird because I don't remember any of them coming to class the day I gave my lecture."

When it was time for Lauren's report, she set her poster-sized illustration on the easel and started her talk. All the Middle Eastern men stood up and walked out en masse. It was as though they refused to learn anything from a woman. The rest of the class sat nonplussed.

Lauren didn't turn to watch the men go or glare at them for their rudeness. She continued her well-researched lecture, pausing now and then to make squiggly drawings on the chalkboard. In response to someone's question, she sketched a land configuration thousands of miles from the subject of her report. This was Chris's first hint of her amazing grasp of geography.

When class was over, Chris planned to introduce himself to Lauren and discuss her lecture with her, but the wolfish professor, Don Weber, had waylaid her, and the two were having an animated discussion as Chris left. *No wonder so few women study geology*, he thought. *Male geology students and professors either demean them or hit on them.*

Graduate-level geology classes at Tex Poly weren't exactly teeming with women. Chris remembered the first day of Geo Chron class when he and other male students had watched as Lauren hurried into the classroom, settled into a seat at the back, and brushed her long brown hair from her eyes. Her earnest expression and absolute focus on the professor's lecture showed she hadn't the faintest idea of the effect she was having on her male classmates.

Even though Lauren wore a wedding ring, Chris noticed within a few weeks that her presence in class had diminished the scruffiness practiced as a religion by geology students and professors. They still rolled out of bed, threw on last night's jeans and T-shirt, and rushed to class without washing up, but now they paused outside the classroom to run their fingers through their hair in a last-ditch attempt to look civilized. Occasionally, someone even showered and arrived with his hair slicked down.

Chris was no exception. He had gone home that first day and surveyed his closet with a critical eye.

Why do I do this to myself? he wondered. *Move from one climate extreme to another.* When he got out of the air force after being stationed in Hawaii for two years, he had moved to Northern Idaho for grad school with Aloha shirts, shorts, old uniforms, and his snorkeling gear. Now he shoved the flannel shirts and sweaters he had bought in Idaho to the back of his closet. Too bad Tex Poly was located in Pasadena, Texas, where the humidity made it feel like the tropics.

He hadn't admitted to himself that he was suddenly taking an interest in his clothes because a beautiful girl had shown up in one of his classes.

>>

On a Sunday night in late October, Chris and Bryan, a fellow PhD student, arrived at their Volcanics professor's front door at the same time. His white clapboard house had an old-fashioned air about it, with dark green shutters and dormer windows on the second story, through which long-ago children might have peeked.

"Hey, Chris," Bryan said, using the brass door knocker to announce their presence. "I'm glad I'm not the only one who showed up."

"Yeah, the night before our Geo Chron exam isn't good timing. I should be home organizing my notes. But people say you can't miss an evening at The Mumper's in case he starts telling volcano stories."

"Exactly."

The door opened and Mrs. Mumper ushered them into a study, where several students were gathered around Dr. Mumper in his big leather chair. He was dressed in his usual Abercrombie & Fitch khaki shirt and trousers that turned into shorts by zipping off the bottom half of the legs. As far as Chris knew, no one made fun of him for dressing like a big game hunter, as though he expected to be called to Africa at any moment. Dr. Mumper had monitored more volcanoes and seen more eruptions than anyone in the department—or maybe in the US. If students, behind his back, referred to him as "The Mumper," it was because his outsized personality made him more legend than professor. No one called him Melvin, even though most professors insisted grad students call them by their first names as a gesture of collegiality.

Dr. Mumper caught sight of the two new arrivals. "Boys, bring in a couple of chairs from the dining room."

Chris and Bryan joined the circle.

"Now everybody, look around you." Dr. Mumper paused for a few seconds.

Oh, great, Chris thought. *This is where he tells us only half of us will make it and the rest will flunk out.*

"These guys will be your buddies for life," the professor proclaimed.

Chris chuckled, relieved it wasn't a dire prediction of failing students. He glanced around the room to see the reactions of the other guys.

"The rugby shirt Bryan's wearing got me thinking," Dr. Mumper went on. "My new theory is geologists are the rugby players of scientists."

Chris noticed everyone had the same puzzled look on his face.

"Rugby players are tough," he explained. "They don't wear helmets or pads. No matter who wins, both teams meet for a drink up at a local tavern. They've done battle together. They're friends. Same with geologists. We're tough, outdoor people. We rely on our fellow geologists. After doing battle with erupting volcanoes, electrical storms, snowstorms, wild animals, or emergencies like running out of beer, we have an unbreakable bond."

The students laughed. Even those with a midterm the next day relaxed in the moment.

"Speaking of beer . . ." The professor smiled. "Will a couple of you guys help me open some Heinekens?"

When everyone had a beer, Dr. Mumper said, "Now to war stories . . ."

"After Pearl Harbor was attacked, I joined the Twelfth Army Air Force because I was sure it was my destiny to fly bombers. The army had other ideas. They made me an airplane mechanic." Dr. Mumper chuckled, as though laughing at his foolish younger self.

"We were stationed in Italy, and our engineers built Pompeii

Airfield, a temporary base a few kilometers east of Mount Vesuvius. The 340th Bombardment Group was deployed there with a fleet of B-25 Mitchell medium bombers. They had bombed the German evacuation beaches on Sicily and provided air cover for the Allied landing at Salerno on the mainland. But they'd taken a lot of hits, especially on the drive for Rome. Too many guys got shot down. Their planes were a wreck."

The geology students listened to Dr. Mumper's every word as though he were FDR or Winston Churchill telling them the real story of World War II. At first Chris wondered, *How does this relate to geology?* Then the mention of Vesuvius gave him a clue.

Dr. Mumper continued, "One night in March of '44, I was outside smoking a cigarette and talking to some buddies. We'd had a hard day scavenging parts from a wrecked B-25. Suddenly, the ground shook. A dark, mushroom-shaped cloud of ash and tephra erupted from Vesuvius's dome. Ash, volcanic bombs, and rocks the size of basketballs rained down on the slopes. It sounded like artillery fire."

"We were all thinking, *Did we survive the war only to get bombed by lava rocks?*

"Our commanding officer, who was only a captain, talked to someone on his walkie-talkie and then announced, as though the army could control a volcano, 'The eruption will be confined to the cone. We aren't moving. Carry on with your assignments.'

"Try concentrating when you've got a live volcano a couple of miles from you. Sometimes it was quiet, and we thought the crisis was over. Other times the ground shook like the world was ending. Then more explosions. The sky was gray with ash.

"One night the whole top of the mountain was burning. Spouts of fire and lava shot into the air, spilled over the sides of the crater, and ran in red streams down the slopes. Our unit was called to help evacuate the little town of San Sebastiano. We piled into Jeeps and raced to the village. A rolling tide of fiery lava thirty to ninety feet deep had reached the upper town. Everything combustible in its path was on fire. Smoke and ash filled the air and blotted out the light. Trees, boulders the size of cars, and other debris carried in the lava roared down the mountain.

"We stared in horror at the oncoming disaster. Hundreds of villagers were trying to escape with their household goods. People scrambled into our Jeeps and we hauled them to nearby towns. Where was safe? Nobody knew. A short time later lava buried what was left of San Sebastiano. I've never seen people so beaten down by war and then devastated by a volcano."

Dr. Mumper shook his head as though he still hadn't recovered from seeing such troubled people.

After a pause, he said, "That, boys, was my first volcano. And it was a doozy. Vesuvius put on quite a show. I've seen twenty or more eruptions since then, but never so close-up or one that affected me more."

Chris couldn't help envying Dr. Mumper's good fortune at having witnessed an eruption of one of the most famous volcanoes in history. And survived it—unlike the unfortunate people of Pompeii in 79 AD. He hoped he would be lucky enough to see an erupting volcano sometime during his career.

"Why didn't the army move the planes?" one of the students asked.

"Good question. If they'd moved the planes right away, they could've saved them. But there wasn't anywhere to go, and the brass couldn't make a decision. By the time they realized it was an emergency, the air was so heavy with ash it was too late. We saved ourselves."

"Did they have a monitoring system?" Chris asked.

"A man peering at the summit through binoculars." Everyone laughed, including Dr. Mumper.

"Now, because it's so close to Naples, Vesuvius is one of the most monitored volcanoes in the world. I'm happy to say they use my tiltmeters as part of their data collection. Without enough warning, a pyroclastic surge from Vesuvius could bury Naples and kill a million people."

Dr. Mumper let the ominous prospect of such a disaster hang in the air for a time before changing his tone.

"Now we're in for a treat. Millie has made her famous cherry cheesecake."

>>

After declining a ride from Bryan, Chris walked slowly back to his apartment. He needed a few minutes to clear his head before studying for his next day's exam. He thought back to when he'd explored Volcanoes National Park on the Big Island in Hawaii. He had loved the park's strangeness: steam emanating from a jumble of rocks tinted unearthly green, lava tubes you could walk through, flowering shrubs growing out of black lava, and a geyser where a thin stream of molten lava from Mount Kilauea poured into the Pacific. Primordial forces, the real nitty-gritty of the planet, were on display there.

Kilauea had been well-behaved when Chris saw it. At other times, he knew, massive tides of fiery lava from Kilauea had slowly obliterated towns and farms on the island. Watching a wall of lava ninety feet deep roar down Vesuvius and engulf a village must have been spectacular. And traumatizing. He understood now why Dr. Mumper had developed a passion for predicting volcanic eruptions.

>>

Two days before Thanksgiving, Chris found his sister Nancy sitting on the front porch of his apartment building when he returned from class.

"Nancy, what a surprise!" *She must be having a crisis. I wonder what's going on.*

Chris gave her a hug when she stood up.

"If you ever answered your phone, I wouldn't be such a surprise," Nancy said with a teasing grin.

"Really? You couldn't get a hold of me?"

She seemed cheerful; he supposed that meant everything was all right. But her surprising him like this was not good timing. He'd planned to spend the break writing a paper.

"Truthfully, I just decided this morning to skip my class tomorrow and fly down here," Nancy said, handing her suitcase to Chris.

"Great! I'm glad you're here, but isn't Mom expecting you for Thanksgiving?" He hoped their mother wouldn't resent the two of them spending the holiday together instead of going home. On the other hand, she actually might be pleased. While he and Nancy were growing up, their mom had tried to convince them they were best friends, even when it was ludicrous, as when he was in high school, and she was still in grade school. No doubt the loss of their dad so young had motivated his mother to make sure her children were bonded so they would have each other in the future when she was gone.

"They won't miss me," Nancy said as they walked upstairs to Chris's apartment. "Aunt Elsie and Uncle Alvin will be there. And Mom's dentist friend is bringing his daughter and her husband and their bratty kids."

Elsie and Alvin, their jolliest relatives, could hold their own with the dentist and his daughter's family, Chris thought. "Yeah, Mom tried to get me to come home, but I've got a paper to write."

"I thought maybe you were staying away because of Mom's boyfriend."

She's right, of course, but I won't admit it. "Hmmm . . . well. I do have work. Here we are."

Chris turned his key in the lock and opened the door.

Nancy looked around. "Hey, not as bad as I thought it would be."

The tiny living room was attractive, even though there was only a small, blue-patterned sofa, a beige chair, bookcases, and a floor lamp.

"All I need. And by the way, it came furnished, so I can't take credit."

Nancy plopped down in the chair. "How about a margarita for a thirsty traveler?"

"Sure—if I had any tequila. Or limes. Or triple sec," Chris said, walking into the adjacent kitchen. "How about a Lone Star?" He held up a beer from the refrigerator.

Nancy shrugged. "If that's my only choice."

Chris grabbed another beer and joined Nancy in the living room.

"So what do you really think of Dr. Benson?" Chris asked. "Other than he has bratty grandchildren?"

"At first I liked him because Mom seemed happy. Then I got to know him, and he started to seem a little ghoulish. As though he couldn't wait to drill into your most painful molar."

Chris laughed. "He seemed okay the only time I met him."

Chris marveled at how grown-up his sister was. He was accustomed to thinking of her as his little sister. The seven years' difference in their age meant they hadn't been close as children. Now she seemed independent and confident. He was grateful their mom and Nancy had come to visit during his last year stationed in Hawaii. The ten days they had explored all the sites on Oahu was the most time they had spent together since childhood. They'd found they shared a similar sense of humor and a practical approach to life. Now, he considered her his best friend. Given enough time, their mother's wish for a strong bond between Chris and Nancy had come true.

"It doesn't matter whether we like Dr. Benson. Mom's happy, so we have to be happy. But please tell me you're coming home for Christmas," Nancy said.

"I am. Probably for a couple of weeks."

"Yay! There's a chance I might bring home this guy I've been dating. I think you and he would really like each other."

"Great." Chris got up and carried Nancy's suitcase into the

bedroom. "You can have the bedroom. I'll take the couch, where I've been known to sleep anyway when I'm studying."

"No, let me sleep on the sofa. I'm way shorter than you."

"If you're in the bedroom, I won't have to worry about waking you if I turn on the light. Let's go get some dinner!"

>>

Later at Smitty's Grill, Nancy asked, "So what happened to you and Linda?"

"It's a long story. Wait. Did Mom send you down here to interrogate me?" He wished his mom would quit worrying about him. She had married young, so she thought Chris was a confirmed bachelor at thirty, like her two uncles who had stayed on the farm.

"Nope."

Chris took a deep breath. "It all came down to a wedding."

"It always does! She wanted to get married, and you weren't ready." Nancy looked up and studied her brother's face. "All my graduating friends are going through it."

Chris relished being unpredictable and said in a gleeful tone, "Wrong. One of her older brothers got married this past summer. She wanted me to be an usher in his wedding, but my fieldwork was scheduled to start two weeks before the wedding, so I told her I couldn't."

"You couldn't take a weekend off?" she asked, cutting her unmanageably large burger in half.

"It would've been a four-day ordeal, counting travel time, rehearsal dinner, and wedding—not to mention renting a tux." Chris took a chug of beer as though still stressed from a narrow escape.

"Ordeal! That's not how most people describe weddings," Nancy said, laughing.

"I think it was a test. Linda wanted to know how serious I was about our relationship and how eager I was to make a good impression on her family. I couldn't go to the wedding so soon after starting fieldwork, and I stayed in the field all summer." *It turned out to be a lonely damn summer,* he remembered.

"You flunked the test," Nancy said.

"I did," Chris said, nodding.

"Didn't you date for almost a year?"

"Yep. Despite being extreme opposites."

"Being opposites isn't all bad. Here, eat the other half of my burger," Nancy said, handing her plate across the table.

"At the party where we first met, I asked her to describe herself in one word. She answered 'Festive.'"

"Well, what do you expect someone at a party to say? Grumpy?"

Chris laughed grudgingly. "Yeah, but I'm serious and introverted."

"You're not introverted. Just a little quiet—and grumpy."

"Listen to this. Her family belongs to a country club." Chris shook his head as though it were hard to believe. "Their whole life revolves around it."

"Isn't it okay if you can afford it?"

"Geologists don't belong to country clubs! We like wide-open spaces. Wilderness."

"Golf courses are wide-open spaces."

"Funny. Golf clubs are closed places. There's no chance an interesting person, a stranger, maybe a scientist, might drop by for dinner. I went to their club one time. Friendly. Good food. Giant glasses of wine. And I mean giant. But what troubled me was that no one had just wandered into the restaurant spontaneously. No, it's all planned. You join. You pay. You see the same people over and over."

"Yes. They become your friends." Nancy rolled her eyes. "What's wrong with seeing a bunch of friends when you go out to dinner?"

"Nothing. But you aren't seeing my point." Chris was annoyed. "It's homogeneous. They all have a certain level of financial success to afford to join a private club. And a certain amount of leisure to spend six hours playing golf." Maybe she was still too much of a kid to understand the way the world operated. Or maybe he was focusing on country clubs so he didn't have to deal with his feelings for Linda, Chris thought in a rare flash of insight into his own emotions.

"You can't blame Linda for what her parents are like," Nancy said, shaking her head for emphasis.

Chris frowned. "I'm not blaming her, damn it!"

"It's not fair. You're assuming she's exactly like her parents."

"Whose side are you on, anyway?"

They sat in hostile silence while they finished their beers.

He felt bad they were arguing. She had flown all the way from Ohio to Texas to see him, and her concern for him was genuine. *How did I let the conversation get out of control?*

"Don't you see? We would've made each other miserable," Chris said, feeling miserable. "Every decision would've been a clash. What to do on weekends, where to live, who our friends would be, what music to play." Chris sighed. "The truth is I miss her. But extreme opposites don't work."

Nancy started to say something but sat back, seemingly resigned.

>>

After class the day before Christmas break, Chris, Bryan, and Matt, another geology grad student, converged on the graduate assistants' cubicles on the second floor of the Geo Sciences building. Bryan sat down at his desk, Chris grabbed a chair from the adjoining cubicle, and Matt leaned on Bryan's desk. They all flipped through their papers that had just been returned to them.

"Okay, so what grades did you guys get?" Matt asked.

"A," Chris and Bryan answered simultaneously.

"Damn. Don gave me a B," Matt said.

"Did he say why?" Chris asked.

"No, but I'm going to talk to him and find out what's going on."

"I wonder what kind of grades that girl gets," Bryan said.

"You mean Lauren?" Chris asked.

"Oh, yeah, that's her name. After her lecture, I thought she was going to be the star of our class. Then she kind of faded away."

"You noticed that, too," Chris said. "She slips into class and sits in the back row. When class is over, she hurries away. I don't think anybody ever talks to her."

"All those guys walking out on her report probably pissed her off," Matt said.

"Or demoralized her," Chris said.

He remembered being dazzled by Lauren's presentation. Her passion for geology showed in the sparkle of her green eyes as she had described two unyielding tectonic plates, the Indian Plate and the Eurasian Plate, colliding slowly and causing the jagged Himalayas to uplift. It was as though she wished she could time travel back fifty million years to see the whole process begin. He couldn't imagine the joy of dating someone who understood geology. What great conversations they could have. Of course, she was married, so he was wasting his time thinking about her.

Chapter 3

Bermuda Triangle

Lauren, 1976–77

"I'll stay only if you ask me to," Lauren said to her husband of five years.

She paused in the doorway to their living room while Kenny, silent, stared at the television screen. Tears streamed down her face as she walked into the bedroom and started throwing clothes into suitcases. She had to get out. She wouldn't stay where she wasn't wanted. Jan, her one friend in the area, had offered to let her sleep on her sofa if she were ever in a predicament. Two suitcases of clothes, a backpack of books, and a corkscrew were all Lauren took from the apartment. Moving out of her marriage and her apartment at the same instant was the hardest thing she had ever done.

After loading her suitcases into the car, she sat behind the wheel and sobbed. Her soulmate and best friend wanted her gone. Their relationship had always been a protective shell around her. Now it was cracked, and large pieces were falling away. She felt raw and exposed.

Shit! My life is shit! Kenny doesn't love me. Nobody loves me. Not even my own mother. What am I going to do? I don't have a place to live.

She had to get away from there. What if Kenny looked out and saw her sitting in the car? But she couldn't go to Jan's place looking like a wreck. When she stopped crying enough to see, she drove to Jan's apartment and knocked on her door.

>>

Just months earlier, she and Kenny had moved to Pasadena, Texas, so Lauren could get her master's in geology at Texas Polytechnic. After their Grand Canyon adventure, they had stayed in Philadelphia two years to help Lauren's mother, Betty, cope with Lauren's grandmother's final illness and the settlement of her estate. With Betty well provided for in a trust, Lauren and Kenny had felt free to move to Prescott, Arizona, where Lauren spent two years getting an undergraduate degree in geology. When she was offered an assistantship to work on her master's at Tex Poly, Kenny had been eager for a new adventure and transferred to an investment office in Pasadena of the same national firm he had worked for in Prescott. He was postponing the inevitable: going back to school to get an MBA.

At first, everything was great. But when the excitement of being in a new place wore off, Kenny grew increasingly moody. He complained his boss assigned him too many worthless clients. Some days he didn't have enough to do, and other days he had to work late.

Lauren was troubled by his behavior. She had never seen him so gloomy. Something had changed, and she didn't know what. Maybe he was blaming her for their move to Texas.

Kenny walked in the door from work one night and said, "Life is hell and then you die."

"Wow. I guess you didn't have a good day." Lauren stood back and looked at him. "What happened?"

"Oh, nothing. Or maybe everything," Kenny said, brushing by her.

"What does that mean?"

"It doesn't mean anything, okay?" Kenny said from the bedroom.

She was trying to understand what was bothering him, and he was talking in riddles. And being rude. After her initial annoyance, she felt sad this was the state of their relationship. He wouldn't talk to her or tell her what was wrong.

"Do you want a beer? If we have one?"

Lauren looked in the refrigerator and rummaged among takeout containers, a pizza box, and cans of soda but didn't find any beer. "Sorry, thought we had one."

"Damn. I parked three blocks away. Now I've gotta go to the store," he said, walking out the door.

Why did I apologize for not having any beer? He was the one who always bought it. And drank it. A couple of minutes later, she looked down from their balcony at his receding figure as he walked toward his car. She was losing him, and she didn't know why.

When Lauren was home evenings, Kenny acted restless and irritable. When she stayed at school to study or do lab work, he stayed out late. He didn't seem to want their paths to cross, let alone lead a normal life with her.

On another night when he arrived home from work, he asked, "What's for dinner?"

"I stopped at the grocery and picked up deli meats and salads," Lauren said, leaning back in her desk chair and stretching.

"Not again. Sandwiches are all we eat around here," Kenny said with a frown. "When we were in Prescott, you used to cook."

"Yeah. Sorry. I miss my cooking, too," she said with a laugh. "Undergraduate geology was way easier than what I'm doing now. Maybe tomorrow I'll have time to make a nice dinner."

"Tell me in advance when we're having deli, and I'll go out."

He grabbed a beer from the refrigerator.

Lauren's mouth dropped open in surprise at Kenny's testy attitude.

"There are worse things than deli foods. I practically grew up on them, you know."

"It's not very appealing," he said, turning on the television.

Lauren couldn't help tearing up. She hurried into the bedroom so he wouldn't see her crying. His meaning was clear. Everything about her was unappealing. So much of her life she had felt unlovable. Kenny had changed that. But now something was wrong. She was desperate to save her marriage.

The next night Lauren made Kenny's favorite meal: roast beef cooked with carrots, onions, and potatoes. He didn't come home. At nine o'clock she dialed his office number, but no one answered. The meat and vegetables sat untouched in a pan of juices and congealed fat. At eleven o'clock she went to bed and lay awake waiting for him to return. When he finally slipped into bed, he smelled of beer and something undefinable. She reached over and touched his arm, but he turned his back to her.

The ultimate rebuff! Kenny didn't even want her to touch him. It was foolish of her to think their broken relationship could be repaired with a good dinner.

"How am I supposed to know when you're suddenly going to start cooking?" Kenny said the next morning when Lauren asked him why he hadn't come home until late. "Besides, you're always studying."

"Tomorrow's Friday. I promise I'll finish my work by five. Let's try a new barbecue place—maybe one with live music."

"Sorry, our office is having a dinner for one of the secretaries who's moving."

Kenny didn't seem to notice Lauren's shoulders slump or the corners of her mouth turn down.

A pattern developed where he either worked late or went out for drinks with colleagues. The work environment he complained of at first had turned into his preferred life.

>>

"How could Kenny have changed in just a few months?" Lauren asked Jan the next night as they ate pizza in her cozy apartment. "I couldn't do anything right—from the groceries I bought to my books and papers scattered over the desk. It was as though he couldn't stand my presence in our apartment."

"How demoralizing," Jan said.

"I finally figured if I can do nothing right, then I might as well stop trying. I had to move out. Not only does he not love me, he doesn't even like me." Lauren wiped a tear from her cheek.

"Maybe he's just out of touch with his feelings."

"Yeah, maybe." She paused. "It's strange because we were happy in Prescott. We hiked and explored almost every weekend. We seemed more compatible than ever."

She thought back to their Grand Canyon trip, which had inspired her to get a geology degree and prompted Kenny's and her move West. They had been excited to travel down the road together. Nothing was more joyful than being in love with someone who was in love with you. She wondered if she would ever have that feeling again.

>>

Two days later, when in good conscience Lauren couldn't stay on Jan's sofa any longer, she found a drab apartment near campus from an ad tacked to a bulletin board in the student center.

After unpacking her meager belongings in the partially furnished apartment, she looked at her surroundings. The main feature of the living room was a swaybacked maroon couch along one of the smudgy green walls. In the dining area, a lamp hung over what should have been a table, but there was nothing there. *I'm going to hit my head on that lamp a hundred times,* Lauren thought.

In the kitchen there was a linoleum-topped metal table and two upholstered metal chairs. It would be her study place. A tiny bed-room was furnished with a dresser and a three-quarter bed. Lauren recognized the odd-sized bed because her grandmother had had one in her guest room. Apparently, it was designed for one and a half adults, three small children, or one pet lover whose dog slept on the bed. The only one that fit Lauren was pet lover, but she lacked a dog.

At least now she had her own place and wouldn't have to feel her husband's indifference daily.

>>

Although classwork absorbed all Lauren's time and more, emotional pain didn't seem to require time. It suffused everything. She remembered the sunburns she and her childhood friend Ginny had suffered as teenagers when they lay on the beach too long at the Jersey Shore. A soft, cool bed sheet drawn over her red and blistered skin had been unimaginably painful. Kenny's abrupt rejection caused pain as searing as the sun. He had been the first person to tell her she was beautiful. He was her friend, lover, and protector. Now feelings of shame and loneliness cycled through her psyche. Her soul felt sunburned.

Lauren went to class, sat in the back row, didn't talk to anyone, and went straight home. She didn't feel worthy of friendship. The person in the world who knew her best—her husband—wanted nothing to do with her.

Aside from the year they'd spent at different colleges, Lauren and Kenny had been together since they were sixteen. Their friends had envied their compatibility. If Kenny met his friends at a pool hall, he had wanted Lauren there, too. She could always count on him to acquiesce to her plans for trips and adventures. They were a good balance for each other. He was street-smart and ambitious to acquire a secure life in the middle class. Lauren, on the other hand, had been well supported by her trust-funded grandmother, and both her grandparents and mother had graduated from college.

Kenny's strength and confidence had filled a need in Lauren that she described as a windy place in her belfry because she hadn't known her father. She had no idea what part of anatomy a belfry was—maybe her heart or spirit. A belfry was where her mother's bats resided, according to her grandmother, who wasn't afraid of using hurtful platitudes in their home.

Now, without Kenny filling that place, Lauren felt like an outline of her former self, with nothing within the borders. All the joy, love, laughter, plans, and future were missing.

>>

On a Saturday night when Lauren could no longer stand the quiet of her apartment, she walked two and a half miles to a movie theater playing *Annie Hall*. For the next hour and a half, she sat and nibbled popcorn and laughed. Kenny didn't cross her mind once.

After the movie she walked to McDonald's and used a pay phone to call Jan on the off- chance she was home and in need of a chocolate shake. When Jan said she was more in need of a glass of wine, they agreed to meet at a bar a few blocks away.

Lauren and Jan had known each other since they waited tables at the same steak house during summers in college. After graduation, Jan had followed her boyfriend to Tex Poly, but they had broken up almost immediately. She now worked as an administrative assistant to a dean.

Lauren walked three blocks to the bar and appropriated the last available booth. When Jan arrived, she waved her over.

"There was a big reception at school tonight that I had to oversee," Jan said, out of breath, as she slid into the booth. "One of my roles was making sure everyone else had a drink, so yes, I'll have a glass of wine!"

Lauren laughed and scooted out of the booth to get Jan a glass of red wine from the bar.

When she sat back down, she said. "You must see *Annie Hall*. It's hilarious."

"I've heard that. Who did you go with?"

"Nobody, but it was fine. I'm getting used to doing things by myself."

"Personally, I like Pasadena, but there must be something about moving here that busts up relationships. Pete and I lasted about a month. He freaked out about the difficulty of his graduate-level classes and decided he didn't have time for me. Fortunately, I'd found a job by then, so I was okay."

"That must have been awful. I'm so lucky you're here."

"No word from Kenny?"

"Nope. I'm sure he's seeing someone. He left our marriage but forgot to tell me."

"Really unfair."

"Yeah, but what can you do?" Lauren drank the last sip of her wine. "Those three summers of waiting tables were fun. I remember meeting Pete and thinking he was a great guy, and Kenny was madly in love with me back then. Ah, the romantic past."

"Do you know what I miss from our waitressing days? Our black aprons at the end of the evening—stuffed with money!"

They both laughed, and Lauren felt happy for the first time in a long time. Was it possible she was going to survive without Kenny?

>>

Spring showed itself early in Pasadena, but Lauren was oblivious to its beauty. There had been occasional bright spots in the months that had passed since she'd walked out, like nights out with Jan, but inevitably she found herself back in her sad apartment, alone and missing Kenny. She kept hoping for a call from him, asking her to move home, but so far, he hadn't shown any interest in getting back together. She couldn't imagine life without Kenny.

In the meantime, her professor invited her "as one of my graduate assistants" to his house for a swim followed by dinner. Don was Lauren's major adviser for graduate work in volcanology and a recognized scholar in oceanic basalts, the most common rock covering the ocean crust. It would be fun to get to know him in a social setting. He greeted her at the front door with a wide smile, his white teeth flashing in his tanned and bearded face.

"Thanks for the wine," he said. "We now officially have more than two people can possibly drink."

"Two people?" Lauren asked, peering around him with a frown as she stepped into the hall of his modern, ranch-style home.

"I try to meet with each new graduate assistant individually." Don gestured for her to follow him.

"Oh, I thought it was a department thing." *Damn,* Lauren said to herself. *I have to carry on a conversation with a famous scientist all by myself—and in a swimsuit!*

"Since I'm your thesis adviser, we should get to know each other better. Let's go out by the pool, drink a glass of wine, and then maybe take a swim."

After a glass of wine, Don took a quick dip and excused himself to finish dinner preparations. Lauren couldn't help noticing his lean, athletic body. She dangled her feet in the warm water and then slid in and swam the length of the pool a few times. She toweled off and let the late afternoon sun dry her swimsuit as she sat in a lounge chair and finished her wine.

After pulling shorts and a T-shirt over her suit, she walked inside to find the living room lit from above by candles on the mantel, and from below by Sterno. Three fondue pots bubbled and sizzled on a low table.

"You did all this for me?" Lauren couldn't help but ask. She was flattered he had gone to so much trouble. *This is so romantic.*

Don indicated a pillow on the floor by the fondue pots where Lauren should sit while he poured wine. Distracted by the gurgling pots, she missed her pillow and sat down on the hardwood floor instead. She laughed and scooted over to her assigned pillow. After handing their wine glasses to her, he lit the pre-laid fire in the fireplace and sat down on a pillow next to her. Lauren took a big gulp of wine.

"Here, try dipping bread in the melted cheese fondue, which, of course, is redundant as fondue means melted," he said as he passed her the tray of bread cubes.

"I didn't know that. I thought fondue meant cheese," Lauren said while skewering a piece of bread and dipping it into the pot.

"This is an authentic mixture of Swiss and Gruyère with a little white wine and kirsch. The kirsch gives a hint of sweetness to the cheeses."

Lauren wondered if she should eat directly from the skewer or put it on her plate first. To be safe she shook the gooey cube onto her plate and then speared it with a fork.

Don put his hand around her back, squeezed her shoulder, and said, "I was glad to see you signed up for the first research cruise of the summer."

Lauren felt flustered by his hand on her shoulder. To cover her confusion she said very fast, "The main reason I came to Tex Poly was to study ocean volcanoes. I just hope I get chosen."

"I can safely say you'll be selected since you're one of the top students to sign up."

"Really? I'll get to go?" Lauren was thrilled. Finally, she had something to look forward to in her dreary life.

"Absolutely," Don said as he topped off their wine glasses.

He continued, "We leave from New Bedford, Massachusetts, and it will take eight days to get to our destination: the Mid-Atlantic Ridge, a section of the great chain of underwater volcanoes that encircles the earth. Mountains of basaltic lava rivaling Mount Everest and canyons ten times deeper than the Grand Canyon are found in other parts of the oceanic ridge. Because there is no erosion, the fault scarps are sharp and clearly defined."

Don paused to take a swallow of his wine.

"Of course," Lauren said, relaxing now that the subject was science. "There's no rain or wind or waves crashing to erode the rock. It's obvious, but I never thought of it before."

"Exactly." Don refilled her wine and continued his description, "Contorted chimneys belch gas and lava. The chimneys stand like sentinels over an alien landscape of eyeless fish and crabs, and fragile jellyfish. Just a month or two ago, researchers discovered eight-foot-tall white tube worms living near volcanic vents in the Pacific a mile below the surface. Their red, plume-shaped heads absorb the scalding, poisonous vent fluids. That these large animals can live on poisonous chemicals is revolutionizing biology. Chemosynthesis has implications for life in space." He paused for dramatic effect. "Someday we'll see all these wonders from submersibles."

"Wow, wouldn't that be fabulous?" Lauren asked, enthralled with his descriptions. She felt her face flush. *Probably from the wine*, she thought.

She positioned a chunk of beef in the pot of hot oil.

"Let's talk about you," Don said, turning toward her.

"Me? Uh, what about me?" Lauren squirmed on her cushion, which slid backward. She struggled to hold on to the skewer.

Don didn't seem to notice her discomfort. "I don't get many smart, beautiful girls in the graduate geology program. How did you get interested in volcanology?"

"My undergraduate degree was in art, but in 1972 I saw my first volcano near Flagstaff, and I was hooked. I went back to school and got another degree—this time in geology—at the University of Arizona at Prescott. And now here I am."

"Does that ring mean you're married?" Don asked, leaning forward.

Lauren felt her heart beating fast. She took a deep breath and made herself respond, striving to keep her voice from shaking. "Yeah.

I've been married to Kenny for almost six years, even though we're temporarily separated. But I'm sure we'll get back together."

"Is Kenny a geologist?"

"No. Right now he's working as a financial planner. But he's probably . . . for sure going back to school to get an MBA."

"It sounds a lot like my situation. My wife is a petroleum engineer. We lead totally separate lives. Right now, she's detailed to the Gulf for six months. And I'll be at sea virtually all summer."

Don placed his hand on Lauren's thigh and massaged gently. She noticed how the warmth of his touch spread through her whole being. A thrill of excitement caused her to shiver. *Oh, dear. Now he knows how turned on I am.*

"You seem tense," Don said. "I happen to have some brownies that are particularly relaxing."

"Oh, I'm not tense. Just a little ticklish, is all. But I do love chocolate," she said, watching him stand up to reach a plate of brownies.

"Now let's talk about us," he said, handing her a brownie on a paper napkin as he sat down again.

"Us?"

"Yes, the minute I saw you in my class, I knew we were meant to be together."

Lauren considered this for a minute, chewing a bite of brownie. "You thought that the very first day of class?" Her voice trailed away as Don kissed her ear.

His beard tickled her cheek. He kissed her lightly near her mouth and then sought her lips. She let him lay her down on the bearskin rug in front of the fireplace. They kissed deeply as they faced each other on the surprisingly soft bearskin. Every cell in Lauren's body tingled with desire. Wood burning in the fireplace hissed and crackled as they made love for what seemed like hours.

Lauren's loneliness left her completely. She felt like the world's most desirable woman.

>>

Later that night as she lay in her own bed, she pondered her surprising behavior. *What have I done? Was I actually naked with my professor? How will I face him in class without blushing?* She felt disloyal to Kenny, despite his absence and indifference. Lovemaking had always been something wondrous between them—two people who knew each other's soul as well as they knew each other's body. Evenly matched intimacy. Disproportionate intimacy, as with Don, was disconcerting.

The next morning a bouquet of red roses sat outside the door to Lauren's apartment with a note from Don inviting her to dinner that night. She was thrilled she wouldn't have to spend the whole day and night by herself as she usually did on Sundays. But then a few guilty thoughts intruded on her happiness. Don was her professor and major thesis adviser. And he was married. What if someone from the university saw them together? If Don wasn't worried, maybe she shouldn't be, either?

>>

In February when she had signed up for the month-long voyage to study ocean volcanoes, she never dreamed she would be having an affair with her professor, the director of the voyage and an icon in volcanology. Lauren could not believe her good fortune. She, whose husband rejected her, was wanted by a man who was her idol. And she was going on her first real expedition at sea. Scientific research and romantic adventure were an intoxicating mix.

At the end of May, Don and Lauren flew to Boston and drove to New Bedford, their embarkation point. Lauren stepped out of the car and breathed deeply of the salt mist. It brought back wonderful childhood memories of walking along the beach in Atlantic City with her grandfather.

The night of their arrival, Lauren and Don ordered lobster and crab dinners at The White Whale Restaurant overlooking the harbor. They talked of ocean basalts and the hope of bringing up something spectacular like gabbro or serpentine. Perhaps they would map an erupting volcano. Lauren was living a dream too good to be real, yet so real nothing else mattered.

"I'm glad we have a day before the rest of the crew arrives," Don said. "It will be trickier when we're on board ship. We'll need to keep up appearance of professor and student, but we'll find a way to be together."

The other Tex Poly students, of course, knew Don was married. Lauren wasn't as troubled by this as she thought she would be. His wife didn't seem to be part of his life. She was rarely home, he said, and they hadn't had sex in two years. *That explains why they don't have children*, Lauren had thought at the time. She had never envisioned herself in an illicit love affair.

During her freshman year of college when she and Kenny were at different schools, a married teaching assistant had given her a ride home from study group. He had tried to kiss her when he parked in front of her dorm. She had glanced in the back at an infant seat and scattered toys. Picturing an innocent baby, she had fled from his car. She wouldn't put a mother with a baby on one vertex of a triangle. It was too precarious. Now here she was having an affair with a married man. How had this happened? Who was being hurt? She would sort out her conscience at a later date.

>>

After lunch the following day, Don and Lauren boarded Tex Poly's research ship, *The Coriolis,* with its dark blue hull and white smoke-stack painted with the school crest. Compared to the yachts and fishing boats in the vicinity, *The Coriolis* was ungainly. Three research labs shaped like boxcars perched on the deck.

Before splitting up and walking in different directions on the ship, Don whispered,

"We'll get together as soon as we can."

Lauren checked in and then went below deck to find her assigned student cabin. Her two roommates—Sherry, a marine biology major, and Greta, an oceanography student—were already getting settled in the very small space. Two sets of bunk beds took up most of the floorspace.

After introductions, Sherry asked, "Shall we flip for the bottom bunks?"

"Not necessary. I'll take an upper bunk," Lauren said. A bunk bed was a bunk bed, she figured. Up or down—the same narrow bed with a thin mattress. She was happy her roommates seemed lively and good-natured. A month in close quarters could be disastrous with the wrong mix of people.

"I feel like a little kid at Girl Scout camp," Greta said, sitting down on a bed and peering out from under the top bunk.

Lauren laughed. "Yes, except instead of canoeing, you'll learn to launch a lifeboat. Speaking of which, we're supposed to be on deck in a half hour for a safety drill."

Just then a loud explosion made the ship lurch.

"Oh, my God!" Greta said.

"Yikes! What's happening?" Lauren said, holding on to the wall for balance.

The three of them ran for the stairway. A series of smaller explosions vibrated the ship and then settled into a rhythmic snorting.

"It's the engine!" Sherry said, stopping halfway up the stairs.

They walked back to their room, which, they now realized, was directly above the engine room. A chorus of grinding gears, rolling thuds, belches, and bangs rose through the floor. They stood listening. The noises were so outrageous and hilarious, at the same time, that Sherry started laughing. Greta and Lauren joined her.

When they recovered, Greta asked with a look of disbelief, "How will we ever sleep?"

"I have no idea," Lauren said. "Let's get out of here and see what's happening on deck."

>>

Around eleven o'clock that night after a safety drill, orientation, team meetings, dinner, and a welcome party in the galley, the roommates headed to their room with trepidation. Greta and Sherry settled into the lower bunks. Lauren crawled up to her bunk and tried to lie still. She was sure she would never sleep, but the gentle rocking and rolling of the ship counteracted the hideous noises. She was at peace on the ocean. Perhaps because her mother had been inadequate, she found comfort in the sea, the great "mother element of life," as described by one of her favorite writers, Loren Eisley. She soon slept and dreamed of gentle waves slapping against the pier in Atlantic City, where she sat with her grandfather.

>>

The next day Lauren and Sherry made their way to a makeshift classroom on the main deck to hear Don's talk. Geologists shared the cruise with oceanographers and marine biologists, all with their own projects. They took turns giving each other lectures. Research and discovery were the essence of science, always searching for an elusive truth.

They joined students already settled in scattered chairs. Lauren noticed how attractive Don looked in his khaki shorts and navy shirt rolled up at the sleeves. He leaned casually against a table at the front. They listened as he gave an overview of the geology project.

"Mountain building. Volcanic eruptions. Earthquakes. Before plate tectonics, no satisfactory explanations existed for these phenomena. Plate tectonics has revolutionized geology as dramatically as evolution transformed biology."

Don paused for a moment and then launched into his lecture on the progression of discoveries and evidence supporting the theory of plate tectonics. Sherry listened intently while Lauren, who knew all the information by heart, let herself drift into reverie.

She blushed at the thought of their lovemaking the night they'd arrived. Their hotel room had come with an oversized, jetted bathtub, which they filled almost as soon as they set their duffels down. They had soaped and caressed each other like sleek water creatures, reveling in every touch. She had never been so uninhibited. At home they usually stayed at Don's house, where she couldn't help sensing the presence of his wife, even though she was away. If they spent the night at Lauren's apartment, instead, one of them was always on the verge of falling off her skimpy, three-quarter bed. A hotel room was heavenly.

When she realized Don's talk was reaching its conclusion, she changed her focus to what he was saying.

"Geology now has a comprehensive theory for understanding Earth's subterranean movements. Active volcanoes and frequent earthquakes along the Pacific Ring of Fire demonstrate that subduction of the ocean floor at the trenches causes most of the volcanism on Earth and the majority of earthquakes. Plate tectonics can be likened to a conveyor belt, making new earth every day at the ridges and destroying that same rock millions of years later at the subduction zones by recycling it back into the mantle, melting it, and forming new volcanoes and new land all around the Pacific. In the process, of course, it causes chaos and destruction for humans to deal with: quakes, tsunamis, and volcanic eruptions.

"Plates converge, diverge, or slide by each other. But what causes them to move? That's the question driving our research today. The answer can only be found by looking at the chemistry, structure, and composition of the ocean floor lava flows. When we are on station at the Mid-Atlantic Ridge, we'll be dredging twenty-four hours a day for rock samples that we hope will yield clues to why plates move."

How lucky am I, Lauren thought, *to be doing research on the most compelling geology issue of our time?* Too often in her life she had felt vaguely discontented with her work or studies, as though she were missing her true calling. Now everything felt right.

>>

After four days at sea Lauren was impatient for the time she and Don could be together. So far, they had stolen only a few moments to hug and kiss when they were alone. Finally, Don slipped her a note asking her to meet him in the geology lab.

"Lauren, darling," Don said, taking her into his arms the minute she walked into the lab that night.

They kissed before realizing the door had swung open and anyone walking by could have seen them.

"There's no doorknob! Or lock!" she said, laughing.

"Right. The wood around the doorknob kind of rotted out, so either someone removed the doorknob, or it fell out."

A couple of extra bunk bed mattresses were stored against the wall.

"Let's move one of the mattresses so it blocks the lower part of the door," Don said.

They moved the other mattress next to the one blocking the door. Lauren hesitated, and then sat down on the mattress.

"If our hotel room the other night hadn't been so luxurious, the lab wouldn't seem so lacking in amenities," Lauren said, chuckling.

Don glanced around and frowned. "This is pretty rough, but we're together, and that's all that matters."

Before sitting down, he reached under one of the work counters and produced a bottle of wine, an opener, and two plastic glasses. "An amenity," he said, smiling.

"Nice."

After a glass of wine, they undressed each other and lay down face-to-face on the narrow mattress. Don stroked and caressed Lauren's body with his hands and tongue. He was slow and gentle, and his beard tickled. Even with a sea breeze, they were soon covered with sweat. They made love all night to the rolling of the ship.

>>

In the morning they awoke to an amazing sight. An image of the ocean, the ship's rail, and the pinks and oranges of sunrise undulated upside down on the back wall. Light streaming through the hole from the missing doorknob produced the pinhole camera effect. It was a perfect awakening—a gift from the sea and sky to commemorate a beautiful experience. They saw the image at the right time, for it was fleeting.

Lauren lay back with her hands behind her head while Don dressed hurriedly. She had a sudden sense their relationship was too exciting to last. The last few weeks she had felt so loved—or at least desired—that it had blotted out the rejection and loneliness from her failed marriage. The short-lived image of the sunrise seemed to say beauty can't stay. She tried to shake the feeling, but it stayed with her for a while.

>>

The sea was kind and smooth the whole month. The geology dredging operation ran efficiently despite the inexperience of the students. The water was clear thirty meters down. Sunsets lasted for hours. The entire ocean mirrored vivid reds, oranges, pinks, and golds that flickered on small swells as though seen through a kaleidoscope. When the sun finally sank beneath the horizon, the curvature of the earth was revealed.

One night on the flying bridge, Lauren asked Don, "What's that light on the horizon?"

"We're in the middle of the Atlantic. Land is hundreds of miles away. It's got to be a ship."

They watched for over an hour as it grew brighter.

Lauren ran down to the galley to alert others to come up top.

"Put down your cards. Come see the approaching ship!"

Scientists and crew members gathered on deck with Don and Lauren. As they watched, the light grew in intensity until a small crescent moon broke the horizon.

"What the?"

"Hey! Where's the ship?"

Everyone talked and laughed at the same time.

"Moon ahoy!" One of the other geology professors clapped Don on the back. "You better warn Captain he's on a collision course with the moon!"

Don's laugh sounded forced. "Very funny. That little shit of a moon fooled me."

The others wandered off, but Don and Lauren stayed on deck.

"That bastard! Turning everything into a joke. At my expense," Don said.

"He was just having fun. He didn't mean anything by it."

"No? He asks the most asinine questions about my journal articles."

"What does that have to do with tonight?" Lauren asked.

"There's an opening on the Board of the American Geosciences Institute. I'll make sure he doesn't get it."

"The board you're on?"

"Yep. He's applied for it."

"Don, you can't do that! He's a well-respected geologist. You told me that yourself."

"Wait and see."

Lauren shook her head in exasperation and moved a few steps away from Don.

"At least we got everybody out of the galley into the fresh air," she said after a long pause. She wasn't going to let Don's foul mood ruin the beautiful night.

As the moon ascended, its light softened and stars repossessed the sky. At that moment Lauren knew exactly how ancient peoples had seen the night and why they invested stars with the power to guide not only their ships, but also their lives.

>>

Toward the end of the thirty-day voyage, the ship's store of fresh food was nearly depleted. Every leaf of green lettuce and carrot stick had long since been consumed. Apples tasted like the potatoes near which they were stored. Suppers consisted of unidentified canned meat over noodles, rice, or potatoes. Far worse than the food situation was the fact that every drop of rum, vodka, tequila, and wine students had brought aboard had been drunk, mindfully or drunkenly, as the case may have been.

On the final leg of its journey to Miami, *The Coriolis* cruised slowly and carefully through the heart of the Bermuda Triangle in the Sargasso Sea. Lauren had read fascinating tales of planes and ships disappearing because of magnetic field aberrations that shut down electrical systems and set compasses spinning. Boats and ships found adrift with no passengers or crew led to a crazy hypothesis that aliens used the Triangle to kidnap Earth specimens. Another equally fantastic explanation for wrecks and disappearances was that forces from undersea civilizations crippled travel in the Triangle.

Even though she didn't believe the fanciful tales, it was a bit unnerving. The Sargasso Sea was a warm, calm body of water with weak currents. The waters were filled with brownish-green seaweed that trapped weather moisture. The air was eerie and misty. The sun appeared larger than normal—a gray-green-yellow with undefined edges. Lauren heard peculiar sounds from birds that rested on seaweed mats on their journey across the ocean. An ugly brown booby bird landed on the ship's crow's nest, where it stayed for an afternoon and a night. Luckily, the ship's larder contained enough canned meat to allow the bird to escape its time-honored role as easily acquired food for hungry sailors. *The Coriolis*, with cheering students lining the deck, glided smoothly into the Port of Miami. The Bermuda Triangle had proved powerless over the ship on its charmed voyage.

Chapter 4

Land

Lauren, 1977

The phone rang as Lauren barged into her apartment with luggage from the cruise. She grabbed the receiver and answered out of breath.

"Lauren," Don said. "I'm glad I got you. I stopped for Chinese takeout on the way home. I'm heading over to pick you up."

The two had flown from Miami to Houston with other Tex Poly students and professors from the cruise. To be discreet, they had traveled home from the airport to Pasadena in separate cars. She longed to spend an evening alone after a month of living in such close quarters on the ship. Also, time away from Don might give her a perspective on their relationship.

"Oh, no. I just got here. I need to unpack. And I was so looking forward to a shower that doesn't move around when I'm trying to stand under it."

Don laughed. "I've got one of those land showers, too. You can shower here. I'll be at your place in ten minutes."

Lauren hung up the phone. As exciting as life with Don was, she didn't seem to have much say in it. For a second, she had thought it might be Kenny on the phone. She wondered if her husband even knew she'd been at sea for a month. There was no note or telephone message at her apartment building to indicate he had checked on her. It made her sad to think he was gone from her life.

>>

When they arrived at Don's house, the kitchen gave off wonderful aromas of garlic, sesame oil, and soy sauce. White cartons of takeout food sat on a cookie sheet in the partially open oven.

Lauren took one look at the backyard where the swimming pool glowed blue in the dusk, and said, "Last one in the pool's a rotten egg."

She ran out the door stripping off shorts, tank top, panties, and bra. Don followed, laughing and tearing off his clothes. Lauren dove into the deep end and swam to the middle of the pool. The water was warm and clear. Don surfaced near her, slipped his arm around her waist, and pulled her toward him. They kissed. His body was lean and hard. Hers was soft but slender. He kissed one breast and then the other. His hands traced her inner thighs, causing small ripples of water to undulate between her legs. The tension became unbearable. She wound her legs around him and took him into her.

Later as they toweled off, Don said, "I wanted you so badly that day on the cruise when we were trying to go for a swim."

They had been poised to jump into the Atlantic, but the captain had stopped them when he spotted sharks.

Don continued, "We could have gotten out of sight under the stern. I was tempted to say, 'Sharks be damned!'"

"You're crazy. No way was I going to swim with sharks," Lauren said, laughing.

As quickly as they could set cartons and plates on the kitchen table, they feasted on kung pao shrimp, sesame chicken, and sweet and sour pork. After being deprived of vegetables for almost a week on board ship, Lauren relished the crunch of peppers, carrots, and celery, and the smoky undertones of mushrooms.

"I'll make reservations for tomorrow night at The Steak Place so we can celebrate my flawless research voyage. I accomplished everything in my grant proposal." Don smiled and sat back with his arms crossed.

"*You* accomplished? What about all of us students dredging and hauling rocks?" she asked, raising her eyebrows. Don hadn't taken a shift on the dredge. Every time she had gone down to the galley for meals, he had been there drinking coffee with other professors.

"Yes, yes, of course."

He seemed annoyed at having to acknowledge the work of others.

"I can't go to dinner tomorrow. Jan and I are getting together." Lauren was glad she had plans. It would be a relief to take a break from Don.

"Now why would you do that when you can go with me to the best restaurant in town?" he asked, frowning.

"Jan's a dear friend. She let me stay with her when I moved out of Kenny's and my apartment. We made plans before the cruise to go out when I got back." Spending time with an old friend sounded wonderful. Talking to Jan always helped Lauren sort out her own life.

"You know, my wife is coming into town in a couple of weeks. I won't be able to see you while she's here, so you better take advantage of the time we have."

There was silence for a few seconds. A wave of guilt washed over Lauren.

"Oh, dear. I've been repressing that we're both married to other people. I feel horrible."

She covered her face with her hands.

Don reached across the table and uncovered her face.

"I've told you before, my wife and I lead totally separate lives."

"Yes, but the fact is, you're married. And the fact is, I'm married." *How did I get into this mess?*

Lauren was suddenly uncomfortable in another woman's kitchen and wanted to go home.

"Maybe we should take a break to try to figure out what we're doing."

"Nonsense. We're made for each other. We'll go out and celebrate the next night."

She really didn't know what she was doing. She needed space. Her affair with Don and the excitement of the cruise had distracted her from her unraveled marriage. Sooner or later, she would have to face Kenny and settle things. She dreaded hearing him say he wanted a divorce.

>>

July in Pasadena was as miserable a month as Lauren could remember. Hot, humid weather continued day after day. She had a sense she had caught a fast-moving train and couldn't get off. Don continued to ply her with romance: flowers, poems, and fancy dinners. The night before his wife was to arrive, Lauren broached a subject she and Don had avoided lately.

"You know, Kenny and I have never talked about what we're going to do about our marriage. Most of the time I'm convinced he'll want a divorce, but then I don't know. . ." She was frustrated by Don's refusal to acknowledge how unsettled her life was. She wished she could get through to him.

"I can only guess what my wife has been doing alone for six months with a bunch of male petroleum engineers."

"Maybe while she's here you can resolve some of the issues between you?" *Please, let him reconcile with his wife,* Lauren thought. Lately, she had worried Don's and her relationship would cause them trouble at the university. The fact that he was her thesis adviser meant he had to approve every aspect of her research and thesis. People in the department might question whether her work was legitimate or tainted by favoritism.

"Highly doubtful."

Damn. It would be so much better if Don broke it off with me. She needed to be alone. And he would expect her to resume their relationship when his wife left town again. Lauren should have known she couldn't forget Kenny so easily.

>>

During the time Don's wife was in town, Lauren was relieved to have space to try to understand what was happening in her life. Kenny had called twice in the last week, once to ask where she'd been for so long, and once to inquire if she needed money. During the second call, he'd suggested they meet for a beer at a bar near their old apartment, where he still lived.

She and Kenny had discovered the dark, dank bar when they first moved to Pasadena. The wood floors smelled of years of spilled beers. It reminded Kenny of the bar where his older brothers had taken him when he was underage and used a fake ID. For fear of finding Kenny there with another woman, Lauren had stayed away from the bar since she moved out. Now, with her heart beating fast, she walked in the door.

Kenny swiveled around on his bar stool and gave her a big smile.

"Hi, babe. How's it going?"

Seeing his smile and having him call her "babe" almost undid her. Suddenly, she was back in their marriage when they loved each other. It was all she could do to not tear up. She looked away for a minute and then tried to act casual.

"Hey. What's up?"

"We haven't seen each other in a while. I thought I'd check in." Kenny ordered two beers, and they moved to a booth.

Lauren admired his smoothness. He acted as though being separated and meeting at their old bar were perfectly normal events in their married life.

"The cruise was fantastic," Lauren said with a nervous smile as she settled into the booth.

"Now it's a cruise? You told me you just got back from a research expedition in the Atlantic." He looked doubtful.

For just a second Kenny seemed vulnerable. Maybe he still had feelings for her, after all.

"Of course. That's what it was—a working voyage, not a vacation." Lauren had a guilty flashback to Don's and her lovemaking. "When we got to the Mid-Atlantic Ridge, we dredged for rocks twenty-four hours a day."

Why do I feel guilty when he's the one who wanted the separation? Maybe it's because I still love him.

"A ridge in the ocean sounds weird."

"Undersea, of course. It's part of the longest chain of mountains on Earth. Two tectonic plates come together there. North America and Europe are slowly moving away from each other because they're on different plates."

"Then I'd better get to Europe before the cost of travel goes up."

Lauren laughed. "You've got an era or two before that happens. How's your work going, by the way?" She was glad to see Kenny had recovered his sense of humor, which had been missing the last few months before Lauren moved out.

"The good thing about a bad job is that it's forcing me back to school. Right now, I'm taking a GMAT prep course."

"That's great. When are you taking the test?" Lauren sat back and relaxed. She was encouraged that they were talking easily, like old times.

"I haven't decided. My workload has doubled at an inconvenient time."

In a world-weary tone, he described his clients, his boss, and the petty politics of his office.

"Sounds a little annoying."

"It's a lot annoying. I assume you're on vacation now?"

"Heavens, no. We have tons of work. Literally. The tons of rocks we dredged on the voyage have to be physically and chemically analyzed. Also, I've been assigned some rocks brought back from Surea by a previous expedition. What I discover about them will be my master's thesis."

"Do you really get off on this stuff?" Kenny sounded skeptical.

"Yep, it's the most exciting thing I've ever studied," she said with a smile.

"That's good." Kenny downed the rest of his beer in one big gulp. "I think we should go out again when I have more time." His friendly manner had turned almost businesslike.

"Sure. Anytime." *What's going on?* she wondered.

"Maybe not right away, but soon. What with work and studying for the GMAT, my life is pretty hectic. Look, I've gotta go. Can I give you a ride to your apartment?"

"No, that's okay." She didn't want him to see how hurt she was by his abrupt departure.

"See you around, then?" Kenny said as he paid the bill.

Lauren sat in shock and finished her beer. Even though he apparently didn't want a divorce, he also didn't seem passionate about getting back together. She felt as though she'd been put on layaway.

Chapter 5

Grand Cayman

Lauren, 1977

Barranquilla, Colombia, was where they would meet *The Coriolis* for the second cruise of the summer. Lauren located it on a National Geographic map of South America. It was a major port city on the Caribbean coast, north of where Panama formed a bridge between Costa Rica and Colombia. The prospect of another research cruise was exciting, but Lauren did not want to go.

After meeting at their old bar, she and Kenny had gotten together a couple of other times to talk. While they were taking what she hoped were small, tentative steps toward reconciling, Don was taking Paul Bunyan-like leaps into marital chaos. He had separated from his wife and relinquished their custom-built house and pool to her custody. He was trying to solidify his relationship with Lauren by convincing her to move into his newly rented Victorian house. Everything was happening too fast.

Kenny had been her first love, her only sexual partner until Don. She wanted nothing more than to have his love back, but she didn't trust her own judgment at the moment. In the past she and Kenny had stood by each other through a whole range of good and bad times. She had thought they were partners for life. Maybe they could be again. Ending her entanglement with Don would remove one roadblock to reconciling with Kenny. Lauren resolved to tell Don she couldn't go on the second voyage.

>>

"Of course, you're going," Don said, looking up from his reading.

Lauren had just stopped by his office to deliver the news of her withdrawal from the trip. *Damn.* He was going to fight her on this.

"But I need to spend time on my research," she said, plopping down in the chair in front of his desk. She couldn't go on another cruise with Don. It would be a disaster. And she was behind in her research. Worrying about how to end things with Don had kept her from getting much work done at school.

"You can do that when you get back." Don said.

"Why couldn't you find another student to go?"

"What do you mean? We leave in ten days! You signed up for it. Besides, I want you there with me."

Lauren felt trapped. It was true she had signed up for both cruises in February when they were first announced. At the time, Kenny was absent from her life, and her relationship with Don had not yet begun. Now her professor, major thesis adviser, and lover were all the same man.

Don controlled too much of her life. She had no choice but to go on the second cruise. She felt like a child again, under the direction of her autocratic grandmother.

>>

The next week their team flew from Houston to Miami to Barranquilla, where they planned to spend a day before taking a bus to Bogotá. After arriving midevening, Don checked them into a white stucco hotel with a red tile roof and Moroccan arches. The open hallways were tiled in a checkerboard of black and white. He handed Tyler and Craig, the other two students from Tex Poly, their oversized room key.

"You guys are sharing a room. We'll meet at nine for breakfast in the dining room," Don said in a brusque manner.

After an awkward pause, Lauren could feel her face turning red with humiliation. He should have given her a key.

Tyler and Craig stood for a few moments before picking up their backpacks and duffels and heading up the wide staircase.

"That was embarrassing!" Lauren said with a frown. "Where's my room key?"

"You're sharing a room with me, of course."

This was not starting off well. He was assuming their relationship was back to normal despite all the times she'd told him they needed to take a break.

"No," Lauren said, shaking her head. "You always say we should keep up appearances of professor and student. It was obvious to Tyler and Craig that we're in the same room!"

"Grant money is tight. Besides, it will be friendlier if we're together." He picked up his duffel and used his free arm to guide her toward the stairway.

That was what she was trying to avoid.

"I didn't want to come on this trip. You should've let me stay back if there wasn't enough money to cover a hotel room for me."

Don turned to face her when she shrugged his arm from around her back. "What's the matter with you? Why are you in such a bad mood?" He sounded petulant.

Lauren wasn't worried about Don forcing himself on her. She knew he would be more annoyed and hurt than angry when she refused sex. It just wasn't possible in his world that a woman could resist his charms.

Lauren reluctantly trailed Don up the staircase.

>>

After breakfast the next day, the Tex Poly team walked toward the harbor. Barranquilla was a large, shabby, industrial city. Even near the hotel, modest houses had bars on their windows. Trash lay everywhere. Painted murals decorated long stretches of walls along city sidewalks. Residents drove American cars from the 1950s and '60s or small European cars. Their group stopped at a fruit seller and marveled at the array of fruits, most of which they didn't recognize. One specimen looked like a giant, unripe avocado with prickly spikes covering its skin. Another was a bright pink orb with light green leaf daggers sprouting down its sides. They bought bananas and mangos.

Their route took them by a complex of prison cells with straw on the floor and no roof. The stench of human waste and rotting garbage was overwhelming. Prisoners, some with outstretched hands, pressed against the bars. Lauren pitied the men kept like caged animals. As they walked by a brown-uniformed soldier with a submachine gun, a cloud passed over the sun, adding to the sense of foreboding Lauren felt.

The Coriolis was a welcome sight. It was taking on diesel fuel and supplies for the month-long voyage when they arrived. Neither the captain nor any of the other English-speaking crew were around. Craig and Tyler, who had not been on a previous voyage, went aboard. Don and Lauren idly watched the harbor traffic and discussed whether the rest of their research team—five Oceanography Institute students and their professor—had arrived yet. When Craig and Tyler rejoined them, they walked in the direction of their hotel by another route to avoid passing the prison. They had spotted a street lined with jewelry stores near the hotel.

"Colombia has the finest emeralds in the world, bar none. Ultimately, emeralds will become rarer and more valuable than diamonds," Don told the others as they walked.

"So, an emerald would be a good investment?" Tyler asked.

"For sure. But watch out. They'll try to sell you topaz or sapphire stones that have been irradiated or dyed to turn them green. You can pick out the fakes because they lack the distinctive feathering of emeralds."

As they roamed from store to store, Tyler said, "Geologists are no doubt the finest connoisseurs of gemstones but also the least likely to afford them." Everyone laughed.

At one store the owner spoke English well. He was happy to have avid and knowledgeable shoppers. Lauren helped Don pick out a modest but beautiful emerald for a ring for himself. On display was a rock that showed tiny, rough emeralds carried in the intrusive fluid, and then frozen in time when the molten rock cooled. After a half hour, the owner went into the back room and brought out his prized emerald of nearly two inches in diameter. They held it to the light and admired the intense green color and its complex internal pattern. He would be willing to part with it for ten thousand dollars.

"It would be worth two or three times that in the States," Don told the group after they left the store.

Lauren had splurged and bought the store owner's display rock. She was thrilled. The beauty of raw nature was always preferable to anything with man's touch. Not only did the rock demonstrate the fluidity of the earth, it hinted at the larger picture of plate tectonics and the constant three-dimensional movement of everything people perceived as stable. The incredible fluidity and motion of the earth were the essence of geology.

For lunch Don took them to a small restaurant with wonderful smells of garlic, onions, and roasted corn. He insisted everybody try a Colombian specialty—*cuchuco*, a heavy soup of ground corn, pork, potatoes, carrots, and herbs. Like everything else in Barranquilla, lunch moved at a slow pace.

"So, you're saying diamonds aren't a girl's best friend?" Lauren returned the conversation to gems.

"Emeralds, I tell you." Don matched her light tone. "Kimberlite pipe formations from the deep mantle that produce diamonds are relatively plentiful around the world. But it takes a hell of a geological coincidence to make an emerald."

He sketched South America on his napkin. "First, there must be volcanism in an area where there are carbonates—like the volcanic arc that was located off the west coast of South America millions of years ago." He drew an island shaped like a parenthesis. "The back arc basin accumulated skeletons, shells, and other carbonates. Tectonic plate action that pushed up the Andes also caused a collision between the island and the continent. The basin was obducted onto the continent. The magma chamber in the vicinity was squeezed in the process. Hot fluids containing beryllium combined in the carbonate zone, and emeralds precipitated out. In a joke of nature, emeralds and some other precious minerals are made up of the rejected elements in the magma chamber. No other crystals wanted them."

Lauren couldn't help but be charmed when Don was at his best as an impassioned professor explaining geological wonders. She had to remind herself why she needed to end things with him.

Their bowls of soup arrived with corn nubbins floating on top. A half-moon of bread made from the yuca tuber, *pan de yuca*, accompanied the meal.

"I always like to make a pitch to students before they specialize," Don said to Tyler and Craig as they ate. "Please, don't even think about becoming a soft rock geologist. You would be working for Big Oil. You'd bounce seismological waves to discover oil pockets ad infinitum and you'd be doing a boring amount of boring. Hard rock is where it's at. You could become a volcanologist, mine geologist, tectonophysicist, or marine basalt expert—my specialty."

"Wow, it's something to think about," Craig said.

Tyler and Craig seemed like good guys. Lauren was glad Don was taking the trouble to advise them about their careers.

>>

After lunch, they boarded *The Coriolis*. Lauren discovered she would be sharing a cabin with Cassie and Kathy, two women from the Oceanography Institute. She was glad for roommates, even ones with confusing names. It would be easier to deflect Don's advances. Last night at the hotel, she had begged off sex, claiming cramps. How was she going to tell Don she was hoping to reconcile with her husband? Don refused to recognize she was pulling away, even though she'd told him several times they were moving too fast in their relationship. In retrospect, Lauren's first passionate response to Don had misled him, when, in truth, it had been fueled by her intense loneliness. One way or another, she and Kenny needed to resolve their marriage.

>>

The Caribbean was not calm like the Atlantic had been earlier in the summer. *The Coriolis* pitched and rolled during the seven days it took to get to their station over the Cayman Trough. The scientists spent hours in the galley. Some days it was too dangerous to go outside because of large swells and stormy seas. Even nicer days were misty and gray. The excitement of research was tempered by the ominous atmosphere and rampant seasickness. The contrast with the first cruise could not have been greater.

The universe seemed to agree with Lauren that she shouldn't have gone on the second cruise. Stormy seas would make the dredging operation difficult. Worse, Lauren had resolved to tell Don their relationship was over, regardless of whether she reconciled with her husband.

Inklings that Don was not right for her had been growing stronger over the past few months. At first it was fun to have someone take charge of her life, which had been badly fractured by her separation from Kenny. Don was wonderfully romantic, but the more she needed space, the more he suffocated her with demands on her attention. It was not the love of a soulmate, but rather a desperate, clutching love.

Lauren was relieved when they were finally on station and her mind was occupied with work. Dredging required a twenty-four-hour vigil, with everyone taking four-hour shifts until the mission was completed. The dredge was a chain link bag three by five by three feet. A crane lifted it off the fantail. One or two people had to steady the bag as it went over the edge of the ship into the water, so it didn't swing back and forth. It was a dangerous operation. One errant move, and an operator could be pulled overboard. Sharks routinely followed the ship. As the bag was lowered into the ocean, the metal chain moved with sawing speed across the fantail and up to the crane. A person could trip over the chain and lose a foot or leg.

Furthermore, the Cayman Trough required deep dredging. It took eight to ten hours to get the bag down to the top of the undersea mountains that formed the northern margin of the trough. All the while, someone had to watch the "pinger" trace on the Precision Depth Recorder to make certain the dredge bag was on target. A sonic device attached above the bag reflected sound waves from the ocean floor and revealed the mountain topography and translated it into an ink trace on the PDR. The room housing the PDR was tiny, with an overpowering smell of ink.

Scientists already feeling seasick often couldn't make it through their shifts in the PDR room.

While on duty one day, Lauren pondered the randomness of their sampling technique. Dragging a chain link bag over the tops of undersea mountains seemed as imprecise as trying to communicate with someone by dropping a bottle with a message into the ocean. Was this really the best way to find relevant samples?

>>

The next night Don stopped Lauren on her way to PDR duty.

"Lauren, there you are. Let's go up to the flying bridge for a minute."

Reluctantly, she followed him to the foot of the rusty iron stairs. "I think it's too windy."

"You're right. We can talk here. Is it my imagination, or have you been avoiding me?"

So many times, she'd tried to tell him their relationship was over, but he'd refused to listen. Now she couldn't seem to get the words out.

"Uh, no . . . it's just with the storm coming, everybody's so sick, and I've been working extra shifts on the PDR, so I guess that's why you haven't seen me."

Don put his arms around Lauren and gave her a hug. "I just wanted to tell you how much I love you. When we get back, I want you to move in with me. I know the house is a little dilapidated, but we can fix it up. We'll have a wonderful future together."

"No, I can't," Lauren said, gently pushing on his chest and stepping backward.

"Hey, what's going on? Now I can't even put my arms around you . . . and you can't move in with me?"

"No, I can't." She paused. "Once the cruise is over, Kenny and I are going to see if we can make our marriage work. I'm sorry."

Don stroked his beard. "You can't possibly mean you're thinking of going back to him."

"He's my husband. We're meant to be together."

"Except when it's convenient for him not to be together with you— like these last few months. Don't you realize I've given up everything for you? My house, my pool, my wife. And now, just like that, you say you're thinking of going back to your husband."

Lauren was speechless with guilt.

Don covered his face with his hands.

"I'm so sorry. I really have to go on duty."

She walked quickly to the PDR room. Her thoughts raced. She wondered if she had done the right thing. It was true Don was brilliant. Maybe she was a fool not to be with him. But she still loved Kenny. She belonged with him. But she had hurt Don badly. She watched the PDR trace. The rough seas made the dredge bag skip and move erratically. It would be a miracle if they snagged anything worthwhile that night.

>>

At dawn when her shift ended, she walked down to the galley for ham and eggs.

Craig slid onto the bench beside her. "Can you give me a hand with the dredge? When you're done eating, of course. It's really rough."

"Sure, I can be ready in five minutes."

She knew she was too upset to sleep. She might as well do something useful.

"Don says there's a hurricane forming to the east of us. I'll see you on deck."

Craig left as quickly as he had arrived.

Lauren stopped at her room, grabbed a sweatshirt, and went up top. Craig was helping one of the crew hook the bag onto the chain. The arm of the crane pivoted. The chain link dredge bag swung wildly back and forth. Lauren steadied the left side of the bag while Craig steadied the right. Just then a large swell hit the ship. Lauren's left hand slipped off the bag. She tried to grab hold again and caught her thumb in the chain link. Sharp pain made her cry out and pull back. Blood spurted from her thumb.

"My thumb!"

"Oh, my God! You've hurt yourself!"

Craig released his hold on the bag and rushed over to look at Lauren's thumb. She shrieked with pain when she grabbed her left thumb with her right hand to try to stop the bleeding.

"We've gotta go down to Captain!" he said.

Craig put his arm around her back and directed her down the stairs to the galley. Lauren's left thumb dripped blood the whole way, even though her right hand was wrapped tightly around it.

I knew I shouldn't have gone on this cruise!

"We need a bandage!" Craig called to Don and Captain, who were having breakfast.

They both jumped up. Lauren stood there shaking.

Captain yelled to the cook to find some gauze. "And bring aspirin," he added.

When the cook returned, Lauren let go of her thumb and felt blood gush. She showed it to Captain while Don blotted some of the blood away. A jagged piece of bone protruded from her thumb. Don wound gauze around it to stop the bleeding.

"It's pretty bad. We'd better get her to a doctor," Captain said before he left the galley.

Lauren wept quietly. *Damn it hurts!* She couldn't think of anything but her throbbing thumb.

Don said quietly to Craig, "You better go find the tip of her thumb in case they can sew it back on."

The cook handed Lauren some aspirin and a glass of water. "Here, take four. It will help with the pain. Captain's already changed course for Grand Cayman."

When Craig came back, he reported to Don the tip of Lauren's thumb was so mangled it wasn't salvageable. Don took Lauren down to her cabin and sat beside her on her bunk.

"I'm so sorry this happened to you," he said, shaking his head in disbelief. "We've never had an accident before."

Lauren was in so much pain she just nodded. She held her left arm high to stop the throbbing.

>>

"Hello, I'm Dr. White." The Black man in the white uniform introduced himself to Lauren as she and Don walked into the open-air clinic on Grand Cayman. "I'll be doing your surgery."

In the examination room Dr. White steadied her arm and asked her about the accident.

She had been holding herself together for almost seven hours without screaming or passing out. She couldn't answer. She just shook her head. If Dr. White had unwound the gauze at that moment and she had had to see her bone sticking out, she would have come undone. Lauren gathered her thoughts while a nurse gave her an injection of morphine.

As the pain receded, Lauren worried about the imminent surgery.

"You can't take my whole thumb," she told Dr. White as he unwound the gauze and examined her injury. "You have to save it."

"Unfortunately, we can't save what has been crushed, but so far, it looks like only the first joint is badly damaged."

"I won't be able to pick up anything or play the piano. Without an opposable thumb, I'll go backward on the evolutionary scale."

Dr. White chuckled. "Don't worry, girl, you'll be able to do everything you did before, except maybe you won't reach a whole octave on the piano."

In surgery the nurse held her arm while Dr. White sawed off the end of her thumb at the first joint. Lauren felt no pain, but her arm jiggled slightly with the back-and-forth movement of the saw. She watched flies buzzing at the windows. *I'm not sure how sanitary flies are,* she thought. But she was grateful the torturous pain was gone.

Dr. White talked as he worked. "I've got to remove all of the nail bed, or you'll have fingernail growing out of the tip. I'm going to save some subcutaneous fat to cover the end of your thumb so the bone will have some padding."

>>

After surgery, Lauren slid down from the operating table, and the nurse escorted her to the lobby where Don was waiting.

As Lauren and Don walked out of the hospital, Don said, "We've got a room at a nearby hotel. Why don't we go check in and put you to bed?"

Don's ignoring what I told him. He assumed they were back together because she was a wreck, and he'd been super solicitous. She was annoyed.

They started walking toward an area of hotels.

"I need my own room, Don. I'll pay for it."

"Now you can't even be in the same room with me?" Don asked, stopping and turning toward her with a frown.

How many times do I have to tell him? He thought he could manipulate her because she was vulnerable and dependent on him.

"No, I can't. I need space," she said, as gently as she could manage.

>>

Lauren sat by the telephone in her hotel room and debated whether to call Kenny to tell him about her accident. She had already spoken to her closest friends and her mother. Her mother's response had been to say she should never have gone on the research cruise in the first place. She finally dialed Kenny's number, fearing a woman would answer.

After hearing her story, Kenny said, "Now, tell me again what happened." It was as though he couldn't believe what he'd just heard.

"I'm in Grand Cayman. I had the first joint of my thumb sawed off. A nice doctor did the surgery."

"But why?"

"The end of my thumb got crushed in a chain link bag we use to dredge for rocks."

Kenny paused for a second before he responded. "Oh, my God, are you all right?"

A few tears ran down her cheeks. No, she wasn't all right. Her life was a disaster, and now half her thumb was gone. There was a slight catch in her voice when she answered. "I'm fine. I'm flying to Houston tomorrow."

"Are you sure you're okay?

"Yeah, so far. But maybe the morphine hasn't worn off yet."

"I'll pick you up. When do you get in?"

"At three, but don't do that. Really. Tex Poly will provide transportation." *I can't let Kenny and Don meet,* Lauren thought. *It would be a disaster.*

"If I can get off work, I'll be there."

Lauren hung up the phone. Kenny's concern warmed her heart, but her stomach felt jittery at the prospect of his seeing her with Don. Kenny would be able to look at her face and tell she'd had sex with Don. *Yikes! I wish I had a better poker face.*

>>

The next day Kenny, waving a bouquet of red roses, greeted Lauren and Don at their airport gate. Her spirits soared the moment she saw Kenny. He had come to the airport despite her telling him not to! She had often dreamed of being loved again by her husband. With the right person, everything else in your life was better. How could she have thought an exciting affair with Don could take the place of love?

"Oh, Kenny. You brought me roses." Lauren wiped away a tear and gave him an awkward, right-armed hug.

"Who's this?" Kenny asked, looking back at Don, who stood behind Lauren.

Lauren turned around. *Oh dear. Here we go. Very awkward.*

"This is my professor, Don Weber."

Kenny and Don looked at each other for a few seconds and then shook hands as though they were opponents in a boxing match.

"Can we give you a lift to Pasadena, Professor?" Kenny asked after another pause.

She wished he hadn't offered Don a ride.

Don acceded by trailing them through the airport.

"Hey, how's the old thumb feeling?" Kenny asked, putting his arm around Lauren's shoulder.

She felt warm and protected with Kenny's arm around her.

"It's fine. At least, what's left is fine. They gave me morphine, and I even stayed awake during surgery."

"You're kidding. They didn't give you anesthesia?" Kenny asked as they walked toward the parking garage.

"Nope."

When Kenny located his car, he settled Lauren in the front passenger seat. Don climbed into the back, and they headed for Pasadena.

"We missed several days of research because of me. I practically ruined the trip. All because I caught my thumb in the dredge."

"It wasn't your fault. Conditions were bad . . . and getting worse," Don said, leaning forward from the middle of the back seat. "But the worst part was what happened to you." Then he changed his tone from sincere to sly and addressed Kenny. "By the way, Lauren is my star student. She excels in everything in and out of the classroom."

Damn him! He was being a real jerk—hinting at their affair so she and Kenny wouldn't get back together.

Kenny was focused on heavy freeway traffic and seemingly wasn't paying close attention to what Don was saying.

Lauren jumped into the conversation in desperation and said very fast, "Maybe I didn't ruin the trip, but think how much more research we could have accomplished if I hadn't had my accident. Kenny, you haven't heard all the details. I was on deck and the wind was blowing like crazy. I was holding onto one side of the dredge bag—you know, the chain link bag we bring up rocks in—and a big wave smacked the ship. The bag swung wide and I tried to catch it and the edge snagged my hand and tore all the skin off the top of my thumb. There was blood all over the place. My bone was sticking out. Have you ever seen any of your bones? It's not fun. You feel like a skeleton before you're dead."

She leaned back. At least Don had shut up.

Kenny looked over at Lauren with surprise and concern. "I'm taking you back to our apartment. You shouldn't stay by yourself," he said.

Could it be that her husband wanted her back? Or was he feeling sorry for her after she blurted out all the gory details? She couldn't help feeling hopeful. Even a little joyful. She wished to hell Don weren't in the backseat. She feared what he would say next.

She smiled and looked over at Kenny. "Sure."

>>

When they arrived at the apartment—the same one Lauren and Kenny had rented when they'd first moved to Pasadena—Lauren walked in with Don holding one of her arms and Kenny, the other. The men sat her down on the couch.

"Put your feet up," Don said, sitting down at one end of the sofa, "and I'll give you a foot massage. It'll help you relax."

Lauren was horrified. It's what he'd done when they were lovers. She froze and looked straight ahead. "Oh no. No. No thanks."

Still standing, Kenny gave Don a sideways glance and then frowned and said, "What the hell, professor, is that part of your job description?"

Don looked flummoxed. "She's been through a helluva trauma. I'm just trying to be helpful here."

"Is that what you call it?" Kenny turned away from Don and asked Lauren, "Do you have prescriptions I need to get filled?"

Oh, God. This is getting worse! What was Don going to say next? She had to get him out of there.

"Oh, prescriptions. Yeah, I think I do. You can't get morphine in

Texas, so Dr. White gave me a few Vicodin to take home. If I have any prescriptions, they're in the flap of my backpack."

She started to feel woozy.

"It looks like there are two: one for penicillin and one for Vicodin," Kenny said as he read the prescriptions.

"Maybe you better get the Vicodin. I took two on the plane when my thumb started throbbing. But now I think the flight made me a little sick to my stomach. Kenny, quick! Bring me a trash can or something!"

Kenny held back her long hair while Lauren vomited into an empty grocery sack. The phone rang.

Kenny answered, "Oh, hi, Beth. Yeah, she's here. I picked her up at the airport. I don't think she can talk. She just barfed. Hold on, she's grabbing the phone. . ."

"Beth, did you hear what happened? No, I feel better now that I threw up." Turning her face to the back of the sofa, she lowered her voice, "You wouldn't believe the bind I'm in . . . can I call you later? My thumb feels fine." Lauren hung up.

Kenny stood at the door. "I'm going to get Lauren's prescriptions filled. Can I give you a lift to campus, professor?" Kenny asked, with sarcastic emphasis on his title.

"Somebody better stay here with Lauren," Don said in an authoritative voice.

"I'm not going out again. This is your last chance for a ride," Kenny said, indicating the open door with a nod of his head.

"I'm fine, Don, really. You need to go!"

As the two men walked out of the apartment, Lauren reached for the telephone.

Chapter 6

A Curious Irishman

Lauren and Chris, 1977

"Dammit! My thumb hurts," Lauren said aloud in an empty apartment.

She held her left hand high. She couldn't take any more painkillers because they made her sick to her stomach. Worse, her marriage was falling apart again. She'd been thrilled when Kenny met her at the airport and insisted she stay at their apartment so she wouldn't be alone. Everything had been great for a couple of days. Their first night's lovemaking had been passionate and joyful, even with the hindrance of her injured thumb. She had felt loved and welcomed home.

Then he had reverted to his moody self. And this morning, only three days after her return home, he had left the apartment without saying a word, taking the welcome with him.

She might as well move back to her own apartment rather than tolerate his remoteness. His concern about her partially amputated thumb had lasted only until he saw she was okay.

Now each negative thought pulsed in the missing joint. She had to get out. She refused to wait for Kenny to return from wherever he had gone. It was demoralizing to feel like an intrusion in her husband's life. She would work at the Geo Sciences building, even though it would be hard to concentrate. She grabbed her backpack and left for school.

On Sundays Tex Poly was deserted, at least near the academic buildings. The day had turned steamy when the sun came out. Puddles from an early morning downpour filled every low-lying area of the parking lot and lawn. Trees heavy with Spanish moss and mistletoe provided shade. She walked up the stairs of the Geo Sciences building to the second floor where graduate assistants had assigned cubicles. Luckily, she had the place to herself. She wasn't ready to face questions about the accident. She also didn't want anyone to see her while she was an emotional wreck, not that she knew many people. She plunked her backpack on the desk, almost knocking over a single red rose in a bud vase. She frowned and shook her head. Even though there was no note, Lauren knew who had left it.

She sat down in her chair, propped her left arm on the desk, and looked through research summaries for her report. No way could she write a coherent sentence now. Writing required focus. If only her brain were an electron microscope beaming on her work, leaving all stray thoughts and emotions quietly in the dark. She longed for Kenny to love her again. Thinking they might reconcile had helped her through the ordeals of the last research cruise—the storms, her accident. She felt lost. Love was supposed to be a safe haven of understanding and friendship that lasted a lifetime. Now it was nonexistent. Tears rolled down her cheeks.

In retrospect, Lauren felt foolish for having been seduced by Don. If she hadn't been mesmerized by his brilliance, if she hadn't been lonely, if she hadn't drunk so much wine and eaten the marijuana brownie, she might have avoided the whole predicament. Don was an incredibly sensual man who had awakened desires in her she had never known, but Don's love was suffocating. She had ruined her life by getting involved with him. At least he wasn't working in his office.

She put her head down on her desk and sobbed quietly.

Someone cleared his throat. *Oh, God, I'm not alone!* She sat up and grabbed a tissue to wipe her eyes and blow her nose.

"Are you all right?" A brown-haired guy from one of her classes approached Lauren's cubicle. He looked concerned and handed her a box of tissues. "Maybe you'll need more of these."

"I'm so sorry," Lauren said, hiccupping. "I thought I was the only one here."

"I couldn't ignore a damsel in distress," he said, leaning on the adjacent desk.

"The distress part is right, anyway. I'm not sure I've ever been much of a damsel," she said, rolling her eyes while she threw crumpled tissues into a wastebasket.

"I'm Chris Connor. My desk's over in the corner," he said, gesturing with his head. "I was just working on a report. We've had some classes together."

"You look familiar. Hi, I'm Lauren Brown."

"I can't help but notice the bandage on your thumb. . ."

"Oh, this." She looked at her thumb and then up at Chris. "I had to have the first joint amputated in Grand Cayman after I caught my thumb in a dredge bag on *The Coriolis*—you know, Tex Poly's research ship. The chain link severed part of it."

"Jeez, that must have hurt."

"It hurts more now than it did during surgery. I didn't feel anything when the doctor sawed off the end of my thumb. Morphine's a wonderful thing."

"No wonder you're upset."

"It's way worse than just my thumb."

"I don't mind listening if it would help to talk about it," Chris said, sitting down in the desk chair of the adjoining cubicle.

Tears welled up in her eyes. Just the slightest bit of sympathy made her feel like bawling again.

"It's just that I've made such a mess of my life." She wiped tears from her face.

"I can't believe you've messed up your life any more than most people."

"Believe it." Lauren half laughed and half sobbed. "First of all, my husband doesn't want to be married to me. We've been separated for months. I moved back to our apartment a few days ago—he asked me to—when I got back from Grand Cayman. At first, he seemed happy to see me, but now he's not talking to me for some reason. After breakfast he left the apartment without telling me where he was going. But you don't want to hear all this depressing stuff."

"Look, I've been working here alone for hours. I don't mind taking a break for human conversation."

"The way I feel, the human part is debatable."

"Don't be so hard on yourself."

"It gets worse. So when we were separated, I started an affair with Don, my thesis adviser."

"Our Geo Chron professor?"

Lauren nodded and then told Chris the whole story. Maybe his kind gray eyes and easy smile made her trust that he would be on her side.

"Now, I'm such a wreck I can't get any work done," Lauren concluded.

"That's too bad because I've been impressed with your work."

"You don't know my work."

"But I do. I was in class when you gave a paper on the formation of Mount Everest and the other Himalayas and the disappearance of the Tethys Sea."

"You were there?" She was flattered that he remembered her report.

"Yeah, and I heard you fired Dr. Mumper as your adviser."

"I can't believe you know about that! Dr. Mumper was my original adviser. On the first day of his volcanics class he started lecturing on expansion of the earth as the cause of earthquakes and volcanic eruptions. I stopped after class to see what he'd say when I brought up plate tectonics."

"I bet I know what he said. He probably said plate tectonics is just a theory. And he's taking a wait-and-see approach until there's more proof."

"That's exactly what he said! Except he ended every sentence with 'my dear.'"

"Believe it or not, I don't think he meant to put you down."

"Well, anyway, I dropped his class and transferred from geophysics to geology, which is when I was assigned to Don—which brings me back to the whole, horrible mess," Lauren said, starting to cry again.

"Lauren, you have so much talent in geology and volcanics, you can't let those two guys derail you from your work. Concentrate on your thesis or whatever you need to do. The rest of your life will fall into place."

Lauren paused to wipe her eyes. Maybe things weren't as hopeless as she thought.

"Really? You really believe that?" He seemed so steady and reassuring. *I need to pull myself together.*

"I really believe that."

"I wish I could. But I've been so focused on my own problems I hardly know anything about you. Where are you from and how did you end up at Tex Poly?" Lauren swiveled her desk chair a little to look more directly at Chris.

"I was born and raised in Ohio. After college I joined the air force for four years. Then I got my master's at Northern Idaho University and came down here to get my PhD."

"And do you like it here?"

"If Tex Poly weren't one of the top schools in plate tectonics and volcanology, I sure wouldn't be in East Texas."

"I guess, compared to Idaho, you probably don't like the heat and humidity. Not to mention, the lack of outcrops."

"Yep. I can't see who would, but then why are millions of people living in the Houston area?"

"Exactly."

"Oh, and I also write science fiction stories."

"I'm a huge sci-fi movie fan myself," Lauren said, leaning back in her chair.

"Yeah, it's fun to try to figure out where science is going next. Uh, what are you doing for lunch tomorrow, by the way?"

"Nothing special."

"Why don't I pick up sandwiches and maybe you can bring something to drink. We can meet on the lawn on the side of the building around noon?"

"I would like that."

"You can keep me posted on what's happening in your life," Chris said, moving back to his own desk and packing up his backpack.

"Oh, I'm sure you want to hear more whining from me."

"No, I really am interested. Call me a curious Irishman. See you tomorrow," Chris said, walking out.

What a nice guy. She wondered why she had never paid any attention to him in class. It seemed as though they could become friends.

>>

The conversation with Chris cheered her, but she still didn't accomplish anything at school. Instead, she walked back to Kenny's apartment and moved out. *At least he's not home*, she thought as she stuffed her things into her duffel bag. When she closed the door on her way out, a wave of dizziness forced her to steady herself against a wall in the hallway. Her thumb hurt like hell. She wiped away a few tears before finding her way to the stairwell and slouching down the steps with her backpack and duffel. On the walk to her apartment, she held her left hand high to calm her throbbing thumb. She felt abandoned.

Again.

>>

The next day Lauren searched her refrigerator for drinks to take to the picnic lunch with her new friend. She found one Lone Star, a can of soda, a half bottle of chardonnay, and a single serving of orange juice. She regretted not having had time to brew tea for iced tea. Using one hand, she loaded the drinks and two plastic glasses into an insulated bag and hurried to campus. Stepping out of her apartment, she felt a blast of heat and humidity even though the day looked deceptively pleasant with blue sky and high, wispy clouds.

Chris was sitting on the stairs on the side of the Geo Sciences building when Lauren, out of breath and perspiring, rounded the corner.

He smiled and ambled down the steps.

"Hi. You made it. Do you want to sit on the bench over there? Or find a shady spot under a tree?"

"Under a tree sounds nice."

They settled on the grass in the shade of what looked like an elm tree.

Lauren filled an awkward silence by apologizing for the motley drinks she had brought.

"Last night was the first time I'd been back to my apartment in a month. Needless to say, my refrigerator wasn't well stocked."

Chris laughed. "Mine isn't well stocked in the best of circumstances." After a pause, he said, "By the way, how's everything going?"

"Okay, I guess. At least I had a place to go to last night. Six or seven months ago when I first moved out, I had to sleep on my friend Jan's couch until I found an apartment. So that's one positive thing in my miserable life," she said with a rueful laugh.

"You can still laugh. That's a good sign," Chris said, extracting from a white paper bag two sandwiches wrapped in deli paper.

"What else can I do? I'm sorry you had to suffer through my moping and crying yesterday."

Lauren held up the bottle of chardonnay as a question, and Chris nodded.

"You had a lot to deal with. How's your thumb?"

"The pain meds make me sick. I'm taking ibuprofen—not strong enough but helps a little."

While they ate sandwiches and drank the bottom half of the bottle of chardonnay, the conversation turned to Dr. Mumper, whom Chris called "The Mumper."

"There's no rational way to explain why he teaches a disproved theory—expansion of the earth—as the reason for volcanic eruptions. On top of that, he's skeptical of the well-supported plate tectonics theory."

"He shouldn't teach something that's flat out wrong!" Lauren sounded indignant.

"At his age he's seen a lot of big ideas come and go. He's not about to jump on the bandwagon of a relatively new theory." Chris gathered their sandwich wrappers and deposited them in a nearby trash can. When he sat back down, he continued, "The Mumper has a fascinating history with Tex Poly that you would never guess. Five or ten years ago, as I understand it, he patented a remote sensor for tiltmeters."

"Tiltmeters for monitoring volcanoes?"

"Yep. He and Tex Poly supposedly got a boatload of money, and royalties keep rolling in," Chris said. "Unbelievable!"

Lauren looked surprised at first and then nodded, as though she had just found out Dr. Mumper worked for the CIA instead of learning he had invented a high-tech improvement to volcano monitoring equipment. "That explains a lot."

She poured the last bit of chardonnay into Chris's glass and then set out the beer, soda, and orange juice. "Our second round of drinks."

"Next time The Mumper invites our class to his house, you should go with me," Chris said with enthusiasm. "That's when he really gets going on the volcanoes he's monitored and the eruptions he's seen."

"Yikes! I wouldn't be welcome after I argued with him about plate tectonics." Lauren said, shaking her head.

"Oh, not true. At one time or another everyone in Geo Sciences has tried to convince him of the existence of plates. He won't even remember your conversation. If you think about it, his passion is trying to predict volcanic eruptions," Chris continued. "Plate tectonics explains why there are eruptions and earthquakes but doesn't help much in predicting them."

"I never thought of it that way." She was getting a completely different picture of Dr. Mumper.

"At the end of the evening when we're at his house, Dr. Mumper's cute, grandmotherly wife serves us her special cherry cheesecake."

Lauren relaxed and leaned against the tree trunk. Chris's broad view of life and his nonjudgmental approach to Dr. Mumper warmed her heart.

"His wife sounds dear. Unlike my grandmother, who was a tyrant," Lauren said, rolling her eyes.

"Really? I can't picture a tyrannical grandma."

"When my uncle and aunt gave me a present, as soon as they left, my grandmother would throw it in the trash. She couldn't control my uncle, so she controlled my toy box."

"A grandma who throws away her granddaughter's toys!" Chris looked amazed.

Lauren laughed. "She didn't want me to like my uncle and aunt. Here's something else bizarre. Even though she was a very plain woman, she thought she looked like Marilyn Monroe."

Chris laughed. "Your grandma was unusual, I'll say that."

Lauren looked at her watch. "Oh, dear. I've got to get to my two o'clock. Thanks for lunch. This was fun. Maybe we can meet for a beer around campus?"

Chris grinned. "Sure. How about Thursday at Smitty's?"

"Never been there, but I'll see you Thursday."

>>

Lauren sat in her cubicle and looked at the red marks on the stack of pages of her report. Don had scrawled "See me" across the top of the first page. Work on her report had been going slowly, but finally she had ten decent pages. *This is a nightmare. I'll never get my master's.* Some of the changes were ones he had told her to make two weeks ago. Now he was requiring her to change them back to the way they were before. He was just trying to get her into his office again.

Dreading another scene, she walked slowly across the hall to Don's office.

"You wanted to see me about my report?" she said, knocking on the door frame since the door was ajar.

"Lauren, come in," Don said, getting up from his desk and closing the door behind her.

She sat in the chair in front of his desk. "I don't understand your comments or the changes you want me to make," she said, looking up at him.

"I have a surprise for you," he said, sitting down and opening a drawer. Reaching across his desk, he handed her a small, antiqued silver box.

"I don't want any gifts . . . please."

"Go on. Open it."

Don watched Lauren's face as she lifted the lid. On red satin lining lay the gorgeous emerald that she had helped him select in Colombia, supposedly for a ring for himself. It had been set as a pendant with a delicate silver chain. Lauren was speechless.

"It's a token of my everlasting love."

"I can't accept this," she said, shaking her head. *This is awkward. What am I going to do?*

"You must. I had it designed especially for you."

"Please, no. I'm not making any decisions about relationships. I just left Kenny—again. I need time to be alone. To think and figure out my feelings." *Damn.* She wished she hadn't told him she'd just left Kenny.

"No matter what happens, no matter whom you choose, this is for you. You must have it."

"It's way too valuable." *This is horrible. He's trying to buy me.*

"I won't take *no* for an answer."

Lauren sighed, picked up her report and the silver box, and stood up to go.

Don came around his desk and put his arms on her shoulders. "Listen, I know you think you need to be alone. But what you really need is someone to talk to. Let's go to dinner tomorrow night and talk."

"No, I can't go out with you," Lauren said, backing to the door.

"Come on," Don said in a whiny voice. "It's just dinner. Please. We can still be friends as professor and student."

"Oh geez, I guess we can go to dinner," Lauren said, hurrying out of his office to get away from him.

Lauren returned to her cubicle and set the silver box on top of the pages of her report, the red marks unresolved. She berated herself. Why was she so weak? She shouldn't have accepted the necklace or agreed to go to dinner.

>>

The next day Lauren propped open the door to her apartment so she could hear Don's approach. She wanted to be ready to leave the instant he arrived, so he didn't have time to corner her. She feared the evening would end badly. A peanut butter sandwich at home sounded more digestible than a fancy dinner with attendant heartburn. When she saw Don's car pull up, she hurried out to meet him. On the drive to the restaurant, she leaned against the car door and let a warm breeze blow across her face.

Don looked over at her. "You're looking exceptionally lovely tonight. Did you do something different to your hair?"

"Nope. It's just getting long 'cause I haven't had time to get it trimmed."

"Well, don't cut it. It looks great the way it is."

"My neck gets hot if my hair gets too long."

"I thought we'd go to The Steak Place tonight."

"That's fine. I don't care where we go."

This night was a big mistake. *Why did I agree to go to dinner?*

Thinking back to the last few months, if she hadn't been in such a depressed emotional state, maybe she could have navigated her life without going down wrong paths and making bad decisions. Having an affair with Don was probably the worst thing she could have done. She feared the harm couldn't be undone. Here she was on her way to dinner with him. The only good thing that had happened lately was meeting Chris. He seemed grounded and focused on his work. How peaceful it would be to think only about her studies. Instead, she was distraught about Kenny's absence and Don's insistence she resume their relationship.

"The local restaurant critic praised their wine cellar as the best in town," Don said, pulling into the restaurant's parking lot.

To Lauren's annoyance he put his hand on the small of her back as they walked into the restaurant. *As though I need to be guided!*

"We've got your table ready for you, Dr. Weber," the maître d' said as he picked up copies of the menu and wine list.

Their table was in the back corner of the dining room. The maître d' pulled out Lauren's chair for her and eased her closer to the table. Don seated himself to her left, even though his place setting was across the table from her. When the waiter approached, Don studied the wine list, selected a bottle of Italian pinot grigio, and ordered a shrimp cocktail for an appetizer.

After the waiter left, Lauren asked in a peevish tone, "What's with pinot grigio? Everyone my age drinks chardonnay."

"That shows how little they know. Pinot grigio is light, fresh, and young—kind of like you, my dear."

"Speaking of fresh." Lauren couldn't help smiling as she shook her head.

"By the way, for your edification, *grigio* means gray in Italian," Don continued. "The grape is purplish-gray. Pinot grigio is perfect for an aperitif. It's fermented in steel barrels and, therefore, doesn't taste oaky like chardonnay."

"I'll remember that the next time I'm not in the mood for oak."

"What would you do without my tutelage? And by the way, I'm only twelve years older than you. In the broad scheme of things, we're in the same generation."

"Indeed. That reminds me, I'm completely stalled on my report. I can't go forward with my research until I get the scope of my project narrowed down. And I can't do that without resolving the issues you raised." *How many times will I have to ask for help on my project?*

"Let's not talk about work tonight. What's happened to us?" Don asked, reaching under the table to squeeze her thigh.

"Hey, there are people around. Don't do that!"

Don withdrew his hand. "Seriously, Lauren, you're the most sensual and alive woman I've ever been with. We're meant to be together."

Sex is all that's on his mind, she thought.

She delayed her response while the waiter served their shrimp cocktail and poured the wine. "I've been married to Kenny for almost six years. He was my high school boyfriend. Even though we've been apart for the last few months, I can't abandon my marriage without fighting for it," Lauren said with conviction.

"You can't give up on us just like that. We're great together. Sex with you is incredible. I'm guessing if there were anything between you and Kenny, you'd be together now."

Lauren's thoughts flashed to the drops of hardened candle wax she had seen on the nightstand in Kenny's and her old bedroom.

They had not been there when she moved out. Obviously, Kenny had been seeing someone. He had never bothered to light candles when he made love to her. She felt a stab of pain in her chest. Tears welled up in her eyes.

Don reached across the table and took her hand. "You have to see you'd be better off with me. Our life would be exciting. We could go to sea every summer. We could have a house with a swimming pool. Remember how we were the only two willing to swim in the Atlantic on the cruise last summer?"

"That's not the point. I can't be with anyone right now. I just can't." Lauren dropped her voice and withdrew her hand as the waiter approached.

"What may I bring you for dinner, miss?"

"She'll have . . . actually, we'll both have the French onion soup to start, and then for our main course we'll have the Caesar salad prepared table side. And another bottle of pinot grigio."

Don failed to notice Lauren's closing her menu with resignation. The restaurant was dim, and cool air blasted from a vent above their table. Wishing her linen napkin were wool instead, Lauren tucked it around her knees. She folded her arms across her chest to keep from shivering.

Don reached over and rubbed her shoulder.

"Don't, please." *So inappropriate!* He acted as though they were still lovers.

"I'm just trying to warm you up."

"Oh, is that what it's called?"

"But Lauren, I can't stand to be apart from you. You're driving me crazy! Can't you see what you're doing to me?"

"I'm so sorry. You don't know how sorry I am." She felt bad that she'd hurt him, but how many times would she have to apologize for a relationship he had initiated?

"My new house is a wreck. I don't have any motivation to fix it up. Everything is just where the movers left it. I'm living out of boxes."

"Maybe you should go back to your wife," Lauren said, looking directly at him.

"I've told you there's nothing there. How can I go back to her when I've met someone with your warmth and passion? No. You must come back to me. I insist."

"You're ordering me back into our relationship?" The thought made her want to drop out of school. But where would she go? *This is a nightmare.*

"Well, I am your major professor. I can facilitate your thesis. When *The Coriolis* sails to the Red Sea next summer, we'll dock in Surea long enough for you to resample the identified locations of your thesis rocks."

"But only if I get back together with you?" She felt like a hostage.

"No, no, of course not. But don't you see it would make everything so much nicer if we were together?" Don said, looking on the verge of tears himself.

When their French onion soup arrived, the viscous melted cheese required all their attention and dexterity. Just as they finished their soup, the waiter rolled the salad cart to their table with a tip-inducing flourish. Like a Roman emperor and his empress, Don and Lauren sat back to be entertained by motions of mortar and pestle, whisk, and flying lettuce.

Lauren found herself relaxing when Don turned the conversation to the formation of the Red Sea thirty million years ago and how her thesis project could add key information about geological forces that caused the African landmass to pull away from Asia. If he only knew how attractive he was when he focused on the wonders of geology. . . he might have stood a chance of wooing her back.

>>

Later as they drove out of the restaurant parking lot Don suggested they stop by his new house.

"No. I'm not going to your place," Lauren said. "No."

"But I need advice on arranging furniture."

"You said we were just going to dinner. I need to go home."

"I've been so lonesome for you. You can't do this to me."

Don pounded the steering wheel in frustration.

Now he's having a tantrum, Lauren thought with disgust. Her spirits dropped another notch. Missing Kenny and battling Don took too much out of her.

"You don't want to be with me in my present state. Trust me. I'm a total wreck," she said.

"We could make each other feel so much better," he said, turning toward her. "Why can't you see that?"

"Please, take me home . . . please."

When they stopped on Lauren's block, Lauren hopped out of the car before Don could turn off the engine. She walked quickly up the sidewalk and turned only when she had unlocked the apartment building door. Don was still sitting in his car.

>>

The next few days were a blur of disconnect between desire and fulfillment. Lauren wanted Kenny to want her. He was absent. On the other hand, Don was insistent. He turned surly when Lauren refused to resume their relationship. Lauren's course work and thesis research were thwarted by her reluctance to seek advice from Don or even be in his presence. In her dreams she ran in slow motion as a strange man chased her. When she finally reached a telephone, her shaky hands repeatedly dialed wrong numbers on a rotary dial.

>>

Some two months later the ringing of the telephone in her apartment woke Lauren.

"Lauren, you sound like you're half asleep," Chris said when she answered.

"I am."

"It's two o'clock in the afternoon. Are you sick?"

"I'm not sick. Just very, very tired."

"You must be sick or you wouldn't be so tired."

"I'm not sick! I'm depressed. I don't feel like getting out of bed."

"Then I'm coming over to drag you out of bed."

Since meeting, Lauren and Chris had become study partners and best friends. They often met for dinner at a campus hangout.

Lauren opened the door when Chris arrived, but walked right back to bed and fell in.

Chris followed her and handed her a paper cup of coffee.

"Drink this. It will get you going."

"But I hate coffee."

"Drink it. You need it. I'll make you tea when you finish your coffee. Then we're going to the Arboretum to take a walk. Sunshine will cheer you up."

She grudgingly dressed and plodded after him on his way out the door.

>>

Lauren and Chris wandered around the Arboretum reading labels on trees and shrubs and realizing how little they knew about Texas native plants and botany in general.

On the drive home Chris said, "Let's stop by school. I'm having a hell of a time with the phase diagrams assignment. Somehow my calculations are off."

Though she felt better after going to the Arboretum, the minute she thought about school and the complicated situation with Don, her gloom returned.

"I guess we can stop by school. But I don't have any reason to be there. I'm taking incompletes in both my courses."

"That's nonsense." Chris turned to look at her. "You can't quit your classes."

"My life is a disaster. I can't work," Lauren said, slumping lower in her seat.

"Lauren, don't let Don and Kenny derail you."

"I can't help it. I can't think, and I'll never get my master's."

"You'll never get your master's if you don't complete your courses. Besides, you have a great thesis project. You're traveling to the Red Sea next summer."

"Summer's a million years away. Anyway, to get to the Red Sea I have to go on *The Coriolis* with Don."

Chris parked illegally by the Geo Sciences building, and they walked up to the graduate assistants' offices. Lauren followed him to his cubicle in the corner.

"I can help you with the calculations, if you want me to," Lauren said. "I'm pretty sure I understood it when Don walked us through the first problem."

They sat elbow to elbow at Chris's desk. After checking his calculations on one problem, they attempted another with more components and variables. Lauren's focus seemed to increase with the complexity of the problem. They both exulted as lines and shapes on the diagram emerged from plot points. The more time Lauren spent in Chris's benign presence, the more her spirits rose from negative to positive territory.

"I understand it better, but you understand it extremely well for someone who's going to drop the course."

"I don't mind math, but I can't think clearly enough to write papers, let alone a thesis."

"Math requires the highest level of abstract thinking. If you can do these problems, you can do anything."

"I thought I heard voices," Don said, making his way through the maze of cubicles to the back corner where Lauren and Chris were working.

Lauren turned to Chris and made a face before assuming a neutral expression.

"Now let me guess which problems you're working on," Don said, tugging his beard. "Could they be petrology problems, per chance?"

"What else?" Chris said.

"Lauren, I need to see you in my office. I've had some thoughts about your research."

"What's the use," Lauren said, following Don across the hall to his office. "I'll never get it done to your satisfaction."

"Well, I am your major adviser. You've a lot to learn."

Don shut the door.

Lauren braced herself for battle.

"But you're making it impossible for me to get anywhere on my reports or research!"

She slumped in the front chair. *This is just another attempt to corner me,* Lauren thought. She wished he would actually talk about her project.

"You're making my life impossible!" Don paced around his office. "Why won't you give me a second chance?"

"I've told you and told you. I can't be with anyone right now. I'm too confused." *How many times do I have to go through this?* She stood up to leave.

Don caught her and pulled her toward him. "Your confusion would evaporate in a second if you let me hold you."

"Hey, don't!"

Lauren maneuvered out of his reach. Don walked back to his desk chair and sat down. He ran his fingers through his hair and groaned.

"I feel terrible. But you're the one who won't let things be over," Lauren said, sitting back down in the chair. "You said you wanted to talk about my research."

"How can you expect me to focus on your project when you've turned my life upside down?"

Chris knocked on Don's door and opened it. "Sorry to interrupt but I need to talk to you about yesterday's lecture—after you're through helping Lauren, of course. I have some questions from my notes."

Chris looked at Lauren out of the corner of his eye.

Don scowled. "Can't we talk on Monday? I don't keep office hours on Saturday."

"I thought since you were here you might be able to clear up my questions."

"Dammit, Chris, I don't have time for this now." Don's face flushed red.

"It's okay, Don," Lauren said. "We can talk about my research next week."

She gave Chris a quick smile before slipping out the door.

>>

Later that evening, Lauren joined Chris at Smitty's.

"You look a little more cheerful than you did earlier," Chris said as she slid into the booth.

"Your barging into Don's office so I could escape made me laugh." *Thank God for Chris,* she thought. Her dear friend had come to her aid twice that day.

Chris grinned and poured her a beer from a pitcher.

"When you left," Chris said, "I plunked myself down and asked him a bunch of questions about his lecture. He nearly became apoplectic!"

"Before you walked in, he tried to hug me, but I pushed him away.

Then he wouldn't answer any of my questions. My whole project is stymied." She sighed audibly.

"That bastard! I'd get another thesis adviser."

"Believe me, I've thought about it, but so much of my work would be wasted if I changed projects. Even if he delays me, it will be faster than starting over. By the way, I'm thinking of turning in back assignments this week instead of taking incompletes."

"Hey, that's great. If you're caught up by next weekend, you should go with me to Dr. Mumper's on Sunday night."

"After what I said to him, I'm reluctant to go to his house."

"He loves to have students over. We don't talk theory. We talk volcanoes. And it's a blast."

Lauren chuckled. "Nice pun. I'll think about it."

>>

"Boys, come in, come in. And young lady. How delightful."

"Lauren Brown, you've met Dr. Mumper," Chris said.

Dr. Mumper smiled broadly and directed the students to his study.

Lauren was relieved he seemed welcoming and apparently didn't resent her arguing with him about tectonic plates.

A tray of cold Heinekens sat on a polished wood desk.

"Help yourselves while I get the door."

The mere presence of beer raised the fun status of the evening from slightly above study group level to near party level. Chris introduced Lauren to Bryan and Matt, who opened beers for all of them.

While Chris, Bryan, and Matt traded fieldwork stories, Lauren excused herself to look more closely at framed pictures of volcanoes on the walls. The subjects ranged from a serene, snow-capped Mount Fuji to an unknown volcano spouting fire. As she stood before a photograph of a fiery cauldron of lava labeled Nyiragongo Crater, Dr. Mumper stopped beside her.

"That crater holds the most dangerous lava in the world," he said. "Or did."

"Didn't it erupt recently?" Lauren asked, turning to face Dr. Mumper.

"Yep. In January of this year, the crater walls fractured, and the lava lake drained in less than an hour—the fastest lava flow ever recorded. It raced down the upper slopes at forty to sixty miles an hour. Hundreds of people died. They couldn't outrun it." He shook his head with a sorrowful look on his face. Then after a pause, he said, "No land animal except a cheetah could've outrun it."

Lauren drained her beer faster than she meant to.

"Why is Nyiragongo's lava so fast?"

"Its composition. Low-silica, alkali-rich lava, essentially free of feldspars. Very different from other lavas. Most lavas are so slow they don't pose a danger to humans."

Lauren was rethinking her opinion of Dr. Mumper. He seemed competent. Maybe she had been too hasty in judging him?

Chris and Bryan and a couple of other students joined Lauren and Dr. Mumper.

"Ms. Brown and I are talking about Mount Nyiragongo in the Congo," Dr. Mumper said to the joiners.

"Call me Lauren, please. So now the lake is empty?"

"We don't know. Nyiragongo sits on a geologically active site. Magma can rise quickly from deep in the earth," Dr. Mumper said. "The sides of the crater are so steep it's not easily accessible. The locals rightly fear the volcano."

"The crater looks full in this picture," Bryan said.

"I took that back in fifty-nine. For years people suspected the crater contained a lava lake. Steam rising from the crater glowed with a reddish light. Scientists finally confirmed it in forty-eight. According to legend, doomed souls are sent there to atone for their sins.

"Now, let's get comfortable," Dr. Mumper said, assuming his place in his big leather chair, and gesturing for the students to sit.

When everyone was settled, he continued, "In fifty-nine when I took that picture, two other volcanologists and I were part of an international expedition. The rest of our team were crazy mineralogists. Speaking of doomed souls!" He chuckled.

Lauren realized Dr. Mumper had lived the life she wanted for herself. To be part of an official expedition would be thrilling. And if the expedition advanced scientific knowledge of the earth, it would satisfy her need to do something worthwhile.

"The mineralogists came loaded with climbing gear—harnesses, ice screws, crampons, bolt anchors, ascenders, descenders—you name it. You'd have thought they were climbing Everest, instead of hiking up a steep, vegetation-covered volcanic cone.

"We collected samples, mostly by hammering off chunks of hardened lava from various locations. But the mineralogists wanted hot samples from all over the mile-wide lake. It took the whole group to figure out how to attach the descenders and ascenders to the ropes and harnesses. It must have been the sulfur I was inhaling, but I volunteered to do a test descent with one of their guys. When we got down to just above the lake, they lowered a bucket of water for the other guy to hold while I dropped hot lava samples into it. Of course, the crazy mineralogists wanted enough samples for all their colleagues, so we'd send up one bucket and they'd send down another. It was hot as Hades. At some point I signaled, no more.

"The geologists were satisfied with the samples we got, but the mineralogists wanted even more samples—this time from two corners of the lake where boiling lava was sending up fountains of fire. One of their guys was halfway down, maybe fifteen feet above the pool, when the belt on his harness gave way. He nearly fell into the two-thousand-degree lava. Luckily, the leg straps caught him and he dangled upside down. You should have seen him flopping around trying to get the harness back around his waist. We had to pull him up. All of us grabbed hold of the rope and hauled the guy—upside down—to the top. He got some pretty good scrapes, but he survived.

"I could tell you more goofy mineralogist stories, but we have more important things to think about. Millie has made her famous cherry cheesecake."

Lauren walked into the kitchen to introduce herself to Mrs. Mumper, who gave her a hug.

"I'm thrilled young women are studying volcanology these days. You know, I've been on a few expeditions with Melvin to Africa and South America, when he was researching various volcanoes."

"I didn't know that," Lauren said. "How exciting!"

After chatting a couple of minutes, Lauren carried plates of cheesecake to the study and handed them around.

As everyone ate and talked, Chris moved to sit next to The Mumper.

"Was there a monitoring system for Nyiragongo?" Chris asked.

Several students stopped their chatter to hear Dr. Mumper's answer.

"None. Villagers living on the slopes had no warning. A quake opened big fractures in the thin crater walls, and lava poured out. As I told Lauren, Nyiragongo's lava is the fastest in the world. Everyone in the lava's path died. It was a terrible tragedy."

Dr. Mumper sighed and shook his head.

"Volcanoes are all-powerful. They can kill you in a hundred ways. A massive release of carbon dioxide from a caldera can snuff out everyone in a nearby village. Or innocent children playing near a volcano can die from carbon dioxide seeping from the ground. A shock deep in the earth can send millions of tons of earth and rocks down the side of a volcano to bury a town. Another volcano explodes with all the violence of the end of the world."

He paused for a few seconds. "Now Nyiragongo has killed. It will kill again. We've got to develop better methods for detecting threats from volcanoes."

Everyone was quiet for a couple of minutes. Lauren looked around the room and saw all the students with serious expressions as though they had been charged by Dr. Mumper with saving the world from volcanoes.

Chapter 7

The Day the Earth Stood Still

Lauren and Chris, 1978

Organization was usually one of Chris's strengths. Now it eluded him. Papers flew when he dropped a library book onto the kitchen table. He scowled as he gathered his research notes from the floor. A full sack of garbage teetered on the edge of a kitchen chair when he bumped it. His bed was filled with piles of clean and dirty clothes. Order existed only in the brick-and-board bookcases that filled all available wall space in his small apartment. Besides geology textbooks, science fiction novels, phonograph records, and rocks, the shelves housed his Star Trek collection.

He decided to pack for his move to Idaho. At the back of a closet, he found two small, flattened cardboard boxes. He double wrapped the *Enterprise*, Captain Kirk, Spock, Scottie, and the rest of his collection and packed them loosely among crumpled sheets of newspaper in the two boxes. Satisfied he was well underway, he grabbed his backpack and headed for campus. Lauren and he planned to see every movie in the on-campus science fiction film festival, lasting the better part of the weekend. Next week would be soon enough to finish his packing. If he'd known he was going to stay in Texas for such a short time, he wouldn't have brought all his gear, certainly not his rocks or Star Trek collection. Moving was a pain in the ass.

Maybe Lauren would be working at the Geo Sciences building.

Just thinking about her excited him. He struggled to keep their relationship casual. Every time he looked into her green eyes, he felt his resolve disappear. She was a clear-eyed seeker of truth, yet, at the same time, a sad-eyed child. He longed to hold her and love her until every trace of sadness disappeared from her eyes. Instead, they were best friends who exchanged quick hugs when they greeted each other. Lauren's husband neither appreciated nor deserved her.

Then there was the fact that he was going back to Northern Idaho University. He had ridden into a box canyon at Tex Poly. His conflict with Don was complicated. First, there was Lauren. Even though Chris's relationship with Lauren was platonic, Don didn't know that. He saw Chris as a roadblock to his succeeding with Lauren. Almost as soon as his friendship with Lauren began, Chris's paper and test grades in Don's classes dropped from A's to B's, then to B minuses. Now a C in his petrology final. That pretty much sealed his fate. In grad school, a C amounted to an F.

Don was an exploiter of people on a slightly greedier level than Chris had seen among officers in the air force. Not only had Don used women students for his sexual needs, but he also usurped the ideas and achievements of all his graduate students. He selected their projects, which conveniently supported his research. It was shortsighted of Don to force Chris out of Tex Poly, taking with him his grant to study flood basalts in the Columbia River Basin. With Chris's fieldwork under Don's belt, he could have laid claim to the title of "Dr. Basalt"—qualified in both oceanic and continental basalt. The man was blind.

Besides despising Don's selfish, exploitative nature, Chris disagreed with Don's approach to science. Fieldwork was key to geology. Don's emphasis on geochemistry and other lab work meant he was only getting further removed from the discipline of geology. The grab bag approach to rock sampling would never achieve the results of hands-on mapping and studying strata and structure. Geologists couldn't solve problems without seeing field associations. Don was stuck in his own world of ocean floor basalts where he, indeed, was master, but he had lost sight of the big picture. Scientific truth couldn't be found with tunnel vision.

>>

Chris bounded up the stairs of the Geo Sciences building and opened the door to a well-lit, seemingly empty set of cubicles. Maybe it was hard for him to get serious about packing because he knew he was moving away from Lauren. He'd found the perfect woman, but she was still in love with her husband.

He heard someone pecking away at a typewriter and made his way to Lauren's cubicle.

"Hi, Chris. Whatcha up to?"

"Hey, you. Oh, I've been doing a little packing at the apartment. Got a good start on it, anyway."

"I'm working on a rewrite of my lab report." Lauren resumed her two-fingered typing.

"Is your thumb still hurting? Is that why you're using only two fingers?

"Yeah, my thumb hurts. But that's not why I'm typing with two fingers. I'm a lousy typist."

"Didn't you take typing in high school?"

"Of course, but I got a D in it." She looked up with her eyes crossed for comical effect.

Chris laughed. "Well, no kidding. Here, show me where you are in your notes, and I'll type."

"But don't you have work of your own to do? The first movie—*Journey to the Center of the Earth*—starts at one thirty."

"I can do your typing in half the time. Then we can go to the auditorium early to get tickets," Chris said, rolling his chair in front of Lauren's typewriter and nudging her out.

"I walked over this morning and bought us tickets for the whole series."

"Then I owe you some typing," Chris said, studying her notes. With Lauren looking over his shoulder and sharing the same small space, typing transformed from a chore to a pleasure.

>>

"So, what do you think—a pitcher of margaritas?" Lauren asked, as Chris slid into the booth across from her at The Vineyard.

They'd come straight from the last showing of the first night of the sci-fi festival, and it was late; the only customers were students like them, full and empty beer pitchers strewn across their tables.

"Sure." Chris nodded. "And how about the cheese platter?"

"Perfect."

Chris waved the waitress over. After they'd placed their order, Lauren leaned toward him across the table.

"I forgot to ask you earlier if Don raised your petrology grade," she said.

"Hell, no. I'm marshaling my evidence and arguments to make one last attempt to change his mind."

"That's outrageous. I feel terrible that I'm to blame."

"Believe me, you are not to blame. He and I have clashed since the beginning."

Lauren knew that wasn't true. Chris had received A's before they met. Don resented Chris because of his relationship with her. How could she ever make it up to him? Besides receiving a bad grade from Don in his petrology final, Chris's whole life was being upended by his move back to Idaho. Don's resentment of him seemed to have no limit. As reluctant as she was for Chris to leave Tex Poly, it was probably the right decision for his career. She didn't know what she would do without her best friend, who had sustained her through all the emotional upheaval of the past year.

As soon as the waitress delivered their pitcher of margaritas, he poured them each a tall glass.

"What did you think of *The Day the Earth Stood Still*?" Lauren asked, taking a swallow of her margarita.

"No, you first. I've probably seen it four or five times."

"I thought it was fabulous. I'm sure I saw it with my grandfather when I was a little kid, but the only thing I remembered from back then was how scary the robot was. I had no idea it was about world—or, rather, galactic—peace."

"It's so wise. It was released in the early fifties, but twenty-five years later, it's still relevant to the Cold War. 'If there isn't security for all, then no one is free.'"

"You have seen it a few times—to be able to quote from it." *Chris always has something interesting to say,* Lauren thought. Not just about geology. Time spent in his company always seemed too short.

"Did you catch the line from Professor Barnhart that it isn't faith that makes good science, but curiosity?"

"There you go again. You've got this movie memorized."

"Maybe I've seen it more like eight or nine times. Who knows?" Chris chuckled. "Wasn't it cool a scientist was the only one to grasp the idea of interplanetary cooperation while the rest of the world panicked?"

"Our trigger-happy army shoots first and asks questions later."

"Man is a warlike animal," Chris said, pouring them each another glass from the pitcher.

"You're always saying that."

"I didn't say it. Thomas Hobbes did. Back in the sixteen hundreds, I think."

"Yeah, and if I remember my philosophy class, Hobbes was an idiot. Wasn't he the guy who thought monarchy was the best form of government?" Lauren gulped her drink as they argued.

"He may not have been politically astute, but he was right on about human nature."

"But seriously, how can you have such a dismal view of human nature? My Quaker upbringing won't let me believe war is inevitable," she said, shaking her head.

"The guys I knew in the air force were itching for war—and not just the lifers. The younger pilots were disappointed they missed 'Nam."

"Surely, we can learn from our mistakes. Vietnam was such a . . . such a hideous disaster that we'll never do that again. . ." Lauren's voice drifted off.

"Hah! Well, I know one thing is inevitable— more margaritas!" Chris said, pouring the rest of the margaritas into their glasses.

"This is too much fun to stop now," Lauren agreed, laughing and hiccuping.

"Lauren, you're drunk."

"Well, so are you."

"How else are we gonna solve the world's problems?" he asked with a big grin.

"But we can learn from our mistakes—like Vietnam."

Lauren knocked over her margarita glass with an emphatic gesture. "Whoops." Giggling, she used a flimsy napkin to sop up the liquid. "I . . ."

"Waitress!" Chris called toward the kitchen.

After a flurry of activity to clean up the spill, they resumed their escalating argument.

"Thousands of years of history prove war is here to stay," he said in a loud voice.

"No! No! Not true. Humans are basically good. We just have to look deeply," she argued, placing a hand over her heart.

"Of course, there's good in humans, but war is always ready to break out. Don't you know that?" he asked in an even louder voice.

By now, everyone was looking at them. The manager walked over to their booth. "You two have had enough to drink. Please pay up and leave."

"We've just begun—" Chris started to tell him.

"No. You're done. I'm sorry, but you have to go. I can't have you disturbing the peace."

"Okay. Okay. We'll go." He held up his hands in mock surrender.

They wove a crooked path to the cashier's counter.

"I can't believe they kicked us out," said Chris as they set off in the direction of Lauren's apartment. "We're two of their best customers."

"Sure, we're drunk, but we're talking about important stuff."

She linked arms with Chris.

"That's right. Now that I think about it, I'm outraged! We're trying to save the world."

"Yeah, and if we don't save the world, who will? Tell me that," Lauren stopped in the middle of the sidewalk to make her point.

When they arrived at Lauren's apartment, Chris walked her in, sat her on the bed, and brought her a big glass of water. "Here," he said, "drink this before you go to sleep, and you won't get a hangover."

After he left, she sat for a few moments while her brain, in all its fuzziness, arrived at a piece of truth. If she weren't married to Kenny, and if they weren't trying to get back together, Chris would be a wonderful man to fall in love with. She crawled under the covers and slept.

>>

The next morning Lauren lay in bed cursing Margarita, whoever she was. Her head ached, and she felt woozy as though she weren't quite sober. She tried to recall Chris's and her brilliant thoughts from last night. She couldn't think of one. *We should have written them down,* she concluded.

After trying to get back to sleep and not succeeding, she got up and turned on the burner under the teakettle. It was eleven thirty. Only two hours until the first sci-fi movie of the day.

When Chris knocked on her door, she was still wearing her clothes from the night before, and tea hadn't cured her hangover.

"Chris, come in." She drew back to look at him. "You're looking fairly normal for someone who's surely as hung over as I am."

"No, I'm really not. I feel pretty good."

"That's not fair. I feel horrible, even though I've had a cup of tea."

"Tea's not going to do the trick. You've gotta fight fire with fire. Do you have any tequila?"

"Somewhere," she said, gesturing in the direction of a kitchen cupboard.

He poured a little tequila into a glass of orange juice and brought it to her in the living room, where she sat.

"This will get you going."

She wasn't sure orange juice made tequila a health drink, Lauren thought. *But it's worth a try.* She didn't want to feel under the weather for the last day of the film festival and maybe the last day she would see Chris.

He jotted notes for a new science fiction novel he was writing while she drank her orange juice and then showered and put on fresh clothes.

"I think the first movie of the day is *Invasion of the Body Snatchers,*" Lauren said as they left her apartment. "Followed by *Twenty Thousand Leagues Under the Sea.* Then there's a long intermission. *Forbidden Planet* is the last one at six o'clock."

Lauren and Chris grinned at each other. A perfect day lay ahead of them.

>>

Walking out of *Forbidden Planet*, Chris said, "Let's go out for a nice dinner."

"Sure," Lauren said. "Where shall we go?"

"Anywhere but The Vineyard," he said, chuckling.

"Yeah. I'm even madder today. They were happy to sell us a giant pitcher of margaritas, but when we actually drank it, they threw us out."

"I think the operative word from last night was *outraged*."

"Mind if I change first?" she asked. "I can make it fast."

"Of course," Chris said in his easy way. "I'm not in a rush."

Lauren considered outfit options on the drive there and decided to wear her favorite long, multicolored dress with tiny blue and red flowers. When they got to her place, she jumped out of the car. "Be right back!" she said.

"I'll be here," Chris assured her.

Grinning, she dashed up to her apartment.

>>

When Lauren arrived back at the car, Chris was leaning against the hood, but he straightened his posture when he saw her. "What a great dress," he said. "Turn around."

She twirled around on the sidewalk.

"Wow. It's perfect for you."

His openly admiring look warmed her heart. She realized he had probably never seen her in anything but jeans or shorts. He held open the door to his blue Dodge Dart, the back seat of which was piled with boxes of rock samples, papers, and books. Lauren sat down and tucked in the long folds of her dress. She felt like a queen going to a ball. Chris's insistence on opening doors had slightly annoyed her when she first met him, but now it felt marvelous to be treated like a treasured person. It brought back memories of walking down the street with her grandfather, who tipped his hat to all the ladies.

"Do you want to try The Steak Place?" he asked as he started up the car.

"Sure. I haven't been there in a while."

As they drove to the restaurant, Lauren recalled previous visits to The Steak Place. She didn't mention to Chris that Don had taken her there numerous times, but she had yet to try their famous prime rib. Don had insisted she share what he wanted, which was usually French onion soup and Caesar salad. No wonder their relationship had lasted only a few months. Brilliance in ocean basalts didn't necessarily translate into brilliance in menu analysis. *Why go to a steak house if the only protein you got was anchovy paste and raw egg?*

>>

"*Forbidden Planet* is such a classic," Chris said after the waiter took their order for a bottle of California cabernet.

"I agree," Lauren said. "It may be my all-time favorite sci-fi movie."

"If the monster had been an extraterrestrial instead of the embodiment of the psychologist's id, the movie wouldn't be nearly so interesting," Chris said.

Lauren nodded. "I guess the movie supports your idea that people have evil tendencies."

She looked on with amusement as the waiter extracted the cork from the wine bottle and laid it in front of Chris, who said, "I'm sure it'll be fine. Just pour it."

Lauren and Chris both took large sips as though thirsty from a visit to a dry planet.

"Not everybody has evil tendencies, but I do think people have the capacity for cruelty and violence, even supposedly civilized people." Chris said, picking up the conversation.

"But at least the psychologist regretted that his id monster killed off the rest of the crew."

"Yeah. Sometimes people are just weak, greedy, fearful, childish—in other words, human. Not necessarily evil. Hey, now I sound like you, defending basic human goodness."

Lauren laughed. She thought how comfortable she felt with Chris. She could say anything, agree or disagree with him, and they could talk about it. It was all okay. He challenged her thoughts and opinions but never her essence. He accepted her and cared about her even though he knew her weaknesses and mistakes. She realized at that moment he was a great man, and how lucky she was to have him in her life. A vague thought from the previous night tried to form but she couldn't quite capture it. She wondered if she were ever free, would she want to be more than just friends with Chris?

After the salad course, the waiter brought two plates nearly covered with slabs of pinkish-brown prime rib. Melted butter oozed over the sides of giant baked potatoes and mingled with the meat juices. Lauren's steady diet of peanut butter sandwiches made the first bite of succulent meat an experience to be savored. She chewed slowly, letting the flavors swirl around her taste buds. She looked up to see Chris watching her.

"I hate to see it end," Chris said with a serious look on his face.

"The prime rib?"

"No. The festival. Science fiction is such great escapism."

"I do, too. It's pretty hard to be depressed when your adrenaline is flowing."

"I didn't once think about the battle with Don over my petrology grade. He can't give me a C. It won't transfer, and I'll have to take the class over at Northern Idaho. I'm going to talk to him again."

"And I didn't once think of Don or Kenny and the mess I'm in. When will you leave for Idaho?"

"Sometime next week. I've got to finish some lab work and get packed. I can start my fieldwork as soon as I get there."

"I wish I were escaping from here. At least, from Don."

"Why don't you apply for a grant from Rockwell this summer? They're trying to map vast areas of basalt flows in Washington, Idaho, and Oregon. I bet they'd jump at the chance to hire you."

"This summer is the only time I can concentrate on my thesis. If I don't finish it now, I'll never get my master's."

"You're right. Get your degree and then come to Northern Idaho for your PhD."

"I'm thinking I'll be lucky to get a master's." *What a dear friend he is to want me at the same school,* she thought.

"Oh, you're on the road to a PhD, all right. Your last lecture on the kinematics of plate tectonics sounded like a doctoral level presentation."

"Wow, that makes me feel good. I did a ton of research."

"It was the most difficult topic selected all year. I was astounded you picked it. No one but you understood enough math to approach the subject, let alone make it understandable to the class."

"Well, thank you. But back to this week. I wish I weren't going to Corpus Christi tomorrow. I won't be here to help you pack."

"What's in Corpus Christi?" Chris asked, looking up.

"Barbara—my roommate from my semester in England—is in med school at the university there. I've been promising her for months I'd come visit."

"Believe me, I don't have that much stuff to pack. Everything will fit in my car."

Lauren felt bereft at the thought of Chris actually driving away in his car. There had been too many losses in her life the last year or so. She had lost her marriage, her husband, and the apartment they shared in one devastating moment when she moved out. Ending her affair with Don resulted in losing an adviser as an adviser should be: neutral and reasonable. Instead, he'd turned into a tyrant. And she had lost part of her thumb—the least of her losses. She would miss Chris and his steady friendship. Even though she didn't know when she would see him again, she was sure their close friendship would continue.

>>

After leaving the restaurant, Chris drove slowly back to Lauren's apartment as Lauren mulled over the evening's conversation. *How incredibly insightful Chris is*, she thought. Scientists usually didn't understand human nature. They preferred to gather and quantify facts. Human emotions were far too unpredictable for most scientists.

When they arrived at her apartment, they both got out of the car. A light breeze had reduced the humidity and turned the night pleasant. The landlady's half barrel of purple and white petunias gave off a sweet, summertime smell. Clouds hid the moon, but quite a few stars were visible. Lauren stood in awe of the night sky. Infinite possibilities of life elsewhere made her feel small and unreal, yet part of a greater reality of the universe. Looking upward was looking backward in time. The darkest part of space held secrets to the beginning of the universe.

She stood next to Chris on the sidewalk and studied the sky. "I wonder where *Voyager* is now," she said.

"It's still a long way from Jupiter, but even before its closest approach, it will send better photographs than we've ever seen."

"Jupiter's cloud patterns are breathtaking from a telescope. Imagine a close-up of the Red Spot." She turned to face Chris.

"Ah, the artist in you can't wait to see the pictures."

"The Red Spot is caused by wind patterns and makeup of the atmosphere. But what exactly is the atmosphere?"

"I guess we'll know more in a year. Jupiter is fascinating in itself, but then you add all the moons. It's an astronomer's dream."

The earth stood still then, as surely as though acted on by travelers from another galaxy. Lauren and Chris looked at each other in the dim light and their lips met, drawn together by an irresistible force.

They kissed gently and then more intensely. They pressed into each other. Lauren's mind reeled with surprise and possibilities. Warmth suffused her body and immersed her in tenderness and desire. When the kiss ended and Chris tipped his head back, his arms stayed tightly wrapped around her and he looked into her eyes, a smile filling his entire face.

She knew then what she had not known. He loved her. *I didn't mean for this to happen.*

"Oh, geez, I'm sorry," Chris said, releasing his arms from around Lauren and running his hands through his hair. "I don't know what came over me. I'd better go."

Lauren nodded. "But don't be sorry. It was nice."

"It's just that I don't know when we'll see each other again . . ." His voice trailed away and he shrugged.

"We'll get together." She gave him a quick hug and then watched as he turned, walked toward his car, and drove away.

>>

Why did I let him leave? Lauren asked herself when she entered her empty apartment. She fell into bed reliving the kiss and how wonderful it felt to be in his arms. She missed the warmth of sleeping with a man. Chris's passionate kiss had astounded her. All along he had been counseling her about getting back together with Kenny. This new dimension to him was confusing. She was still married, she reminded herself. What if she and Kenny reconciled? Then she would hurt Chris. Just like she had hurt Don, only Chris was her dearest friend.

Lauren knew she struggled with loving and being loved. During her childhood, her grandfather had been the only one who gave her unconditional love. He had been gone for seventeen years. She had married Kenny in the exuberance of youth and sex and adventure. Now they were apart. Too much of her life was missing. With Don, she had mistaken sexual desire for love. Then just a few short months later she realized she not only didn't love him but didn't even like him.

The universe, with all its mysteries, was more understandable than her life. That night she dreamed tornadoes flattened all the buildings on campus except the Geo Sciences building, where she and Chris worked on math problems.

Chapter 8

A Man in Flight

Chris, 1978

Chris trudged up the stairs to the second floor of the Geo Sciences building. After reviewing his final petrology paper and Don's comments, he was certain his paper deserved an A, not a C. He hoped Don would raise his grade when presented with the evidence. The door to Don's office was open. He was watering a row of plants along the windows.

"Don, I need to talk to you," Chris said, as he walked through the doorway.

"Now's not a good time." Don continued watering his plants without looking at Chris.

"Well, I don't have much time," Chris said. "I'm leaving in two days for fieldwork in Idaho."

"I've got a department meeting in five minutes," Don said, looking at his watch, and then turning back to the row of plants.

"It's about my paper. I reread it, and it's better than a C paper."

"You were lucky to get a C."

Chris flipped through pages of his paper and tried to remain calm.

"Here, where you say I didn't explain one of my thesis statements, there are nine pages of explanation. So, you're wrong about that."

Without looking at Chris's paper, he said, "Your topic is your first mistake."

"But you approved my topic!" Chris frowned and looked with disbelief at Don.

"You told me you were going to research mantle composition as it relates to Earth's origin."

"That's the first part of my paper—" Chris crossed his arms across his chest.

Don interrupted, "Yeah, but then you veer off into meteorite analysis. From there you plunge into disproving differential volatility's role in the formation of planets."

"Why does doing more than required result in a lower grade?" Chris demanded.

"Did you happen to note the name of the course when you enrolled—Petrology of Earth's Mantle?"

"This is outrageous! You can't understand formation of the earth without understanding formation of other planets."

"Besides not sticking to your topic, your paper lacks the rigorous intellectual analysis demanded by the department," Don said, watering the prolific spider plant cascading in the corner.

"Damn it! I doubt any other student did more rigorous analysis than mine!" Chris said.

"Face it, Chris. You are not a PhD caliber student. The sooner you realize that, the better."

Chris pointed at Don. "You can't handle the fact that I'm not obsessed with ocean basalts."

Don gave Chris a malevolent look and walked out the door. "Clearly, you don't belong at Texas Polytechnic."

Chris stood for a minute in Don's office and then crossed the hall to his cubicle. He was glad no one was around to hear Don's denunciation.

"Shit!" he said out loud, dropping into his desk chair.

He looked over at Lauren's deserted desk and wished she weren't in Corpus Christi. She would have been able to cheer him up and provide a little perspective on Don's behavior. Talking to the head of the department about his final grade wouldn't help. Chris had already told him he was transferring to Northern Idaho. The department head wouldn't confront Don—a nationally recognized scholar in ocean basalts—on behalf of a soon-to-be former student. Nothing would make Don happier than to hear Chris was transferring. Chris wouldn't give him the satisfaction. He would have to hear it from someone else.

>>

When Chris arrived home later that day, he looked at his apartment with new eyes. Its condition resembled the state of his life: trashed. He remembered how pleased he had been when he was admitted to Tex Poly. Now, apparently, he didn't meet the standards of either the Geology Department or the university. He hadn't fallen from grace. He had plummeted.

Like all spoiled children, Don was a master of manipulation—and as an adviser, he was useless. Continental basalts might as well have been Shakespearean sonnets, as far as Don was concerned. They were so far from his field of interest that he hadn't been able to guide Chris into a workable science. Worse, Don was willing to subvert the mission of the department and all the people in it to satisfy his own ego. If Chris were inclined to be exploited by an adviser, which he wasn't, he would have chosen a more desirable geographical location. East Texas stank.

Chris rose with a sigh of disgust and made his way down to the alley to gather boxes for packing. There he encountered the same disheveled hippie he'd seen the previous day, digging through trash cans.

This time the man, holding a bottle wrapped in a paper bag, sidled up to him singing, "Oh, I want your money, oh, I need your money, oh, give me your money."

"What the hell," Chris said. "Are you trying to rob me?" The man looked a little drunk but not violent.

"No, man, I just need money."

"Do you think I'd be walking down alleys looking for free boxes if I had money?"

"I bet you've got more money than I do. I haven't eaten since yesterday."

The man looked unkempt enough to be either homeless or a geology professor, so Chris handed him five dollars. "Here, get a burger."

"Thanks, man. I bet you're a Tex Poly student," he said, examining the five-dollar bill as though it might be counterfeit.

Chris shrugged. "Was."

"Why? Didya flunk out?" He looked at Chris with new interest.

"In a manner of speaking." *Not far from the truth,* Chris thought. He felt like a failure even though he knew the low grade Don had given him was based on pure nastiness. Chris had always been at the top of his class. Now Don had damaged Chris's academic record and could harm his professional reputation as well because of Tex Poly's prestige.

"Tex Poly is a worthless fucking institution, if you ask me."

Chris chuckled inwardly. *I couldn't have said it better myself.*

"I was there in sixty-seven, and it never got me anywhere but to 'Nam," the man said.

"You were in 'Nam?" Chris asked, resuming his search through the dumpsters.

"Yeah. Combat base outside of Da Nang." He tagged along behind Chris.

"I was in the air force for four years, but it was after Saigon fell."

"You a pilot?"

"Nope. I did intelligence mapping."

"Hey, there's a cricket in one of your boxes."

Chris started to turn the box upside down but changed his mind. He turned to the man.

"Do you want to help me catch a bunch of bugs?"

"What do you want a bunch of bugs for?"

"A farewell present for a friend."

"Far out, man. Where's your friend going?"

"I'm the one going."

"Grasshoppers are hopping all over the place in the park," the man said, pointing down the alley.

>>

It was late Friday afternoon by the time Chris had packed up his apartment and loaded all the boxes into his car. The back seat was stacked to the ceiling, and the trunk barely closed. He realized he had better get to the university and clean out his office if he were to get on the road in the morning.

He parked what he now thought of as the getaway car adjacent to the Geo Sciences building. The second floor was lit but seemingly deserted. He returned heat lamps, mortar and pestle, and sample bottles to Room 6. Once he had packed his rock samples, books, and files from his cubicle, he sat down and wrote a three-page letter to Don outlining his deficiencies as an adviser and attaching assorted documentation. Then he walked across the hall to Don's office and unleashed five flying beetles, seventeen grasshoppers of two different species, three crickets, and a starving caterpillar on Don's magnificent spider plant. He laid the letter on Don's desk, positioned his chair so he could sit down without having to move it, and placed a tack where it would do the most good.

Muttering complaints about the department and personalities, Chris roamed the halls looking for a pushcart to carry his boxes. When he reached the office of Don's close colleague, he was in full fervor.

He stuck his head into the darkened office and said in a loud voice, "You're a rat fink, too."

He turned around and looked into the face of his friend Matt.

"Oh, hi, Matt."

"You're here kind of late. By the way, who're you talking to?"

"I thought I heard someone in Arlen's office."

"A rat fink, perhaps?" Matt asked with a grin.

"Yeah." Chris laughed. "What are you doing here on a Friday night?"

"I stopped by the lab to check my solutions."

"I just packed up my gear. I'm leaving tomorrow for fieldwork in Idaho."

"I envy you. I wish I were getting out of this heat and humidity. Have a great summer," Matt said as he headed down the steps.

Chris returned to his apartment and fell asleep with the light on. At four o'clock he woke with light shining in his eyes. It was still dark outside. He decided to get on the road. With little traffic, he soon drove onto the ramp to Interstate 45 and headed north. A man in flight, he felt disgraced for having to leave this way. His stubbornness always made him stay with a situation until he overcame it or faltered. He should've had sense to transfer at the semester when he first realized the magnitude of the divide between Don and himself.

>>

The drive was not as bad as it had been in other years. Leg aches and back stiffness were offset by the joy of returning to Idaho and seeing the mountains again. The air was crisp and clean and fruit trees were leafing out.

After visiting with an old professor in Coeur d'Alene, he went to fill out paperwork for his research grant at the Rockwell/Department of Energy headquarters in Richland, Washington. When he was done, he met fellow geologists Rob Cordova and Jeff Rutherford at a local pool hall. Except for a couple of old-timers hunched over their beers at the bar, the geologists were the only customers. They signaled for Chris to join them at a pool table.

"You look like a house painter in that get-up," Chris said to Jeff, who, as always, was dressed in white. "I thought you might have turned into a real geologist while I was away."

"Son of a gun, you're back," Jeff said with a big smile. "And by the way, I have turned into a real geologist. I got my degree this spring."

"Hey, congrats!" Chris clapped him on the shoulder.

Jeff handed Chris his cue stick. "You take on this hustler," he said, nodding at Rob. I already owe him a beer."

"Chris. Looks like it's you and me," Rob said, giving him something between a high five and a hug.

"You're up to your old tricks, I see," Chris said with a grin.

"I hear they assigned you the Weiser Embayment," Rob said, picking up his cue stick. "Now that's a big-ass area."

"I'll take it. It's hundreds of miles from the Hanford site, which is a good thing. Have you guys looked around at Hanford? It's alarming." He paused. "Isn't anybody alarmed?" Chris asked, watching Rob rack the balls, line up his shot, and break explosively.

Balls bounced and clacked all over the table, but none went down a pocket.

"Damn! Of course, Hanford's alarming. But don't alarm me while I'm breaking," Rob said.

"Can't handle the slightest distraction, can you?" Chris asked with a glint in his eye, but then grew serious again. "The map shows uranium, tritium, and strontium-90 in the groundwater. And the Columbia River has even more contaminants." He forgot for a minute the setup table that lay before him, balls ripe for the picking. After making an easy shot, he missed a second one.

Jeff sat in a bar booth and watched Rob systematically make shot after shot while Chris missed easy ones and tried ever more complex shots to try to catch up. When Rob sank the eight ball, he and Chris hung up their cue sticks and slid into the booth.

"Looks like Jeff and I are buying."

"Looks like it," Rob said with a goofy grin on his face, as though he had won the lottery instead of a couple of beers.

"Mapping basalts seems like a feeble way to deal with nuclear waste," Chris said, returning the conversation to the Hanford site.

"Yeah, I agree," Jeff said. "Could they have picked a worse site to manufacture plutonium back in the forties?"

"Now they consult geologists. After the fact," Chris said, taking a swallow of his beer.

"I guess one good thing comes from nuclear contamination—money for geology fieldwork," Rob said.

"I picked up on that," Chris said. "When they told me I was getting a field vehicle, I immediately asked for money for rare earth element analyses and strontium dating."

"Anything for the asking. The only thing Rockwell and DOE require in return is permission to publish your thesis in a limited edition. And that doesn't preclude publication in major journals," Rob said.

"Not a bad arrangement. But what a lot of rigmarole they're putting me through just to get on board. Besides requiring pages of forms and an FBI check, they fingerprinted me, and I have to take a physical."

"Yeah, I don't get it either," Rob said, finishing his second beer and getting up. "I've gotta go. But, thanks for the beers, boys."

Jeff and Chris made plans to meet mid-June in a town adjacent to their field areas. After Jeff left, Chris was left to contemplate the Hanford site and toxic fluids percolating through basalts.

>>

The next day after his physical, Chris picked up his equipment and Chevy Suburban and took a southern route home so he could drive through his research area in the Weiser Embayment in Southern Idaho, 250 miles south of Coeur d'Alene. He marveled at its beauty. Although only at an elevation of three thousand feet, there was evidence of an alpine environment. Meadows covered in wildflowers were cut by small creeks. Pine trees peppered the sides of hills. Trucks loaded with logs indicated a thriving lumber industry. Small towns consisted of wood frame houses and a few stores. Sturgill Peak was a dominant landmark, the center of broad ridges stretching across his research area. At four thousand feet, light from a band of snow played with the darker colors of pines and gullies.

Unfortunately, most of the exposed basalt was well weathered, making it virtually useless for chemical analysis. Two areas looked promising as sections to map. At the top of one pass, he identified four basalt flows with well weathered, highly oxidized tops. These four units had characteristics that were traceable. It would be ironic if they outcropped only at this one location.

His heart raced at the thought of the scientific puzzles to be solved.

When he returned to Coeur d'Alene, he checked into an inexpensive motel. Even though he was famished, he decided to write to Lauren before going to dinner. He couldn't stop re-living the last time he saw her. He wanted to say how he could have gone on kissing her forever. How soft and yielding she felt in his arms. How he wished they had made love all night. How they could have been lovers and best friends. Instead, he cleared his thoughts and wrote the letter he'd meant to write two days earlier.

May 26, 1978
Dear Lauren,

When I started this letter, I was so tired from traveling I immediately fell asleep. Today may be the day I finish. I left books at your apartment I meant to give you before you left for Corpus Christi. There are three sets: two field books, an art book and sketch pads, and two notebooks. They represent potential—the tabula rasa of your talents as a scientist, artist, and writer. I am enthralled with what you've done and the possibilities for your future.

As discussed before, this summer may be a critical time. I'd like to call you from Idaho to learn what has happened and generally see how your life is progressing. It's much cheaper to call collect than to put coins in a pay phone, and I do want to call. The enclosed check for $30 is to handle calls from a curious Irishman. I'll let you know in advance when I plan to call. Knowing your penchant for independence, I realize you won't like this arrangement, but practically speaking, you don't have the resources to pay for calls, and I do. And I would really like to talk to you.

Other than meeting you, my time in Texas was for naught. I have accomplished more in two days at Northern Idaho, gained more cooperation, and been treated as an equal instead of a peon, than my time at Tex Poly. I start my field-work tomorrow. They gave me a 4-wheel drive field vehicle, so my old Dodge Dart gets the summer off. If you're so inclined, you can write me in care of General Delivery, Weiser, Idaho 83672.

How is your thesis coming along? Have you cut all your samples? How about Don? Has his strategy changed or is he still a greedy-eyed, hungry-lipped wolf? Has Kenny's confusion ended? I hope everything's going well. As things are now, I'll call you Sunday, June 11th at 9 p.m. your time.

However short it was, I enjoyed our last night together. It's crazy, but it meant a lot to me. And it was without reservation my best evening in Pasadena. I think of it with fondness *and no extrapolations. If I could choose what I want for you, it would be this: to be happy with no feelings of guilt, to fulfill your potential in art and science, and to be at peace. Whatever route you choose, I hope it eventually will lead you to the above. I'll be wishing you on. You are a unique person, Lauren. You have an intellect and creativity few people possess. I've enjoyed our friendship very much.*

Thank you,

Chris

Chapter 9

Rift Zones

Lauren, 1978

When Lauren entered her empty apartment, she noticed a sack sitting just inside the door, as though the landlady had set it there. She ripped open the stapled-shut bag from The Co-op and found journals, field notebooks, and sketch pads. No doubt a present from Chris—her thoughtful, generous friend who was now on his way to Idaho.

As she unpacked her duffel, she thought back to their last evening together and how they had kissed passionately. They could have become lovers. Had she missed a chance to be with an incredible man? A wave of regret overwhelmed her for a few minutes. Then the rational side of her brain took over. *No,* she thought. *If I'm ever with Chris in the future, it'll be because Kenny and I are divorced.* She was thankful that Chris and she hadn't become lovers. It wouldn't have been fair to involve him in her crazy life.

She still yearned to get back together with her husband—the way he used to be. Chris and she could continue to be best friends.

Now she was home and within a mile of Kenny's apartment. She felt his presence and his absence. Because her life improved dramatically when she met him, it was hard to contemplate life without him. She remembered her awkwardness when she transferred from Friends school to public school. The physical education locker room had been a revelation. All the girls wore bras instead of undershirts, and no one except Lauren had unshaved legs. Her ingrained politeness and nonaggression made her an easy target for teasing and practical jokes. She and Hannah, her best friend from Friends school, gravitated toward other less popular students. From the deepest and coldest part of space, their group wheeled around the sun that shone on athletes, cheerleaders, and homecoming queens.

When Kenny's high school in a nearby suburb closed for renovation, their schools merged. Suddenly, a star athlete too new to know Lauren was from Pluto sought her company. He was tough and street-smart. Misconstruing her shyness for elusiveness, he pursued her aggressively. He seemed impressed by the stately neighborhood where she lived with her trust-funded mother and grandmother. On her sixteenth birthday, Lauren and her friends, dressed in tent dresses and go-go boots, danced to 45 rpm records with Kenny and his scruffy friends. After the party Kenny took Lauren for a ride on his motorcycle. Pressed against his back and with her arms encircling his waist, she felt warmth.

The past few days in Corpus Christi, she had thought of Kenny only intermittently. An oldies radio station had played their song, "Ain't No Sunshine," sung by Bill Withers. Then when she and her friend Barbara drank beers at a campus hangout with peanut shells on the floor, it had reminded her of a similar place she and Kenny frequented in college. Throwing peanut shells on the floor was liberating, if not exhilarating, for a Quaker girl. It was one of many firsts she had experienced with Kenny. He had taught her to spin the Frisbee against the sky so it returned to her like a boomerang. In college he had taken her to a pool hall, a place previously associated with trouble, thanks to *The Music Man*. Pool rituals excited her. She had watched Kenny circle the table like a field commander organizing his troops. He had rubbed chalk on the end of his cue stick and then leaned over and pressed his thighs into the rounded edge of the table to take his shot. It wasn't long before she and Kenny had meandered down the garden path to sex—a path paved with chalk dust and peanut shells.

After five years of dating, six years of marriage, and seven months of separation, her happiest memories were of Kenny. Dwelling on the past reminded her of joy that was gone. The present felt dull, and the future, unfathomable. All manner of human time seemed lost to her.

She opened a recorked bottle of chardonnay from the refrigerator and poured herself a glass. Geology dealt with deep time, before human angst clouded the earth. It was a relief to immerse herself in her thesis, whose underlying question was why Africa and Surea began breaking apart from the Arabian Peninsula thirty million years ago. One theory was that the Afar plume in northern Ethiopia had been a significant factor in the rift. Mantle plumes associated with continental breakup often resulted in three-armed patterns. In the case of the Afar plume, two arms had formed seas: the Red Sea and the Gulf of Aden. One rift failed to form an ocean but had produced the volcanically active East African Rift Zone, which could rip Africa apart over millions of years.

Lauren had inherited twenty-one rocks gathered by a Tex Poly researcher two years before on a school expedition to the Red Sea. The chemistry of these gabbros would tell the source and depth from which the magma came. Finding gabbros from the first magma chambers that influenced continental breakup could answer questions about processes that pull continents apart. She was thrilled that next summer she would go on a research voyage to the small, oil-rich country of Surea to resample the sites of the original rocks. After a second glass of wine, Lauren made a list of tasks and a tentative schedule for her research. She would start first thing tomorrow.

>>

The next day began earlier than planned. At six o'clock her mother telephoned to say the building handyman had hung up on her when she reported her clothes dryer was broken.

Lauren guessed she had called him repeatedly prior to calling Lauren. No wonder he had hung up on her. Her mother couldn't put problems in perspective. Unimportant background became foreground, light dimmed into shadow, and minor problems loomed like Goliaths. This nightmarish vision became a fixation. A broken dryer was not life-threatening. Lauren left the telephone receiver off its cradle and went back to bed.

As soon as she woke up, however, she ate, dressed, and drove to her mother's.

As she neared the apartment building, she felt her stomach tighten. Whenever she had to deal with her mother alone, she nearly became ill. Kenny had been good, or at least neutral, in his interactions with his mother-in-law. Lauren had not told her mother she and Kenny were separated.

Since her grandmother Dorothy died four years ago, Lauren had been responsible for Betty. Her mother now lived on the outskirts of Houston, forty miles from Pasadena and a half hour from her mother's brother, Uncle Steven. He and Lauren had tried to convince Betty to move to a supervised home. She'd refused. The mental health test for involuntary commitment was whether a person was a danger to herself or others. Lauren had to admit her mother wasn't a danger to anyone, except, perhaps, to Lauren's sanity.

She longed for her mother to get psychological help but couldn't compel it. She blamed her grandmother for destroying her mother's autonomy. Strong-willed and imperious, Dorothy had been one of the first women to earn a PhD at Swarthmore College. She relished her role of Greater Being in the presence of Lesser Being—Lauren's mother, who was awkward and unsure of herself. Betty idolized Dorothy and stayed dependent on her until Dorothy's death. When the person in the light was gone, did a shadow ever round out? Step out? Dance? Lauren thought not.

She yawned as she pulled her 1969 Chevy Camaro around a plumber's van into the left lane. If she were lucky, she would be back at school by early afternoon to start the work she had ignored for ten days.

She found a parking space close to the apartment entrance and decided to take the stairs to the left of the lobby. When she opened the fire door to the stairwell, she found her mother, dressed in light blue sweatpants and an orange T-shirt, sitting on the first landing. Instead of the elegant woman she could have been, she looked like a lanky, gray-haired kid with a self-inflicted haircut. Sweat beads lined her forehead and upper lip.

"Where's Kenny?" her mom asked.

"It's Monday. He's at work," Lauren said in a flat voice.

"Well, you took your sweet time getting here."

"What are you doing sitting in a stairwell where it's at least ninety degrees?" Lauren asked with a touch of outrage.

"I need to catch Charlie. He never uses the elevator. My dryer made a horrible noise and now it won't go around."

"Come on, let's get out of here. They'll either fix it or buy you a new one. Your apartment is supposed to come with washer and dryer."

Even the simplest problems were beyond her mother's ability to solve. Not because she wasn't smart. She had a college degree, after all. It's just that her crazy emotions tangled up her thinking.

"I don't know what to do." Betty stood up and ambled down the short stairway.

"What did the building manager say?" Lauren asked, opening the door and holding it for her mother.

"I didn't talk to her."

"I've told you and told you, when you have a problem, you need to call Anita."

Lauren was annoyed. She had wanted to start her research instead of driving halfway across Houston.

They walked across the lobby toward the office.

"She can't do anything. Charlie fixes things. But no one really cares. No one wants to help," Betty said.

"Charlie works for Anita. She tells him what to do."

"The ladies on my floor are always boohooing to her about something. I never bother her."

I guess it's good Mother's not a constant complainer, but when she does have a problem, she freaks out.

Before they walked into the office, Lauren turned toward her mother and reminded her, "If Charlie won't answer his phone, you have to talk to Anita."

Anita was using the copy machine in the back office, the main feature of which was a giant board with keys on hooks.

"Ladies, take a seat. I'll be right out."

Betty situated herself in the chair closest to Anita's desk; Lauren took a chair against the back wall.

When Anita came in, Betty said, "What do you expect me to do with my wet clothes?"

Oh, geez. Why does she have to start off that way? She alienated everybody and it was embarrassing.

"Now, Mrs. Wilson, this is the first I've heard of a problem. Your dryer isn't working?"

"I need help. I need a new dryer."

"The dryers on your floor aren't more than three years old. You don't need a new dryer."

"*It*, back in the corner, my useless daughter, said you have to buy me a new dryer."

Tears welled in Lauren's eyes. *My own mother humiliating me!* She stood and rushed out of the office. She thought she was immune to her mother's epithets, but every once in a while, she was taken by surprise.

Her mother hurried after her. "Lauren, Lauren, I told you we shouldn't go see Anita. Don't leave me here alone!"

Lauren continued walking in the direction of the front door but turned and said, "Don't call me when you have a problem. Solve it yourself."

"You owe me. It's the least you can do."

"You're an adult. Act like one."

"How can I dry my clothes? I don't have a clothesline," her mother said, sounding as though she were about to cry.

"I'm sure they'll fix it."

"Don't abandon me!"

"I need to go back to school."

"Mrs. Wilson," Charlie called, walking across the lobby toward them. "I've got your dryer running again. But for heaven's sake, don't call me at four thirty in the morning!"

"Mother, I've got to go." Lauren walked out the door to her car, where she sat behind the wheel and wept for a few minutes. How stupid she was to expect her mother to behave like a normal mother. She never did.

>>

Driving back to Pasadena, Lauren forced herself to put her mother out of her mind, choosing a safer topic to ponder—her dilemma about the summer's field trip. On the one hand, the Guadalupe Mountains National Park was a geologist's dream. She longed to explore El Capitan, the 290-million-year-old marine fossil reef exposed during uplift a few million years ago. The reef had developed in a semi-circle around the Delaware Basin, which was part of an inland sea connected to the Permian Ocean. The uplifted reef could be explored in three places: the Glass and Apache Mountains in Texas and the

Guadalupe Mountains on the Texas–New Mexico border. By far the largest exposed section of El Capitan was in the Guadalupe Mountains. Unlike modern reefs built by stony corals, in Permian time reef-building organisms had been mainly calcareous algae, bryozoans, and sponges. It would be a reef like no other she had seen.

On the other hand, she suspected Don's requiring her to go on this trip was a ruse to get her alone. She decided she wouldn't go. A few days later when she saw him leave his classroom, she followed him down the hall.

"Don, I can't go on the Guadalupe field trip this summer. I'm behind in my lab work, as you know."

Don turned and frowned. "You can do your lab work when you get back."

Why does everything have to be a struggle? she wondered.

"Couldn't you find somebody else in the department to go?"

"I assigned you this trip a month ago. Besides, I'm short of graduate assistants this summer."

Most geology expeditions are voluntary, Lauren thought. *Not this one.*

"I really can't go. I'll never catch up," Lauren said, shaking her head.

"I'm your professor, and you have to go. That's final." Don turned abruptly and continued walking down the hall.

Lauren's shoulders slumped. She watched until he turned a corner. Then she crossed the hall to the graduate assistants' offices, dropped a load of books on her desk, and looked around. Chris's cubicle in the back corner was abandoned. She was happy he had arrived safely in Coeur d'Alene. Inadvertently, she had poisoned his chances at Tex Poly. She felt guilty, but she was relieved he had transferred to a school where they would appreciate his talents. However, this was not a good time to lose a best friend. She sat down and wrote him a letter.

June 4, 1978

Dear Chris,

Thank you for the journals, field books, and sketch pads. Their blankness is thrilling, but also a little intimidating.

Are you enjoying the cool, dry mountain air of Idaho? Pasadena is particularly humid and roach-infested this summer. A critter scurried out of my toaster when I toasted. I bought a new, pesticide-free product, Roach Motel ("Roaches check in . . . but they don't check out!"), in hopes of diminishing my kitchen colony. Maybe it's not surprising East Texas is populated by scurrilous people. This weather encourages low-life forms!

Barbara and I had a great time in Corpus Christi, but now I've got to catch up on work. You'll never believe what happened when I was cutting a slice of one of my sample rocks. The saw blade flew across the room! Luckily, there was no one in the room to decapitate. I think the rock was too big for the blade. Fearing Don's anger at my ruining a diamond-encrusted saw blade, I called him immediately. He said grant money was available for replacements. Whew! I'm sure he was as relieved as I that there was no carnage.

I agree our last evening together was fantastic. Please know nothing could hurt our friendship. I value you and our relationship. I'm confident we will always be great friends no matter where our lives take us. I can't wait to talk to you when you call on June 11th. I want to hear about your adventures in the field.

Your friend,

Lauren

In late June they arrived at Guadalupe Mountains National Park at dusk. Even though El Capitan was in deep shadow, they felt its presence. Don, Lauren, and eight undergraduate students from assorted colleges and universities had made the fourteen-hour trip from Pasadena in one long day. Don had insisted on driving the whole way despite numerous offers by Lauren and others to relieve him. Once inside the park, everyone, including Don, had to get out periodically to push their van out of deep ruts in the dirt road. Using the last bit of daylight, the group set up their individual tents where the road ended, and their hiking adventure would begin. Lauren and two undergraduate girls pitched their tents in a cluster away from the boys' and Don's tents. So far Don had behaved in a professional manner, but she wasn't taking any chances.

The next day after breakfast, the party set off in high spirits on a beautiful desert trail in the lower elevations of the park. Prickly pear cacti showed blooms of red, white, and yellow. Ocotillos waved their spindly arms tipped with reddish-orange flowers. Don strode ahead. The undergraduates joked and laughed among themselves. They seemed pleased to be on a lark that gave them geology credit for a week of field camp. When Lauren caught up to Don, she implored him to rethink their hiking plan and to shorten the first day's hike. Most of the students were inexperienced hikers.

"Nonsense. They're kids. They have energy to burn."

"Ten miles with elevation gain is too far with heavy packs."

"No. We're camping at Wilderness Ridge tonight. To have enough time for McKittrick Canyon tomorrow, we'll hike to Pratt Cabin, backtrack a little and then head up the trail. By the time we reach the campsite, we'll be in a treed area with shade."

He's so rigid and dictatorial, Lauren thought. She couldn't believe she was ever involved with him.

Lauren glanced back. Two hikers had already fallen behind the other six. "Look, some are already lagging."

"I'm in charge here. We'll follow my plan. If you're so concerned, stay back and make sure everyone keeps up."

He acts like a jerk and I have to deal with the consequences.

Lauren sat on a rock until the two New York boys caught up.

"How's it going?"

"I think my boots are giving me blisters," Luke, the taller of the two, said, wincing.

"Guys, are those new boots?" Lauren asked, looking first at Tony's tan leather lace-up boots, and then at Luke's camouflage-printed canvas and black leather boots that reached to mid-calf.

They're even more inexperienced than I thought.

"These are jungle boots from Vietnam. I bought them at an army Surplus store," Luke answered.

"This is desert." She gestured at the surrounding landscape.

"Yeah, but they're mostly canvas. I think it's the leather that's rubbing on my heel."

"Mine are new," Tony said, looking pleased.

"A hiking trip is not a good time to break in new boots."

The boys sat down on the ground while Lauren dug through her backpack.

"I hate this backpack. It's like carrying lead. It's pinching my neck and giving me a headache," Tony said, letting his pack drop.

Lauren handed the boys moleskin patches for their blisters. "These will keep your blisters from getting worse. Let's get moving. We're already behind."

By the time they were underway again, the others were out of sight around a bend. The three walked fast for the next hour or so, once catching sight of the group from a ridge. A figure in the distance was getting closer. It was Don, who had doubled back to tell them the plan. "Not too far ahead we'll be leaving the marked trail. Follow the cairns."

"Don't you think I should have a map?" Lauren asked.

"You don't need a map. We'll leave cairns all along the way. Just follow them."

Lauren watched, dismayed, as Don hurried ahead with the only map flapping from his back pocket. Luke and Tony sped up, and in another half mile they saw four balanced rocks beside an arrow of smaller stones pointing toward a faint path strewn with rocks and boulders. They followed the arrow. Almost immediately, Luke stumbled and complained he had twisted his ankle. Lauren was glad she had brought a couple of stretch bandages. She wrapped Luke's ankle even though it wasn't noticeably swollen. He stood up and hobbled a few feet.

"We don't have to go fast. It's all right if we lag behind the rest of the group."

"I don't think I can walk any farther," Luke said. "A helicopter's going to have to come get me."

Lauren had to stifle a laugh at Luke's idea of helicopters being readily available.

"Helicopter! What helicopter are you talking about? There's no helicopter. We're a hundred miles from El Paso."

"Well, I can't walk."

"Maybe you'll be able to walk after we rest awhile."

The boys had long since taken off their packs from which they now extracted giant cans of ravioli and spaghetti.

"We don't have an opener!" Tony said. "Kimberly from Boston is the one who has the can opener. We'll have to catch up with her if we want to eat."

"You don't have any food that's not in cans?" Lauren asked.

"Nope."

Luke and Tony turned their packs upside down and more cans tumbled onto the ground.

"No wonder your packs are so heavy. Didn't you see the list of what to bring? It was the last sheet in your packet."

Luke and Tony looked at one another and shrugged.

Oh, geez, what am I going to do now? The rest of the group was so far ahead, it was doubtful they would catch them.

Lauren handed them each a smashed peanut butter sandwich from her pack. She unwrapped a chunk of cheese and some crackers for herself.

"Where do we get water?" Tony asked. "My canteen's almost empty." He swallowed from a small, round, canvas-wrapped canteen, the kind that comes with children's camping kits.

"That's all the water you brought?" Lauren asked, her eyes widening.

"I'm almost out, too," Luke said, holding up an identical canteen.

"Shit," Lauren said under her breath. Their water supply was several miles away at Pratt Cabin.

This is getting worse all the time!

"You guys wait here. I'm going to hike ahead to see if I can catch the group. I'm leaving you my extra bottle of water. Don't drink more than half of it. We're going to need it later."

Lauren jogged north along the path which ended in a huge outcropping of silicified dolomite. No cairn. She slowed her pace a little and jogged across the outcropping to the east. Sweat dripped from her face. She was beginning to panic. No cairn. She returned to the start of the dolomite in case she had missed a sign left by Don and the others. Next, she hiked across the outcropping and veered west. Still no cairn. When she had hiked in all directions, she returned to where Tony and Luke were sitting on boulders, waiting. This was a nightmare! She told herself to calm down and think of solutions.

"Guys, I've got bad news. I can't find the trail. We're on our own for tonight. And we've got to find water. A couple of ridges over is a fault. We're likely to find water there."

"But I can't walk," Luke protested. "I think we should signal a helicopter by building a fire."

"Have you seen a lot of helicopters flying over? You'll have to walk the best you can. We can't stay here without water."

Lauren had studied the morphology of the surrounding area as she searched for cairns. The dolomite outcropping descended into a valley defined by faulting. A tree in the far distance looked as though it might be a cottonwood, which would be a good omen for finding water. If she could just drag the guys with her. . . she was exhausted and doubted whether she and Tony could carry Luke, who, though slim, was six feet or more.

"Leave your cans here. We'll retrieve them on the way back. I have enough granola bars for us to survive."

Luke shifted his lightened pack onto his shoulders.

Tony stacked their cans into an arrow. "I'm setting a can cairn so the helicopter will know which way we went."

They picked their way carefully around boulders and rocks.

"Ow, ow, ow!" Luke complained as he limped along.

By the time they had traversed the barren face of the exposed dolomite, they were thirsty and out of water.

Now it's getting desperate, Lauren thought. *I've got to find water before dark.*

As daylight faded, they slid on their backsides down the steep slope of loose rock to the valley below, hiked over the next ridge and down into a fault-bounded valley. The vegetation thickened and soon they fought their way through low shrubs until they came upon a trickle of water.

"Hey, guys. Water!"

They followed the trickle to a large, spring-fed pool, where they fell to their knees and drank the icy cold water from their hands before filling their canteens. Lauren splashed water on her dust-caked face and used her bandanna as a towel.

"How did you know there would be water here?" Tony asked.

"It's not hard if you understand a few natural laws." She paused to take a long swallow from her refilled bottle. "First, nature follows the path of least resistance. Always. From basic geology you know that a fault is a break in the earth's crust along which there has been relative movement. When it rains, water flows downhill along the easiest path and winds up in fractures in the crust, or faults. Also, vegetation is a sure indicator of water. See that cottonwood tree over there? Cottonwoods usually mean water isn't too far underground. If water weren't bubbling to the surface, we could probably dig down to it."

The boys looked impressed.

Lauren sighed with relief and then smiled. Her first major hurdle in keeping the guys and herself alive.

For dinner they ate granola bars and shared a bag of almonds. Despite Luke's complaints, his ankle didn't seem worse for all the hiking and scrambling. He and Tony cleared rocks from a flat, sandy area not far from the pool as a place for their sleeping bags. Even though it was a warm summer evening, they wished they had brought their tents, which they had left in the van in anticipation of clear weather.

Lauren was exhausted, as were Luke and Tony, judging by their eagerness to stake out places to sleep. She crawled into her sleeping bag but sat up to admonish them.

"Remember Don said there are rattlesnakes and scorpions in the park," she said. "It's not likely, but snakes seeking warmth have been known to crawl into sleeping bags with people. Be sure to tighten the cords at the top of your bags."

"You're freaking me out!" Tony said.

"Shit! Me too. I hate snakes! I won't be able to sleep."

"I have a plan," Tony said. "We can take turns keeping watch."

"Yes!" Luke said. "Each person can do a two-hour shift. Who's going first?"

"I'll take the first shift," Tony said.

"Okay," Luke said, "but you have to promise to watch for every kind of critter. I don't like bugs, either."

"Good plan, guys. Night," Lauren lay back down.

Within minutes, all three were asleep.

>>

The next day Tony shook Lauren. "Wake up! Something's wrong with Luke!"

Lauren scrambled out of her sleeping bag to find Luke blue-lipped, shaking, and dripping water.

"What happened?" she asked Tony.

"I think he lounged in the pool."

"Quick! Grab his sleeping bag. We've got to warm him up."

Luke continued to shake uncontrollably while Lauren and Tony helped him into his sleeping bag.

"I think I'm dying," he told them.

They wrapped their sleeping bags around him, as well.

Lauren was pretty sure Luke wasn't dying but she couldn't help worrying. Clearly, he was suffering from hypothermia.

He continued to shake until midmorning when he drifted into a deep sleep. They woke him at noon. He drank some water and ate a few bites of granola bar before falling asleep again. By nightfall he was hobbling around camp. For supper the three shared the last one and a half granola bars.

"We're out of food. The water we're drinking may or may not be contaminated with giardia. We've got to get back to civilization tomorrow," Lauren said.

"Tony and I think we should build a big fire to signal a helicopter."

"I keep telling you. There are no damn helicopters!"

"But there will be helicopters if they think there's a forest fire!" Tony said.

"A few wisps of smoke from our fire will not alarm anyone watching for forest fires. We would have to build an inferno to get anyone's attention—and kill ourselves in the process. No, we have to hike out of here."

Tony and Luke groaned and looked glum.

Lauren had no idea where they were. They had wandered so far afield, anyone looking for them wouldn't know where to start searching. *How did I get into this predicament?*

>>

Early the next morning, Lauren climbed to the top of the taller peak adjacent to their campsite and surveyed the surrounding area. She wished she had a pair of powerful binoculars. She was about to hike down and over to the next peak when she caught sight of a line of telephone poles toward the north in the far distance.

"Eureka!" she said aloud.

Skidding on loose rocks, she clambered down the slope, thinking as she went that it was too bad a vacuum cleaner company had preempted Archimedes' exclamation. *Eureka* should be saved for big discoveries like telephone poles or finding a method for assessing the purity of gold, which had incited Archimedes' outburst in the first place.

The thought made her laugh aloud. She lost her footing and sat down hard, laughing until tears ran down her face. The view from the top had put everything into perspective. She felt a wave of affection for the New York boys, although that isn't how she would have described her feelings for them on the previous two days. She was still chuckling when she returned to camp.

"Why are you so happy?" Luke asked.

"Fill your canteens. Pack up. We're going to hike out of here."

>>

Nearly two hours later, before reaching the telephone poles, they met the search party: three park rangers, Don, and the geology students. Don hugged Lauren and clapped Tony and Luke on their backs. The others cheered.

Hooray! Lauren thought. *I'm no longer in charge of keeping Luke and Tony alive.* She felt like celebrating.

"Why didn't you follow our cairns?" Don asked.

"What cairns? We turned at one cairn and then the trail ended at an outcropping of dolomite."

"What outcropping?" Don asked.

Lauren laughed. "It was a huge, silicified dolomite slab at least a mile across."

"I don't know what's so funny. You could have died of thirst or been attacked by a bear," Don said with a frown.

"I guess I'm just happy to be back with the group."

Don and the students thanked the rangers and hiked in the direction of their van so they could drive to Whites City, New Mexico, to resupply before resuming their explorations.

"Hey, everybody, watch for my cans of ravioli on the way back!" Tony said.

>>

Lauren looked up and down the hall, which was deserted. Don's office was dark. She hurried into the grad student cubicles and shut the door.

She had been avoiding Don since the Guadalupe Mountains trip. He had sent her a bouquet of red roses the day after they returned, and twice had left notes telling her to see him about her research. She decided she would type results of her lab work and write a status report for him rather than meet with him. If he still wanted to see her, she would stop by his classroom when other people were around.

She sat down at her desk, wound her dark, glossy hair into a bun, and placed a pencil through it to secure it. She laid out four pens and tested each by scribbling on her calendar. If she had had sleeves, she would have rolled them up. In further avoidance of her task, she swiveled her desk chair around to face her rock collection on the shelves behind her desk. She glanced at assorted rocks collected over the past ten years. Even before she knew she wanted to be a geologist, she had picked up rocks along the way. Rocks carried the spirit of the land and were far superior to doodads sold in souvenir shops, with the possible exception of fudge and saltwater taffy.

Rocks were history books of the earth. They told of volcanoes erupting, seas coming and going, continents moving, and mountains forming. Rocks chronicled everywhere they had been and everything that had happened to them. They revealed what earth's atmosphere had been like and the kind of weather they had experienced. If a meteor had struck the earth while rocks were forming, if earth's magnetic poles had been reversed, or if rocks had seen life—all was recorded within. One only had to know the language to read them— and a few torture techniques known to geologists.

Lauren had inflicted various types of torture on the twenty-one rocks that would form the basis of her thesis in the last few months. The first was slicing them an eighth of an inch thick, sanding them, and subjecting them to the University of Texas's electron beam microprobe in Austin. The next step was pulverizing them into a fine powder the consistency of flour, mixing the powder with hydrofluoric acid to dissolve it, and using Tex Poly's atomic absorption machine to burn the dissolved matter in each test tube, thereby revealing the mineral content of her sample rocks.

Irradiating her samples using the nuclear reactor would be the last major phase of her research. She had watched as other researchers set their plastic vials of powdered rock in a cage in the chamber surrounded by a large pool that emitted neon blue light. The uranium core bombarded the samples with neutrons, causing the samples to become radioactive. Then the samples had to sit for three or four weeks until enough of the major radioactive elements had decayed away so minute quantities of rare earth elements could be seen. The elements were so rare they were measured in parts per million or parts per billion.

As to her immediate problem—her memo to Don—she would use excerpts from the report she had been required to send to Prince Malouf in Surea after each step in the analysis as part of the arrangement with the geologist who had collected and imported the rocks that formed the basis of Lauren's thesis research. In fact, the Surean government had been adamant about receiving chemical analyses of the rocks. To comply, Lauren sent a summary of results at the end of each research phase. Because certain gabbros contained minable quantities of chromium and platinum, she theorized, they were suspicious that the US planned to exploit Surea's mineral resources. They didn't realize true scientists were interested in learning more about the geodynamics of plume activity and how it related to plate tectonics. Even if Surea wasn't interested in how Africa split from the Arabian Peninsula and the Red Sea formed, Lauren was. Come summer, she would travel there in person to collect the final rocks for her thesis.

She marked sections of the Malouf report that she would reuse for Don and organized her lab reports. The sound of the door opening and closing interrupted her thoughts. She peered around her cubicle and saw Don approaching.

Just when she was making progress. *Please let him be professional. I can't take another scene.*

"Ah, Lauren, at last."

"I was just putting my lab results into a report for you."

"No need. No need. An oral report is fine."

Don paced and tugged his beard as Lauren told him the results from the microprobe.

"Lauren, you don't know how frantic I was when you didn't show up at camp last week," he suddenly said, interrupting her.

She looked up from her report and calmly said, "I told you I needed a map."

"Those two bozos could have gotten you killed," Don said, scowling.

"They were sweet guys. The only other place they'd ever hiked was Central Park."

"What kind of geology student is that?"

"Young and inexperienced?"

"I don't know why you're so nice to them and so cold to me."

Now he's jealous of two nineteen-year-olds!

He sat down with resignation in the chair of the adjoining cubicle.

"I'm just trying to keep our relationship professional."

"How can you say that, after what we've meant to each other?" he asked, raising both hands, palms up, as though to direct his question to the universe.

He won't even try to be professional.

"I've apologized and apologized to you for our previous relationship," Lauren said. "You won't let it go."

"I've tried to move on with my life. I've dated other women. I always come back to you."

"I'm trying to move on with my life, too. My life is my thesis. Right now, I need to go down to the lab to check my solutions," she said, standing up and walking toward the door.

"Wait." Don followed her and grabbed her hand. "I know I can never love another woman—ever." He pulled her closer to him. "Just give me one more chance. Please."

She disliked whining and begging above all else. *Doesn't he have any pride?* She couldn't be forthright and tell him there wasn't a chance in hell she would ever be with him again. He had already made her work difficult. If she told him what she thought of him, he would never approve her thesis.

"Don't, please," Lauren said, backing toward the door. "I came to

Tex Poly to get my master's. That's the most important thing in the world to me. You of all people should understand."

He maneuvered her against the closed door and tried to kiss her.

"Stop!" Lauren said turning her head to the side. "I need to leave."

She reached behind her back and turned the doorknob. The opening door made them both step aside, and she escaped down the hall.

Chapter 10

Flying Dutchman

Chris, 1978

Chris slid into a booth at a café on State Street in Weiser, Idaho. After driving from Coeur d'Alene in his assigned four-wheel-drive Suburban, he had stopped at the post office, where a forwarded letter from Don awaited. He ripped open the envelope and read the letter with disbelief. Then he read it two more times, all the while oblivious to the waitress who consistently refreshed his coffee and inquired whether he was ready to order.

> *June 5, 1978*
> *Dear Chris:*
>
> *The sum effect of your poor course grades in quantitative courses, your disparaging remarks concerning quantitative approaches to your science, and most seriously, your lack of originality in your science have convinced me that I do not wish to serve as your PhD committee chairman. Basically, you have not shown the ability to contribute an original concept to our science; I consider such ability the foremost trait necessary above dedication and hard work. Furthermore, I am disturbed that you insist upon staying in the field for two semesters against our advice.*
>
> *I strongly suggest that you consider entering another*

university to continue your studies and will help you do so if
you wish. My advice in this matter certainly does not prevent
you from returning here, finding a new professor with whom
to work, and completing your degree as planned.

  I considered your complaints about the grades you received
from me and considered the petrology exam score of 71 that I
assigned was actually an 83 or an A minus. You still have Bs
in both courses primarily because you did not show the origi-
nality that I associate with PhD candidates.

  Sincerely,
  Don Weber
  Associate Professor
  cc:
  Dr. Marvin Mayer
  Dr. Edmund Wilkinson

Chris was stunned. Don had now denounced him in writing
and sent copies to two other professors in Tex Poly's Geo Sciences
Department. At least Don had raised his grade in his petrology final
from a C to an A-, although combined with his lack of "originality,"
the A- had turned into a B for his course grade. Now he wouldn't have
to take petrology again. Don's mentioning lack of originality three
times in the space of a short letter made his message clear: Chris
didn't have an original thought in his head. Exercising free speech
seemed to diminish Chris's originality in Don's view, as did failing to
kowtow to Don's ideas about Chris's dissertation project. It was lucky
Chris had already been accepted at Northern Idaho.

He stuffed the letter into his backpack and dug in his pocket for
money. He left two crumpled dollars on the table for his bottomless
cup of coffee. He was glad Don didn't know he had transferred. *Let*
him suffer thinking I might be back next fall, he thought, as he walked
out of the café.

He drove north on Highway 95 toward Mann Creek Reservoir for his first night in the field. The day had turned gloomy. Chris's elation at starting his research ebbed. He gripped the wheel of the truck tightly.

I might as well face it. I'm dull as dirt. Who am I pretending to be? Some world-famous adventurer? Mapping basalts wasn't going to change anything. Hazardous wastes had harmed the earth already. He was just reverting to his Boy Scout camping days to avoid the real world. Maybe Don was right. Chris should focus on geochemistry instead of cavorting in the great outdoors of Idaho.

A memory from fourth or fifth grade edged into his consciousness. It was before speech therapy had taught him to control his stuttering. He was giving a report on Ohio's capital city, Columbus. He tried to say, "capitol building." He enunciated "capitol" but stalled on "building."

He stood in front of the class in a stuttering zone.

"B-b-b-b-b-b-b-building."

A few children in the class laughed while others stared. At some point his teacher told him to sit down until he was ready to give his report.

Over time Chris had built his self-confidence block by block, layer by layer: an oral report on Pompeii from his *Weekly Reader*, a science fair prize, dean's list in college, air force promotions and commendations, a master's degree. Now his self-confidence crashed to the basement like a broken elevator, accelerating past all the carefully laid blocks. Chris wondered if everyone suffered as he did, or if his childhood stuttering had doomed him to free-falling self-worth.

Snow-capped Sturgill Peak loomed over the area. He drove into the park and made his way on a rutted road past campsites occupied by Winnebagos and pickup trucks with camper tops. As the road deteriorated, the number of campers diminished. He downshifted carelessly and almost stalled the truck. A quarter mile past the last occupied site, he parked. He was in no mood to be near drunken fishermen.

Chris hauled his old tent from its canvas bag. Even if he ended up sleeping in the back of the truck because of the cold, he decided he would pitch his tent. After many frustrating attempts to drive wooden stakes into packed earth, he had invested in new metal ones this year. Now the sight of the shiny pegs pleased him. The ritual of stretching the canvas, driving the stakes, smoothing out the floor, and running a rope to a nearby tree to stabilize the pitch of the roof soothed his mind. When he surveyed his site, the only thing missing was fire. He gathered twigs and pinecones for kindling and lit a fire in the crude metal grill set in the rocks. Because he had forgotten to bring wood, he threw charcoal briquettes on the fire among the sparse flames. He was home.

He sat near the glowing coals, ate sardines from a tin, and drank boiled coffee. Don was a self-serving bastard. That much he knew. He had taken advantage of Lauren and who knew how many other female students. While at Tex Poly, Chris hadn't been troubled by his and Don's verbal sparring. To be honest he had enjoyed being a thorn in Don's side—interrupting Don's attempts to be alone with Lauren, arguing against the all-importance of ocean basalts, insisting on the value of fieldwork. He had paid the price of coming back to Northern Idaho. When he was accepted into the doctoral program at Tex Poly, he had thought he was moving up in the academic world. Now Don had broadcast Chris's inadequacies to Tex Poly's faculty. It was humiliating.

Feathers flew when he rolled out his old down sleeping bag to use as padding for his good sleeping bag. He lay in the top bag with only his head uncovered. Studying the dark insides of his tent wasn't as inspiring as looking at the night sky, but at least he was warm. People spent their lives earning money for a house with a floor to insulate them from the ground and a bed to insulate them from the floor. Now here he was, about as low as he could get.

The earth felt solid and unmoving, yet it was anything but stationary as it revolved and rotated through the heavens.

He might as well take a spin on Planet Earth tonight. His spirits lifted.

>>

Chris had spent the morning reconnoitering and the early afternoon sampling basalt flows in the area; now he was eating chicken-fried steak and a baked potato at his favorite State Street restaurant in Weiser and studying for his comprehensives, even though they were some fifteen months off. The great thing about fieldwork was it distilled his life down to its essence: study of the earth. No office, apartment, possessions, bills, or other distractions of actually living someplace. Letter writing was his main communication tool. He stifled his desire to write to Lauren since he had arranged to telephone her Sunday night.

When the waitress brought his check, he said, "I hear the National Oldtime Fiddlers' Contest is coming to Weiser. Do you know when it starts?"

Without looking up from his newspaper, an old man in an adjacent booth answered, "Starts the nineteenth. But it's not like it used to be. Now they got them amplifiers and electric guitars, and they make noise they call music. Few years ago, use to have a bunch of Black fellas play the fiddle; you know, guys from Nashville, real bluegrass music. Ain't seen any of em last few years. Guess they went in for the loud music, too."

"Could be." Chris shrugged.

Still not looking up from his paper, the old man continued, "Some hippies came in last year, you know the type—long hair, beards, real dirty. Local boys taught 'em a lesson. Don't think they'll be back."

Fiddling sounds peaceful, Chris thought as he paid his bill. He never would have thought it caused violent culture clashes. He headed back to his campsite.

>>

The first sign of the fiddlers' contest came in mid-June. An orange Volkswagen Beetle parked in an adjacent campsite, and a young man climbed out. He set up camp, took his shirt off to expose white skin to sun, and read a book. He stayed to himself while Chris worked on his notes and drawings.

At sunset, the young man took a fiddle from his car. With one foot marking time on the picnic bench, he played his repertoire. His bow skipped over the strings when he played upbeat songs. On sad pieces his bow pressed the strings until they cried. The only song Chris recognized was "Orange Blossom Special." As sole audience, Chris nodded his appreciation when the man put his fiddle back in its case.

Aligning your brain waves with music keeps your soul from screeching, Chris concluded. Not that his soul screeched often. Only when Don was in the picture. Maybe he would attend one of the fiddling sessions this weekend, just to make sure he stayed on a harmonic course.

>>

Then the others came, crowding into all available campsites. When Chris returned to his camp at dusk on Friday night, he was greeted by a young man in cutoffs who was drinking a Budweiser.

"You a gov'ment man?" he asked, slurring his words.

"Geologist."

"Oh. Thought maybe you was a gov'ment man come to give us the word."

"He'll be along later," Chris said with an inner chuckle.

He laid his day's rock samples on the picnic table. The young man and his friends watched as Chris labeled them. To have a geologist in the campground was apparently like having a two-headed dog or a large, smiling Buddha among the campers.

After the others left for the fiddlers' contest, Chris enjoyed a beer they had given him, then went to bed—only to lurch awake in his sleeping bag at two in the morning, when people started returning from town.

Car stereos throbbed with rock music. Chris sat up in disbelief at the actions of his neighbors, who left music blaring even after their car doors slammed. When the car stereos finally went silent, he heard them trying to find music on a staticky portable radio. Resigned, he lay back with his hands clasped behind his head.

Despite the noise, he drifted back to sleep.

>>

The next evening when Chris asked his neighbors if they could keep the noise down when they came back in the middle of the night, the young man Chris now knew as Doug answered, "It's because you're working and we're on vacation."

My point exactly, Chris thought.

"That still doesn't explain why you can't be quiet when you return from town."

"Don't you understand? This is our chance to relax, unwind, and take in some music. You don't do this because you're working."

"That's right. I get up early in the morning and hike for nine hours. I need my sleep. You guys sleep all day and then go into Weiser at night and raise hell. Jesus, it's a bloody morgue here at seven a.m."

"But you don't understand," Doug said.

This is hopeless, Chris thought. *I might as well have some fun.* He gave up trying to get his point across and decided to probe Doug's mind, instead.

Doug's main concern was the growth of the federal government.

"It's too large. Too impersonal. That's why the youth of today are revolting."

"Are they really?" Chris asked. "Like the sixties and early seventies?"

"No. Then it was different. The kids were too radical."

Chris remembered being more idealistic than radical in those days.

"But we had the Vietnam War to stop. And who do you think started the ecology movement? Now, c'mon, don't you think the best word to describe kids now is apathetic?"

"Mellow," Doug said. "I think our age is mellow."

That word. Made famous by Paul Simon, Woody Allen, and Gary Trudeau, *mellow* had come to symbolize a philosophy, an attitude, an excuse.

Chris couldn't resist asking, "How are you feeling today?"

"Mellow, man."

"And do you think President Carter should have intervened in the coal strike when he did?"

"Look, I don't know nothing about a coal strike, but I'm sure it will turn out mellow."

"Do you think the Soviets and Cubans will invade Somalia?"

"Man, you're harshing my mellow."

Chris laughed. "Is that anything like marshing your mallow?"

"Very funny. Hey! That's what we'll do tonight—roast marshmallows and make s'mores."

"Will that be at two a.m. or three a.m.?"

After the exchange Chris retreated to his truck and drove across the reservoir to sample basalt. He listened to the sigh of the wind across yellow flowering currant bushes. He decided the revolution of the 1960s had been nothing more than a ripple in time.

>>

On Saturday Chris drove into Weiser, where plywood fiddles hung from wires strung across streets. Store windows were plastered with posters of hillbilly caricatures, some with their print streaking from a recent rain. Sagebrush and wagon wheels were tied to lampposts. Everywhere signs welcomed fiddlers and visitors. Loudspeakers blared fiddle music.

Chris wondered about the young man in the orange VW bug, who had left the campground when the crowds came. He would try to hear his performance if he was a contestant. He bought a bratwurst in a bun with peppers and onions and strolled through town eating it. He walked over to the high school where contest events were taking place that afternoon. People stood in line to buy tickets. Another crowd was milling at the entrance.

Suddenly, the thought of waiting in line or sitting in a crowded gymnasium made him feel claustrophobic. He tossed his bratwurst wrapper into a trash barrel and walked back in the direction of his truck.

June 22, 1978

Dear Lauren,

The fiddlers' contest is in full flower in Weiser. I was tempted to attend an event today but decided I would rather be outside than in a crowded gym. At the ripe old age of thirty-one, I show definite signs of becoming a hermit.

After two abortive attempts, I finally located the volcano I was looking for: McIntyre's Vent—almost a square mile of pyroclasts. This is the second vent I've mapped thus far. A few days ago I discovered my first, a small one on a hillside that I encountered late in a traverse. I was really excited and more than a bit annoyed I hadn't recognized it immediately. My excuse was that I was hot and tired. I was tracing a very sparkly basalt flow across a ridge when I saw this bench in the distance. Thinking it to be a fault or a new flow, I went over and sampled it. Nuts, I thought, a new flow and something to complicate my already fragile map. The rock was frothy. What the devil, I thought, on top of everything else, a frothy lava. Then it occurred to me, slowly, that the features I was looking at were compacted, much like what would be expected from an all-volcanic feature. The more I looked, the more convinced I was that this was a source, perhaps a vent. It was a good find.

If you feel ornery sometime, you might mention to Don I'm making good progress and have discovered two vents, not merely dikes that are prevalent on the Columbia Plateau. He wants me to fail so he won't have to acknowledge he made a mistake and missed an opportunity to further his career as a basalt expert. You can cause discomfort by pretending innocence about this sore point.

When are you going on your adventure in the Guadalupe Mountains? I'm sorry you are forced into Don's company. I wish I could send you some of the joy I'm feeling here. This summer has been so pleasant, relaxed, yet eventful and filled with mystery and discovery. If you could just rid yourself of one tearful baby, you'd be able to work in peace on your science and art. Keep making progress on your thesis and finish it quickly. There's an exciting world waiting for you, and the sooner you finish, the sooner you can enjoy it. I must write my sister Nancy and congratulate her. She just graduated with a degree in art education from Case Western. I'm quite pleased.

So much for being alone. Four cars from Oregon just moved in, and one has its radio blaring. Sigh. I'll have to move to a new campsite if I want to get any sleep tonight. One more day in the field, and then a day off to take a

shower. My clothes are so potent, to get dressed I have to
wrestle them on.

Stay strong, Lauren.
From the wilds,
Chris

In late July Chris was camped near Sugarloaf Mountain and
Deadman's Gulch to try to map the flats in as short a time as possible. He preferred to work in the mountains where it was cooler. He
was feeling a little down. He blamed it on the hot weather that made
his work harder. Even though he had written regularly to Lauren, he
hadn't received a response recently. He told himself letters were more
important to him because he worked alone all day. He hoped it didn't
mean Don was giving her more trouble—or even worse, that she had
reconciled with her husband. He tried to keep from thinking negatively.

The following week, he ran into his first series of Snake River
Plains basalts, which confused him for a couple of days. Besides
reversed polarity, the samples were unlike any he had seen in his two
summers of fieldwork. He began documenting a case for the cessation
of Columbia River basalts in the area, which would require sampling
another whole section on private land.

He feared doing more damage to the rancher's property where he
was currently camped. He had already run over an irrigation pipe,
which now formed a perfect contour with the road. When Chris saw
what he had done, he drove to the rancher's house and apologized
profusely.

"Well, it's done now," the rancher said with a heavy sigh.

He had let Chris camp on his property, but Chris didn't know
what he would say if he asked for more time, or for permission to
bring a troop of geologists to look at his findings. He would wait a day
or two before asking more favors.

The road to the ranch house was the worst Chris had ever driven.

The insides of the Suburban were shaken to a shambles. By the time he reached his campsite, the cap to his five-gallon water jug had popped off, leaving only two quarts for a day's mapping. At the end of the next day, having had no water for the last three miles' traverse, Chris's throat was dry and dusty. Because his backpacking stove and pot were small, he spent an hour and a half boiling water just to get a decent supply for evening and the next day.

August 2, 1978

Dear Lauren,

Even though I'm eager to move on from Crane Creek, my observations say the Rosetta Stone lies here. Reading the language of basaltic ooze from millions of years ago is surely as difficult as deciphering Egyptian hieroglyphics. I've been getting indications of another volcano in the area: ashfalls, pumice. But I can't quite pin it down. Previously, I found three pyroclastic units.

Where is the source? The hunt is on, my dear Watson, and I'm enjoying the chase.

Whenever possible I try to get permission from ranchers to cross their lands. Actually, I use this as an excuse to jump onto other lands. If I stray too far in my mapping and violate ownership boundaries, oh well. Overall, the ranchers have been very cooperative, although, admittedly, suspicious about my driving a government truck. Few ranchers will smile, but all are full of information and quite willing to part with what they know; they have ideas and are eager to have them confirmed by an expert. All want to know what's on their land, although few have any use for volcanoes as I've learned these past weeks. No one has the same enthusiasm. I am jumping up and down with excitement about my findings, and nothing but a "ho-hum" from the rancher.

I had to defuse the anger of one rancher who was mad at geologists in general and the USGS, in particular. The USGS surveyed the hot springs on his property and promised to send him a copy of the report but didn't. Worse yet, they cited him in the report as an oral communication source, which he discovered when I showed him my copy. So I gave him mine. By the time I left, he was thanking me profusely for stopping by and he offered any assistance I might need. At times like these, I marvel to find myself, the focal point of bitter, denouncing letters from Don on the one hand, and a diplomat of some skill on the other. What a comedy.

It won't be dark for another 45 minutes, but I'm exhausted. I think I'll read more of Gail Sheehy's Passages. The woman annoys me so much I stay awake late formulating arguments to demolish her theories. If the movie schedule is right, Coma will be shown at the People's Theatre in Council tomorrow night. Might grab a hamburger, a couple of beers, and go see it.

Lauren, keep active. Work on your thesis. Paint. I'm confident you'll do fine. I'll call you in a couple of weeks.

From the Weiser Embayment,

Chris

P.S. By the way my belt fits, I think I've lost at least five pounds.

Chris was happy to find a letter from Lauren in his postal box the next day. Hiding beneath it was a letter from Don. He tore open the one from Don. By the time he had read it, his hands were shaking. Don had learned of Chris's transfer to Northern Idaho University and had taken the opportunity to congratulate him on his recognition that he didn't meet Tex Poly's standards. Furthermore, this time he had sent copies to the head of the department as well as to three other professors. Chris felt a familiar slipping sensation, as though distinctions between himself and the universe were blurring. Then he stopped and got angry instead. He left the post office and sat in his truck to calm himself.

I transferred. What more does he want? Blood? Don would have to carry on the vendetta by himself. Chris wouldn't let some jerk of a professor beat him down. His fieldwork would vindicate him. He saved Lauren's letter to read when he arrived back at his campsite. He started his truck and headed out of town but then drove around the block, returned to the post office, and parked near a phone booth. He placed a collect call to Lauren. *Let her be home,* he hoped as the phone rang.

"Chris, what a surprise. It's good to hear your voice."

"I was in Weiser and thought I'd take a chance you might be home."

"You sound kind of down. What's going on?"

"I just got another letter from Don."

Chris wandered outside the phone booth as far as the telephone cord would allow. Even though he was tired, Don's letter had made him angry and restless. If the cord had been longer, he would have paced.

"But why? He already told you he raised your grade."

"Yeah, he did. But he just found out I transferred to Northern Idaho and congratulated me on realizing I didn't meet Tex Poly's standards. The worst part is he sent copies to Jacquez, Zachary, Gallamore, and Griffith—the four people in the department I most respect."

"I can't believe it. Didn't he raise your test grade to an A minus?"

"Yeah." He sounded glum even to himself.

"That means you received one of the top grades in his petrology final. How can he say you don't meet Tex Poly's standards?"

"Yeah, I guess you're right." His mood brightened momentarily. "But my course grade turned into a B because I failed to show 'originality.'"

"How mean and spiteful of Don!"

"The fact that he's broadcasting my deficiencies to other professors in the department is what makes me angriest. I plan to be a geologist for a good long while."

"Maybe you could call the faculty members he copied on his letter and tell your side of the story."

"That would just prolong the fracas."

"Oh, you're right."

"Besides, Don sounded so peevish and disagreeable in his letter, I'm not sure he didn't do more harm to himself than he did to me. Now that I think about it, it's actually kind of funny."

"Next you'll say, 'What a comedy,'" Lauren said.

Chris chuckled. "I don't know why I let him get me down. Thanks for listening."

He felt like his old self when he hung up. How lucky he was to have a friend who understood him—and could even predict what he might say next!

>>

Chris worked the Crane Creek valley. He sampled and remapped to try to verify his contact points. Columbia River basalt poked through at irregular places throughout the plateau. He had to define how many of the flows were of the odd, reversed polarity unit.

The next day Chris crossed a field with a herd of cattle to get to his starting place for an ascent up a canyon. His prior experiences had taught him that if he mooed when he approached the herd, they wouldn't stampede as soon or as far. He felt ridiculous mooing to stupid cattle, but it kept the dust down. In his first attempts at taming cattle, he had sung to them, which made them stampede quicker. One time when he had sung *My Wild Irish Rose*, the herd panicked, and a dusty chaos ensued. This time his mooing was effective with most of the cattle. A big bull stood his ground. Chris skirted the bull and just kept walking, stifling his desire to run.

August 25, 1978

Dear Lauren,

Campers are always asking me about geology. Twice I've been roped into lecturing to children at the Youth Conservation Corps. It seems most of the kids and virtually all the counselors suffer from narcolepsy. No sooner do I begin my talks than their eyelids droop, their mouths open wide and then close, and their heads start bobbing. What a blow to my ego. Here I am, working like a new convert, spreading the good word about my research, and all I produce is a cure for insomnia.

Yesterday I did charm a mother and her two young daughters in my explanation of Earth's volcanism. The older daughter, about fourteen years old, seemed quite taken with the Irishman, so much so that sibling rivalry manifested itself, and she made efforts to stifle her younger sister. It's well known that once an Irishman turns on his charm, there isn't a female alive who can resist his blarney.

You mentioned in your last letter your desire to be someone, to accomplish something important. I do not consider this to be "merely a childish dream." If it is, then I've been deluding myself all these years. It's important to strive to the limits of your potential. To settle for anything less is unfair to yourself, and you fail to live up to your point in history. This is our stage now, at this moment—our opportunity not only to play out our dramas, but if we are cognizant of our environment and ourselves, to write our script. That said, the toxic environment in the department where you are makes it imperative that you get out of there as fast as you can. Write up what you have and give the draft to Don for "wordsmithing." If he thinks he can get a joint paper from it, fine, let him write it up, submit it with both your names, and allow him to

*get the honors or the hits. The important thing is to leave Tex
Poly with your degree in hand.*

*I'd better close as I'm about to be thrown out of this restau-
rant. The waitress is amazed at the great volume of coffee I can
drink. If you get another chance to write, please do. If not, no
problem. You still have a friend.*

Chris

As summer neared its end, Chris continued to have problems
with two Forest Service topographic maps from the 1950s and '60s.
Neither was sufficiently accurate to show new roads or the demise
of old roads. Thinking Long Gulch Road was a pass between two
mountains as indicated on his newer map, he drove down a narrow,
twisting mountain road with a steep hill on the upward side and a
nice cliff on the downward side, only to find the entire road washed
out. He backed up for miles, dodging deadfall and boulders.

On another day Chris tried to find the one road that twisted
and turned for twenty-five miles before finally ending in Fruitvale.
Alternative roads, of course, ended in never-never land. After considering all possibilities, he made a command decision and turned
his truck onto a likely candidate of a road. The tarmac, all-weather
road gradually changed into a gravel road, then a Jeep trail, which
degraded into two narrow ruts surrounded by trees and shrubs. He
was lost.

Completely immersed in nature, he stopped his truck to contemplate his situation. He was sure a new myth was in the making.
Like the *Flying Dutchman* of the high seas, he envisioned the ghost
of his truck driving madly down dirt roads, creating large clouds of
dust. Ranchers would be unable to see any substance of a vehicle. His
flashing headlights would pass through the night, and other than a
shadowy Department of Energy truck and an occasional low moan,
there would be nothing for locals to define. Stories would emerge

of cowboys, tourists, and woodcutters stopped by a ghostly figure and always asked the same plaintive question, "Is this the road to Fruitvale?"

He turned his truck around and finally arrived at a newly developed road that led to another road that led to a crossroads. After twenty-five miles of driving, he had arrived at the exact place where he had begun his journey. He had had enough. He bought a six-pack of Oly, drove to Mann Creek Reservoir, and waited for the rains to come. He didn't have long to wait.

As he drank a beer and watched the skies open up, he outlined a plan for finishing his fieldwork in time to get settled in Coeur d'Alene before classes began. If only the rest of his life were as easy to map. When would he see Lauren again? Unknown. Would Lauren reconcile with her husband? Unknown. When would Don stop badmouthing Chris? Unknown. If life were a math problem, Chris's had too many unknowns to be solvable. Luckily, life was more mystery than mathematics. He had an affinity for mysteries.

Chapter 11

Texas in My Rearview Mirror

Lauren, 1979

Lauren walked into Don's office without knocking. "You want me to retype my entire lab results to correct three typos?"

"I think I made that clear in my note," Don said, looking up from his reading.

"But this is a draft. Only two people besides you will see it."

"I won't have sloppy work leaving my office."

"With all due respect, it's not sloppy work—just bad typing. Surely, you're not going to force me to hire a typist for a rough draft."

"Do what you must to meet my standards."

She turned and stalked out. Her hands shook as she opened the door to the graduate assistant offices. She dropped down in her chair and shoved the carriage return on the typewriter so hard the machine wobbled on the edge of the typing credenza. An empty bud vase tipped over but didn't break.

"Hey, what's going on over there?" a voice from across the room asked.

"Who's here?" Lauren rolled her desk chair around and looked in the direction of the voice. "Oh, hi, Bryan."

"What's all that racket?" Bryan walked over to Lauren's cubicle.

"My typewriter and I are fighting over whose fault my bad typing is," Lauren said, gesturing at the typewriter.

Bryan laughed. "Thank God my wife types my papers, or I never would have gotten out of undergraduate school," he said, leaning against the desk of the adjacent cubicle. "By the way, what do you hear from Chris Connor?"

"I talk to him all the time. He's doing great at Northern Idaho."

Unlike me—still struggling with Don, she thought. *How I miss Chris!*

"I was surprised when I heard he had transferred."

"He and Don were at loggerheads. I think Don resented advising someone whose passion was continental basalts. He told Chris he didn't belong at Tex Poly."

"That's outrageous!" Bryan said, shaking his head in disbelief. "I'm glad Don's not my adviser."

"Lest I say too much, I'd better start typing," Lauren said, rolling back to her typewriter as Bryan walked to his cubicle.

How many years will I spend getting my master's? she wondered. It had taken a year and a half to complete lab work on twenty-one rocks, make her calculations, draw conclusions, and write a draft of a partial thesis. Now she had wasted an extra month haggling with Don over sentence structure, punctuation, and typos. Instead of being finished with the first phase, she was still typing and retyping.

What kept her from screaming was the thought of the summer's trip to the Red Sea. In a good novel, all that goes before, all that is foreshadowed, and all that must be culminate in the climax. Truth is revealed. The research voyage would be the climax of her project. Receiving her degree would be mere denouement.

On site in Surea, she would see the field relationships of her present rock samples and determine where to collect rocks to complete the gaps. Scientists from several departments and other universities had pooled their grants to finance the expedition. Lists of participating researchers had been sent to the Surean government. In a couple of months, *The Coriolis* would be outfitted for the trip.

>>

When Lauren returned to her apartment two hours later, a note in Kenny's handwriting was taped to the door. Surprised he remembered where she lived, she stared at the note that read, *Call me.*

She didn't allow her heart to lighten, but she couldn't stop it from beating fast. Maybe he wanted to get back together. More likely, he wanted a divorce. His silence for the past few months made it clear how little he cared about her or their marriage. She couldn't bear to call him.

The next day, Kenny telephoned at nine in the morning while she was still in bed. He told her his brother Rich had injured his back at work and was in the hospital.

Lauren sat up. "Oh, dear. I'm sorry. How badly hurt is he?"

"He's going home today, but he can't work for six weeks. His girl-friend's going to take care of him."

"I'm glad he has help." *At least Kenny wasn't calling about a divorce.* She played with the phone cord while waiting to hear what he really called about.

"I thought you might want to maybe send a card."

Lauren paused. "Won't he think it's weird to hear from your estranged wife?"

"Uh, he doesn't know we're not together."

"Really?" She wondered what it meant that he hadn't told Rich about their separation.

"No one in my family does."

"I guess I didn't tell my mother, either." *Maybe we're both ashamed we failed at marriage.*

"Anyway, I thought you should know about Rich."

When Lauren hung up the phone, she lay back on her bed and contemplated what it meant that Kenny wanted her to send a card to his brother. Maybe the thinnest threads of family ties still connected her to Kenny. Even though the pain of separation had not diminished much in the year or so since she first moved out of their apartment, the hope that they would reconcile had nearly disappeared.

>>

Later that day on returning from school, a letter bearing Prince Malouf's gold-embossed emblem awaited her on the mail table of her apartment building. She ripped it open. It would contain landing permission from the Surean government for the summer's voyage. As she read down the page, she grasped that she had been refused entry to the country because they had realized the L. Brown with whom they had communicated was Lauren Brown, a female. Lauren reread the letter in shock.

Her hand shook as she turned the key in her apartment lock. On entering, she shut the door and leaned against it to steady herself from the sensation of spinning and losing her balance.

The thought of going to sea this summer for her thesis project had kept her sane in the face of the disaster that was her life: a husband who didn't want to be married to her, a crazy mother, her best friend at a faraway university in Idaho, and a vindictive professor blocking progress on her thesis. Now she would never get her degree. She would be stuck forever at Tex Poly with Don's unreasonable demands. How could she fight a prince? The Surean denial was insurmountable.

She threw herself on her bed and cried until she slept.

>>

The ringing of the telephone woke Lauren. After fumbling for the phone, she answered to find Chris on the other end.

"Those pricks. Damn them! They don't know what they just lost," he said when she told him she had been barred from Surea.

"All that time and work wasted. I'll have to start over."

"Oh, surely not. You've already done more research than most people do for a master's thesis."

"I'm going to talk to Don, but I don't think there's any hope."

"You've got to get your degree and get out of there. You can get a grant to study Columbia River basalts for your PhD. I'll send you the forms and help you apply."

"It would be heavenly to be in the Northwest."

"The Columbia River basalts are massive, mysterious, and in need of good geologists. And they're in the US—no visa required."

Lauren managed a feeble laugh at his attempt to cheer her. When she hung up, she felt a slight hope for other possibilities. Chris's long view of life always reassured her when the present was clogged with problems.

Her tears now were because she missed his daily presence in her life since he had moved to Idaho. Strong feelings for each other were always on the fringe of their friendship. It was possible they could end up together, after all. She had almost given up on Kenny, who'd been gone too long. She and Chris had so much in common, but maybe they were meant to be just friends. At the moment, she wasn't sure of anything in her life.

>>

The next day as Lauren walked to Don's office, she thought about her situation. She knew some Middle Eastern men held women in low esteem from the way they acted in geology classes at Tex Poly. When they had stood up and walked out during her lecture, she had wondered if it was because they were so brilliant, they knew they wouldn't learn anything from her. However, their brilliance was never tested, as they didn't deign to give reports themselves. American universities opened their doors to Surean students. For the Surean government to forbid her from setting foot on its soil was degrading and unjust.

It reminded her of the way she had been treated at the University of Arizona at Prescott. Even though she was a student in the mining geology program, on field trips she was not allowed to go into mines owned by Mormons. A woman's presence in a mine was considered bad luck. Discouraged by Mormon professors from going on field trips, Lauren had participated anyway. She had sat outside the mine entrance while male students and professors explored below.

Each year a gold-plated Brunton compass, the most important field instrument in geology, was awarded to the graduating senior most likely to contribute to the field of geologic science. When Lauren graduated, she had the best grades by far of any student in the program. Her adviser warned her that, despite being the best student, she wouldn't receive the coveted Brunton because five of the ten professors on the board were Mormons. They would vote only for a man because they believed a woman could never contribute anything to the field. A male student with substantially lower grades than Lauren's had received the gold-plated Brunton that year.

Then and now, Lauren felt like a fool for aspiring to be a geologist. She was carrying the weight of this thought as she reached the threshold of Don's office.

"Lauren, you look terrible!" Don rose, ushered her inside, and shut the door behind her. Looking at her with concern, he put his arms around her.

"I know. My eyes are puffy." She couldn't help sobbing on his shoulder. "They won't let me into Surea!"

"Two women students from other universities have been denied landing permission, as well. The whole voyage is in question."

Lauren disentangled herself and sat in the closest chair. "What am I going to do? I can't finish my project."

"It's not your fault."

"No, it's the damned Surean government. How can they treat women this way?" Lauren had battled so long to get her thesis project to its current stage that being stymied now was unbearable. It was like reading an Agatha Christie mystery and never finding out who did it. But much worse. It was her life that was on hold.

Don tugged at his beard and walked back and forth along the row of plants near the windows. "I've been thinking. Your detailed chemical experiments and analyses should be enough to grant your master's."

"No." Lauren shook her head. "It's not complete." She might have been able to contribute knowledge about continental breakup. Now she couldn't.

Don stopped and faced her. "Your analyses have more integrity and detail than most theses."

Lauren shook her head again. "It's not good enough."

"You're not listening to me. I'll get it approved."

>>

Lauren didn't know what to think. Kenny had invited her for a beer at their old bar, and now he was acting as though they weren't separated, and everything was as before. For the last fifteen minutes, he'd been updating her on news of his family, including his sister Evie's acceptance to community college, as if months hadn't passed since they'd last seen one another.

"Why are you telling me all this?"

Kenny raised his eyebrows. "I thought you'd want to hear the good news about your sister-in-law."

"Of course I'm happy for her, but given the state of our marriage, I'm not sure it's relevant to me," she said in a neutral voice. She leaned back as though she were an observer of the conversation instead of a participant. Lauren had been telling herself to harden her heart so she wouldn't get hurt again.

"That's why we're here. To get our marriage back on track."

I've heard this before, she thought. "Nothing would make me happier, but being apart has been so destructive, I wouldn't know how to fix things," Lauren said, crossing her arms across her chest.

He looked at her with an earnest expression. "I miss you. I miss our life."

Lauren considered this for a few moments.

"Maybe I was deluding myself, but I thought we were happy in Prescott. What changed when we moved here? You wanted me gone from our apartment. After my accident you asked me to stay with you, but then you stopped talking to me. Now you suddenly miss me?" She paused. "The last year and a half have been miserable. Am I supposed to forget how shitty you've been to me?" Lauren took a deep breath.

"I don't know why I've been such a jackass since we moved to Texas." He shook his head and rubbed his temples. "There's no excuse. I thought I could fool around, and you wouldn't notice. I was on an ego trip. But I didn't feel good being such a jerk, and I took it out on you. You were smart to move out. You didn't deserve to be treated that way."

"No, I didn't." A few tears rolled down her cheeks.

"When I heard about your accident, I freaked out. I realized how important you were to me. But when I saw you with your professor, I knew something was going on between you. I ignored it at first because I was so happy to have you back in my life. Then it started to drive me crazy thinking of you with another guy. Somehow, I justified my bad behavior because you'd been with somebody else. I convinced myself I deserved to screw around. It distracted me from my bad job and the fact that I didn't have the balls to look for another job."

"I feel terrible I've hurt you," he continued. "I know I shouldn't expect you to forgive me, but I love you."

Lauren sat quietly. Kenny had never spoken so openly about his feelings. Or failings. He sounded sincere, but she had fought too hard to get her master's. She wasn't going to let him derail her from her plans. "I don't know what to say."

Kenny looked glum.

"All my professors have signed off on my thesis."

"What does that mean?"

"It means I'll get my degree this spring."

"Congrats! Let's go out to dinner and celebrate."

Lauren smiled but shook her head. "I'm giving a lecture tomorrow on my thesis. I have work to do." Suddenly, she felt lighthearted. Over a year of a heavy heart was a long time. "Maybe we can go out tomorrow night."

>>

The next night, Kenny took Lauren to a Mexican restaurant near their old apartment. He scooted into the booth on the same side as she until their shoulders touched. Her heart jumped wildly at his nearness.

"I have more good news," she said, turning to face him. "Spokane University has given me a grant for next year to work on my PhD. I'm so excited! The Geology Department there is leading the research on the Columbia River Basalt Project."

Lauren had finally become accustomed to planning her life without thinking of anyone else. She wondered if Kenny would try to influence her plans.

"Wow. Congrats again," he said in a subdued voice.

He sounded a little down, but he had to know she wouldn't wait around to see what he would do.

"This summer's fieldwork will give me data for my thesis."

The waitress interrupted to take their order. Lauren opened the menu and ordered the first combination plate. Kenny ordered the same. She didn't care what she ate. What Kenny had said yesterday and the way he was reacting to the news of her grant from Spokane, had given her hope for their relationship.

"So you're moving?" he asked, his eyes round and questioning.

"Yep. I can hardly wait to get out of Texas," Lauren said, smiling. The struggle to get her master's degree had been so monumental and soul-killing that she wouldn't stay at Tex Poly one day more than necessary.

"When will you leave? After graduation?"

"Or sooner. I don't think I'll stay for graduation. I need to start my fieldwork."

"What am I going to do here without you?" he asked, looking worried.

"I'm sure that's not a problem," she said, her eyes narrowing a little. "At least it hasn't been for over a year." *He's not going to get any sympathy from me,* Lauren decided.

When their food arrived, they concentrated on eating.

He said, "I can't lose you. You're the best thing that's ever happened to me. I'll go with you."

Lauren didn't know if she could trust her own judgment at the moment.

"But what about your job?"

"The office where I'm working is the worst place I've ever worked. I'll look for a job in Spokane."

Lauren couldn't help smiling as she named barriers to their getting back together. They both laughed when she said he couldn't leave Pasadena because there would be no one to water the poison ivy on his balcony.

"*Our* balcony," he said, brushing his hand along her inner thigh. "Let's get out of here."

>>

After leaving their food half-eaten and paying the bill, Lauren and Kenny drove together to his apartment building, where they parked in a spot near the alley. As they left the car, the mewling sounds of a newborn baby emanated from a dumpster filled with construction trash.

"What the hell?" Kenny said, pulling odd lengths of two-by-fours from the dumpster while Lauren threw soggy cardboard boxes over the side.

Please let the baby be okay, Lauren thought.

A gray striped cat struggling against a mass of used duct tape changed his cries to distinct meows when Kenny lifted him out. Lauren freed his right back leg, but his front paws were caught in a ball of tape.

"Oh, dear! Do you think someone did this to him?" she asked.

"I doubt it. He probably jumped into the dumpster looking for food."

"Let's take him inside so we can cut the tape."

After taking the cat into the apartment and cutting the tape from his fur, they gave him milk and a can of tuna and then bathed him in shallow water at the bottom of the bathtub. Kenny found an old sleeping bag and turned it flannel-side out on the sofa for Tom, as they were now calling him. Kenny's concern for Tom warmed Lauren's heart.

While Tom slept in his nest, Kenny spread a comforter on the floor and took Lauren's hands and pulled her down to him. They stood on their knees and kissed. Kenny traced around Lauren's nipples with his thumbs. When clothing became an unbearable impediment to skin against skin, they undressed each other with practiced hands. They kissed and caressed each other's bodies as though assuring themselves the other was truly there.

Body heat melted irreconcilable differences. Purring pervaded the room.

>>

"Let's throw our own going-away party," Lauren said to Kenny a couple of weeks later.

She had moved back to their old apartment a few days after they found Tom.

"We can invite people from your office and grad students and faculty from the Geology Department."

"You're not inviting the foot rub guy, are you?"

Lauren laughed at his description of Don. "I can't invite the department and not him. He's the one who got everyone else to approve my thesis."

The night of the party, things didn't get lively until the fire. Kenny had laid out four fondue pots of assorted shapes and colors on the concrete block-and-board bookcase. Just before guests were due, he turned on all four electric burners on the stove and heated oil in two pots, melted Velveeta chunks with salsa on the third burner, and a pot of chocolate squares on the fourth. When the pots were hot, he moved them to the serving area and lit Sterno canisters under them. Lauren had never known him to be so involved in party preparations. She could see he was in his element—fire. She remembered his tales of the Fourth of July in his hometown. He and his friends had all but blown each other up with cherry bombs and M-80s placed under inverted coffee cans.

As guests arrived, Lauren brought out bowls of chips, raw beef, and chicken chunks, plus strawberries and banana slices for the melted chocolate. The great thing about a fondue party was that guests did the cooking. Hosts were superfluous once everything was set out. She found a measuring cup with a handle to use as a dipper for tequila sunrises, which she had concocted in a new plastic bucket.

The Sterno can under the oil for chicken had been low initially, but it soon completely burned out. Kenny opened the hall closet and rummaged through their camping gear. He found a can of kerosene they used for their camp stove and poured some into the empty Sterno canister.

When he struck a match, kerosene flamed three feet high with an audible *whoosh*.

"Oh, shit!" Kenny said.

"Oh, shit!" Lauren echoed. "Someone call the fire department!"

They both stood gaping. Don stepped away from the conversation he was having, grabbed the handle of the fondue pot with its flaming canister and carried it to the kitchen sink, where he smothered the flames with dish towels and potholders. Everyone clapped and laughed with relief to see the fire extinguished. They refilled their drinks as though the averted disaster had caused parched throats and gathered around the three remaining fondue pots.

Looking sheepish, Kenny said to Don, "Hey, thanks."

"We're lucky the oil in the pot didn't catch fire. By the way, kerosene and Sterno are very different chemically. They're not interchangeable."

Damn! Kenny isn't going to like being lectured to by Don. She hoped he wouldn't lose his temper.

"Except when you're camping. We always carry a few Sterno cans for when we run out of kerosene. But I agree, they don't mix," Kenny said, laughing.

He'd apparently had enough to drink that even Don couldn't ruin his happy mood.

"Good comeback," Lauren said to Kenny in an aside.

>>

One by one the fondue pots went dark. After most guests had left, the remaining seven or eight people sat talking on the sofa, coffee table, and floor. When Matt and his wife said they had to leave, Lauren walked them out. Don brushed by Kenny and hurried behind them. When the couple turned to walk away, Don came from behind Lauren, put his arm around her shoulder, and turned her toward him.

Taking a step backward, she said, "Thanks for coming to our party—not to mention putting out the fire."

"Lauren, I don't understand you. Do you really want to be with a clown who almost burned down your apartment?" Don asked with a scowl on his face.

Oh, no. Here we go again. Can't he ever just let things go?

"What do you mean? He's my husband! We were high school sweethearts." Lauren's defense of her husband sounded feeble, even to herself.

"My point exactly."

"I'm happy." *He can't argue with that.*

Don put his hands on her upper arms as though to shake her. "I know you think you're happy. And I know you're moving to Spokane. But I don't care who you're with or who I'm with, I'm here, and I want you back—no matter how long it takes or how far into the future it is."

Don let go of her arms, looked down, and turned and walked in the direction of his car.

Lauren watched him leave. She felt bad she had hurt him, but he had exacted so much revenge by his outrageous treatment of Chris and his irrational demands on her work, that she could feel only relief that she was leaving Don and Tex Poly behind.

What he said about Kenny, though, was troubling. She knew Chris was skeptical of him, mainly because of the way he had treated her. Did she herself have doubts about her husband? He'd been unfaithful in their marriage, but then so had she. She only felt slightly guilty since her affair had been prompted by the misery and loneliness Kenny had caused. Surely her joy at being reunited with him told her she was making the right decision.

She returned to the apartment and slipped her arm around her husband's waist as he said goodbye to guests at the door.

>>

A few days later, Lauren sat down to write Chris a letter. He needed to know she and Kenny had reconciled. *Please let him be okay with the new situation.* Chris was the dearest of friends, and she may have already hurt him by her obliviousness to his feelings for her. She wondered how she would react to seeing him for the first time since that kiss a year ago. Would it be awkward for Kenny and Chris to spend time together? She hoped not. Both were congenial and liked hiking and camping. *Well, here goes,* she thought.

May 14, 1979
Dear Chris,

I have so much to tell you. First and most important, Kenny and I are back together. Our incompatibilities and misunderstandings seem to have fallen away. He's willing to move to Washington with me. Since we're not staying for graduation, we'll arrive in Spokane by the third week in May. You'll already be in the field by then, so we'll plan to visit you right away in Weiser or wherever you are working. I can't wait to see you.

All my travails with Don are over. The Kafkaesque requirements he imposed on my research and thesis caused me at least an extra semester of work, but when I was denied entry to Surea, he facilitated approval by the department of my thesis in its present form. I'm still disappointed that I couldn't complete the last phase of my project. What a nightmare! Or, as you are always saying, "What a comedy." Maybe I will be able to think that way when I get a little perspective on the situation. Right now, I'm eager to leave Pasadena.

My second most exciting news is I've been assigned the Picture Gorge Basalts in Oregon as my field area. It's almost as spectacular on my topo map as it is in photographs. I wish there were canyons in Pasadena to practice my climbing. As it is, I've been walking and jogging around campus to get in shape.

Thank you again for getting the application forms sent to me and for writing a letter of recommendation. Knowing I had a grant for a summer of fieldwork helped me when things looked bleak. If you call me next Sunday night, we can make plans to meet in your field area.

As always,

Lauren

"I thought happiness was Lubbock, Texas in my rearview mirror." The radio station played a new Mac Davis song as they began their long drive to Washington.

"That goes double for Pasadena, Texas," Kenny said after the song ended.

"I couldn't agree more," Lauren said with a smile, glancing at Kenny.

Lauren had a sense they were back in high school or college and experiencing one of many firsts together. Tom, their newly adopted cat, snuggled on Lauren's lap, or at times, peered out the window as tractor-trailers roared past. Truckers grinned when they saw the traveling cat. Kenny and Lauren's new Jeep with its burly tires seemed overqualified for driving on the smooth interstate, but they both liked sitting up high in a vehicle that promised adventure: exploring back roads, driving through ditches, and fording streams. The future unwound in front of them as endlessly as the highway.

Chapter 12

Slow-Moving Dreams

Lauren and Chris, 1979

Lauren and Kenny met Chris at his favorite café on State Street in Weiser. He greeted Lauren with a hug and shook hands with Kenny. "You're here. How was your drive?"

"Texas to Washington in a Jeep was a long damn trip. We barely moved into our new apartment, and now here we are in Southern Idaho," Kenny said as he slid into one of the turquoise-upholstered booths. He looked disheveled.

Chris and Lauren stood looking at each other for a few seconds before they, too, slid into the booth.

"It's been a while," Chris said. His face was tanned, and he was slimmer than he had been at Tex Poly.

"Almost exactly a year," Lauren said, feeling herself blush when she thought how attractive Chris looked.

"So you two patched things up?" Chris asked after a waitress took their order for burgers.

"Yeah, finally," Lauren said with a smile. *Chris seems okay with Kenny and my being together—at least he's acting like it.*

"What's this incredible thing you mentioned in your letter that you have to show us?" she asked.

"I'll take you there as soon as we eat, but I'm not telling you anything until then."

He resembled a schoolboy who could barely contain his excitement at having something spectacular for show-and-tell.

"I hope it doesn't involve more driving," Kenny said with a frown.

"Don't worry, it's just a few miles out of town," Chris assured him.

Lauren was surprised at Kenny's irritability. His usually affable nature was nowhere to be seen. But then, she and Kenny had been on the road for days, and he had done all the driving. As much as they both loved their new Jeep, they realized it was exhausting to drive and ride in.

>>

After lunch, Lauren and Kenny followed Chris in his car as he drove out of town on the river road and then turned onto a gravel road that dipped down to the river. Part way down the gravel road, they parked their cars.

Lauren jumped out of the Jeep and looked at the river. "You wanted to show us the river?"

"No, but the Snake is a magnificent river. I think Kenny will like the fishing here. What I want to show you is down this direction."

They walked along a path to where a large expanse of basalt lay exposed above the river. They climbed to the dark gray flow with rusty streaks.

"Look at these huge crystals." Chris said, pointing to white rectangular prisms in the basalt. For Kenny's benefit, he explained, "Crystals grow in a cooling magma chamber. The large size of these crystals shows they erupted from a magma chamber that had been cooling for an unusually long time."

"Does that mean there's a volcano around here?" Kenny asked, stepping up to take a closer look at the crystals.

"Yeah, there are some volcanic edifices, but mostly in this setting, the basalt oozed from fissures rather than erupted in a violent sense," Chris said.

"It's rare to see crystals this big," Lauren said.

"Besides the beauty of the crystals, the basalt offers another treasure." Chris paused and grinned. "The force of the motion of the lava as it poured out of the vents aligned the rectangular crystals lengthwise in the direction of the flow. They show flow lines and eddies perfectly."

"Really? They look so random." Lauren was doubtful.

Chris held up a few pieces of white chalk. "I thought you might be skeptical, Dr. Watson. I am prepared to make a believer of you. Shall we proceed?"

Lauren laughed. "Do I have a choice?" *This is fun. Chris always comes up with something interesting.*

"I'll let you two play detective while I do some fly fishing," Kenny said. "I hear the trout calling."

Chris and Lauren watched as Kenny hiked back toward the river. They turned toward each other.

"So, things are going well?" Chris asked, passing the chalk back and forth between his hands.

"Kenny's been great. Really supportive." Lauren leaned against the rock wall.

"It's good to see you happy."

Poor Chris, he's seen me at my most miserable.

"How are you? I've missed you. I've missed our talks," she said. *He seems good.*

"I'm doing well. My research is exciting."

"You look fit." *That's what fieldwork does for you,* Lauren thought. They stood awkwardly for a few seconds.

"Let's get started," Chris said, showing Lauren how he made chalk marks down the middle of each rectangular crystal the long way and then connected the line to the next closest crystal. "Maybe you could start marking over there and I'll continue here. Then we'll meet in the middle."

Lauren was dubious but worked diligently because she didn't want to hurt Chris's feelings. She felt like a math teacher writing an endless problem on the blackboard with nobody paying attention. After an hour, she was sweaty despite the cooling breeze from the river.

The longer they worked, the more their chalk lines revealed the main flow direction of the lava as well as currents and eddies. Near the bottom of the flow the lines descended into chaos where lava flowed over obstacles and encountered general friction from the land's surface.

Lauren stood back to better see their lines. "Hey, you're right. This is incredible! It shows the inner workings of fluid flow."

"I know! Everyone thinks something like this massive wall of basalt is solid, but over time, it's fluid."

When they were done, Chris photographed their masterpiece.

>>

They walked down to the river where Kenny had pitched a tent and was starting a fire with driftwood. When he saw them coming, he reached into the cooler and held up five rainbow trout, each over a foot in length.

"Hey, nice going," Chris said.

"Yeah, it takes a business major to put food on the table," Kenny said.

"You did well," Lauren said. "But so did we. Chris was right about what the crystals showed. You should see our lines."

Lauren rummaged in the back of the Jeep to find fry pan, plates, and forks while Chris set up his tent a discreet distance from Kenny and Lauren's. Kenny cleaned the fish and then cooked them in a little beer since they didn't have cooking oil. At the last minute he emptied a giant can of pork and beans into the skillet. They drank beer and feasted on fish and beans in the shade of a cottonwood tree.

After dinner, Kenny walked up to look at the chalk lines and explore the surrounding area. Chris and Lauren moved lawn chairs nearer to the fire to chat.

A year's worth of scientific wonders had accumulated since they had last seen each other. They dipped into them at random and examined them like stones.

"Weren't the pictures from the two *Voyagers* incredible?"

"Beyond what I hoped for," Lauren said. "The photos of the cloud patterns of the Red Spot on Jupiter are as compelling as the first pictures of Earth from space."

"It's hard to fathom the Red Spot is a hurricane three times the size of Earth, and it's lasted for over three hundred years. Talk about a storm."

Lauren had almost forgotten how thrilling it was to exchange ideas with another scientist.

"I know! And all the moons that have been detected in the last year or two. Even poor little Pluto has a moon almost as big as itself."

Once examined, each discovery was put away—smoothed and polished by two minds.

>>

Kenny joined them for a beer by the fire at dusk, and they paused their science talk for a time. When he finished his beer, he rose.

"I'm exhausted," he said. "See you in the morning." He kissed Lauren and headed for the tent.

As soon as he was gone, Lauren returned the conversation to space. "What do you think about black holes, Chris? Do they exist?"

"They better. I've written about them in one of my stories."

She laughed. "No, seriously. Is there such a thing?"

"Even though we can't prove they exist, we've now proved light bends around the sun."

"I know. So if gravity bends light, then black holes must exist according to Einstein's theory back in the early nineteen hundreds."

"Exactly. I think that's where everything is leading, Chris said. "It will have taken us almost eighty years to prove Einstein correct. I mean, the poor guy died without knowing whether he was right about black holes."

As the fire subsided, their conversation turned desultory. They basked in the soft light of the moon rounding to full.

"I guess I'd better call it a night," Lauren said, putting empty beer bottles into a paper sack.

"I think I'll sit here and finish my beer. See you in the morning."

As Lauren walked to her tent, she glanced back briefly at Chris's profile dimly lit by the dying fire. What a good guy. He deserved to find a wonderful woman. How would she feel if he were with someone? She hoped she would be happy for him. Love and all its complexities still mystified her, but she knew she was glad to be back with her husband.

>>

No one rose early the next day. When Lauren and Kenny emerged from their tent, Chris was assembling a row of peanut butter sandwiches on the picnic blanket.

"Ah, neighbors, just in time to eat," Chris said with a grin.

After breakfast, the three hiked to Chris's favorite overlook, where they could see for twenty miles. He pointed out Sturgill Peak and the faults and contact points between various basalt flows.

Clearly, he was at home. For some strange reason, Lauren also felt as if she had come home. Spending time in Chris's company always made her feel that everything on Earth was as it should be.

On the way back to their campsite, he said, "The conclusions I'm reaching about the basalts in my area don't necessarily agree with the opinions of my supervisor and colleagues."

"Is that a problem?" Lauren asked, shading her eyes to look at Chris.

"Mostly, it's not a problem. The Columbia River Basalt Project involves dozens of geologists working in three states. It's an exciting time. The search is just beginning. Lots of questions remain unanswered."

"But that's good. They need answers from geologists." *This must be concerning, or he wouldn't have mentioned it.*

"Every geologist has a strong theory and is trying to prove himself or herself right. There's disagreement."

"What are you telling me?" Lauren asked, stopping to concentrate on what Chris was saying.

"Only after all analyses are completed will we have answers. Don't let any preconceived ideas get in your way. You've got to stick to your guns when you make a discovery."

"I can do that." Chris was always trying to help her along and protect her. She hoped she wouldn't let him down by failing at fieldwork!

"I know you can. Truth will be revealed in time."

"Luckily, if I have any questions, I know a brilliant geologist I can consult."

Chris laughed, shrugging off the compliment. "You've got a great field area. Picture Gorge Basalts has canyons, exposed flows, dikes, and who knows what else. I'm sure you'll find out."

When they returned to where their cars were parked, Lauren paused by Chris's car and said, "I guess we won't see you until the end of summer." She wished they could talk this summer and compare notes, but it was impossible with his fieldwork in Idaho and hers in Oregon.

"Nope. I'm determined to finish my fieldwork by September. After that I'll be back in Coeur d'Alene."

"Hey, let's get on the road." Kenny sounded impatient as he leaned on their already loaded Jeep.

Lauren handed Chris a piece of paper with their Spokane phone number written on it.

"Call us when you're back at school. We're only thirty-three miles from you."

She gave him a quick hug and walked over to the Jeep.

>>

Chris sat in his truck for a few minutes after Lauren and Kenny started down the road. *I don't think I can do this,* he thought. *It's killing me to see them together. But I'd be even lonelier if Lauren and I weren't friends.*

It had been a lot easier at Tex Poly, when she'd been separated from her husband. Even though he knew she wanted to get back with Kenny, he never thought it would happen. Then a week ago he'd gotten the letter telling him she and Kenny had reconciled and were moving to Washington.

Since then, he had worked his field area in a daze, thoughts of Lauren circling through his mind. Sometimes he had to remind himself to do simple tasks like making notations about his rock samples. Other times, he shook himself from a reverie and wondered where he was for a moment.

He'd tried to talk himself out of loving her. It hadn't worked. Sitting by the fire with her last night after Kenny had gone to bed, he had felt as though he and she were the only two people on Earth. Her warmth, her beauty, her voice, her lips—everything about her drew him to her. With sparks from the fire shooting skyward, and their thoughts wandering the universe, he'd felt as though they had reached a mystical place.

Then she'd gone to bed, and he had crawled into his tent alone.

>>

"Good luck with your interviews," Lauren called to Kenny as he drove off.

He had driven her to Richland, Washington, to the Department of Energy Rockwell Hanford site so she could complete paperwork for her grant and pick up equipment and a field vehicle. She walked into a drab building marked "Badging" and identified herself to the closest secretary. After receiving her badge, Lauren was handed a multipage form on a clipboard with a pen attached by a dingy string.

"You can use the conference room down the hall."

As Lauren walked down the hall, she paged through the form titled, Questionnaire for a National Security Position. This was reminiscent of a major, scary exam. When she found the room, she laid the questionnaire on the conference table and sat down in a metal chair with a cracked gray leather seat. She wrote her name and then paused at Line 2. She fumbled in her backpack for the scrap of paper on which she had written her new address.

Not a good sign I'm stumped by my own address, she thought. Two hours later she turned in her questionnaire. Next, she was fingerprinted and then directed to a doctor's office in another building where she was given a complete physical examination. When she emerged from the doctor's office, the young man who had taken her fingerprints was waiting for her.

"There's a problem with your fingerprints. There are no whorls, loops, or arches on your left thumb print. I can't get it accepted by the higher-ups."

"Look at my left thumb. I had to have the first joint amputated two years ago in a school-related accident."

"Did you chop it off with a paper cutter?" he asked, his eyes round with curiosity.

"No, I was on the Tex Poly research ship and caught my thumb in a chain link."

"Fence?"

"No," Lauren said, laughing. "A chain link bag used to dredge for underwater rocks."

"I thought it was strange to have a chain link fence on a ship.

Well, they won't accept it because the ridges go straight instead of in whorls, loops—"

"I don't have any whorls because I don't have a tip!" Lauren interrupted. "They threw the tip into the ocean because it was so mangled. That's where the whorls are."

"In the ocean?"

"No, on the tip of your thumb."

"Well, obviously. But I have to turn in a set of ten good prints. If the whorls, loops, and arches are even a little blurry, the higher-ups reject it. I know I can't turn in a print without any whorls, loops, or arches at all."

"There must be an exception for somebody who's missing a joint. What if I were missing my whole left arm?"

"That wouldn't be a problem because I'd only have to turn in five good prints."

"I can't put the tip of my thumb back on. Surely you can figure a way to get my prints approved. Who are these higher-ups you keep talking about?"

"Buildings Three and Five."

"How can buildings make decisions?"

"That's where the higher-ups are."

"Please, I have to get my fingerprints approved today so I can get my vehicle and start my fieldwork. My husband drove me all the way from Spokane, dropped me off, and returned home. If I don't get my vehicle, I won't have any transportation."

"I'll try to get Building Three to sign off on your prints. Come to my office at four forty-five, and I'll let you know."

Lauren ate her peanut butter sandwich in the conference room and then spent an hour walking up and down the halls reading bulletin boards. At 4:45 the young man told Lauren he could get her prints approved if the physician would certify the tip of her left thumb as missing.

"I'm sure it's not a problem. I'll run back to his office."

"He's gone for the day. He only comes here if he has a physical scheduled. His next physical is ten tomorrow morning."

Lauren felt like laughing and crying simultaneously. She asked one of the secretaries if there were a shuttle to town so she could get a motel room. She told Lauren she would give her a ride to town, but there was no need to get a motel room as she and her husband had plenty of room and loved to have guests since their children were grown and gone. Lauren accepted. Generous and gracious people compensated for moments of bureaucratic insanity.

When Lauren went back the following day, the physician photographed her left thumb with a Polaroid camera and certified her thumb's condition as having no first joint. With signatures from two witnesses, Lauren's prints were accepted. She picked up rock hammers, magnetometer, safety glasses, field books, and stipend. Released into the wilds at last, she fled south to Oregon in her Chevy Suburban.

>>

Before dawn two days later, Lauren parked her new government-issued Suburban partly in the ditch and partly on the dirt road that ran parallel to a creek. She had decided to start her rock sampling on the smallest canyon, seven hundred vertical feet, and work her way up to the steepest, some of which were five thousand vertical feet. Until now her fieldwork had been an exciting mental adventure. The reality was humbling.

Lauren had been thrilled when she was assigned the Picture Gorge Basalts. Yesterday on her way to her field area, she had driven through glorious countryside—the Painted Hills with great swaths of mustard yellow and cinnamon red; stunning canyons layered with pastel rocks ranging from pink to rose to peach to creamy white, reminiscent of giant birthday cakes. There was a reason for the spectacular scenery—Oregon's checkered past. Hundreds of millions of years ago, the state didn't exist. The Pacific Ocean lapped the shores of Idaho, instead. Then 150 to 90 million years ago, the North American tectonic plate had collided with the islands, volcanoes, and coral reefs off its coast, which had become Oregon's landmass. Sections of sea floor had been thrust onto the continent, where, to a geologist's delight, they could be examined without the need for a submersible.

She was the sole researcher detailed to the area, so she had a proprietary feeling about her five hundred miles in north central Oregon. Its beauty and mysteries were hers to enjoy and solve. The area was especially intriguing because it encompassed many of the feeder dikes that were major sources for the Columbia River basalts. Were eruptions such as these associated with continental breakup? Did the North American continent almost pull apart? Why didn't it? Lauren's job was to map the Picture Gorge Basalt flows in the area and chemically analyze samples to help answer these and other questions.

As she looked up at the canyon walls, they looked dark and foreboding and not at all pastel. Of course, she knew she would be working with basalt and not sedimentary rock. Basalt layers bore no resemblance to a birthday cake. She felt small and inadequate and terribly alone. To get herself in shape for fieldwork she had walked and jogged ten miles a day around Pasadena, Texas. Her leg strength was good, but she knew her arms and back were weak. Before getting out of the car, she closed her eyes, took a deep breath and prayed an inchoate prayer to the universe for strength to accomplish her research.

When Lauren had scouted this particular canyon yesterday, she estimated it had eight or nine flows. She loaded her backpack with a giant water bottle, peanut butter sandwich, apple, safety goggles, floppy sun hat, and two sledgehammers—Samson, weighing 6.6

pounds, and Delilah, 3.2 pounds. The predawn morning was cool, and her vest felt good over her long-sleeved shirt and jeans. She hefted her pack onto her shoulders. *Heigh-ho, heigh-ho.*

A mere sixteen to twelve million years ago, layer upon layer of basalt had flowed over northwestern United States. Lauren was required to get two fresh, non-weathered samples from each basalt flow, nearly impossible on a water planet, where most outcroppings were well weathered.

She started at the bottom contact, where basalt had flowed over the sedimentary deposit known as the John Day Formation. With what she thought was a mighty blow from Samson, she broke off a quarter inch of surface rock and nearly toppled over. Luckily, she was still at the bottom. A quarter of an inch was not nearly deep enough to get a fresh sample.

Bracing herself, she swung her hammer again. This time she penetrated a little deeper into the rock. Her ears rang. She donned her safety goggles and struck a third blow and broke off a two-by-three-inch sample. To measure the rock's polarity, she pulled her magnetometer from a vest pocket and checked the needle. It was normal, so she marked the rock with an N. Because basalt erupted as fluid with crystals full of iron, the iron aligned itself with the magnetic field of the earth at the time. When it cooled, the magnetic compass was frozen in the flow. By studying basalt magnetism, scientists had learned the earth's magnetic field had reversed itself many times. During the course of the summer, Lauren expected to find samples with reversed polarity, meaning the flow had cooled when Earth's pole was south rather than north.

Next Lauren checked the height with her altimeter, made notations, and drew the details of the flow in her notebook. She decided not to rely entirely on the altimeter, which was subject to weather changes and other vagaries. She would also measure the thickness of each flow by eye heights. She knew her eyes were sixty-four inches from the ground. She eyed her first marker and then climbed to it. She took her second sample on a protruding rock where she could use her smaller sledge. This sample, too, showed normal polarity. She climbed eye height by eye height up the canyon, taking time after each sample to correlate altimeter readings, eye heights, and topographic maps with field data. The contact between each flow—where two flows came together—had to be drawn on the topographic map at the correct altitude.

By midmorning the dark basalts were radiating heat, and Lauren was hot and hungry. Having sampled only 350 feet of the canyon so far, she decided to sample one more flow before finding a shady place to rest and eat lunch. Her slow progress was discouraging. It seemed doubtful she could finish the canyon today.

She scrambled over rocks to reach her next eye-height marker before climbing higher. This flow was massive. Finally, she reached the contact point. She was amazed at how different each flow was from the previous one. One had columnar jointing, another had crystals, and some were glassy. She decided to use her small sledge to take the last two samples. With a shaky arm she swung hard at the rock face. Delilah's head flew off and tumbled down a steep gully.

"Damn!" she said out loud, her voice reverberating across the valley. Now she would have to use Samson the rest of the day. Her arms and back were so sore she could hardly lift it.

By the time she stopped for lunch, she was too tired to eat. She drank to the halfway level on her water bottle and lay down on a flat outcropping partially shaded by a spindly pine tree. She covered her face with her sun hat and instantly fell asleep. When she woke forty-five minutes later, her hair was sweaty and matted. Her legs and back were so stiff she could hardly stand up. She moved farther into the shade to eat her sandwich and apple.

Climbing canyons with a heavy backpack was difficult. Stopping in precipitous places to swing a sledgehammer, adding rock samples to her pack, and then continuing up the mountain bordered on the irrational. Were they crazy? They expected her to keep this up day after day, week after week, all summer. Thousands of vertical feet for hundreds of miles.

Not humanly possible, she decided.

>>

By six o'clock the sun was behind a canyon wall, and Lauren had sampled almost six hundred vertical feet of the canyon. She could go no higher. Her arms shook as she slung her pack onto her back. It must weigh ten pounds more than it had when she started, and her water was gone. She knew she should quit while it was still light enough to find a reasonable route down the canyon.

She picked her way back down to her Suburban carefully, then drove her truck to a deserted campsite a few miles along the dirt road, close to where she would resume work in the morning. After pitching her tent, she rummaged through the back of the Suburban for a bowl to use as a washbasin, splashed water over her face, and took a quick sponge bath. It was a long time until Friday, when she could check into a motel and take a hot shower. Unheated Dinty Moore stew in the can was her dinner. If she took two peanut butter sandwiches for lunch the next day, maybe she wouldn't be so desperately hungry by nighttime.

Suddenly, she felt an overwhelming urge to hear a human voice. She wished she could call Chris to tell him about her first day, but he was probably in as remote a location as she. If she drove thirty miles to the nearest town, maybe she could call Kenny. In the end, exhaustion won out, and she crawled into her sleeping bag with a flashlight beside her. She was asleep before it was completely dark.

>>

At the end of the fourth day, Lauren's whole body felt sore and bruised. It hurt to hold a pen in her hand, yet she could hardly wait to write her thoughts to Chris. She sat on the passenger side of the Suburban at her campsite and wrote him a letter.

June 12, 1979
Dear Chris,

I very much want to talk to you, but the odds of our having access to a telephone at the same time are not good. Letter writing will have to do.

How is your fieldwork going? Have you discovered any other volcanoes? Do you have trouble getting reliable magnetic field readings at the top of your sections? The top flows in my sections frequently give both normal and reversal readings. My theory is it's due to lightning strikes. So far, I have discovered only one good reversal in sampling several sections.

After being serenaded by a pack of coyotes my first night, I gave up setting up my tent. Sleeping in the Suburban feels more secure. Besides a rattlesnake, I've seen countless scorpions. Of course, I shake my samples before I put them in the back of the truck. Scorpions would not make good bedfellows.

The lack of human company has me talking and singing to myself. If someone were to come within earshot, they would no doubt call me the "crazy lady of the canyons." Kenny will come down this weekend to help get samples with Super Samson, my 8.8-pound sledge. I have knocked myself over (literally) trying to hit rock forcefully enough to get a fresh sample. Many flows are heavily fractured and, thus, have a thick, weathered coat to bang off. I have acquired many nicks to my face and hands from flying glass shards. Safety goggles protect my eyes, but I could use a welder's helmet, although it would have to be air-conditioned.

Climbing up a canyon with a heavy backpack makes me acutely aware of gravity and its downward pull. The earth

seems to want me at the bottom! Then a strange thing happens
when I finally get to the top; I feel light and airy and not at all
subject to gravity. The first couple of days I couldn't imagine
surviving the summer. Now I'm pretty sure I'll make it.
   Your friend,
   Lauren

Four weeks into Lauren's fieldwork, she found a marker in the middle of the dirt road when she hiked to the top of the Holmes Creek section. Three sticks held by a rock pointed to an overlook she especially loved, where she could see for miles, although the forest reached almost to the ledge. Many middays she enjoyed eating lunch in the shade.

She walked in the direction of the marker and found a wooden sign nailed to one of the tall trees with LAUREN'S OVERLOOK carved on it. Cowboys and ranchers near where she worked were beginning to accept her. One ranch foreman, in particular, had taken an interest in her work. At first, he seemed stunned that a woman would take on the task of climbing canyons and collecting rocks. He no doubt thought she would be gone in a week. After a few weeks, he must have realized she was determined to map the area. Now she had her own overlook. She guessed it made her famous, or better yet, one of them.

Lauren spent the next several days sampling a huge section of the Holmes Creek area which was over two thousand vertical feet. As she approached the top, it became more difficult to sample because there were two flows in the last hundred feet, with sheer vertical exposure of about thirty feet. She had to hug the base of one of these flows for about a half mile before she could find an eroded area to climb up to the next flow. Once she reached the third flow, it wouldn't be so steep. As she ascended the second flow, she pulled herself onto a ledge and looked into the yellow eyes of a mountain lion. Bones lay everywhere in front of an entrance to a shallow cave. She'd invaded a mountain lion's nest! Turning abruptly, she jumped down onto a boulder, and fought to keep from plunging down the canyon. Simultaneously, the big cat leapt to the ledge above its den.

Oh, God! It's going to pounce!

She ran along the ledge in the opposite direction. One of her sledgehammers clattered down the canyon. Glancing back to the high ridge, she saw the cat was running away from her. She slowed to a safer pace and scrambled down the canyon to where her truck was parked.

When she reached the Suburban, she glanced in the side view mirror and saw a red face framed by a wide-brimmed straw hat.

She laughed out loud. Her head with its huge hat appeared as big as that of a wild-maned African lion. She must have been a fearsome sight to a mere North American cougar. Tomorrow she would climb to the top to finish sampling the flows, avoiding the area around the mountain lion's den. And she would wear her secret weapon.

>>

A few weeks later Lauren and her intern, Katie, walked into one of the few bars in Spray.

"Let's get a drink and maybe play some pool," Lauren said.

"But I've never played," Katie said. "I don't even know how to hold the pole or stick or whatever it's called."

"It's a cue stick, not a pole. And I'll show you how to hold it. I bet you were good at geometry in high school. Am I right?"

"Yeah, I was pretty good at math."

"Then you'll do great at pool. I, myself, am a tragically bad pool player, but the guys here don't seem to mind," Lauren said, looking at the rough group of cowboys gathered at the bar. "And I do understand the game even if I can't hit the shots."

The two women put their backpacks on a table and walked to the bar and ordered margaritas. Lauren looked around, unsurprised that, aside from an older woman, they were the only women in the bar. They sat down with their drinks and sighed with pleasure as cold, salt, and pain relief for their aching hands were provided courtesy of Margarita. After relaxing and ordering another round of margaritas, Lauren suggested they play a game.

"Ping-Pong would be way more fun than pool," Katie said, licking salt from her lips.

"Ping-Pong! This is a cowboy bar. Cowboys don't play ping-pong. It's not dignified."

"I don't see why not."

"Can you imagine their leaping around in their boots and hats to hit a bouncy little ball? They're big on pride."

Glancing at the men at the bar, Katie said, "Judging from some of the beer bellies around here, I recommend a little leaping around."

Lauren chuckled. "True. But you're naturally slim."

Despite her slight figure, Lauren's intern from Oregon State was surprisingly resilient. Other than acquiring a bad sunburn when she wore a spaghetti-strapped top instead of a long-sleeved shirt, Katie had been a competent field researcher.

"I used to weigh a hundred and ten before all this climbing and sweating. I'm probably down to a hundred pounds."

"I haven't weighed a hundred pounds since third grade."

Katie laughed. "You're as slim as I am but you're six inches taller."

Lauren moved to the pool table and inserted two quarters in the slot. The balls rolled down and she racked them.

"Somebody will always rack the balls for you. You don't have to learn this for a while," she said, lifting the rack. "This is how you break. The white ball is the cue ball. You hit the other balls with it. Place it anywhere behind this mark and then hit it hard with your stick so balls scatter. One or more balls ought to go down a pocket."

A burly rancher in his fifties and one of his hands, a young cowboy dressed in black, walked over to Lauren and Katie. "We saw you workin' over at Monument Mountain today. You was so high up we thought maybe you was mountain goats," the older man said.

"Yeah, it's steep but interesting. We found dozens of dikes up there," Lauren said, leaning on her cue stick.

The rancher laughed uproariously at the mention of dikes.

He's kind of a jerk, Lauren decided.

She ignored him and continued her explanation. "Millions of years ago, lava poured out of dikes and covered this area. Dikes are fissures in rocks, by the way."

"My ranch backs right up to that ol' mountain."

"Really? We may need to cross your land to get to one of our research sections."

"I got no problem with that. Where're you girls sleeping tonight?"

"Oh, we have our campsite," Lauren said, giving Katie a meaning- ful look to warn her not to reveal where they were camping. *We don't need unwelcome visitors to our camp.*

"I've got a mighty nice ranch house on my spread. Wouldn't you like to take a hot shower and sleep in a nice, soft bed?"

"Thanks, but we have to get up before dawn and start sampling another section," Lauren said.

"Well, then, how 'bout we join you girls in your game?"

"I don't know what I'm doing, but you're welcome to play with us," Katie said, looking to Lauren for agreement.

"Sure. Let's play girls against guys."

She proceeded to break, although no ball went down a pocket.

"Who goes next?" Katie asked, looking at the others.

"I do. Call me Wayne." He dropped two solids before missing his third shot.

"Let's get you girls some more drinks. Me and Tex been drinkin' here since noon. Curt! Two more beers and a couple of margaritas for the girls."

Wayne and Tex won the first game handily. Wayne manipulated the next game so he and Lauren were partners.

"What do you raise on your ranch?" Lauren asked Wayne as he took a swallow of beer before picking up his cue stick.

"Oh, 'bout a thousand head of cattle and a couple hundred pigs. Tex here is my right-hand man."

Wayne broke and sank a striped ball and then missed on his second shot.

As Lauren and Wayne stood watching Tex advise Katie about her grip on the cue stick, Wayne slipped his arm around Lauren's waist and pulled her close to him.

"With those long legs of yours, you could give a man a good lovin'," he whispered.

Lauren removed Wayne's arm and moved away from him. "Hey, don't do that! And by the way, I'm married." *I had a bad feeling about him.*

"That don't matter," Wayne said, slurring his words. He watched Lauren knock in a solid ball that Katie had left hanging on the lip of a pocket. "You girls can at least come by for one drink."

"Two drinks are my limit, and I think I've had three," Katie said, giggling.

Katie was young and innocent, Lauren decided. She had no idea how creepy Wayne was.

Lauren's run of one ended when she tried to make two solids follow each other into a side pocket. The balls went two different directions but not down. While Wayne lined up his shot, Lauren told Katie he was getting aggressive. Next Katie sank her first ball ever before missing her second shot, leaving Tex a nice table with easy marks.

Wayne sidled up to her and put his arm around her shoulder and said in a low voice, "You and me both know you wanna fuck me."

He was drunk and Lauren didn't trust what he would do next.

Lauren shrugged his arm off her shoulder and moved to the other side of the table. "We have to leave after this game."

Even with Katie as a liability, the young cowboy won the game for them by sinking the last two stripes and sending the eight ball into an end pocket.

Lauren whispered to Katie, "Let's get out of here! It's turning bad."

They gathered their backpacks and walked quickly out to the dark street where the Suburban was parked. Katie opened the passenger door and got in.

Wayne, who had followed them, called after Lauren, "Hey, wait a minute, I need to talk to you."

Lauren hesitated for a few seconds since her research might require access to his land. He walked up to her, grabbed her arms, and pressed her against the side of the truck. She could feel him hard against her belly.

"Stop. Let me go!" Lauren screamed, trying to free her arms.

Katie opened her door, ran around the truck, and grabbed Wayne's right arm from behind. Without turning around, he knocked her to the ground. He yanked Lauren's blouse up over her shoulders and grabbed her breasts.

Shit, he's going to rape me right here, Lauren thought. "Help!" she yelled as loud as she could while fighting him. She hoped someone in the bar would hear.

She pushed against his head with both hands and tried to kick him.

At that moment Tex emerged from the bar and ran to them. He shoved Wayne away from Lauren and struggled to hold him.

"Get in your car and go like hell," he said to Lauren and Katie.

Lauren started the Suburban with a shaky hand and ground the gears getting into first. They screeched away from the curb and drove out of town. Even though no one followed, Lauren passed the road to where they were camped and then doubled back.

"I think we're in the clear," Lauren said.

When they reached their campsite, they sat in the truck for a moment and breathed.

"Wow. I can't believe that old guy attacked you!"

"Did you get hurt when he knocked you down?" Lauren looked over at Katie.

"Just a scraped elbow, but he was strong."

"You took on a guy more than twice your size! That was gutsy. Thank God Tex rescued us," Lauren said as she reached into the glove compartment for a first aid kit and handed Katie bandages for her elbow.

"Yeah, what a good guy."

"Tex will either lose his job, or the rancher will thank him in the morning for saving him from jail," Lauren said.

The women slept with rock hammers beside them.

>>

When Katie left a week later to return to Oregon State, working alone seemed strange and a little scary to Lauren. She noted the irony that more danger lurked in town than when she climbed steep canyons. Except for mountain lions, she felt safe working outside because she was armed with rock hammers.

During Katie's three-week internship, the two of them had devised a system whereby they covered at least a third more territory each day than when Lauren worked alone. Time, instead of creeping along at the speed of a lava flow, had leapt into the present with conversation, commiseration, and laughter. Lauren would no doubt revert to talking to herself.

>>

By August Lauren was a seasoned geologist. She had a geologist's tan—darkly tanned hands and lightly tanned face. Her hands were covered with nicks, cuts, and calluses. Once she finished her sampling that summer and associated lab analyses during school term, she would possess the partial makings of a dissertation. She was proud of her notebooks filled with sketches and data entries. She had gone back and resampled some of her first flows and found her measurements surprisingly accurate. A few she had corrected or improved.

She was spending her last week in the field sampling the Bronson Creek canyons. On her second to last day, she arose before dawn, ate her usual breakfast of deviled ham, drank a bottle of Gatorade, and began her climb. That particular canyon had more trees and brush than many of the desert canyons she had sampled earlier in the summer. Before long she heard a close whizzing sound, like the buzzing of a huge bee. *No bee could be that big*, she told herself. Then another *whish*. Out of the corner of her eye she saw an arrow fly past her right ear. *Hunters!*

"What the hell are you doing?" she shouted. "Don't you look where you're shooting?"

A far-off voice called, "Sorry."

Lauren shook her sun-hatted head. Hunters assumed anything that moved was fair game. It didn't seem to matter that bow hunting season was restricted to elk and deer. She regretted not wearing orange clothing rather than faded denim. As soon as she climbed above the lower areas of brush and trees, she felt safer.

By the time she returned to camp she was exhausted from work and from watching for goofball hunters behind every rock and bush. She remembered what her friend who served thirteen months in Vietnam had said about his last week in-country. His passionate desire to live devolved to every cell in his body. The danger he had taken for granted and routinely guarded against for over a year suddenly seemed to take aim at him. Each step he took he was sure he would step on a mine. All the incoming rockets seemed headed in his direction. Lauren wasn't deluded into thinking fieldwork was in any way comparable to Vietnam, but she was superstitious about her last day of work. All the dangers, great and small, she had faced over the summer could be lurking in the woods and brush. Especially hunters. To take her mind off the risks of the next day she sat down and wrote a letter.

August 24, 1979
Dear Chris,

This summer has been amazing in every sense. My head is swimming with artistic visions. The quiet time spent under the hot, blue sky looses my imagination. I could fill canvases with fantastic shapes and forms of dikes, columns, and veins. I feel impelled to paint eruptions happening: red lava pouring out of fractures—contrasting with the frozen, cooled black lava. I can imagine violent eruptions with gray ash billowing above a volcano.

At night I feel time, real geologic time. It's comforting to see myself as part of the universe, but oh, so humbling. I agree with you when you say you can't think of anything greater than to be a Renaissance scientist—someone who can see beyond one narrow field of science and make connections by coupling knowledge with leaps of imagination. No doubt one of the sources of friction between you and Don was the difference in your perspectives. He had a narrow view of science and felt threatened by the breadth of your vision.

After tomorrow I leave for Richland to turn in my Suburban and equipment. I realize you're staying another week in the field. Call us as soon as you get back to Coeur d'Alene and we'll have a cookout at our place. Kenny assures me the apartment is all settled. It will be wonderful to be within thirty miles of each other.

As always,
Lauren

Chapter 13

A Sleeping Giant Awakes

Lauren and Chris, 1979–1980

As soon as the installer from the telephone company left, Chris dialed the phone number Lauren had given him. They hadn't seen or spoken to each other since late May—over three months ago—when she and Kenny had visited him in his field area. Kenny seemed easygoing enough, and he wasn't evil like Don. Even with Kenny on the periphery, the time spent in her company had been worth the pain. Lauren knew Chris better than anyone and shared his love of science and adventure. He could not think of a more intriguing woman. At least Lauren had escaped Don's clutches.

He was glad she, not Kenny, answered the phone on the second ring.

"Chris. I'm so excited you're back at school—and you have a telephone!"

Her warmth and enthusiasm made Chris smile. He was lucky to have such a friend.

"Yes, it's amazing what they invented over the summer."

Lauren laughed. "I'm still adjusting to newfangled things like microwaves, not to mention computerized registration at school."

Chris laughed. "Exactly."

"We want you to come for a barbecue. How's tomorrow?"

"Sounds great. I'll bring the beer."

He was excited to see Lauren but wasn't looking forward to Kenny's presence.

>>

Early the next evening, Lauren answered the door to find Chris standing on the threshold, two six-packs of Olympia in hand.

"Chris, welcome," Lauren said. She smiled and gave him a beer-encompassing hug.

"Lauren, great to see you." He followed her into the kitchen and set the beer on a counter.

"By the way, have you met Oly, your new state beer?" he asked, indicating the six-packs.

"I think I ran into a few of those in Oregon this summer," she said, laughing. "Kenny's not home with the grilling supplies yet. Let's have a drink while we wait for him."

She opened two beers, and they sat down at the kitchen table. They clinked cans and grinned at each other.

"To surviving fieldwork," Chris said. They each took a swallow.

Lauren thought how wonderful it was to be with someone who knew exactly what fieldwork was like.

"But you actually finished yours?"

"Pretty much." He nodded. "That's why I stayed an extra week."

"Let's celebrate. It seems like old times when we were both at the same school."

"Better. Don's not here. Working outside for the past summers has cleared my mind of so many unimportant things, including Don. I didn't think of him once this summer."

"I barely did either. Negative thoughts just fly away when there's no ceiling to contain them," she said, her hands gesturing upward.

"Hey, I like your theory," Chris said, laughing.

"Actually, the sky didn't take care of all my negative thoughts. I spent my last two days in the field cursing archery hunters. One of them mistook me for a deer and shot arrows in my direction."

"God, that's dangerous," he said, shaking his head. "Just think what an arrow designed to kill a deer would do to a human. What did you do?"

"Besides yelling at him, I hurried to get out of the brush and trees so I could see who was nearby and they could see me."

"I didn't run across any hunters while I was working, but on my last night I came back to camp, and the whole place looked like an army basic training post. All the hunters were wearing their new camouflage outfits."

Lauren chuckled. "You'd have thought I was camouflaged by the way they shot at me. How I wished for some neon orange."

"For sure." He paused and then added, "The guys next to me invited me for a couple of beers. They reminded me of my dad and all the preparations that went into his fishing or hunting expeditions. He'd spend weeks sorting his tackle box, concocting new recipes for bait, or cleaning his gun. A couple of years he bought a deer license but never took a shot, according to my mom. She said he was way too softhearted to kill a deer. I guess he liked being outdoors with his buddies."

"Yeah, I don't see how anyone could kill a deer. I mean, really," Lauren said, rolling her eyes. "Think about Bambi."

Kenny walked into the kitchen and set a sack of groceries on the counter. "Who's killing Bambi?"

"No one. I'm glad you're a fisherman and not a hunter." Lauren said, looking up and smiling at Kenny.

"I hunted up these steaks, if that counts."

Chris stood up, and he and Kenny greeted each other with a quick handshake.

Kenny put the steaks in the refrigerator and flicked his new lighter to make sure it worked.

"Grab a beer and pull up a chair," Lauren said.

"Not till I get the coals going."

Kenny tossed his blazer on a living room chair, rolled up his sleeves, and went out onto the balcony where the tools of his trade—fire—awaited. When a strong smell of lighter fluid reached the kitchen, Lauren turned on the vent fan above the stove and looked out at the conflagration in the grill.

"I think you've got it going," she said in a droll voice. "Why don't you come inside and shut the door?"

Kenny gave the fire another squirt of lighter fluid, then came inside to join them.

They were all in agreement that it was good to be in Idaho and Washington and away from the heat and humidity of Texas. Lauren could tell Chris was ill at ease in Kenny's presence. She struggled to think of a conversation topic of mutual interest to them.

After an awkward silence, Chris said, "From what I've read, you two will like hiking and exploring around here."

"Does exploring for a good dive bar count?" Kenny asked.

"Only if you found one."

"Palm Garden. Dollar drafts. Pickled eggs. Pool table."

Lauren and Chris laughed.

"I've identified a few bars like that in Coeur d'Alene. Except maybe the pickled eggs," Chris said with a chuckle.

Lauren turned to Chris and said, "Spokane is supposedly surrounded by amazing geological features. Weird landforms left by ice age floods. Canyons not carved by any river. A massive dry waterfall bigger than Niagara Falls. At least that's what my guidebook says."

"Yeah, sounds interesting."

As the evening progressed, Chris and Kenny fell into an easy bantering, interspersed with a few sarcastic remarks. Lauren was relieved they were getting along, although they didn't really have much in common. As Chris was leaving, he suggested they all go sailing on

Lake Coeur d'Alene sometime in the next couple of weeks before the weather changed.

"You're on," Kenny said. "Right, babe?"

"Sure. Night, Chris." *Sailing! Maybe that's what Chris and Kenny can bond over,* Lauren thought as she watched as Chris walked down the hall of the apartment building.

On his drive home Chris thought how Lauren exuded a new lightness and self-confidence. Surviving a summer of geology fieldwork was life-changing in itself. Then for her to be free from Don's harassment and all the obstacles he had placed in her path, it was as though she had found her way out of a dark cave into the sunlight.

Damn. Why the hell did she get back with Kenny?

The week classes started, Lauren was troubled by thoughts of her mother stranded in Houston. Her uncle's work had transferred him from Houston to New York, so Betty no longer had relatives nearby. Lauren needed to relocate her.

She and Kenny decided to move her to Spokane to be near them. The next weekend, they found an apartment for her in a complex with a swimming pool. Betty loved to swim, and it was important to have recreation on site, since she didn't drive. The apartment was within walking distance of a grocery store. The stress of purchasing furniture would have undone Betty, so Lauren and Kenny bought simple furnishings.

It would be challenging for Betty to get on a plane by herself to fly to Spokane, but at least the apartment would be ready when she arrived. Lauren wasn't exactly looking forward to living in the same city, however. In a conversation a few years back, she had asked her mother the definition of love. "Service," her mother had been quick to reply.

Betty had served her own mother, Dorothy, off and on from the time she was a child. So long as she did her mother's bidding, Betty hadn't worried about playing her own cards. So humbled was she by Dorothy's exalted status as one of the first women to receive a doctorate from Swarthmore that Betty had passed up the opportunity to attend Swarthmore, choosing to go to Ursinus College instead. Though she was five feet nine inches and weighed only 140 pounds, Betty thought of herself as "fat as a sausage" and feared her lumpish presence at Swarthmore would embarrass Dorothy.

Lauren had seen pictures of her mother in college. They showed a willowy, dark-haired beauty.

After college, Betty worked at Friends University in Wichita for a year, after which time she came home, having been briefly married and newly divorced. She'd brought her three-month-old baby girl with her.

Betty never left home again. She served her mother until she was as empty as the silver tea service displayed on their buffet. During her mother's final illness, Betty had sat at her bedside all day long—and when Dorothy died at eighty-five, Betty was no more capable of fashioning a life for herself than an inmate released after decades behind bars. Lauren was pressed into service as Betty's only offspring. By default, Kenny also found himself responsible for his mother-in-law.

Lauren was amazed by how tolerant her husband was of Betty. Having grown up in a modest neighborhood, he automatically granted undue respect to people who came from money. When Lauren's grandmother had been alive, invective and recriminations filled their home, but Kenny had been impervious to these splashes of vitriol. A childhood spent in a boisterous family apparently gave one a tough hide. Even now he didn't sense the hysteria that underlay Betty's every word and action, as Lauren did, nor did he see Betty as a failed mother. Although he noted her craziness at times, he believed he and Lauren should do their best to care for her.

Lauren and Kenny would help her mother get settled when she arrived in Spokane in a few weeks.

>>

By spring, Lauren, Kenny, and Chris had settled into a pattern of meeting every few weeks for hikes, sailing, dinners, or parties. Spokane and Coeur d'Alene, compared to Houston, were paradise for outdoors people.

On March 21st, Lauren came upon a small article in Spokane's newspaper, *The Spokesman-Review*, about a 4.2 magnitude earthquake that had occurred the day before at Mount St. Helens in western Washington. A series of smaller quakes had been recorded earlier in the month. She immediately dialed Chris's number.

"Something mysterious is happening at Mount St. Helens," she said when Chris answered.

"I know! One of my professors mentioned it yesterday."

"Do you think it's going to erupt?" Lauren was glad she could call Chris when something exciting like an earthquake happened. They were equally passionate about geology.

"I don't know. It's been quiet for over a hundred and twenty years. We'll have to wait and see."

"Wait and see are not my best skills."

Chris laughed. "Nor mine."

"Let me know if you learn anything, and I'll do the same."

>>

Kenny arrived home from work on March 27th with a four-pack of Guinness and two six-packs of Budweiser just as the pizza delivery man drove away.

"Hey, great timing," Lauren greeted him. "Dan should be here any minute. I'm glad you remembered he drinks Guinness. I don't know when Chris will get here. I'm going to run upstairs to shower, 'kay?"

Kenny nodded and opened a beer, and she darted upstairs.

She'd heard the news as she was driving home from class that day: Mount St. Helens had erupted! She was amazed at her good fortune to be living in Washington. She'd invited Chris and Danjuma, a PhD geology student from Nigeria, to what she was thinking of as her Volcano Party that evening—although it would likely be only four people.

She finished showering and dressing in record time and arrived back downstairs just in time to hear Kenny asking Dan, "Are you as excited about Mount St. Helens as Lauren is?"

The two were sitting at the kitchen table with beers in front of them.

"Very much so. We do not have active volcanoes in my country, although we have many extinct ones in the northeastern provinces. An active volcano like St. Helens is quite a drama."

Lauren couldn't believe Kenny was discussing volcanoes with Dan. They usually talked football, or soccer, as most Americans called it. It had taken a volcanic eruption, but Kenny was finally showing some interest in geology! The thought made her smile. She retrieved a Budweiser from the refrigerator and joined them.

"Hi Dan. Don't get up." She patted him on the shoulder as she sat down. "I heard you say Nigeria has extinct volcanoes. I didn't know that." Dan was a dear guy. Since his wife had returned to Nigeria at the end of the semester, he'd seemed a little lonely. Lauren was glad he'd come to the party.

"Lauren, my friend. Our volcanoes are not situated along plate margins. They are emplaced within the continent and associated with mantle hot spots."

"Of course."

When Chris finally arrived, they filled their plates with pizza and salads and gathered around the television. Aside from occasional news flashes, they would have to wait for a special report on Mount St.

Helens on the ten o'clock news. Lauren found it hard to sit still. After dinner she served bowls of vanilla ice cream with fresh sliced strawberries. At exactly ten, Kenny turned up the volume on the television.

"It's starting!" Lauren said. Volcanoes always seemed exotic and far away. Having a volcano in Washington was fascinating—but having it erupt was thrilling. *If I were still stuck at Tex Poly, I would be unbelievably frustrated,* she thought.

Mount St. Helens was the lead story. Film from different locations showed dark gray smoke in convoluted, coral-shaped formations billowing through the clouds that obscured the top of the volcano. Compared to the fluffy clouds surrounding the mountain, the ash and gases clearly had a more sinister origin.

"Oh, my God, this is unbelievable!" Lauren looked at the others, who were as riveted as she by the pictures and film clips of the eruption.

A scientist with the US Geological Survey estimated the plume rose seven thousand feet above the new crater, which was 150 feet deep. The summit had dropped, and long cracks had formed along east–west faults. People in the vicinity reported hearing two loud explosive booms about a second apart.

In Cougar, Washington—only ten miles from Mount St. Helens— reporters who poured into town found residents nonchalant about the event. They were accustomed to notoriety, what with adventurers looking for Bigfoot, the FBI searching for parachuting hijacker D. B. Cooper, and now the eruption of their mountain.

"How great is this? We're studying volcanology, and a volcano erupts," Lauren said, turning to Chris and Dan.

"It's ordained," Chris said.

Lauren jumped up. "Let's go to Mount St. Helens this weekend! Dan, can you go?"

"I cannot. My professor says I must finish some lab work for him by Monday."

She turned to Chris. "Maybe you, Kenny, and I can go tomorrow after work?"

"I'm tempted, but I can't go for at least a month. I need to organize my dissertation and do some XRF work."

"A month! It'll be dormant again. Kenny and I will have to go without you."

"Not me," said Kenny. "Our office has had computer problems all week. I have to work this weekend."

"Damn! Mount St. Helens will erupt, and we'll miss it. The Forest Service has already closed the mountain above the tree line because of avalanches. By the time we go, we won't get within ten miles of it." *I might as well be in Texas*, she thought, feeling sorry for herself because nobody could go with her.

Lauren sat back down on the floor and started rummaging through her volcanology books on a low shelf.

"I seem to remember the last time Mount St. Helens was active—in the mid-eighteen-hundreds—it erupted intermittently for fifteen years or more," Chris said.

"I know. But with a Washington volcano awake, I'll never be able to sleep."

Chris laughed. "I want to go as much as you do," he said as he took his leave, "but I'm at a crucial point in my thesis."

Lauren wondered if Chris was reluctant to go with Kenny and her because he feared it would be awkward—even though, as it turned out, they couldn't go that weekend. Last spring when they had visited him in his field area, everything seemed fine. It would be so much more fun and interesting if he would go with them on a trip to Mount St. Helens. Kenny was a good sport, but he was more interested in fishing than in volcanoes.

After their guests were gone, Kenny stood up and yawned.

"Can we go to Mount St. Helens next weekend since we can't go this weekend?" she asked.

"Yeah, probably. I have to admit it's exciting."

"Yay!" Lauren clapped her hands together.

"Night, babe," Kenny said, already heading upstairs to bed.

"Night," she called after him. "I'm going to do a little reading."

She felt a vast, all-consuming excitement about Mount St. Helens. *Mother no doubt will accuse me of wanting to go to the volcano because I love danger,* she thought. Since high school when she'd straddled the back of Kenny's motorcycle, her mother had railed against her putting herself in harm's way. Perhaps her mother was right to a certain extent, but Lauren didn't think she needed danger to feel alive. In this case, curiosity about Earth's infrastructure and fire, so often imagined and now maybe visible, drove her to explore and see things.

Volcanoes were almost unknowable. Much of their mystery lay four thousand miles down at the center of the earth, forever hidden from human eyes. Lauren sprawled on the sofa and read books on Cascade volcanoes. Eruptions had happened on the site of Mount St. Helens for thousands of years. Under the relatively new cone lay an ancestral volcano. Lauren studied a chart of the past eruptions of St. Helens. Sometimes it was dormant for four thousand years. Other times it was quiet for four to five hundred years before an eruption.

Glowing avalanches, ash clouds, a mud flow that flooded the Lewis River valley for a distance of forty miles—all these were part of St. Helens' history, she read. The Cave Basalt above the Lewis River that she and Kenny planned to explore had been formed by Mount Kilauea-like lava streams that emanated from fissures on St. Helens.

Holy smoke! That's quite a repertoire, Lauren thought. Unpredictability was frustrating. Not only do we not know when, we don't know what. She continued to read until almost two in the morning.

>>

A week later Lauren and Kenny loaded their green Jeep CJ-7 prior to picking up Betty to take her with them to Mount St. Helens. It was Kenny who had suggested they include her in their weekend excursion. Lauren feared Betty would ruin the trip, but he had reminded her Sunday was Easter.

"I thought you never left your mother alone on a holiday," he had said.

"I try not to, but geez, I don't want to ride in a car with her for hours. Oh, all right. I guess we'd better."

And now they were on their way, Betty riding in the front with Kenny while Lauren shared the back seat with a big cooler. This was Betty's first ride in their Jeep.

"Where are the sides to this car? Is this window plastic?" she asked with alarm. She poked her finger onto the zipped shut plastic window, which yielded to her touch.

"Yeah, isn't it cool? The doors come off and you can unsnap the top. It turns into a convertible," Kenny said.

"But convertibles have thick metal doors!"

He pointed to the roll bar and big fenders as safety features. Betty was like a child for whom everything was new and astounding.

"I dare not go to sleep. I might fall through the plastic!" Betty braced her hands against the dashboard.

"Your seat belt is buckled. You'll be fine," Kenny reassured her.

"And the top is so thin. What if it hails?"

"We'll park under a tree."

Lauren rolled her eyes when she saw Kenny look at her in the rearview mirror. She was happy to let him interact with her mother. If she leaned back, she couldn't hear their conversation. The Jeep, with its big tires, roared down the road at fifty-five miles per hour. It felt as if they were going seventy-five or eighty. Now that she thought about it, she had never seen a Jeep pulled over for speeding. Exceeding the speed limit wasn't possible, she decided. At a high rate of speed, you would either bite your tongue off or be shaken to death.

She sighed. She might as well settle in for a long trip.

>>

As they were getting back on the road after a late lunch on the outskirts of Yakima, Lauren pointed to a bank of clouds. "If the sky clears over there, we might get to see Mount Rainier. Now that's a volcano. It's nearly twice as high as Mount St. Helens."

"Then why aren't we going to Mount Rainier?" Betty asked.

"Because Mount St. Helens is erupting, and Mount Rainier is not." Lauren vowed to be patient with her mother, even if it was hard.

They came within a few miles of the entrance to Mount Rainier National Park on US Highway 12, although they couldn't see the top of the volcano, which remained shrouded in clouds. Lauren shushed Kenny and Betty's conversation when a local radio station described Friday's activities of Mount St. Helens. Eruptions almost hourly had sent plumes upward from the crater, and seismometers had recorded six earthquakes between magnitudes of 4.0 and 4.6. The reporter added that two episodes of harmonic tremors had also been recorded.

"Wow! That's fabulous. We're almost guaranteed to see some action," Lauren said.

"I bet they won't let us near the volcano." Kenny sounded disappointed.

"We still can get pretty close. The harmonic tremors are the most exciting part of the news."

"What the heck are harmonic tremors?" Kenny asked.

"A quake is more of a distinct jolt or a series of jolts. Harmonic tremors are continuous, rhythmic ground shaking that might mean magma is moving under the volcano and the mountain is getting ready to erupt."

"Earthquakes? Eruptions? We're heading smack into harm's way!"

Betty said in a high-pitched voice as she turned to face Lauren. Her eyes showed fear.

I knew it, Lauren thought. *She's taking all the fun out of the weekend.*

"Really, Mother, think about it. Would they let all these people drive their cars into the area if it weren't safe? We'll be fine. It might not erupt for months." Even though it was difficult, Lauren used her most reasonable tone.

She noticed Mount St. Helens was clearly visible to the south. Its glacier-covered peak rose majestically above green forests. Younger and less eroded than other Cascades volcanoes, Mount St. Helens was sometimes compared to Mount Fuji for its symmetry and beauty. Lauren understood why the Japanese worshipped their sacred mountain. The mysteries of the earth lay inside.

She shook herself from her reverie in time to point out Mount St. Helens. As they passed north of it, a puff of steam rose from the newly formed crater.

"That's its welcoming toot," Lauren said with a smile, as she leaned forward between the two front seats.

"That little bit of steam? What's so great about that?" Betty asked.

Lauren sighed. *Why do I even try to make this trip pleasant?* "It's just an indication the mountain is awake," she said in a flat voice.

In Longview they found inexpensive rooms in a motel near the highway. Following dinner and a walk to get ice cream, Lauren and Kenny bade her mother good night.

>>

After going out for a beer, Lauren and Kenny sprawled on the bed in their motel room and watched the day's news on television. Washington's governor, Dixy Lee Ray, had declared a state of emergency and urged people to stay away from Mount St. Helens. The executive order restricted access to extremely dangerous areas of the mountain and its surrounds—a so-called Red Zone.

>>

After breakfast the next morning, they drove north on the interstate before turning east on State Highway 504 toward Mount St. Helens. Traffic was bumper-to-bumper.

"I guess we should have gotten an earlier start to avoid traffic," Lauren said. "Everyone's excited about seeing an active volcano."

She noticed her mother seemed more relaxed than she had been yesterday. Maybe she was reassured by all the cars driving toward Mount St. Helens. Lauren hoped the day would go better than yesterday.

In a few minutes they drove by Seaquest State Park on the left, and Silver Lake came into view on the right. The lake was large and shallow with marshy edges populated by blown cattails. Several people in motorboats trolled the lake for fish. In the distance Mount St. Helens looked fresh and clean with new-fallen snow on its glaciers. As they drove slowly by the lake, the pine forest intermittently blocked their view of the lake and mountain. Traffic ahead of them stopped. Cars were parked on both sides of the road. They decided to pull over where they had a clear view of the lake and the volcano. Kenny plunked the cooler on the hood of the Jeep and then walked down toward the lake.

I wish he hadn't left me alone with my mother! Lauren worried what they would talk about.

She climbed up on one fender and indicated the other as a place for her mother to sit. Betty balanced herself on the bumper, instead. They faced the mountain as though waiting for a drive-in movie to start. Children in Easter finery ran about. Teenagers leaned on their cars, radios blaring, and visited each other back and forth across the road. The atmosphere was more reminiscent of a rock concert than of Easter.

At least all the hoopla around us is entertaining.

She was relieved when Kenny returned from his reconnaissance mission.

"Are they catching any fish?" she asked.

"They claim they catch largemouth bass here but all they showed me was a string of little bluegills."

He reached into the cooler on top of the Jeep and retrieved a Miller Lite.

"Ladies?"

Just then a gray ash cloud burst silently from the vent on Mount St. Helens and rose several hundred feet into the air.

"Woohoo!" Lauren shouted as she jumped down from the car and did a little dance. "How cool is this."

People across the way cheered.

Betty looked at Lauren as though she were crazy. "What's so great about another cloud of steam?"

Here she goes again, Lauren thought.

"Don't you get it? It's not just steam. It's an eruption of ash." Lauren hadn't meant to sound strident.

She softened her voice when she continued her explanation. "See where gray ash has fallen on the white snow? Ash is tiny pieces of rock blown apart by steam bursting out of the crater."

"How about that!" Kenny said. "My first volcanic eruption."

"It's the first eruption for all of us." Lauren said, looking at her mother.

Betty looked bewildered, but Lauren could see in her eyes some acknowledgment that she had been brought here to share something important. Even though she couldn't express emotions, she seemed grateful to be included in the trip.

>>

On the drive back, Lauren planned to talk to Betty about Lauren's father, whom she had never known. During her childhood, she had overheard occasional whisperings between her grandparents about her father. She perceived there was something shameful about the subject.

Let's see how this conversation goes, Lauren mused. Talking to her mother had always been difficult.

"Mother, I need you to tell me about my father. I might be able to apply for a grant for school because of my Native American heritage."

"Lauren Brown, you are German not Indian."

She's repressed the fact that I ever had a father. No wonder I feel fatherless.

"You told me my father was part Cherokee."

"That doesn't make you an Indian."

"But, Mother, yes it does. Was he half Cherokee? A quarter?"

"Who?"

"My father—your husband!" Lauren said, becoming exasperated.

"Oh, dear, that was so long ago," Betty moaned. "I can't remember much from back then."

"Try to think. It's important."

Lauren was discouraged and doubted she would learn anything about her father.

"Why do you keep asking about the past?" Betty clasped her hands in front of her mouth.

"Where was my father from before he came to Kansas?"

"I don't know . . . maybe he had a sister in Missouri?"

"Do you remember her name?"

"No. I never met her," Betty said in a higher voice than normal. She squirmed back and forth in her seat. "Don't ask me any more questions!"

With a defeated sigh, Lauren sat back and covered her eyes with her hands. It was futile to try to have a rational conversation with her mother. It was also futile to want a close emotional connection with her. After years of puzzling over what was the matter with Betty, she had come to the conclusion her mother lived in a constant state of near hysteria, as though she heard shrieking violins in her head—like music from the movie *Psycho*. She couldn't process information or emotions in a normal way.

Lauren lamented not knowing her father. She would never find him. The only information she had was his name on her birth certificate: Jonathan Harold Wilson. That wasn't enough to go on. Tears welled up in her eyes. She missed her one true parent, her grandfather. When she was eleven, he had died of a massive heart attack. He was an artist who had shown her small miracles of nature. They had observed a sapling in their yard grow, split its skin, and form welts, which became bark. Every Saturday morning, he had taken her to see cartoons at their local theater. When she was older, he had taken her to science fiction movies and encouraged her interest in art and science. How could such a nice man have been married to her grandmother?

Dorothy had the sense of entitlement of an only child raised by doting, wealthy parents.

Dorothy's trust fund had given her power to manipulate her husband; her daughter, Betty; and Lauren. Her son, Lauren's uncle, had escaped his mother's control when he was drafted into the army shortly after Pearl Harbor.

Lauren's grandfather had worked in his family's modest bakery and painted landscapes and seascapes that a local gallery sold. Because his income merely supplemented Dorothy's trust fund, she had held all the power. Lauren remembered feeling sorry for her grandfather when her grandmother had painted three children's paint-by-number canvases and hung them on their walls instead of her grandfather's paintings.

Lauren had asked her grandmother, "Why did you take down Poppy's paintings?"

>>

Betty hadn't seen Dorothy's faults. In fact, she had worshipped her, and Dorothy had needed an underling to dominate. She issued so many orders to Betty that she had dithered and fumbled. When Betty made foolish mistakes, Dorothy had complained, "*It* can't do anything right." Betty hadn't been able to give Lauren unconditional love or be a real mother because pleasing her own mother had consumed her life. Betty and Lauren had been two fish darting to the surface to retrieve the same fleck of food.

>>

Her grandmother had regulated Lauren's life down to the contents of her toy box. When she arrived home from school in the afternoon, her grandmother had completed her homework for the next day. If she argued, her grandmother retaliated by telling her she had the personality of a fish. *Maybe that's the best you can do if you're trapped in a fishbowl*, Lauren thought in retrospect.

Science had saved her. It was the only academic area that hadn't interested her grandmother. When Lauren took biology, Dorothy had to bow out. The same with physics and chemistry. There was something magical about science. It couldn't be controlled by her grandmother. It was wild and adventurous, yet rational. Scientific truth came from a higher power. The search for it could take a lifetime. Often, when Lauren felt herself adrift, her passion for science anchored her. It was something to focus on outside of herself or her fractured family.

By the time they reached Spokane, Lauren's resentment of her mother had dissipated. Betty hadn't had a chance against Dorothy.

Lauren felt a profound sense of loss—for her deceased grandfather, for her unknown father, and for her mother who couldn't be a mother.

Kenny and Lauren accompanied Betty into her apartment, turned on lights, and laid her suitcase on the bed. When they were walking out the door, Lauren turned and gave her mother a hug. *Maybe I need to learn to be a daughter*, she thought.

Chapter 14

Disappointment Ridge

Lauren and Chris, Spring 1980

Lauren was overwhelmed with the lab work she needed to finish before starting another summer of fieldwork. The previous summer she had collected three hundred rocks from her research area in Oregon. So far, she had analyzed two-thirds of them. Each sample rock was keyed to a lava flow that had erupted anywhere from sixteen to twelve million years ago, or MYA as everyone abbreviated million years ago. MYA was having difficulty competing with *now* in Lauren's priorities. Mount St. Helens was erupting, and she wanted to be part of the action. Geologists from all over the world were flocking to Washington. Here she was in Washington, but on the wrong side of the state.

Just as she was making progress at school, news and pictures of yet another eruption diverted her. The mountain seemed to be communicating in smoke signals. Puffs, plumes, and billows were secret ciphers belched forth in the deep voice of the earth. What did they mean? No one knew. Something Lauren had read in the newspaper kept reverberating in her mind. David Johnston, a USGS geologist monitoring Mount St. Helens, told reporters that standing next to the volcano was like "standing next to a dynamite keg with the fuse lit. We just don't know how long the fuse is." She pictured a lit fuse running under the mountain. It made her heart beat fast.

Time was short.

>>

On April 9th the mountain erupted for three hours, and the summit dropped two hundred feet. Chris telephoned Lauren late in the afternoon.

"We missed a big one," he said.

Mount St. Helens was like a soap opera they were addicted to. One of them had to call the other every time there was a new episode. Lauren smiled at the thought.

"I know! The one I saw on Easter lasted only a couple of minutes."

"At least you've seen an eruption. I keep telling myself there's no urgency, that it will be erupting for years to come, but still, it's driving me crazy not being there."

"I'm hoping Kenny and I can scout an observation site in a week or two. Why don't you come with us?"

"You don't know how much I want to go. But I'm thinking, if I just stick to my work—I'm so close to finishing my dissertation—I can go to Mount St. Helens after I'm done and spend a couple of weeks camping. Then I'll really get a chance to see the mountain in action. Maybe mid-May."

"I'm disappointed, but you're right. Finish your dissertation."

She wished Chris could go with them. His input would have been valuable. Besides, it would have been fun to have his company when Kenny went off fishing.

>>

Two days later when the mailman delivered the atlas of Washington topographical and backcountry road maps Lauren had ordered, instead of going to school to organize lab work, she tore open the wrapping, laid the book on the kitchen table, and sat down to study Cowlitz, Skamania, and Clark Counties, which surrounded Mount

St. Helens. Her observation point needed to be away from the high-way and tourists. Since she would be driving from the east, it would make sense to find a site east of the volcano, but there was no high-way through the national forest. Too much time and too many miles would be spent driving on back roads. South of the mountain was even more inaccessible. On the north side, Mount Margaret, just north of Spirit Lake, was high enough at almost six thousand feet to be a good viewpoint but lacked protective ridges between it and the volcano.

Besides, hiking to the top of Mount Margaret carrying cameras, camping equipment, and food would be daunting. Finding a place west of Mount St. Helens seemed the only solution. Lauren's atten-tion lingered on Disappointment Ridge, northwest of the volcano and fairly high at over four thousand feet. At least three ridges lay between it and the volcano. She would explore Disappointment Ridge and other possible observation sites on her next trip.

>>

By the end of April, Lauren was frantic to get back to Mount St. Helens. The crater on the volcano was now the size of twenty-four football fields, and the north side was fractured and bulging.

But Kenny was reluctant to fight the crowds. Instead, he wanted to make the short drive to Lake Coeur d'Alene, camp on the beach, and rent a sailboat.

On a Saturday morning, they sat across from each other at the kitchen table. Lauren was pasting news articles about recent erup-tions into a scrapbook.

"Think how peaceful sailing on the lake would be," Kenny said, taking a swallow of his coffee.

"Of course, it would be peaceful. Nothing's happening there! Why would we go to Idaho when the biggest event of our lifetime is hap-pening in Washington?" Lauren looked up from her scrapbook and waved two pictures of eruptions at him. *Why didn't he realize how extraordinary an active volcano was?*

"It may be the biggest event of your lifetime, but it sure as hell isn't the biggest in mine. Not even close." Kenny crossed his arms across his chest.

"But this is what I'm studying. I may never get another chance to see an erupting volcano." She put aside her scrapbook and turned her full attention to Kenny. *Oh, please, please, please go with me,* she pleaded silently.

"I don't want to spend the whole damn weekend driving to Mount St. Helens, along with the rest of the population."

"I promise I'll go with you to Coeur d'Alene this summer when it will be warmer and way more fun, but, please, go with me this weekend. We'll explore back roads away from the crowds. You can fish."

"I can fish in Coeur d'Alene and not spend hours on the road."

"Oh, come on! We've got to get back to the volcano before the big eruption. I'll drive. You can relax."

"I suppose you're not going to let up till I give in."

"Yay! So that means we can go?"

"You've worn me down."

>>

When Kenny came home from work the following Friday afternoon, camping equipment, jackets, maps, and a cooler full of beer and food were sitting by the front door of their apartment.

"I guess you're serious about going to Mount St. Helens this weekend," he said in a droll tone, looking at the array of items.

Lauren laughed. "Did you think I'd suddenly forget? Let's get on the road! Remember, I'm driving so you can take it easy."

After two hours of driving, their AM radio station faded as it grew dark. Kenny twiddled with the dial trying to find a station without static. He finally gave up and turned it off. The intimacy and charged air of riding side-by-side in a Jeep on the way to an adventure were too much for Kenny. He leaned over and massaged Lauren's thighs.

She shrieked and laughed at the same time. "Kenny, don't! You'll make me drive off the road. This is what happens when you have too much time on your hands. You should be driving."

Next, he touched her breasts lightly with a backhanded reach. "You're right. Pull over at the next turnout. I want you to come over to the passenger side."

In a few miles she parked the car in a deserted scenic overlook and walked around to his side. "Now we have no driver," she said, slipping off her jeans.

Kenny drew Lauren onto his lap. She tried to rest her bent right leg on the driver's seat, but it was awkward.

"Hey! There's nowhere for my leg to be." She couldn't help but giggle. "Let's move the front seats forward and get in the back."

Kenny wrestled the giant red-and-white cooler out of the back and set it on the ground. They crawled into the back seat. Trying to lie in the narrow space, they were half on the seat and half on the floor. When Kenny sat up to assess the problem, he banged his head on the angled support of the roll bar. They both laughed.

"Damn! This isn't working. Let's go over to that low wall and you get on me." He laid down a sweatshirt before sitting on the wall.

"What if someone drives into the parking lot?" Lauren asked, guiltily looking over her shoulder as Kenny pulled her to him.

They hadn't made love the previous night in their king-sized bed at home, but the impediment of a cold, rock wall was of little concern at the moment.

Kenny was a good partner, Lauren thought. Especially on adventures. He was fun, sexy, and unpredictable. It felt right being back together with him.

>>

Saturday morning after a quick breakfast, they headed east on Highway 504. They wanted to avoid crowds of tourists and explore back roads. While Kenny drove, Lauren studied a map of backcountry roads and tried to guide their forays into the forest, but roads on the map were not always marked with signs, and logging roads not on the map crisscrossed the area. By afternoon they still hadn't located a place to observe Mount St. Helens. Kenny was tired of driving and wanted to fish the North Fork of the Toutle River, so they set up camp down by the river, even though Lauren pointed out that it would not be a safe site if the mountain erupted, despite being outside the Red Zone. Debris flows would race down both forks of the Toutle, devastating everything in the vicinity. They decided to take a chance that the mountain wouldn't erupt on their one night of camping. While Kenny fished, Lauren hiked along the river. Late in the afternoon he returned from upstream with a fair-sized steelhead trout that would make a delicious dinner.

"I think I've figured out how to get to Disappointment Ridge," Lauren said as Kenny cleaned the fish. "We need to get back to 504 and go east a little farther. Let's give it another go before dinner. Then we can relax."

Forty-five minutes later, they arrived at the top of a ridge with a magnificent view of Mount St. Helens as well as more distant views of Mount Rainier, Mount Hood, and Mount Adams. Steam emanated from fissures on the north side of Mount St. Helens.

"We're here," Lauren announced. "How perfect is this? Now we just need to remember which road we took."

She traced their route on the map with a marker before they headed down to their campsite by the river.

>>

"I wish you could have seen us driving around the forest," Lauren told Chris when they chatted on the phone first thing Monday morning.

"We would come to a dead end or arrive where we had been before, turn around, start forward, back up, and then veer off in another direction. You'd have thought we were in one of those herky-jerky silent movies."

"At least you had a four-wheel drive for your stunt work." Chris chuckled, picturing a Charlie Chaplin film. *Lauren can be funny*, he thought. *In addition to all her other wonderful qualities.*

"In the end, I think we found a fabulous observation point for when we all go. We came to the top of a ridge, and there was Mount St. Helens in all her glory."

"Fantastic. I'm aiming to get my work done in the next two weeks so I'll be free to go. Oh, by the way, I booked back-to-back times for us on the XRF Tuesday and Thursday nights. They were the only times I could get." The exhausting and tedious work on the XRF would be made bearable by teaming up with Lauren.

"I'm glad you got at least two nights. I'm so far behind I'll have to work every available shift. See you tomorrow night."

>>

Because Spokane University and Northern Idaho University were only thirty-three miles apart, geology and other science departments cooperated to time-share laboratory instruments. The X-ray fluorescence (XRF) machine was the last step of chemical analysis in determining the history of a rock and the flow from which it was collected, and Spokane's XRF machine was available to grad students from both universities between midnight and eight in the morning.

Whenever possible over the past year, Lauren and Chris had booked back-to-back, four-hour sessions on the XRF machine. During marathon analyzing sessions, they made time go faster by discussing new theories about Earth's volcanism and, lately, advances in knowledge likely to result from a major eruption of Mount St. Helens.

The last week before they were to leave for the volcano, Lauren and Chris worked three consecutive all-nighters in the lab. They took turns making food runs and alternated taking naps in their sleeping bags on the floor. By Friday morning, they had finished. They both went home to pack so they could leave when Kenny finished work that afternoon.

>>

Caravanning during the four-hour trip to Mount St. Helens would ensure they all arrived at the same place. Chris honked his horn three short beeps when he pulled up in front of Lauren and Kenny's apartment complex. He knew they were eager to get on the road.

They were soon underway. Chris led the way to I-90 while they followed in their Jeep. He had packed clothes, organized notes for his dissertation, and cleaned out his refrigerator in record time. His landlady had reduced his rent for the next three months so he wouldn't have to move out for the summer when he would rarely be there. He was thankful for that. After three all-nighters on the XRF, he was so exhausted he hadn't felt the exhilaration at the beginning of summers he remembered from childhood.

Strangely enough, the exacting lab work in the bleak hours of the night had turned to pure joy with Lauren as his partner. He would miss their close collaboration on the XRF. Aside from this weekend, he wouldn't see her until midsummer when they agreed to meet in Oregon in her field area so she could show him her discoveries.

Chris thought of himself as a disciplined person. How had he fallen in love with someone who was already married? Of course, when he first met her, she had been separated from Kenny. Now they were back together. Chris and Lauren's friendship was so right and so strong he could not violate its proper bounds. Maybe a few weeks of fieldwork would clear his head and help him sort his emotions. He doubted it.

After two hours on the road, Chris turned on his blinker to signal Lauren and Kenny to pull into a gas station. He needed a cup of coffee to stay awake.

>>

Sometime after midnight, Chris approached what he thought was the silhouette of Mount St. Helens in the distance. He couldn't be sure because it was so dark. With Lauren and Kenny following, he turned off Highway 504 and drove along a side road to a ridge just north of the paved road so they could sleep for what remained of the night. Despite fatigue, everyone seemed in good spirits when they got out of their cars.

"What if it erupts during the night? We'll miss the whole thing," Lauren said to Chris.

"The sun will rise all too soon. Let's get some sleep." He was so exhausted he couldn't talk volcanoes with Lauren, his favorite topic in the world.

He crawled into the backseat of his car and tossed everything but a pillow and blanket into the front. Sleeping in a car was uncomfortable enough without contending with a steering wheel.

>>

Lauren woke a few hours later, just as it was getting light. She slipped out of the Jeep. A cloud of ash and steam burst from the volcano, which was still in shadow.

"Hey, wake up, you guys!" she called to Chris and Kenny. "It's erupting!"

Kenny covered his head with a pillow, but Chris hurried out of his car and watched with Lauren as the cloud dissipated in the wind. She felt the warmth of his presence next to her. This past school year, with their universities only thirty miles apart, their friendship had grown even stronger than it had been at Tex Poly. And Kenny and Chris had become sailing buddies. Now the three of them hoped to see a major eruption together.

"Damn. So that's Mount St. Helens waking up," Chris said. "No doubt she's clearing her throat for what's to come."

"Yep. It's going to be incredible," Lauren said, yawning and stretching.

Earth's internal engine, so complex and unobservable, was displayed in plain sight when a volcano erupted. Tectonic plates moving, continents colliding, seas opening, mountains uplifting—all involved time dimensions so far beyond human existence they were nearly incomprehensible. A million years was but a second. Seeing an erupting volcano was a sought-after experience because for once the earth was in motion in a time frame also experienced by humans. The eruption of Mount St. Helens would be the culmination of six years of education for Lauren and eight years for Chris. The dream event of a lifetime was at hand.

"We're close, but we're not quite there," Lauren said as she reached into the Jeep for a page torn from her atlas of Washington maps. The sun had risen high enough to give good light. She showed Chris the road to the ridge above Disappointment Creek she and Kenny had discovered on their last trip. Lauren was pleased Chris concurred that a high ridge almost six miles from Mount St. Helens would be a safe observation point.

"And it's outside the Red Zone," she added as an afterthought.

>>

Lauren and Kenny led the way farther up Highway 504 and then turned into the forest on a heavily used logging road. They drove slowly enough that Chris was able to keep them in sight. When his Dodge Dart bottomed out a couple of times on the rutted and winding road, he shifted into low gear and got traction.

They continued to climb until they crested a ridge, and Mount St.

Helens suddenly materialized. It was as if he had come face-to-face with a sumo wrestler, or some other being with heft and presence. He parked his car and hopped out. Three other volcanoes—Mount Hood to the south, Mount Rainier to the north, and Mount Adams to the east—could be seen in the distance. All were enveloped in pure blue sky as though they inhabited a desert environment instead of the rainy northwest.

"Wow!" Chris said. "This is an amazing view."

"I know! An active volcano beckoning us. And three sleeping giants watching and waiting their turn."

Chris set out lawn chairs facing the volcano, and he and Lauren unfolded their tripods, situated them in front of their chairs, and attached their cameras. All three sat down to enjoy the show.

"Have you ever thought that a volcano looks like a big, fat mound of mashed potatoes plopped on your plate by the school cafeteria lady?" Kenny asked, turning to the others.

They laughed.

Lauren said, "Only if you include where she pressed the bottom of her scoop into the potatoes to make a caldera for gravy."

"Naturally," Kenny said.

Kenny can always be counted on for humor, Chris thought. He himself tended to be on the serious side.

"You two are real poets with your mashed potato metaphor," Chris said, smiling. "But you're right. A volcano looks like an oddity in the landscape because it doesn't come in ranges like uplifted mountains. It's supreme unto itself."

"Absolutely. Right now it looks deceptively inanimate," Lauren said, "but watch out. It houses a holocaust. Power on a planetary scale."

>>

After they'd been sitting for a while, Kenny became impatient and left for a walk. Lauren and Chris waited, but the mountain was silent. The sky stayed clear with a few wispy clouds in the west. They talked about their two field areas and what they could contribute to the Columbia River Basalts Project. Would they ever know whether the basalts erupted because of the hot spot that now underlay Yellowstone? Or were the basalts indicative of continental rift? The answers would be revealed by the chemistry of the flows, but as Chris pointed out, much fieldwork also needed to be done. They argued about which chemical elements would be keys to the puzzle.

"Speaking of fieldwork," Lauren said, "I can't wait to show you the dikes in my area when you come visit this summer. Maybe we can decipher flow boundaries our two areas have in common," Lauren said.

Meeting Lauren in her field area will be the best part of my summer, Chris thought.

"Of course. Wouldn't it be intriguing to follow flows from the dikes eastward toward Idaho and see what we can correlate? I bet no one's done that before. And who better than us?"

They both grinned.

They agreed for the third or fourth time that their viewpoint from the west of Mount St. Helens was stellar. Their cameras sat on tripods ready to capture the sequence of the first eruptive surge and the ensuing pyroclastic flows.

Chris said, shaking his head. "It's erupted as many as ninety times on other days. How can it be quiet when the sky is so blue and we are so ready?" He wondered if he had waited too long and missed his chance to see a real eruption.

"Maybe it's playing with us. It could burp and emit steam for years to come," Lauren said.

"Yeah, we'll probably bring our children and grandchildren here to see little eruptive displays." They laughed.

They both knew an active volcano posed huge uncertainties. Anything was possible, but their hopes were high despite their joking. When they could sit no longer, they decided to explore. They unscrewed their cameras from their tripods and hiked north along the ridge to where they could see down to the valley floor and Castle Lake.

The thrumming of a helicopter's rotors drew their attention to the volcano, and they ambled back to their site just in time to watch a helicopter land on the summit.

"Did I tell you Bryan called the other day to let me know that Dr. Mumper's consulting with USGS at the volcano monitoring center in Vancouver?" Chris asked.

"Maybe he's in that helicopter," Lauren said.

"Wherever there's an erupting volcano, that's where The Mumper is!"

Steam billowed from a clearly visible fracture that ran from the summit down the northwest side to the volcano's base on the north as far as they could see. Besides the fracturing, the north side was bulging so dramatically that the volcano's previous symmetry and beauty were all but ruined. That a landslide would fill the valley below seemed inevitable.

"I'll bet if Harry Truman could see the bulge from here, he might leave his place on Spirit Lake. Even a small landslide will inundate the lake and his lodge," Lauren said.

"He's a stubborn old cuss. I think it comes with age. My dad used to call it bullheadedness. Sadly, he didn't live long enough to acquire it."

They lapsed into silence. The two shared an undercurrent of sadness over the early loss of the male figures in their lives.

Chris thought, *I had my dad until I was ten. Lauren never even met her dad.*

"You know," he said, "I dream about my dad sometimes, even though he's been gone twenty-three years. When I wake up, I always have a sense he was trying to tell me something, but I can never figure out what it was. Shortly before he died, my aunt took the only home movie we have of him to record my aunt's and Dad's memories from when they first came here from Ireland. At the time of the filming, he was emaciated from cancer. For years Nancy, my younger sister, begged to watch the movie over and over again. I bet we saw it fifty times. You'd think I would dream about my dad in his frail condition, but in my dreams, he's restored to his stocky, robust self. And he's trying to tell me something."

He continued, "There has to be some sort of afterlife. Not Heaven with streets of gold and flying angels . . ."

"*Flying* angels?" Lauren interrupted. "Are there any other kind?"

Chris chuckled. "I guess that's redundant. Unless angels are modeled after ostriches rather than doves." He tried to picture an earthbound, ostrich-like angel.

Lauren smiled. "I wish there were a heaven. It might take the fear out of dying, but I can't make the leap. I also can't envision an afterlife. Would it be just for humans? What about cats, dogs, and gorillas?"

Chris turned to look at her. "Gorillas? What brought that up?"

"They are gentle souls—at least compared to our ancestors, chimpanzees. But seriously, what would an afterlife be like?"

"After Dad died, my mom always assured us he would be waiting in Heaven, along with our cat, dog, and hamsters that had died. Obviously, I don't believe in that kind of afterlife, but surely life on Earth can't be for naught. Somehow people are transformed at death. If I die first, I'll come back and tell you what I find out."

"You're on. I'll do the same if I go before you. Death is less scary if you're old and you've done everything you've wanted to do."

"I agree. But it's easy for us to say since we're young and have so much life ahead. To me there are only two acceptable ways to die: as an old man surrounded by my wife and children, or in a volcanic eruption doing research I love."

I can't believe I mentioned a wife and children, Chris thought. He never talked to anyone about his dreams for the future, especially to a married woman he was in love with. The way she cocked her head and listened intently made him blurt out his most personal thoughts and memories. Including those of his dad, who'd been on his mind lately. His dad's love of the outdoors was probably one of the reasons Chris had become a geologist. Maybe he would feel his spirit in this beautiful place.

>>

The morning waned, and the mountain remained quiet. Lauren was impatient for something to happen. She paced awhile and then decided to set up the hibachi since it was near lunchtime. Kenny returned from his hike just in time to get the fire going to cook the burger patties she and Chris were making.

The smell of cooking meat attracted a big black Labrador retriever that came bounding toward them. Not far behind was a tall young man in overalls. His luxuriant head of curly blond hair vibrated as he introduced himself as Roy Gustafson, a carpenter from Portland.

"I've been camping here off and on since Easter to take pictures of eruptions," he said.

"We're here to do exactly that." Chris said. "Lauren and I are geologists."

"You're real geologists? Cool! Do you want to see my photo albums?"

"Sure. Why don't bring your pictures and join us for burgers," Lauren said.

Bear, as the dog was known, stayed behind to monitor the meat while Roy walked the short distance back to his camper. After giving the dog several thumping pats on his head, Kenny stood up, apparently to assert his dominance over Bear by pushing his hindquarters down into a sit. When Kenny told him to lie down, Bear just sat and wagged his tail, so Kenny pulled his front feet out from under him until he was prone.

Lauren frowned. *Kenny's kinder to cats than he is to dogs*, she thought. It was annoying that he felt the need to train someone else's dog. Bear escaped Kenny's attentions as soon as he could and sought refuge between Chris's knees.

After lunch, Kenny gathered up his gear and left to go fishing, while Chris and Lauren paged through Roy's photo albums. A series of pictures taken at sunrise showed a crimson sky behind a pinkish-white eruption cloud. The beauty of the photos left Lauren awestruck and eager to get similar shots herself.

Roy peppered Chris and Lauren with questions about volcanoes. She could tell Chris was in his element teaching someone about the earth. He explained that plate tectonics was responsible for most of the world's volcanoes and earthquakes. The subduction zone located off the northwest coast—where the Juan de Fuca microplate plunged under the North American plate—had caused the formation of the Cascade volcanoes, including Mount St. Helens.

"Holy shit! This is exciting," Roy said. "Now here's something I've been wondering for a long time. When will California fall into the ocean?"

Lauren took his question seriously because every geologist is asked that question sooner or later.

A big earthquake could be imminent, she said, "but California is not going to separate from the mainland anytime soon. In a few million years, part of California will break away and head north to Alaska, and the trip will take millions of years."

"What about now? What's gonna happen here?" Roy asked, gesturing over his shoulder toward the volcano.

Lauren said, "No one knows. Volcanoes are unpredictable. Mount St. Helens is probably the most monitored volcano in history. Remote-controlled cameras are focused on the mountain at all times.

Seismometers measure earthquakes in the area. Planes routinely take thermal infrared images."

"Don't forget Dr. Mumper's tiltmeters," Chris said. "They measure tiny changes in the tilt of the ground—deformation caused by moving magma. Geologists are also sampling ash, steam, water, and rock in the crater. We saw a helicopter land on the summit earlier this morning to do sampling, no doubt. And we still don't know when or if a major eruption will occur. Maybe by studying Mount St. Helens we can learn to forecast volcanic eruptions."

Roy said, "Guess what I've got in my camper." He paused, but Lauren and Chris shrugged, apparently puzzled. "An oxygen tank. And two masks: one for me and one for Bear. In case the eruption comes too close."

At the mention of his name, Bear, who was sitting at Chris's feet, perked up his ears. Chris reached down and stroked his head. Lauren and Chris looked at each other, as though wondering why they hadn't thought to bring oxygen tanks.

"That's really forward thinking," Chris said.

Roy grinned, clearly pleased that a geologist approved of his planning.

"Disappointment Ridge is a pretty good observation site," Lauren said. "It looks like the action will be on the north side. Either that, or the eruption will go vertical. We feel safe because of the distance and the intervening ridges. But if the ash gets too thick, an oxygen tank and mask might come in handy."

The mountain remained silent. The three of them sat and watched as the slanted afternoon sunlight enhanced the visibility of fractures on the north side. Over time the summit had slumped along the main fracture, and it was obvious the whole north side was multi-fractured and unstable.

Chris said, "A landslide may well be what we see. It will happen fast, and we'll need to spring into action to get good photos."

"Absolutely," Lauren agreed.

The descending sun bathed Mount St. Helens in pink alpenglow, but the volcano stayed calm and inscrutable.

>>

After Roy and Bear headed toward their camper, Lauren was troubled by the thought that they were not as prepared as Roy for the eruption they all hoped to see. *What else besides oxygen have we overlooked?* she wondered.

"Will we really have a warning before a major eruption?" Lauren asked Chris.

"We just named everything that's being done to monitor Mount St. Helens. Surely, there will be a warning of some kind: higher levels of sulfur emissions or increased earthquake activity," Chris said. "What do you think?"

"Yeah. I agree. But even if we have a warning, we don't know what's going to happen," Lauren replied. "Worst case is always the way to think. Then you're prepared for all possibilities. In this situation, worst case would be an eruption of much greater magnitude and destruction than what the mountain has done before."

"Really? I tend to go with the last few thousand years of Mount St. Helens' history to arrive at most probable, which is how Governor Ray set the Red Zone boundaries," Chris said. "That's where we should be focusing."

"I disagree. Volcanoes are not predictable hazards. Remember what Dr. Mumper said, 'Volcanoes can kill you in a hundred ways.' We don't know every danger Mount St. Helens poses."

"For forty-five hundred years, the eruptive products have been mostly confined to the cone," Chris offered. "Any current eruption will probably affect the same five-mile radius. Statistics help us make the best guess."

"Statistics are good ballpark predictors, but real life doesn't always follow the rules. Don't forget Krakatoa, Pelée, and Tambora and the huge loss of life in those eruptions. In hindsight, clues to potential destruction were obvious, but people ignored the obvious because it didn't fit the desired scenario."

"If you truly believed this volcano were going to be as powerful as Tambora, the biggest eruption in recorded history, you sure wouldn't be sitting in a lawn chair here on Disappointment Ridge," Chris said.

Lauren laughed. "You've got a point. We're a mile outside the Red Zone, and I resent not being inside the Red Zone. If you'd advocated for worst case planning, I probably would've pushed for historical eruptions as a guide."

"It's fun to argue. Someone who finds holes in your argument or contributes observed data or new information helps you enhance and expand your theory."

Lauren and Chris let twilight wash over them. The volcano was dark. Yellow light emanated from Roy's camper across the way. When Kenny returned empty-handed from his fishing expedition, he said, "I can't believe you two can sit this long. And why *would* anyone sit this long?"

"Time goes fast when you're arguing," Lauren said with a smile.

Kenny sounded a little owl-y. Lauren didn't think he was jealous of Chris, but it was possible. Since Mount St. Helens awakened, she and Chris had talked on the phone nearly every day. And then this weekend Kenny, who wasn't as passionate about volcanoes as she and Chris, had been left to hike and fish by himself. If she thought about it, he seemed a little like the odd man out, even though she tried to include him.

"You don't look mad at each other."

Chris laughed. "Not in the slightest. It was more like volcano banter than real disputes."

>>

As it grew darker, the group realized they'd rushed to get to Mount St. Helens and were missing some necessary provisions. Chris planned to stay on Disappointment Ridge for the next week to work on his map and chemical calculations for his dissertation while he watched and waited. Then he'd drive to his field area in Idaho. He'd brought most of his thesis material with him but needed supplies for the next week. Since they'd gotten so little sleep the night before, Lauren and Kenny had rented a motel room for the night.

Chris led the way down the ridge to Silver Lake, where they stopped to talk and plan for the next day. Lauren and Kenny volunteered to pick up hot dogs for the next day.

"Let's meet on Disappointment Ridge at sunrise," Lauren said.

"Sounds like a plan," Chris said. "Wouldn't it be something if we got a picture of the initial surge with a sunrise sky?"

He rolled up the window of his Dodge and headed down Highway 504 with Lauren and Kenny following in their Jeep.

Chapter 15

Eruption

Lauren and Chris, May 18, 1980

No light penetrated the blackout curtains of the motel, but Lauren's inner clock told her it was nearing dawn. She slipped out of bed and lifted a corner of the curtain.

"Kenny, it's starting to get light."

"Hunhh?" He didn't lift his face from the pillow.

"I want to get a picture of the sun rising over the volcano. It's rare for the sky to be so clear," Lauren said, stuffing clothes into her duffel.

"Ohhhh, nooooo. It's still dark." Kenny moaned and turned onto his back.

"We've got to get on the road."

"Rushing like hell to sit around all day is stupid. Maybe I'll drop you at your site and drive down to a spot on the river where I saw fishermen catching trout yesterday."

"Sure. That could work. But let's go. I bet Chris is already up there."

"Steelhead trout—now that's something to get excited about. Twenty or thirty pounds of magnificent, fighting fish."

"Yes, they're fabulous fish, but please get up!"

Kenny rolled out of bed and pulled on jeans and sweatshirt. Before leaving the motel room, he checked all the drawers and under the bed for forgotten items while Lauren, her duffel slung over her shoulder, stood propping open the door and all but tapping her foot.

With their cooler and duffels loaded, Kenny started their Jeep and drove down the road to Highway 504. Now if only Mt. St. Helens would cooperate.

Lauren watched for the dirt road to Disappointment Ridge around every twist and turn of 504. She was excited beyond belief at the prospect of seeing a major eruption. Yesterday when Roy Gustafson showed them pictures of eruptions he had taken since March, she and Chris had practically drooled. On her first trip there, she had captured only a few images of an eruption, which was trivial on the scale of eruptions. And Chris had nothing. This was his first trip to Mount St. Helens since it had awakened. Maybe today.

When Lauren and Kenny reached the turn off, Kenny pulled the Jeep onto the shoulder and made a U-turn.

"We're going back for breakfast," he said.

Lauren faced him. "What? What are you doing? We're already late!" She felt like screaming from frustration. They were so close! Twenty more minutes and they would have been at their site.

"I know, but I'm starved. Cheese and crackers for dinner last night didn't cut it."

"We've got food in the cooler. I'll find you something."

"I want a hot breakfast! And I'm not being unreasonable—after all the hours I've spent driving back and forth to Mount St. Helens."

Kenny sounded adamant. It would be impossible to talk him out of breakfast.

They stopped at a small country café where Lauren worried aloud about being late while her husband, who rarely ate breakfast, ordered the "lumberjack special" with bacon, eggs, sausage, hash browns, and pancakes.

"Don't you feel bad Chris is up there waiting for us?"

"We're not going to be *that* late."

"Just think of the great pictures he's getting," she said, trying to needle him into hurrying.

Finally, they were back on the road. Lauren leaned against the plastic window on her side, putting as much distance between herself and Kenny as possible. She was annoyed. Could he be any slower? Of course, he had to order the sausage that took longer, delaying them even further.

By the time they reached the turnoff to Disappointment Ridge for the second time, it was 8:32—almost two hours after sunrise. A massive cloud of gases and ash burst from the north side of Mount St. Helens.

"Damn! The mountain's erupting and we're still twenty minutes from our site!" Lauren said as she grabbed two cameras from her backpack.

Kenny stopped the Jeep on the shoulder, and Lauren jumped out. Two men in a blue pickup pulled over at the same time and also started taking pictures.

"Wow! This is incredible. Are we lucky or what?" said one of the men.

"Yeah," agreed Kenny. "This is great! Maybe we could get closer."

"It's exploding laterally," Lauren said almost to herself.

Within sixty seconds, the pyroclastic surge consumed the entire Toutle River Valley immediately in front of them. With a shock Lauren realized it wasn't the expected eruption. It was the worst case! It was Bezymianny in Russia. Or Pelée on Martinique—thirty thousand people dead in minutes. This was a disaster! Their chances of surviving were slim.

"We've got to get out now or we'll die!" she screamed at Kenny.

Lauren yelled at the men standing by the blue pickup. "Go back! I'm a geologist. You've got to leave now or you'll be killed!"

Lauren and Kenny jumped into their Jeep. Kenny turned it around and raced back down 504 behind the pickup and other cars escaping. The mountain had lost a massive amount of its north side, and magmatic gases were boiling and billowing over the countryside, heading straight down the North Fork of the Toutle River toward them.

"Go faster! It's coming right at us!" Lauren closed her window and the Jeep's air vents. "That cloud's filled with toxic gases and ash. And no oxygen. It'll sandblast us like a tornado!"

I don't want to die, I don't want to die, raced through her mind incessantly. How had she not seen the danger?

She scrambled into the backseat and then into the far back to see how close the cloud was to them.

"The cloud's gaining on us. Oh my God! And it's filled with lightning! Speed up!"

She snapped pictures as fast as she could, switching back and forth between her cameras, one with a wide-angle and the other with a telephoto lens. So massive was the cloud she couldn't get more than a fraction of it in a frame.

She worried about Chris. Was he already at Disappointment Ridge when the mountain blew? Where was he now? *Please let him be okay,* she prayed and sobbed. She hadn't realized she was crying. She should've told her mother they were coming here. She wouldn't even know they were missing!

"Oh, God! We're losing ground!" she turned and shouted at Kenny.

The silent black cloud bore down on them. The lightning advanced.

They careened around curves on two wheels. Two sedans raced up the road toward the volcano as fast as Kenny was driving down. He flashed his lights and blasted his horn. The cars sped on.

"They're driving right to their death!" Lauren shouted to Kenny.

Another mile down the road, he screeched to a halt to avoid hitting a camper, flinging Lauren against the cooler. From her awkward position, she caught a glimpse of terror on the face of the woman in the passenger seat of the camper as it turned around to join the escape. Kenny pulled the Jeep beside the camper and accelerated around it.

The black specter engulfed the forest as if the trees were part of a miniature stage set. Then it snuffed out daylight around them.

"Why is it dark? What's happening?" Kenny yelled.

"Hurry! Help! It's on us!"

Lauren was now certain they would die. The entire meaning of her life centered on her cameras as she took picture after picture, having changed the film with shaking hands. She wondered why there was no sound. Would flashes of lightning show in her pictures? The black-and-gray cloud looked like smoke, but she knew it was far different. If it reached them, they would be blown apart. In the end, she thought, people would find her cameras. Her photographs would be her only legacy to science.

>>

At dawn Chris parked his Dodge in the same place on Disappointment Ridge as he had parked the day before. He delayed turning off the engine to hear the end of Christopher Cross's song "Ride Like the Wind."

Although the song was probably about a biker escaping to Mexico, it reminded Chris of how much he liked riding the wind in an airplane. The perspective from the air was invaluable to a geologist. Things too big to comprehend on the ground organized themselves into recognizable features from above. Once he finished his PhD and was making decent money, he planned to take flying lessons. Everybody assumed he was already a pilot because he had been a captain in the air force, but his job had been mapping. He turned off the ignition and stepped out of his car.

Sleeping in the back seat made him appreciate morning, even early morning. He stretched and paced a bit before he set up his tripod and bolted his camera to it. Sunrise wasn't spectacular because there weren't enough clouds. Also, it was a little hazy, but he might as well be ready for any puffs or snorts from the mountain. Mount St. Helens looked perfectly tranquil at the moment, just like yesterday. He set up three lawn chairs and sat down in one.

Music put Chris in a philosophical mood. These past summers of traversing and mapping the Columbia River basalts in his research area had given him great satisfaction, even joy. Luckily, geology was a discipline where he could go into the field, touch the rocks, and work directly with the land and morphology. When a geologist relied on grab-bag samples and spent most of his time in labs, or worse, in geodynamic seminars pontificating on the work of others, as his nemesis Don did, he lost the skills and pleasure of solving problems in the field with real strata and structure.

Earth's beauty was exceeded only by its complexity. Eons of violent movements like earthquakes and eruptions, as well as slow rearrangements like flows and upthrusts, had created a planet of many mysteries, a spherical Rubik's Cube over which geologists could puzzle. Volcanoes were portals to the mystery.

His adventures so far had aroused an insatiable curiosity in him. He sometimes felt as though he were following a thin string through room after room of an unseen house, trying from the inside to describe the exterior. Last summer when he had seen signs of an unnamed, unmapped volcano in his area, he had persisted until he found its source. A Sherlock Holmes moment.

What other profession besides geology attempted to know the unknowable? To look millions of years into the past? Well, maybe astrophysicists had it even tougher, he conceded. They looked up instead of down and never touched a moon or star. When a meteorite finally hit the earth, who were there gathering, sampling and claiming it for science? The damned geologists. He chuckled. Anyway, geology and astrophysics both studied the same grand processes.

Now that his major fieldwork was all but completed, he would spend time on campus writing his dissertation. The last batch of chemical analyses should be ready for him when he returned to Coeur d'Alene. His goal was to build a masterpiece, a true piece of art. Everyone needed to erect a monument, to make a contribution to better humankind. Most people were satisfied with producing off-spring and passing the torch to them. Somehow that wasn't enough. His dissertation would be the start of the monument he planned to build.

He had science fiction stories to write, sociology studies to complete, students to teach, and geologic questions to answer. If he wanted to be a true Renaissance man, he had much to learn. Someone born five hundred years ago was a strange role model for a twentieth-century man, but Chris couldn't think of anyone he admired more than Leonardo da Vinci. He hadn't restricted himself to one discipline. He had mastered and understood many areas of nature. Only by crossing into other disciplines could true discoveries be made. While working as a civil engineer, da Vinci had observed rock strata and become convinced Earth had formed over many years. The presence of shells and other fossils high in the mountains could only be explained if the mountains had been heaved out of the sea. In short, da Vinci had conceived of geologic time hundreds of years before it was accepted as scientific fact. Da Vinci still didn't get the credit he deserved for being a brilliant scientist.

Even though Chris was moving on, he never wanted to lose touch with fieldwork. He remembered the young scientists with whom he had gone through orientation on the Basalts Project. They were excited by their profession and interested in making their mark. Geologists who limited or diluted the concepts of excellence in favor of job security were pigeonholed as "Planners and Schedulers."

Over beers one night, fellow field researcher Jeff Rutherford had said, "Goddammit, Chris, there's nothing worse than a manager. They don't understand geology. They don't understand fieldwork. All they understand are papers and memos and meetings."

Chris was determined not to turn into a Planner and Scheduler or, for that matter, a manager, with a matched set of In and Out boxes. He wondered where Lauren and Kenny were.

It wasn't like Lauren to be late. She was as passionate about geology and volcanology as he was. How irresistible was a woman who
loved the earth, mountains, and men? Then if she happened to have
long dark hair, green eyes, and a beautiful face, it was enough to drive
a man mad. He groaned. Here he was occupying the third chair as
usual.

He felt closer to Lauren than to anyone else in the world. The two
of them had never had a short conversation. They spent hours theo-
rizing about the creation of the universe, the inevitable burnout of
the earth, and all the wonders in between. After one lengthy long-dis-
tance call, he had speculated they were a couple of reincarnated old
ladies who had spent their previous lives talking over the back fence.

At least Lauren seemed happier now. Her work in the field had
built confidence in herself as a scientist. Just being in her presence
was a rich experience. A scientist with a wide-ranging mind and an
artistic sensibility was a rarity. And she loved science fiction novels
and movies as much as he did. Her undergraduate degree in art
explained her ability to visualize what was unfathomable to many
geology students. It was a travesty that Lauren sometimes let herself
be held captive by people of lesser ability. Luckily, she had escaped
the clutches of Don, who used everyone for his selfish purposes.
Chris couldn't help feeling jealous of Kenny—even though he had to
admit Kenny was a pretty good guy.

The emotional closeness he felt with Lauren made it excruciating
not to express it physically. He thought she sometimes felt the same.
When they brushed shoulders in the lab. When their eyes met. They
both seemed to know their relationship was too precious to spoil
with an affair while she was married—and so recently reunited with
her husband. His and Lauren's relationship would either be the finest
friendship on record or—if she were ever free—the grand passion of
their lives. He sighed.

He felt a slight tremor in the earth. The air seemed to vibrate, changing the pressure in his ears. The bulging north face of Mount St. Helens collapsed. He ran to his camera and started snapping pictures of the avalanche. An enormous black cloud of gases and ash blasted laterally to the east and west. This was it! The eruption volcanologists dreamed of witnessing. Lauren would be disappointed she missed it.

The cloud was not the type to make a beautiful sunrise. It reminded Chris of smut, a fungus that transformed an ear of corn into masses of dark, ugly spores. Fire and brimstone from the nether world seemed to tumble into Earth's atmosphere. Lightning flashed. Within seconds he felt a cold rush of shit to his heart. He was in mortal danger! The mass would reach him momentarily. After unscrewing his camera from the tripod, he ran to his car, jumped in, and jammed his camera under the front seat. He found a blanket in the back seat and wrapped it around himself.

Why is the eruption so silent? Where is Lauren? Oh, God, let her be safe!

A short distance away the roiling cloud engulfed Roy Gustafson's camper, which rocked with an explosion that blew out the side of the camper. *Oh, no! How can this be happening? Roy can't have survived!* A black shape staggered through the ash in Chris's direction. It was Bear, Roy's dog. Chris got out of his car and tried to run toward the dog against a blast of gray, searing wind. His skin was on fire. His lungs burned. He coughed and spat out mucous and ash. When Chris reached Bear, the dog struggled past him.

Chris turned his back to the stone wind and stumbled after Bear.

>>

About five miles from where they started their run, Kenny and Lauren began to gain distance on the black cloud. "I think we've outrun it!" Lauren said.

Kenny looked over his shoulder. "Thank God!" He slowed the Jeep to a less dangerous speed.

"It's erupting vertically now. But we've got to keep moving. Melting glaciers will cause mudflows down both forks of the Toutle. We need to get to the other side of the North Fork! And we've got to find Chris. Either he's up on the ridge, or he might have escaped another way."

Cars slowed and traffic backed up on 504 as they approached Silver Lake. People lined the railings of both sides of the bridge to watch the eruption as Lauren and Kenny crossed the North Fork into a parking lot filled with cars, campers, and clusters of tourists. They spotted some firemen and raced to them.

"Help! You've got to get our friend out. He's on a ridge above Disappointment Creek." Lauren unfolded her worn map with shaking hands and showed them exactly where Chris was located at their observation site.

"He was supposed to be there at dawn. We got halfway there and then it erupted. We think he got caught by the eruption," Kenny said.

One of the firemen used his walkie-talkie to report Chris's position to his field commander.

Another fireman turned to Lauren, "How long have you been racing for your lives?"

She looked at him completely bewildered. She could not answer. It felt like a lifetime had transpired, even though it might have been only fifteen minutes. She understood with her whole being the meaning of relativity. "I-I don't know. Just hurry and find Chris!"

"Chris must have escaped by a different route," Kenny said to Lauren after the fireman walked away.

"Yes, either that or he's trapped on the mountain because mud flows have choked off the roads."

"I bet they can get a chopper up there—now that it's going vertical."

"I feel so helpless," said Lauren, pacing but glancing frequently at the plume.

"Hey, look, someone's selling T-shirts in the parking lot," Kenny said, pointing to a young man standing at the back of his pickup with piles of T-shirts. "Can you believe it?"

Kenny sounded almost cheerful. *Maybe he's trying to distract me from worrying about Chris*, Lauren thought.

A young man in shorts held up a white shirt with simulated burn holes. It read, "I Survived Mount St. Helens."

"That's pretty clever," Kenny said.

"I bet they've had those printed since the first eruption in March. I should buy one to give Chris when they bring him out."

"Oh, for Chrissake, let him get his own shirt."

"Or, when we're reunited, all three of us can go buy T-shirts together," she said.

"Maybe. A souvenir of an incredible day."

>>

An hour passed. The gases and ash from Mount St. Helens now soared vertically through Earth's atmosphere. Lauren experienced the strangest mixture of fear, wonder, disbelief, and anxiety. A helicopter landed. Kenny and Lauren rushed over to watch as three survivors were brought out. A man who looked from a distance like Chris climbed out last.

"It's Chris! I think it's Chris!" Lauren ran toward the helicopter.

The man was in his early twenties and significantly taller than six feet. Even covered with ash, he didn't resemble Chris. Lauren cried from frustration and fear.

"How long will this continue?" Kenny asked, nodding in the direction of the erupting mountain. "Do you think the ash could move this way?" He looked worried.

"I don't know. Pyroclastic flows must be crashing down on all sides."

"Maybe we should move to another location," Kenny said.

"No. We can't leave until they find Chris." *It would feel like we were abandoning him.*

The eruptive plume was now so high they couldn't see the top. Haze from the melting glaciers filled the Toutle Valley. Lightning continued silently. Lauren felt as though they were watching a silent movie. Where was the sound? Why weren't they being burned by the hellish surge? The wind seemed to be blowing the ash away from them. They were in the eye of a hurricane. A wall of death and destruction surrounded them, but somehow, they were protected.

Ash-covered helicopters continued to land intermittently. Lauren and Kenny hurried over to see if Chris was one of the survivors, but each time they were disappointed. Lauren grew increasingly anguished. When all survivors had climbed down from one helicopter and Chris wasn't among them, she sobbed.

The pilot walked over to her. "I saw a Weyerhaeuser chopper dropping off survivors at Toutle High School not too long ago. Whoever you're looking for, you might check there."

"Oh, thank you!" Lauren said, brushing her tears away.

Still, Lauren was reluctant to leave since she thought Silver Lake was the most likely place they would bring Chris. But what if he was at Toutle High School?

>>

In the afternoon mudflows with timber and other wreckage started crashing down both forks of the Toutle River. A truckload of National Guardsmen arrived at the lake and called through loudspeakers: "Mudflows are surrounding the lake . . . you must leave now! Extreme danger! Form lines and leave!"

Lauren and Kenny jumped into their Jeep and inched into the line of cars in the parking lot leading to Highway 504. No one knew what was happening. Would they be trapped in mudflows? Was the eruption getting bigger? Was the ash changing directions? One driver bolted out of the line and drove into the ditch to get onto the two-lane road, where motorists were driving west in both lanes. Other terror-stricken people followed his example. Drivers yelled at each other. A woman abandoned her car in the middle of the road and took off running between the two lanes of traffic. Kenny drove into the ditch to get around her car.

"She's faster than the traffic!" Lauren said, wondering if they should do the same.

When they finally reached Interstate 5, cars were moving only a few feet at a time onto the ramp for southbound lanes. A National Guard truck pulled across northbound lanes and announced by loudspeaker that north I-5 was closed because of a damaged bridge over the Toutle River. Panicked motorists drove in ditches or forced cars already on the road to move onto the median strip. A man in a car in front of Lauren and Kenny drove down the shoulder onto the median and hit a rock. His car burst into flames.

Kenny slammed on the brakes.

"Oh, my God!" Lauren said, bracing against the dashboard.

Cars drove in every direction to get away from the fiery wrecked car. The man in the car opened his door, rolled out, and stood up. People yelled at him to move away from his car before it exploded.

"We've gotta get out of here," Kenny said, extricating their Jeep from southbound traffic by crossing under the interstate to a local road, where fleeing cars were also bumper-to-bumper.

Lauren nodded her agreement. "Let's not die in a car wreck after surviving the eruption!"

East of Castle Rock they pulled over on the bank of the Cowlitz River and watched the massive eruptive plume. Steelhead trout jumped out of the river to avoid being boiled or suffocated in the mud that had now reached forty miles downstream from the volcano. Lauren felt pity for the hapless fish, doomed to die in air or mud.

After a few minutes, Lauren said, "We can't stay here. We have to find a telephone so we can call Toutle High School to see if Chris is there. If he's not there, we need to report him missing to agencies besides the fire department."

"Yeah, and we need to call our families and tell them we're alive."

"I didn't tell my mother we were going to the volcano because she always freaks out about the danger." *And this time she was right,* Lauren thought.

>>

When they finally reached the town of Longview, they were lucky to find an inexpensive motel room. Soon every motel and hotel would be filled with tourists, scientists, and rescue workers. Lauren called her mother immediately.

"Where have you been?" Betty asked. "I've been calling and calling your apartment."

She must have guessed they were at Mount St. Helens and was concerned about them.

"Don't worry, as soon as we saw the mountain erupt, we drove away from it as fast as we could and made it to safety. We're alive!"

"I don't care about that. The pipes under my kitchen sink are stopped up and no one has come to help me."

Lauren was speechless for a few seconds. She felt dizzy and disoriented. *How can I not be hurt by what my mother says?*

"Your pipes! Don't you realize the volcano blew up and I was almost killed?"

"My sink almost overflowed, and then it got dark here. Why isn't anyone worried about me or my sink?"

"Turn on your TV, Mother," Lauren said, hanging up the phone. "She's oblivious. Totally unable to relate to what we've been through. I should have known better."

Kenny called his mother, who was relieved to hear from him.

Lauren lamented not having had a normal family. It lasted a lifetime.

>>

After repeatedly dialing Toutle High School's number to learn if Chris was there, Lauren cried in frustration when a recorded message advised that evacuees had been moved to a safer, unnamed location.

She called the Cowlitz Sheriff's Department next, and when a deputy sheriff came on the line, Lauren reported Chris missing and his location on Disappointment Ridge. The deputy checked Chris's name against a list of a handful of people rescued. Since he didn't find a match, he added his name to the list of missing people and told Lauren to keep checking back as the list was updated moment to moment.

Among calls to Red Cross shelters and the National Guard, Lauren repeatedly dialed the sheriff's office, sometimes getting a busy signal and other times talking to someone. She couldn't find out either if Chris had been rescued or if he was confirmed dead.

Where was he? Too much time had gone by. Lauren paced and fretted in the small motel room. If she weren't so worried about Chris, she would have been demoralized by her mother's reaction to the news that she and Kenny were alive. No wonder she felt unloved and unworthy of love: she had a mother who valued unclogged pipes more than her daughter.

But she couldn't waste her energy on her mother right now. There were more important things to worry about.

Where are you, Chris?

>>

They watched hours of interviews, replays of the avalanche, and live coverage of the continuing eruption on TV that evening. Lauren felt sure that if they just concentrated, they would see news of Chris's rescue. While Kenny was changing channels, she caught a glimpse of film of a blue car near which someone had been found dead.

"Stop!" she shrieked. "That wasn't Chris's car, was it?"

Please let it not be his car, she prayed.

The picture was already off the screen.

"It looked like an American car, but I couldn't tell if it was a Dodge," Kenny said.

Lauren gasped. Pressure on her chest seemed to prevent intake of air. When she could breathe again, she turned to Kenny, who looked grim.

"They didn't say where the car was," she said.

"No. It could have been anywhere."

Lauren felt slightly better when she thought of the thousands of people and cars that had flocked to Mount St. Helens since it awakened.

"We have to track down film of that car. I'm sure they can blow it up so we can read the license plate. She picked up *TV Guide* and located the channel they had been watching. "It's a Portland station—KOIN."

"We should drive there first thing tomorrow," Kenny said.

"I agree, even though I'm sure it wasn't Chris's car. Not quite the right color. We just need to rule it out."

When they finally went to bed, extreme exhaustion made Lauren nearly ill. She felt like a diver who had dived too deep. Flying high on excitement and then plummeting to the depths of terror was almost more than a mortal could bear.

Chapter 16

Search

Lauren, May 19–25, 1980

The next morning, Monday, Lauren disentangled herself from twisted sheets and nightgown and sat on the side of the bed. Her pillow, its case half off, lay on the floor. She felt heartsick. Chris was missing. How could she find him in the devastation and pandemonium surrounding Mount St. Helens? Taking deep breaths, she tamped down the panic that threatened to overwhelm her.

She glanced at the other side of the bed. Kenny was gone. No doubt he had walked out to get a newspaper, but she felt abandoned.

>>

The door to their room slammed while she was showering. Toweling her hair, she hurried out of the bathroom. "Thank heavens, you're back. Any news?" She felt like crying with relief at seeing Kenny. *I'm an emotional wreck*, she realized.

"Nope. It's dismal out there. I think the mountain's still erupting. Some places are closed, but I found a restaurant open a few blocks away. Do you want to go eat?"

"I'm too stressed to sit in a restaurant. We've got to find out if the car we saw on TV last night was Chris's car. Going to Portland is the only way we're going to know."

"Yeah, I get that, but can we grab some fast food along the way?" Kenny asked.

"Sure, but let's get on the road!"

A thin layer of ash covered the interstate. It was as if an ice storm had slicked the roads. Cars either crept along or drove too fast for the conditions. Ahead of them a black sedan skidded across two lanes of the highway.

"Watch out!" Lauren said.

Kenny maneuvered the Jeep onto the shoulder to avoid a collision with the sedan.

"That was close," Kenny said. "No one knows how to drive in ash."

A few cars ended up in the ditch. One car slid in a half circle and faced the wrong way on the other side of the highway.

Lauren was relieved when they made it to their destination without further incident. The hectic scene inside the KOIN station mirrored the chaos on the highway. She felt panicky. How were they going to track down a film clip amid such commotion? The receptionist's desk was abandoned. A woman briefed a group of people gathered around her.

A man, hoisting a heavy camera to his shoulder, turned to talk to a high school boy trailing behind him, and almost ran into Lauren and Kenny. When they explained the urgency of their quest, he directed them to the editing room. A young woman was sympathetic but didn't remember seeing film of a blue car. They polled several reporters, one of whom remembered the clip, but he couldn't locate it.

Lauren was unbearably frustrated. It seemed they were on the verge of locating the film but then it would disappear into some twilight zone for lost things. *The film is here,* Lauren kept telling herself. *Someone knows where it is.*

"Please, we need to know if our friend is alive or dead," Lauren pleaded as they told their story over and over to managers, photographers, news anchors, and secretaries. But no one could find the film.

Disheartened, they sat in the lobby to make a plan. Copies of *The Oregonian* and *The Seattle Times* were scattered over chairs and coffee tables.

"Maybe they've published a list of survivors," Lauren said as she sorted sections of *The Oregonian*. "This article says helicopter crews have rescued fifty people from along the Toutle River. Chris could have made his way down to the river if roads were blocked and he had to abandon his car. We need to find where they took the survivors."

Lauren's spirits lifted as her thoughts shifted from finding the film clip to finding survivors.

"Was Cascade Middle School in Kelso one of the evacuation centers you called yesterday?" Kenny asked as he skimmed through *The Times*.

"No. That doesn't sound familiar. What about it?"

"There's a story about a logger who was rescued by a military chopper yesterday and they let him bring his two pet boa constrictors on board. But the interesting thing is, two hundred and fifty people are at the shelter. That's a lot of survivors."

"This is hopeful! Surely, Chris is one of the fifty or two hundred fifty. He wouldn't know how to contact us to tell us he's okay. I'll bet he's as worried about us as we are about him. He doesn't know my mother's last name, so he couldn't get her phone number in Spokane. Did they pick up the logger anywhere near Disappointment Ridge?"

"It just says they rescued him from the Toutle River Valley, and he worked at Camp Baker."

Lauren and Kenny left the TV station after extracting a promise from a film editor to call their motel if she found the tape of the blue car.

>>

The interstate was just as bad as earlier, but with more cars.

When they reached the evacuation center, they hurried through the front door of the school where a Red Cross volunteer greeted them.

"Please, help us. Our friend is missing. Can we find out if he's here?"

"He was most likely brought in by helicopter," Kenny said.

"We have a registry of the people who stayed here last night. I can check for you, but it's not alphabetical so it will take some time."

While the woman reviewed the handwritten names in a lined theme book, Lauren and Kenny looked around the school. People milled about. Children ran up and down the hallways. Lauren and Kenny studied the face of every man they encountered, but they didn't see Chris.

After the frustrating experience at the television station, it was energizing to see children playing and adults talking animatedly. *Now if only Kenny and I could be reunited with Chris*, Lauren thought.

"As far as I can tell, there is no Christopher Connor on our registry," the volunteer finally told them. "And I wasn't here yesterday, but I'm pretty sure most people arrived by car, not helicopter. Nearly everyone is from Toutle or Castle Rock. People were evacuated because of flooding."

Another fruitless stop, Lauren thought.

They left a note for Chris with the name and telephone number of their motel, and then drove to a second Red Cross center in Longview, where they left another note when told Chris wasn't on their registry, either.

"We've got to get help from professionals," Lauren told Kenny.

From there they stopped at the Cowlitz County Sheriff's office where they learned Chris's name was on the Missing list but not on the Confirmed Missing list. A clerk explained that hundreds of people had been reported missing by relatives and friends who failed to reach them by telephone because of downed lines and busy circuits. "The vast majority of these people are not missing at all."

"But Chris *is* missing!" Lauren said. *What kind of idiot office keeps a Missing List and a Confirmed Missing List?* She looked down while she gathered her thoughts and tried to calm herself.

"He's a geologist who was on Disappointment Ridge, six miles west of the volcano, when it erupted. He wasn't sitting at home with a telephone that didn't work. You've got to help us find him! We told this to a deputy yesterday."

"I can move his name to the Confirmed Missing List if that will help," the clerk said.

"That's all you can do?" Lauren was furious. "Someone's got to fly to Disappointment Ridge in a helicopter to see if he's trapped there!"

"This office is not coordinating helicopter rescues. I think you need to contact the Washington National Guard."

They went straight to the National Guard Armory, where they were told Disappointment Ridge was an area where they were actively looking for survivors. With that vague reassurance, they spent the rest of the afternoon checking hospitals and evacuation centers, where helpful people suggested additional avenues for searching for Chris. Continually sent from one place to another, Lauren felt like a pinball kept in motion by a mysterious player pushing the flipper buttons. Sometimes they were refused help because they weren't Chris's family.

She tried to keep her emotions under control so she could function effectively, but being thwarted caused her to feel outrage, followed by disappointment so deep she could hardly go on. Then she heard of another center where survivors had been taken, and her hopes rose again.

>>

After dinner at a restaurant near their motel, they bought two local newspapers— Longview's *The Daily News* and Vancouver's *The Columbian*—and settled in front of the television to read papers and watch news of the eruption, survivors, missing people, and problems caused by ash deposits.

"This is unbelievable! Canadians two hundred miles away heard the blast we couldn't hear a few miles from the volcano," Kenny said. "A loud boom would have made the danger more real. It might have saved lives."

"True. It was eerily silent. It says here David Johnston from US Geological Survey is missing. He was northwest of the volcano. Oh, that is sad. And Harry Truman is missing and presumed dead. His lodge is gone, and the area is covered in deep mud and debris. Remember, he's the guy who wouldn't leave his place on Spirit Lake?"

"Yeah, vaguely."

"He thought he knew the mountain. Someone who's experienced the earth one way for a whole lifetime can't believe that it won't always be that way. A human lifespan is but a moment in time. Worse, we geologists who should've known better assumed Mount St. Helens would act as it had for the last four thousand years. Now look at the disaster." Lauren wiped a tear from her check.

"Babe, you act like you caused it," Kenny said, shaking his head. "Nobody could have predicted the power of the eruption."

Kenny's reassurances made Lauren feel better, though she kept crying.

"But I chose Disappointment Ridge, and it wasn't safe," she sobbed.

"You didn't know. No one knew."

Kenny linked arms with Lauren as they sat slumped against the side of the bed. Leaning against him had a calming effect on her as they watched nonstop coverage of the eruption. She dozed intermittently before finally going to bed at three in the morning. Images of lightning-filled clouds, downed trees, washed-out bridges, and mud-boiled fish followed her there.

>>

Tuesday morning Lauren and Kenny bought every newspaper they could find in Longview. Chris had to be found. Lauren organized notes from their prior days' searches while Kenny scanned articles for names of agencies participating in rescues. The number of people killed in the eruption fluctuated from newspaper to newspaper and from radio station to television station. There was general agreement the death toll would climb dramatically when all bodies were recovered. Search efforts were focused on finding survivors.

"There are forty agencies reporting to the Washington Emergency Operations Center," Kenny said, after reading an article in *The Oregonian.* "Why are we just finding out now? State Patrol, National Guard, FAA, and other search and rescue entities supposedly communicate with the center. This article says aircraft stand ready to get survivors out."

Now we find out, Lauren thought, *after running around in circles yesterday.* With so many agencies reporting to one place, it was their best hope for information about Chris. "We need to call to make sure they have Chris's location. Does it give the phone number?"

"Nope. And it sounds like they don't want the public calling."

"We've got specific information about someone who's missing. They have to talk to us. They could send a helicopter to Disappointment Ridge! It also doesn't say where the center is, but I bet we can find out if we go back to one of the places we stopped at yesterday."

Kenny groaned. "We're both beat, but I guess we'd better get on the road."

>>

They returned to the Cowlitz Sheriff's office to verify Chris's location had been reported to the Emergency Operations Center. A clerk reassured them that every name on the Confirmed Missing List had been given to the center.

"Do you know who made the call?" Lauren asked. "I want to make sure they gave the exact location where to look for Chris."

"Somebody signed off on it. I can't read the initials, but it's definitely been taken care of."

I don't trust these people, she thought.

"I think I'd better call the center myself. Could you give me the number?"

"We're not supposed to give it to the public. . ."

The clerk must have seen the distress on Lauren's face. She relented and wrote the number on a piece of paper and slipped it to her.

Finally, someone willing to help. Getting the phone number felt like a huge victory to Lauren.

They drove right back to their motel, where Lauren called the number the clerk had given her. Her heart beat fast while she waited on hold, fearful of hearing heartbreaking news. But the Emergency Operations Center wouldn't budge from their strict protocol for releasing names of casualties and survivors. Lauren didn't qualify to receive information about Chris even though she and Kenny had been traveling with him at the time of the eruption and were the last to see him.

Knowing they might know something about Chris made her crazy.

She reported Chris's location, and they assured her every missing person would be sought relentlessly. And no, she should not drive to Lacey, Washington, where the center was located. She would not be permitted entry to the premises.

"Shit! Shit! Shit!" Lauren slammed down the receiver. "We'll never find him."

>>

Light rain fell on Wednesday. A plume of ash and steam continued to rise from the crater on Mount St. Helens. First thing in the morning,

Lauren and Kenny drove to the Kelso–Longview Airport in hopes of talking to search and rescue pilots in person.

None of the pilots remembered rescuing Chris, though they all promised to search for him on Disappointment Ridge. Back in their Jeep, Lauren and Kenny felt both better and worse. Rescue teams were looking for Chris, they had been assured. They also believed they would be the last to know when he was found.

They visited every evacuation center, hospital, and agency they had already contacted at least twice before heading back to their motel. They sprawled on the bed and pored through the newspapers they'd bought.

"Oh, no! An article in *The Times* lists a Robert Connor as missing but no Chris or Christopher," Kenny said.

"What? How can that be!" Lauren jumped up and paced the room. "It's beyond outrageous they got Chris's name wrong after the dozens of times we've reported him missing!"

She didn't know where to direct her anger. At incompetence. At everyone who wouldn't give her information. At the mountain for erupting. She felt like screaming.

"Even worse news," Kenny said, looking stricken. "Roy Gustafson is listed as missing. Wasn't that the name of the kid we had burgers with?"

"God, that is bad news. Yes! And his camper was so close to our site." Lauren's anger dissipated, and her mood turned somber.

She lay back down on the bed.

"What's killing me is the thought that Chris is somewhere on the mountain injured and can't get help. He has food and water, but what if he can't reach it?" Lauren worried aloud.

"Somebody knows something about Chris," Kenny said, "but they won't tell us. How come you don't know Chris's mother's name so we could call her?"

"I think she remarried in the last year or two. Besides, I don't know where she lives."

"Damn, we're blocked at every turn. My office has been understanding, but I've got to get back to work soon."

Lauren felt a sinking sensation in her stomach. *We can't give up the search.* She knew she would never forgive herself if she didn't do everything in her power to find Chris.

On Thursday, in an incredible state of frustration, Lauren and Kenny tried one last longshot. Knowing geologists were sampling Mount St. Helens by helicopter, they drove to the volcano monitoring station in Vancouver to see if they could get access to Disappointment Ridge. As they approached the observatory, they were accosted by Secret Service agents and a SWAT team carrying rifles.

"Right," Kenny said, smacking his forehead as he unzipped the window on his side of the Jeep. "President Carter is touring the destruction today."

"What's your business here?" the agent asked Kenny. "I need to see identification, and both of you need to get out of the car while we search it."

"We have information on a missing person," Kenny said, handing over his driver's license and stepping out of the Jeep.

One of the agents took Lauren's camera bag from the back seat and started rifling the contents. "I'll need to confiscate this. You can get it back when you leave."

"No. I'm sorry. Could you give it to me?" Lauren held out a hand. "It's just cameras and film." Being chased by a volcanic eruption was a terrifying experience. But the chance to take photographs of an eruption and its lightning-filled cloud was the scientific opportunity of a lifetime. She was not going to lose her pictures.

The agent looked at her in disbelief. "I'm keeping it while you're on the property. I repeat, when you leave, you get it back."

"We almost died getting those pictures! You're not taking my film and cameras," Lauren said, shaking her head and resting her hands on her hips.

As their argument escalated, a man covered in ash and balancing a boulder of pumice on his shoulder, walked up to them. "Hey, Lauren! What's going on?"

"Dr. Mumper! We need help! Chris Connor is missing."

Dr. Mumper turned to the agents and said, "They're geologists—part of my team."

The agent returned Lauren's camera bag with a surly, "Here."

She told Dr. Mumper they couldn't confirm that a helicopter had flown to Disappointment Ridge to search for Chris. She showed him on the map where to look for him and described Chris's blue Dodge Dart.

Dr. Mumper's face filled with concern when he saw the location.

"We're sampling the crater as conditions permit. We'll check out Disappointment Ridge on our way back," he promised. "But it could take a while."

They watched Dr. Mumper and a younger geologist duck under the whirling rotors and climb aboard. Lauren allowed her spirits to rise as the helicopter lifted off. Certain that Chris was just trapped on the mountain, she expected Dr. Mumper would bring him back. Even though she had seen Dr. Mumper's worried look when she showed him Chris's location, she told herself he was probably troubled by the risks of sampling the crater of an erupting volcano rather than about looking for Chris. They sat in the parking lot in their Jeep and waited. Intermittently, one or the other of them would get out to stretch and pace around.

"He's okay. I know he's okay. He's gotta be okay," Lauren said.

"Sure. We'll all go out tonight to celebrate."

Lauren tried to imagine the joy she would feel celebrating Chris's rescue. For some reason she couldn't summon the feeling. *I'm just so tired*, she thought.

>>

Two agonizing hours later they watched as Dr. Mumper, looking grave, walked toward them from the helicopter. "God, I'm sorry. I have terrible news. We found Chris dead a short distance from his car. Beside his dog."

Lauren wailed as she slumped in her seat, covered her face with her hands and sobbed.

Oh my God, no. Not my friend, not Chris, no. It can't be. It can't be.

Dr. Mumper reached into the Jeep and patted her on the shoulder. "We found footprints in the ash showing he survived the first few minutes of the eruption. Apparently, he got out of his car and ran part way toward a destroyed camper. Then it looks like he turned around, and he and his dog went in the other direction past his car. I brought his camera from the car and what I could of his other belongings."

Lauren couldn't stop crying. She just nodded. *Chris survived for a while. But now he's dead.*

"He didn't have a dog. It was some other guy's dog. Damn. We were just with Chris on Saturday," Kenny said to Dr. Mumper, who was leaning on the Jeep.

"I'm devastated," Dr. Mumper said. "Dave Johnston is missing and presumed dead. And now Chris. Two brilliant young geologists."

He looked down and shook his head in disbelief. The ash on his face was smudged, as though he, too, had been crying.

Lauren glanced at Dr. Mumper as he turned and walked like an old man back toward the helicopter. Chris had been one of his favorite grad students.

As Kenny backed out and turned the Jeep around in the parking lot, Lauren covered her face with her hands and sobbed and moaned. "No. Not Chris."

Kenny drove slowly toward Longview, as though a somber pace was fitting for the day.

"Bear," Lauren said, still slumped down.

"What?"

"That was the name of Roy Gustafson's dog. Roy who is missing. Chris was probably trying to reach them."

It was just like Chris to think of others before himself. He was one of the dearest men she had ever met. And now he was gone. How was she going to survive?

>>

Back at their motel, they were paralyzed by grief. Kenny sprawled on the unmade bed and Lauren sat on the end of the bed. They worried about how to get home through 250 miles of ash that was choking car engines as well as living creatures. It would take them at least two days, they were sure.

Lauren stared at the dirty clothes scattered about the room. How would they ever get packed? Her hands, resting on her legs, looked distorted as though she were looking at them underwater. A pizza box with dried crusts lay on the floor, and assorted beer cans were scattered about. It seemed impossible to go on.

The maid's knocking at their door shook them from their lethargy. Kenny walked next door to the office and told the manager they were checking out. Lauren stuffed clothes into duffels and stashed a box of crackers and a bag of chips into their empty cooler.

They drove to the closest gas station where they bought three air filters. To avoid as much ashfall as possible, they drove south through Oregon and then east into Idaho. Even so, the ash was four inches deep in places. It was like snow that didn't melt. Even the slightest motion caused it to billow into huge clouds, obscuring everything. Periodically, when the Jeep's engine sputtered, Kenny changed the air filter.

The land was covered in varying shades of gray. Lauren's mood perfectly matched the lonely, lifeless environment. When the sky partially cleared, people wearing surgical masks or bandannas over their faces peered out of the bleakness. The eerie landscape and its inhabitants reminded Lauren of the movie *The Andromeda Strain*. It seemed extraterrestrials had landed, and earthlings were in danger of being infected by an alien atmosphere. The sun was a dim circular light far beyond the fog. Even at noon it appeared to be the dawn of a new dark age.

Chris was gone. Lauren and Kenny had survived, but Lauren felt barely alive. The final leg of their trip north from Lewiston, Idaho, to Spokane was a slog. Visibility was limited to thirty feet, and if they drove faster than thirty-five miles per hour, they were enveloped in a gray cloud of their own making.

As they approached Spokane, Lauren worried about the welfare of Tom—and when they entered their apartment, she knew something was wrong. A thin layer of ash covered the furniture and floor—they'd left windows cracked so he would get fresh air. The giant bowl of dry cat food they had left was still half full.

They found Tom hiding in their bedroom closet. He had pushed aside numerous boxes and nestled himself as far back as possible. When Lauren coaxed him out, he was trembling and purring simultaneously. She could feel his ribs.

"Poor Tom!" Lauren opened a can of tuna fish and fed him from her fingers.

The upheaval of the earth on the other side of the state had shaken the most imperturbable of cats and driven him into survival mode. He padded around the apartment meowing for almost an hour to let them know the depth of his distress.

Chapter 17

Aftermath

Lauren, 1980–81

As Kenny and Lauren tried to piece together their lives, it was like solving a puzzle without all the pieces. Nothing fit as it should. Lauren vacillated between disbelief that Chris was dead and realization that he was. She was filled with guilt because Disappointment Ridge had been her choice. "If only, if only" played like a mobius strip in her mind.

The first few days after their return home, she could think of nothing but the eruption. She researched every detail of the devastation. Night after night, she dreamed the scenes exactly as she had read about them. The landslide raced toward her. She was drowning in hot mud. Icy chunks of glaciers rained down on her. She struggled to keep her head above the sludge.

After studying the pyroclastic surge, she dreamed her hair stood on end from the electricity, and she could feel heat from the blast. The ash cloud chased her. When she learned Chris had died of suffocation, she suffocated in agonizing detail in her dreams. She was unable to get air. Hot ash seared her throat. Her skin burned. She wandered in a hissing, hellish darkness trying to escape. She woke just before her last burning breath.

Trauma, real and dreamt, propelled her to action. She accepted every invitation to talk to college and high school science classes,

Elks Lodges, Rotary Clubs, and governmental entities about the eruption and her escape down the mountain. Teaching students and adults about volcanoes and the earth helped release some of the pressure she felt every morning when she woke and felt guilty to be alive. She needed to speak for all the people who hadn't escaped from the eruption. During her speeches she couldn't help tearing up when she told of Chris's death. Appreciative audiences surrounded her with warmth.

Besides telling her story, she became preoccupied with discovering what had happened to every survivor. She researched hikers, vacationers, loggers, and families camping in the area to see if they survived. If she saw a name in the paper, heard one mentioned on television, or read about someone in a journal, she did her own detective work to find them. She telephoned them and exchanged information and pictures. Survivors had a connection no one else understood. They were bonded by a catastrophic, near-death event.

Nothing looked the same. Nothing felt the same. No one else could see it, but survivors knew it. It was as if they had been detached from the real world and lifted into a parallel universe where existence had a higher purpose. Daily life seemed petty. Some survivors had difficulty dealing with the intensity of this detachment and tried to put the event behind them as quickly as possible.

Nearly everyone felt the experience was a negative one. Lauren did not. Yes, she had lost Chris, and it had been the worst loss of her life. Still, the eruption had been incredible. It showed the magnificence of the earth and its renewal forces. To understand, feel, and be part of it was an experience of a lifetime.

Even in her grief, Lauren understood that.

>>

Lauren withdrew from classes and, instead, worked on a committee to finish Chris's thesis. Her job was to finalize the chemical calculations from XRF analyses and make graphs of the data. She completed countless phase diagrams and charts of the varying chemistry of the Weiser basalts, yet she was painfully aware it was incomplete. Valuable notes and too much data had been lost in the eruption. Solving the mystery of the genesis of the Columbia River basalts was to have been Chris's first great contribution to geology. In the end, it was not the masterpiece he planned.

During long days when Lauren worked on Chris's dissertation, Kenny spent evenings restoring a wrecked 1965 Ford Mustang that he kept at a body shop. They saw each other in passing. She understood his desire to make something whole and beautiful again. She wondered if he understood she was trying to make herself whole again.

She often thought about what Chris had said the day before the eruption—that if he went first, he would come back and tell her about the afterlife. She lay awake night after night, waiting, asking, begging him to communicate with her.

Silence.

>>

Under Mount St. Helens lay a monstrous force that had blown a third of the mountain away and changed the landscape beyond recognition. Lauren felt compelled to return to the volcano. In order to photograph every aspect of the destruction, she needed to get close.

Several weekends she and Kenny drove back, each time trying a different road into the devastated area and hiking as close as possible to the mountain. So many roads were gone—buried in mud. Others were impassable because of downed trees. At every dead end they persisted. They hiked through fields of downed trees as big as six or seven feet in diameter. Each tree was a huge obstacle. They either climbed over or squeezed under it. Even a small breeze stirred up suffocating ash. Of course, the devastated area was off-limits. When patrol helicopters flew over, Lauren and Kenny ducked under trees.

Soon they were so covered in ash they were like ghosts in a haunted landscape.

The surge had stripped all the bark and branches from trees and laid them flat in the direction of flow. Solid material and gas that comprised the surge had acted as a fluid. It was a good example. Lauren and Kenny could see eddies and smaller chaotic currents superimposed on the main flow lines. Surmounting all obstacles in its path, the surge flowed up one side of the ridge and down the other, covering the land like a huge, unstoppable flood. There was no place to hide.

>>

In a desperate attempt to locate missing pages of Chris's dissertation and data, Lauren received backing from the Columbia River Basalt Project for Kenny and her to fly to Disappointment Ridge.

They boarded a small red-and-white helicopter in late June and their pilot, who had flown rescue missions on May 18th, flew them over the devastation. As they approached the ridge, they were stunned when they saw the reality of Chris's location. His car had been a quarter mile from perfectly green trees, yet it was covered in gray ash. He had been so close to safety but unaware of it. Lauren felt as though she had been punched in the heart.

"He might have escaped," she said, sobbing.

The helicopter landed next to Chris's car. The blue paint in the front, which faced the volcano, had been sandblasted by ash and rocks. Windows had been blown out and glass lay all around. There were burn holes in the seats. Someone had stripped the tires and engine, and Chris's belongings were gone.

If the perpetrators had found his thesis, they probably would have tossed it aside, so Lauren and Kenny hiked all around the mountain. They found his pillow and a hubcap, but nothing else.

A column of ash and steam burst from the crater.

"It's erupting!" Kenny yelled to Lauren, who was combing the area above him. She jumped down from a low ledge and stumbled over a rock, nearly falling. Kenny dropped the hubcap, and they ran toward the helicopter and arrived out of breath. Their pilot continued to lean nonchalantly against the chopper.

"Now I feel silly." Lauren said to the pilot. "We panicked."

"Look, you survived the Big One. You know the power of this mountain."

>>

Before bringing them back to the airport, the pilot flew Lauren and Kenny straight into Mount St. Helens' crater, over the pyroclastic flow deposits and the north side destruction, and within a hundred feet of Spirit Lake.

Lauren couldn't tell a forest had ever existed near the lake but for logs floating in it. The surrounding area, which was thought of as the first zone, had been stripped clean of everything and filled with mud. The gray-and-tan landscape was alien and devoid of life, like the landscape of Mars. Steam emanated from the ground.

The second zone was a vast area of downed trees. The occupants of cars trapped amid the trees had no doubt perished. The third zone, where trees were upright but burnt reddish-orange, was shockingly narrow. Just beyond, trees were green and unharmed. It looked as though someone had painted a thin, reddish-orange line at the edge of the devastation and spared everything outside it.

Lauren obsessed over Chris's location, so agonizingly close to green trees. If only he had known to go west a short distance.

"If the second he saw the mountain erupt, he had run to his car and driven like crazy, maybe he could have escaped death. But the surge was moving so fast—five hundred miles an hour."

"He couldn't have known," Kenny said.

"If only . . ." was Lauren's recurring lament.

Beaten and exhausted, she couldn't stop thinking about how Chris might have escaped.

"It's ironic," she said to Kenny. "We thought we planned carefully, yet we were wrong. Now I know we walk a thin line in the universe. A second here, a few steps there make all the difference."

>>

On the drive home, they both were quiet. Lauren hadn't recovered from the shock of seeing how close Chris had been to safety. Kenny had an aura of gloominess about him, she noticed. He gripped the steering wheel as though the Jeep would bolt from his control if he relaxed his hold.

"You seem a little tense," Lauren said.

"I'm done with the volcano."

"What? Why? I thought the view of the devastation was incredible."

"Of course." Kenny turned to look at her. "But all our weekends are taken up slogging through ash and mud, or like today, flying around looking at downed trees. We need to forget the eruption and get on with our lives."

"Sure, but it's hard to forget something that almost killed us. We don't have to come here every weekend, though," she added.

"You're not listening. I'm done."

The rest of the drive, Lauren and Kenny kept their conversation focused on uncontroversial matters like finding a veterinarian to give Tom his vaccinations and the upcoming visit from Lauren's high school friend. When they arrived home, the ritual of unloading the Jeep seemed like the end of something.

>>

Staying home wasn't the answer either, Lauren soon realized. She and Kenny had become different people from who they were before the eruption. The qualities she cherished most in Kenny—his sense of humor and his love of adventure—were missing. Lauren realized she was not the fun-loving person she used to be, either. And she knew he was frustrated by what he called her obsession with Mount St. Helens. What was left of their original selves was not enough to make a relationship.

Even the small apartment where they lived seemed too big for them. They couldn't find each other. Or see each other. They were still ash-covered ghosts wandering an unrecognizable landscape.

While Kenny was considering an offer to be a partner in the investment firm where he worked, Lauren received a call from the Geology Department at the University of Colorado. Gary, the department chair, had heard her talk at a conference and invited her to apply to teach geology to undergraduates and work on her PhD. Neither Kenny nor Lauren was willing to pass up the opportunity. In the end, they came to the painful conclusion they could not put their marriage back together. The eruption had irreversibly upended their lives.

Chapter 18

Monument

Lauren, Five Years Later

"How come you're jealous of Chris but not of Kenny?" Lauren good-humoredly teased David, her husband of three months.

He laughed. "Well, you've never mentioned building a monument to your ex-husband."

"Lauren shook her head. I don't hold a grudge against him. But I also don't plan to build him a monument!"

They were eating burgers and beans at a picnic table in early evening at their campsite along the Cache la Poudre River, northwest of Fort Collins. On the drive from Denver, Lauren had shared her idea of building a monument to Chris on the site where he had died. David was skeptical of the project. Like every other man to whom Lauren had told Chris's story, he wanted to put a label on Chris and Lauren's relationship.

"But seriously, you two were lovers. Right?"

"No. Best friends."

"How can a man and a woman be just friends? What were his motives? Chris must have been gay."

"Are you saying people of the opposite sex can't like each other, have interests in common, cheer each other up, and have each other's back?"

"It seems like you've thought a lot about this."

"Chris was not gay. He and I might have become lovers if I hadn't been married to Kenny at the time and hoped to reconcile with him. The truth is," Lauren continued, "Chris and I gave each other exactly what we both needed at the time: true friendship. We forged a bond through long talks about science, life, truth, and the universe. We didn't always agree, but we listened with respect, and each gained another perspective. He was a great guy."

"Now I wish I had known him," David said. "I like your idea of a monument. It'll be a challenge to see if you can make it happen."

Lauren thought David seemed relieved she wanted to memorialize a friend instead of a lover.

>>

Following the 1980 eruption of Mount St. Helens, Lauren had given hundreds of talks about her escape down the mountain and Chris's death. So long as she was thinking and talking about him, his memory was alive. As time passed and she gave fewer talks, her fear escalated that Chris would be forgotten. She had lobbied the US Forest Service to rename Disappointment Ridge in his honor. Following two years of correspondence, she had received an encouraging letter from an associate deputy chief, but then the issue had been referred to the Under Secretary of the US Department of Agriculture. So far, she had not been able to penetrate the Byzantine USDA.

Amid Lauren's efforts to commemorate Chris, she met David. He was dropping off rolls of film from his trip to Costa Rica at a camera store while she was picking up her African safari pictures. They had exchanged phone numbers and soon found they shared a passion for science, travel, hiking, and more. They had married a year later.

Even though Lauren was saddened that she and Kenny had grown apart and divorced in the aftermath of the eruption, the perspective of five years made her realize she and David were compatible on so many more levels than she and Kenny had been. As painful as the divorce was, it had freed her to find David.

On a sleepless night a few days before their camping trip, Lauren had had an epiphany. If there were to be a permanent monument to Chris, she would have to build it herself. On Disappointment Ridge. Something organic. She could collect basalt rocks from his field area in Idaho and form them into a monument from the ground up. Lauren could almost visualize the completed project. It would be a classic pyramid shape. She remembered reading that the earliest pyramid in Egypt had been a step pyramid, which served as a stairway to the heavens for the pharaoh's soul. Maybe Chris's wouldn't be a step pyramid, but it would point to the heavens.

>>

Lauren and David left Colorado the following May on a mission to build a monument to Chris near Mount St. Helens. As they traveled through Wyoming to Idaho, Lauren read aloud from Chris's letters from the summers of 1978 and 1979.

"He sounds like a character," David said after Lauren read a letter recounting Chris's misadventures mooing to a herd of cattle to keep them from stampeding.

"Yeah, he was a character. Not like the class clown is a character, but like the more you got to know him, the funnier and more interesting he was."

>>

As they approached Chris's field area, driving north of Boise, Lauren could feel his presence grow stronger. Beyond Black Canyon Reservoir, they found a place to camp. At dawn Lauren hiked several miles around the park, and David joined her for the last two miles. They collected the first basalt rock for the monument near the dam. Acquiring it felt momentous, a tangible step toward reaching her goal. Chris had referred to his summers of fieldwork as the metaphorical building blocks to his thesis. Lauren planned to collect samples of each type of basalt as he differentiated them. These rocks would be the actual building blocks of the monument that Lauren hoped would represent Chris's essence.

When they returned to camp, David set up the hibachi so Lauren could cook pancakes for breakfast. She walked over and gave him a hug as he stood up.

"What's that for?"

"To thank you for supporting my project—taking time from work, driving for hours, helping me find the right rock. Everything."

He gave her a quick kiss. "A woman who promises adventure and then hauls me off to Idaho in her camper is pretty hard to turn down."

Lauren laughed and stood grinning while David arranged charcoal briquettes in the hibachi.

>>

After breakfast they took a zigzag route toward their destination of Crane Creek Reservoir, collecting rocks along the way from various basalt flows. As there were no other campers at the reservoir, they had their choice of campsites. They settled on a site near the northeast section of the lake. Chris's letters had spoken often of the peace and solitude of this place. Following dinner, Lauren and David sat in lawn chairs near the glowing coals of the hibachi.

After a glass of wine, David said, "You've never said much about what happened after Mount St. Helens."

"I know I've told you how sad and distraught we were when we found out Chris was dead."

"Yeah, you've told me that part. How soon did you leave Washington?"

"About eight months after the eruption. Are you sure you want to hear all this?"

"We have all night. I'm too tired to read by lantern light."

Lauren related her adventures hiking into the devastation of the eruption, searching for stories of other survivors, working on Chris's dissertation, and dropping out of her own PhD program at Spokane University.

By the time she finished her story, the coals in the hibachi had turned to ash. The wine bottle was empty.

Lauren said, "I'm beat. Let's call it a night."

>>

At dawn the next day, they walked around the lake as fish jumped, crickets chirped, and cranes flew overhead on their floppy, double-jointed wings. Lauren could picture Chris working on his thesis at the lake: musing, thinking, and problem-solving, but still finding time to send her encouraging letters in Pasadena, Texas.

Their itinerary for the day was to head north on South Crane Creek Road, where they added another rock to the gunnysack. The more they explored the Weiser Embayment, Chris's massive field area, the more Lauren respected his feat of having completed a geologic map of it. They collected another rock on Hawthorne Road, an area of rolling farm and ranch country, where she especially felt Chris's presence. Fields of violet, pink, and purple penstemons contrasted with snow-covered mountains in the distance. At intervals wire bins filled with rocks anchored the barbed wire fences. No human sounds intruded on the quiet.

All the while collecting rocks, they crossed Hornet Creek Road and drove toward Pyramid Point on a very windy, poorly marked road to a forested area, where they found a protected campsite amid the trees.

The next day they collected another rock and headed down the mountain. The truck was so loaded with rock that by the time they reached the bottom, the brakes were smoking. Trailing a wisp of burnt brakes, they crisscrossed, meandered, and backtracked east to Council, then south, then on to Cambridge, and finally arrived at Mann Creek Reservoir.

Lauren climbed the hill for a good view of the lake. Chris had found this place conducive to working on his thesis, and now she understood why. Again, the magnitude of his task struck Lauren. To sample and map the Weiser Embayment required discipline, drive, and a desire to create a work of art.

It required Chris, she thought.

>>

Lauren felt a huge sense of accomplishment when they secured the final rock from the final site in Chris's field area. It was as though by making a circuit around Chris's field area, they had come to a conclusion or closed a circle.

Leaving Idaho, she felt as though they were leaving Chris behind—his presence was so much a part of the area—but she was also excited to be in Oregon. Its volcanic energy was unique. Not only was it breathtakingly beautiful with its painted hills and canyons, but every kind of volcanism on earth was represented in the state.

At dawn she hiked around the gravel pit, a distance of five or six miles. She and David had finally solved how to meet each other on lake hikes when they started at different times. She always went left, and he always went right. They were assured of meeting somewhere on the circumference instead of chasing one another and never intersecting. Nothing was friendlier than completing a hike together.

Their plan for the day was to drive to Picture Gorge—Lauren's field area from 1979. Besides showing David the spectacular scenery, she planned to collect rocks at various sites. She and Chris had always exchanged rocks for good luck, so it was fitting to include rocks from her field area in his monument. Returning to her field area now was another circle of completion. To what end she was going in all these circles was yet to be seen.

The rain began almost as soon as they started down Highway 26 toward Picture Gorge and continued to torment them for the next four days. Hiking the canyons of her field area was impossible in rainy, slippery conditions. Still, they persisted in collecting rock samples, even if they were ones they found alongside the road. Driving to Washington seemed the only activity not prohibited by the weather.

>>

Mount Hood was shrouded in mist and rain as they drove toward the town of Hood River, where they crossed the Columbia River into Washington. When they arrived at Moss Creek, they turned into a Gifford–Pinchot National Forest Campground. The next morning Lauren and David lay in bed in the camper listening for rain on the roof but hearing none.

"Hooray!" Lauren said, hopping out of bed to open the curtains covering the small windows. "It's clear. Let's hit the road."

They didn't bother to cook breakfast but ate bread and cheese on the road and drank instant coffee heated by an element plugged into the lighter socket of the truck. They were elated by the good weather. The lush greenery of Washington sparkled with drops of water from recent rains, and the magnificent Columbia River accompanied them on their drive to Vancouver, where they bought wood and bags of concrete. David found several discarded drywall buckets in an alley to use for mixing concrete.

>>

In midafternoon Lauren and David presented themselves at the office of the Department of Natural Resources in Castle Rock. Even though they had a permit in hand, Fred, the unit forester, informed them the department needed an exact location where the monument would be built. To provide that, Lauren and David would drive up the winding and rutted roads to Disappointment Ridge, determine where to build, and then drive back down to Castle Rock to report their decision. Before starting up the mountain, they stopped at a park and filled every water jug and tank they had brought. Tons of rock, bags of concrete, and now heavy containers of water weighed down the truck. Even with good directions and annotated maps from Natural Resources, they struggled to find the way. Logging roads were not marked and often intersected with each other. Fog drifted in.

When they passed a field of downed trees, Lauren caught her breath. She was back in 1980. Chris had just died. She and Kenny were trying to make sense of the devastation. Her emotions overwhelmed her. She made a sound like a strangled sob.

"Are you okay?" David asked, looking over at her.

"I . . . I . . . don't know. There are so many memories here. I'm just terribly sad." Tears rolled down her cheeks.

"Shall we keep going?"

"Maybe we should stop for the night. We might be there, or really close."

Hoping morning would reveal where they were, they parked their camper.

>>

The next day they were still enshrouded in fog, but Lauren thought they were in the right place. They spent early morning scouting possible sites. The surrounding steep slopes would make building the monument difficult. Midmorning the fog lifted to reveal Mount St. Helens in the near distance and Mount Adams, Mount Hood, and Mount Rainier in the far distance.

"This is it," Lauren said in a quiet voice. "This is Disappointment Ridge."

She and David leaned on each other companionably as they stood and looked around.

She continued, "Who would think a nondescript ridge above a trickle of a stream would be so perfectly placed on Earth as to view four incredible volcanoes? Although, I must admit, Mount St. Helens is kind of a wreck. She lost thirteen hundred feet from her summit in the eruption."

From where they stood, the volcano looked almost flat on top with a dip to the north side. Newly fallen snow covered its glaciers.

"But it's still impressive," David said.

They resumed exploring. Disappointment Ridge felt like a sacred place despite—or perhaps because of—tragic events that had occurred there. They spotted the little flag Fred told them he had placed at the location of Chris's car. A plastic grill with surge deposits embedded in it looked as though it had come from his car. Just above where it had been parked and above the road was a well-protected, level clearing.

"I think we've found a location for the monument," David said, looking back at Lauren.

"I agree. It won't be obvious to potential vandals, but anyone seeking it can easily find it."

Lauren marked the exact spot where they would build on the Mount St. Helens map. While they were unloading rocks, concrete bags, and water jugs to lighten the truck before heading down the mountain, they heard a truck roaring up the road.

"I wonder who that can be," Lauren said, dropping a bag of concrete near the chosen site.

A Department of Natural Resources truck pulled up, and a man got out.

"Hey, Fred!" David greeted him like an old friend, even though he and Lauren had just met him yesterday. "What's up?"

"Thought I'd come see for muhself where you intend to build this monument."

"Right here," Lauren said, pointing to the area they had cleared.

David resumed dragging gunnysacks of rocks out of the camper, and Fred lent a hand by stacking bags of concrete near the site. Then the two men bolted together wooden forms into a triangular shape to outline the base of the pyramid, while Lauren stacked all the Idaho and Oregon rocks in the middle of the triangle. As she stepped back to assess her piles, she laughed aloud.

"A two-foot-high pyramid won't be very impressive! Don't worry, though, I'll collect a bunch of local rocks for the core."

By the end of the day, all three of them were exhausted, but they had made a good start on the base. They thanked Fred, who promised to look out for the monument. Lauren and David dined on cold canned chili and ibuprofen and went to bed before it was fully dark.

>>

It took them three days to finish building the monument. By four thirty in the afternoon on the final day, they had cemented in place the engraved granite stone. They opted to leave the wooden forms in place for the stability of the pyramid. Lauren took handfuls of surge deposit and rubbed it into the wood so its color would blend with that of the rock. The monument looked wonderful. David opened a bottle of champagne and read Lauren's words from the engraved stone as a toast and benediction to Chris.

IN MEMORY OF DR. CHRISTOPHER PATRICK
CONNOR, KILLED HERE BY MOUNT ST. HELENS
MAY 18, 1980, VOLCANOLOGIST, SCIENCE FICTION
AUTHOR, SOCIOLOGIST, A QUIET, HONORABLE
RENAISSANCE MAN WHO LOVED
HUMANITY AND THE EARTH.

They each took a sip and then poured a little champagne from their glasses onto the monument.

>>

That night while they were sleeping, they heard a knocking on the camper door. David got up to answer it.

Half-asleep, Lauren called from under the covers, "If it's Chris, let him in."

"No one's here," David said, peering out the door.

Lauren threw off blankets, got up, and walked to the door.

"Must've been the wind. I'm going back to bed," David said, brushing by her.

Lauren stepped out into the cold, still, moonless night. Stars and planets dazzled.

"Chris," Lauren said softly as she sat down on the camper steps.

She didn't say his name as though she were speaking to him, but rather, as though she were acknowledging his existence in the beautiful night sky they both loved. It reminded her of the night before the eruption when she and Chris had sat together as sunset faded to grayish purple, and Mount St. Helens disappeared into darkness. So many nights since then she had waited for him to contact her. Tonight, she felt his presence.

A few tears rolled down her cheeks. Chris was one of the dearest men she would ever meet. When he had been gone two years, and she was healing from her divorce, she had yearned to love him as he deserved to be loved—as a woman loves a man. As Elizabeth Barrett loved Robert Browning: to the depth and breadth and height her soul could reach. Sometimes not loving someone hurt more than loving and losing.

No doubt a gust of wind or little disturbance in the atmosphere had caused the tapping on their door just now. That's what Lauren told herself, anyway. But in her heart, she knew Chris was letting her

know his soul was all right. He was where he was supposed to be—
beyond Earth and sky and merged with the stardust of the universe.

Wiping tears with the sleeve of her pajamas, she glanced at the
dark shape of the pyramid she and David had constructed. It pointed
skyward. She looked up and let the night settle around her. If Chris
couldn't come back to tell her about the afterlife, she would have to be
happy with his presence in the stars.

Acknowledgments

I am beyond grateful to the many wonderful people who helped bring this book to publication.

First readers, Nora Jacquez, Susan Simon Van Skoyk, and Eva Lanier (the "Bloomsbury Group"), read a rough draft of the book and, thankfully, saw possibilities in the story.

I appreciate Greta Lindecrantz, Anita Paoli, and Fred Paoli, who shared their insights as well as their friends and contacts with me.

Barbara Bogue and Gary Koopmann offered creative suggestions that enhanced the story. I am thankful to them for their perspective.

I am grateful to Chuck Sizer, Collette Sizer, Jan Sizer Deines, Gayle Gallamore Denney, and Mark Miller for encouragement and thoughtful comments on the book.

Editors who critiqued and edited the book all contributed immensely to its quality. Krissa Lagos, with her extraordinary book sense, guided the book to a higher level. Danielle Dyal gave extensive comments and positive feedback. Jodi Fodor inspired me to add a new, colorful character who recounted the dangers of volcanoes. And Jennifer Caven's finely detailed copyedit was invaluable. I can't thank them enough.

Many thanks to Lauren Wise, my editorial project manager, and to Brooke Warner, cofounder and publisher of She Writes Press. Both are quintessential professionals.

Julie Metz is an amazing designer, and I am so appreciative of the cover design she created.

Finally, I am indebted to my family, who have lived with the book as long as it's been in progress. Besides being supportive, my husband Jeff Bogue read the book several times and made valuable recommendations. Katie Bogue Miller and Zack Bogue encouraged me and shared thoughtful suggestions. Sherry Sizer Griffith read various iterations of the book and contributed creative ideas. They have my everlasting gratitude.

About the Author

Headshot TK

Susan Sizer Bogue is a lawyer who practiced law for a number of years before turning to writing.   She is the author of the script for the musical, *The Christmas of the Phonograph Records*, as well as of many humorous essays. This is her first novel. She lives near Denver, Colorado.

Looking for your next great read?

We can help!

Visit www.shewritespress.com/next-read
or scan the QR code below for a list
of our recommended titles.

She Writes Press is an award-winning
independent publishing company founded to
serve women writers everywhere.